Lynne Graham was born in Northern Ireland and has been a keen romance reader since her teens. She is very happily married to an understanding husband who has learned to cook since she started to write! Her five children keep her on her toes. She has a very large dog, which knocks everything over, a very small terrier, which barks a lot, and two cats. When time allows, Lynne is a keen gardener.

After spending three years as a die-hard New Yorker, **Kate Hewitt** now lives in a small village in the English Lake District with her husband, their five children and a golden retriever. In addition to writing intensely emotional stories, she loves reading, baking and playing chess with her son—she has yet to win against him, but she continues to try. Learn more about Kate at kate-hewitt.com.

THE GREEK'S BLACKMAILED MISTRESS

LYNNE GRAHAM

PRINCESS'S NINE-MONTH SECRET

KATE HEWITT

MILLS & BOON

First Published in Great Britain 2018
by Mills & Boon, an imprint of HarperCollins*Publishers*
1 London Bridge Street, London, SE1 9GF

The Greek's Blackmailed Mistress © 2018 by Lynne Graham

Princess's Nine-Month Secret © 2018 by Kate Hewitt

ISBN: 978-0-263-93546-2

Printed and bound in Spain
by CPI, Barcelona

THE GREEK'S BLACKMAILED MISTRESS

LYNNE GRAHAM

CHAPTER ONE

'I'M TOO BEAUTIFUL to be dumped,' Fabiana told Xan in all seriousness, her perfect face a mask of disbelief. 'It's my poor English, isn't it? I'm picking you up wrong—'

'No,' Xan contradicted with gravity, smoothly switching to her native Spanish. 'The movers will be here in an hour to help you pack. We've been together two months. I did tell you that this arrangement wouldn't last any longer than that—'

'But you can't *not* want me any more—' Giving her reflection an appreciative appraisal in the nearest mirror, Fabiana fluffed up her fall of tumbling dark curls.

'I *don't* want you any more,' Xan countered, losing patience, beginning to wonder how the hell he had enjoyed even one encounter with the brunette, infused as she was with astronomical vanity.

'Where am I supposed to go?' Fabiana demanded abruptly, studying him in frustration, silently recognising that she was unlikely to ever have a better-looking man in her bed. Six foot three and beautifully built, his black hair cropped short over a lean, devastatingly handsome face, the Greek financial guru, Xan Ziakis, would be a very hard act to follow and without him she would lose access to the exclusive events she had so much enjoyed.

'Your possessions will be stored and a hotel room has been engaged for you,' Xan clarified, on firmer ground now because he had been changing mistresses every couple of months for years. There was nothing new about the status quo and Fabiana had benefitted richly from their association even though his visits had been few.

Reflecting on that last surprising truth, Xan questioned his libido. He was only thirty years old. Obviously he was bored with Fabiana, he told himself impatiently. Yet, in truth, work and the pursuit of profit had always won out over the thrill of sex for Xan. *Some day* he would heed his mother's endless pleas and start dating with a view to taking a wife but that day was many years off. His father, Helios, had married five times over, gifting Xan with a costly and troublesome flock of half-siblings, and he was determined not to repeat his father's mistakes. Helios had married too young while Xan intended to wait until he was in his forties, at the very least, and had sown every last wild oat available to him.

Not that Fabiana and her faceless, virtually indistinguishable predecessors had much in common with wild oats, he conceded with wry self-mockery. All his bed partners had been models or minor actresses, the sort of women who understood that he paid generously for everything they wanted in return for their bodies. Framed in those words, it sounded crude, he acknowledged without shame, but that very basic format worked well for him and the one time he had tried another approach, when he had been both young and idealistic, it had gone badly wrong for him.

Xan believed love was a dangerous risk. His father had fallen in love repeatedly with demonstrably unsuitable women. Xan had had his heart broken when he was only twenty-one and nothing would've persuaded him to revisit that learning experience.

A financial genius, who had become a billionaire by the age of twenty-five, Xan was the acclaimed mastermind behind City coups worth billions. He had quickly repaired the giant hole in the Ziakis family fortunes left by his imprudent father, and had simply chosen to organise his sex life much as he organised everything else around him because disorder of any kind put him in a bad mood. He liked his life smooth; he *preferred* a routine he virtually never deviated from. He would not risk the upheaval of marriage breakdowns and hugely expensive divorces that had decimated his father's wealth. He was stronger than that and infinitely cleverer, indeed smarter than most of the people around him, and the only risks he took were in the financial field where he trusted his gut and aggressive instincts.

His phone vibrated, instantly freeing him from all awareness of Fabiana's presence. He dug it out, immediately wondering why Dmitri, the head of his security team, would be contacting him. A moment later, he found out and he was enraged. Someone had *dared* to steal something very precious from him, and he stalked out of the apartment his mistresses used without another word to the brunette. His penthouse apartment was his sanctuary where he entertained neither women nor anyone else. The idea that *any* person could violate his London home in spite of all the security he had put in place sent his hot temper nuclear.

'*The maid?*' he breathed with audible distaste.

'Or her son. She let him into the apartment even though it's against the rules,' Dmitri filled in stiffly. 'I could pursue this discreetly *or* call the police—'

'You call the police and provide them with the evidence,' Xan cut in fiercely. 'You punish them with the full weight of the law!'

Xan collected imperial jade that cost him shocking sums and he had placed that little brush pot in the hall for his own enjoyment because it was a remarkably tactile piece and had once belonged to a Chinese emperor. In his penal frame of mind, whipping was too light a punishment for thieves.

The following day, Elvi's teenaged brother flung himself into her arms and sobbed, 'I'm so sorry…this whole nightmare is *my* fault!'

'Let's calm down,' Elvi suggested gently, framing her little brother's face with both small hands, recognising from the anguish in his green eyes that he had been crying alone in his room for some time. 'I'll make some tea—'

'I don't want tea!' Daniel protested. 'I want to go down to the police station and admit it was me and *not* Mum!'

'No, we're going to talk about this first,' Elvi over-ruled. 'Mum protected you for a reason—'

'Bloody medical school! It doesn't matter—'

Of course it mattered, Elvi thought ruefully, that Daniel wanted to be a doctor like their late father. It was all he had ever wanted to be since he was a little boy and a conviction for theft would totally destroy that ambition. Furthermore, Daniel had already been awarded a place at Oxford to study because his academic results were the very best. She knew exactly why her mother had lied and taken the blame for her son, but what she could not understand or credit was that Daniel would *ever* have stolen anything.

'I *need* to know what happened,' she persisted quietly, seating herself on the bed where her dark-haired brother had flopped down to hang his head. He was getting so tall and lanky at just past eighteen that he was fast growing out of all his clothes, his jeans barely reaching his ankles and his enormous feet. She and Daniel bore not an ounce of resemblance to each other because, although they had had the same father, they had had different mothers. Elvi's mother had died when she was a baby, and her father's second wife had adopted her and brought her up as her own. She was the short, plump one of the family, Elvi conceded ruefully, bright blue eyes troubled, pushing back the white-blonde hair sticking to her perspiring brow because she had run all the way home from work as soon as Daniel had phoned her.

'Yesterday, I called to pick up Mum for her AA meeting but I was a bit early,' Daniel confided.

Elvi heaved a sigh, for both of them tried to ensure that their mother went to regular meetings and since the summer arrived and Daniel had finished school and only contrived to find part-time employment, he had taken over the duty. Sally Cartwright deserved her family's support to stay sober. She had been sober now for three long wonderful years but Elvi was painfully aware that alcoholism was an affliction that never entirely went away. Denying herself the craving for that one dangerous drink was what Sally dealt with every day.

'And?'

'She was cleaning something and had to finish it, so she told me to sit down in the hall and not to touch anything,' Daniel grumbled. 'Like I was a little kid or something and I was annoyed, so I *didn't* listen...'

'What did you touch?' Elvi almost whispered.

'There was this little jade pot sitting on the console table in a patch of sunlight—honestly, Elvi...it was the sort of thing I've only ever seen inside a museum case—and I just wanted to hold it for a minute, so I picked it up and took it over to the window to hold it up to the light because it was so delicate—'

'And then what?' Elvi prompted with anxious impatience.

Daniel studied her in almost childlike discomfiture. 'Then the doorbell went and Mum rushed out to answer it and I kept the pot hidden in my hand because I didn't want her to see what I'd been doing. Unluckily for me, the man at the door worked for Mr Ziakis too and he was there to tell me that I shouldn't be in the apartment in the first place and that I should be waiting for my mother downstairs. He made me leave immediately, like…he was sort of nice about it but I had no chance of putting the pot back with him standing there—'

'For goodness' sake, Daniel!' Elvi erupted in vehement protest. 'You should've handed it to him straight away! The minute you stepped out of that apartment door with it, you labelled yourself a thief—'

'Yeah, you think I don't know that now?' Daniel traded with laden irony. 'But I gave way to panic and I concealed it, brought it home and stuck the blasted thing in a drawer. I planned to ask Mum to put it back for me tomorrow but apparently the housekeeper reported it missing when she turned in for work in the evening, so that was that. I missed the boat and—'

Stupid, stupid, stupid, repeated in Elvi's head but she didn't let the word pass her lips because she could see that her sibling was already painfully aware that he had acted like an impulsive and reckless total idiot. 'When did the police get involved?' she interposed.

'This morning…they arrived with a search warrant and of course they found it. Mum asked me to go into her room to get her handbag and while I was in there she may have confessed to taking it because by the time I came back out again because I couldn't find the blasted thing she was being arrested and read her rights,' he revealed chokily, gulping back more unmanly sobs. 'We need a solicitor—'

Elvi was thinking hard and fast but coming up with nothing. Her brain was still in shock. She wished she didn't know as much about her mother's fabulously wealthy employer as she did. He was the guy with the colour-coded closets and alphabetically arranged books. He had a desk that must never be touched and a bed that had to be changed every day. Her mother's duties in his apartment were hedged in by a very detailed list of do's and don'ts. That in the flesh the same male looked as though he had stepped straight out of a glossy magazine advertisement as a supermodel for designer apparel had struck Elvi as uniquely unfair.

She had read up about her mother's employer on the Internet, learning more that had made her grind her teeth together. *Why?* Because, Xan Ziakis seemed to have been born under a very lucky star, blessed by every conceivable attribute, and all he seemed to have learned from his remarkable good fortune was a marked tendency to behave as though he suffered from obsessive-compulsive disorder. Of course, maybe he did, she allowed ruefully, because nobody could possibly be that perfect in the real world. When she was still meeting her mother out of work to accompany her to AA meetings, she had seen Xan Ziakis coming home on several occasions while she sat waiting in the foyer of the luxury apartment block. And he was gorgeous to look at, absolutely, unmistakably gorgeous.

'I did the only thing I could,' Sally Cartwright confided hours later as she sat with her adopted daughter in the bedroom they shared. In her forties, she was a slender brunette with anxious green eyes now lined and shadowed with strain.

'It wasn't the only thing,' Elvi argued in a low voice,

neither of them wanting Daniel in the next room to over-
hear them. 'You could've told the truth, both of you—'

'And do you really think anyone would have *believed*
us?' her mother demanded tearfully, her cynicism unhidden. 'We're poor and down on our luck. Why? Because *I* wrecked all our lives, brought us down from a
normal happy family to *this*!'

'This', expressed by a shamed hand gesture, encom-
passed the grim surroundings of their council flat in
a tower block. But it was the guilt infused by Sally's
bitten-back sob that worried Elvi the most, fearful as
she was that her mother's distress would drive her back
to alcohol. She knew better than to fall into reasoned
argument with her mother on the score of her culpa-
bility because essentially the older woman was stating
the unlovely truth.

At the time of Elvi's father's sudden death, the Cartwright family had been financially secure. They had
owned their home and Sally had been a respected
teacher in a girls' school but alcohol and a tide of growing debt had washed that safe, comfortable life away.
Inevitably, Sally had lost her job and Elvi had left school
at sixteen to find work. Like bricks tumbling down
in a child's game, everything they had once taken for
granted had been taken from them until they'd reached
rock bottom and became homeless.

From there it had been a slow climb back to security, a *very* slow climb, Elvi acknowledged wryly, but
until this theft incident occurred their lives had steadily
been improving. The three of them had rejoiced the day
Daniel was accepted into medical school because it had

been the first positive event they had had to celebrate in a very long time. Sally was so proud that, in spite of all that they had lost, Daniel had kept on studying and finally won through against such stiff competition because places to study medicine were very much oversubscribed in the UK. The threat of Daniel being ruined by one foolish mistake *could* destroy her mother all over again, Elvi thought with a sick sinking sensation in her stomach.

'No,' Sally declared steadily, her troubled face set with strong determination. 'This is *my* moment to make a sacrifice for everything *I* took from the two of you years ago and nothing you can say or do will change my mind on that score.'

Well, we'll just see about that, Elvi thought defiantly as she lay in her bed that night, listening to her mother toss and turn, as unable to find sleep as her daughter. The mother she loved as much as she loved her little brother. Yet *her* mother had been her father's first wife, a Finnish nurse, tragically mown down by a car in a hospital car park within months of Elvi's birth. Her father had met and married Sally when Elvi was two years old and Elvi had no memories whatsoever of her birth mother. Her Scandinavian background came down to some faded photos and a handful of letters from an elderly Finnish grandma, who had died while she was still a child. For Elvi, family meant everything and she truly wished that her mother would accept that she and Daniel had long since forgiven her for her blunders.

After all, it wasn't as though Sally had *wanted* to become an alcoholic. Shattered by the sudden death of the husband she had adored, left alone to raise a six-year-old and a toddler, Sally had fallen apart in the grip of her grief and had slid into addiction by using alcohol as a crutch. Sally had had no other relatives to turn to for support and no close friends either because shortly before her husband's death, he had moved them all across the country to accept a new job. No, Elvi had sufficient compassion and understanding not to blame her mother for all their woes, nor was she willing to stand by and watch Sally undo all the progress she had made in recent years.

But realistically, what *could* she do?

Go and speak to Xan Ziakis in the hope that there was a streak of mercy beneath that designer suit and that frightening reputation for ruthless aggression and financial self-aggrandisement? Some hope, she mused wretchedly, feeling horribly weak and small and powerless. Xan Ziakis was feared in the City of London for his refusal to ever play as one of a team and his disdain for alliances, temporary or otherwise. He worked alone and her mother had never seen any evidence of a woman having been in his penthouse. Maybe he was gay...

No, not him, Elvi decided, shifting quietly beneath her duvet, remembering with shame a period when she had been almost obsessed by a need to see him daily. She didn't like to think about it but a sort of juvenile crush had engulfed her when she first saw Xan Ziakis. Not before time, she told herself drily; after all, life might have been all swings and not much roundabout throughout her unsettled and unhappy adolescence, but she was now twenty-two years old even if she was still almost as innocent as a child. Even so, she still recalled the single scorching appraisal Xan Ziakis had given her months ago and the flame that had leapt through her like a soaring torch along with the surprise of its effects on her body. No, he definitely wasn't gay, she was convinced. But the shock had been that a man who looked as he did could look at *her* that way.

She was no show-stopping beauty and she bore not the smallest resemblance to the giraffe-legged bone-thin models she had seen on his arm in images on the Internet. Five feet two inches tall, she had white-blonde hair down to her waist, blue eyes and the sort of generous curves that made buying clothes a nightmare. She kept her hair long because the unusual colour was the one thing she liked about herself. As for the big breasts, the overly large bottom and the thick thighs, anyone was welcome to them. If only she had been the gym-bunny type, she reflected, but she hated gyms, hated dieting, hated getting on the scales and loved her food far too much. He must have been looking at the boobs, she thought ruefully.

Would the boobs get her into his presence? Embarrassed by her own thoughts, she winced, but she wasn't in a position to be precious about what it might take to get a meeting with Xan Ziakis. He was a very powerful, influential and wealthy man, whose staff probably guarded access to him as if he were a solid platinum trophy to be seen only by the fortunate and equally rich and important few. So, approach him at home? Or at his office?

He was way too private in his lifestyle to be approached at his penthouse. It would have to be the office. Shortly before dawn when Sally had fallen into a restless sleep, Elvi crept out of bed, having finally decided what to do next. Since she doubted the likelihood of Xan being willing to grant her a personal interview, she would write him a letter, telling him what she needed to say. It was worth a try, she thought limply, and better than doing nothing. *Only just*, her intelligence warned her.

On Daniel's laptop, she began to tell their family history, but only after humbly apologising for both troubling Xan and the theft. She wished it had been possible to tell him the truth but, like her mother, she reckoned it would be too dangerous to put Daniel back in the suspect corner. If she told Xan Ziakis the truth, he could easily drop the charges against her mother and instead pursue her brother and, even worse, he could then use the very letter she was writing against her family. Maybe writing *anything* down on paper was too dangerous, she thought fearfully, stopping in her task several times with a chill on her skin as she tried not to envisage even worse consequences coming their way.

But what other option did she have? Appealing to a man who might well have no heart was the only road she could take, and only then, if he was willing to see her, would she see him and plead her family's case to the best of her ability. Having to lie and state that her mother must have succumbed to an inexcusable moment of temptation distressed Elvi, but since Sally had already owned up to the theft with the police she didn't have much choice. She begged him to drop the charges because he had got his valuable artefact back. Did Xan Ziakis have any compassion? Was it possible that a man who had so much could be decent enough to be human and caring too?

The letter in an envelope squarely marked 'private and confidential' in one corner, Elvi waited on the pavement outside the Ziakis headquarters at eight that same morning. An assistant in a craft shop, she didn't start work until nine. And, according to her mother's idle chatter over the months, Xan Ziakis had a schedule that ran like clockwork. He left the penthouse at eight and travelled by limousine to his office seven days a week. *Seven*, she reflected wryly, a man who worked every day of the week for his success. Well, she could hardly criticise his work ethic.

The big black limousine drew up. The driver only opened the door after another car drew up behind and four men in dark suits sprang out. Looking on in dismay, Elvi registered that Xan Ziakis was guarded by a ring-of-steel protection before he even got a polished shoe out of his limo. Even so, she moved forward, her legs turning strangely wobbly as Xan himself emerged into daylight, blue-black hair gleaming like polished silk, his flawless bronzed cheekbones taut below dark deep-set eyes, his lean, powerful body encased in an elegant suit that fitted him like a second skin, and there she froze.

'Get back!' someone said to her and, disconcerted, she retreated several steps still clutching her envelope.

Her quarry stalked on into the building…out of sight, *out of reach*, and she felt sick with failure, her face drained of colour, her eyes bleak.

A man appeared in front of her then, an older man, and there was something vaguely familiar about his craggy face. 'Is that letter you're gripping about your mother?' he asked bluntly. 'I work for Mr Ziakis too—'

'Oh,' Elvi said, taken aback by his approach. 'Yes, it's about Mum—'

'Then give it to me,' he urged. 'I'll see that it reaches the boss's desk.'

In a daze Elvi looked up and saw the kindness in his gaze. 'You're—?'

'Dmitri,' he supplied, twitching the letter out of her loosening grasp. 'I know your mother. I can't promise that the boss will read it or anything but I *can* put it on the desk.'

Elvi blinked. 'Thank you very much,' she murmured with warmth.

'No problem. She's a lovely lady,' Dmitri told her, walking off again at speed and vanishing into the building while tucking her letter into a pocket.

And Dmitri, whoever he is, doesn't think Sally Cartwright's a thief, Elvi realised as she climbed on a bus to get to work and mulled over that surprising encounter. Just as well, considering that she had frozen like an ice sculpture when she saw Xan Ziakis, not that she thought his bodyguards would have allowed her anywhere near him, because someone had told her to get out of the way. Dmitri? One of the other three men?

It didn't matter, she decided as she stocked shelves

of knitting wool at work. The letter might land on Xan's desk but, as Dmitri had said, that didn't mean he would actually bother to read it or even more crucially respond to it.

But in that Elvi was mistaken. Xan was so disconcerted by the unexpected sight of his head of security covertly sliding an envelope onto his desk, when Dmitri clearly thought he was unseen, that nothing would have kept him from opening up that letter out of sheer human curiosity. Xan skimmed down to the signature first: *Elvi Cartwright*. He knew that name well enough and he also knew he should've been prepared for the tactic in such a situation. Instantly he wanted to crumple the letter up and bin it without reading it. That would have been the cautious way to deal.

Even so, although Xan was *very* cautious with women, he couldn't bring himself to dump the letter unread. A couple of months ago, he had noticed her, well, really, *really* noticed her, he acknowledged grimly, and he had instructed Dmitri to find out who she was, assuming that she lived in the same apartment block. He had, however, learned that she was his maid's daughter, which had naturally concluded his interest. Billionaires did not consort with the daughters of their domestic staff. The gulf was too immense, the risk of a messy affair too great.

And yet, all the same...the letter still unread, Xan drifted momentarily into the past, recalling Elvi Cartwright with intense immediacy. The shining pale-as-milk hair, the wonderful blue eyes, the crazy natural glow of her, not to mention the extraordinary fact that she looked very different from the sort of women he usually slept with and yet, inexplicably, one glance at her turned him on harder and faster than any of them.

She was a bit overweight, he supposed abstractedly; hard to tell when he had only ever seen her in a loose black jacket that swamped her. Very short in stature, not his type, absolutely *not* his type, he told himself sternly as he shook out the letter, more concerned by Dmitri's bizarre involvement in its delivery than by what it might say. If he couldn't trust his head of security, who could he trust? Why had Dmitri got personally involved in so tawdry an incident?

Xan had a scientific approach to everything he read. Elvi's use of English was far superior to what he would have expected and then he began reading and what he read was most educational from his point of view even if, by the end of it, he couldn't think why she expected *him as the victim* to want to do anything about Sally Cartwright's self-induced predicament.

Inevitably he studied the situation from his side of the fence, where all the power lay, and the sort of ideas that had never occurred to Xan Ziakis before when it came to a woman began very slowly to blossom. Xan, who never ever allowed himself to succumb to any kind of unwise temptation. Xan, who usually policed his every thought, suppressing any immoral promptings to concentrate more profitably on work. And once he let those bad ideas out of the box they created a positive riot in his imagination, raising the kind of excitement that only a good financial killing usually gave him...

and that was it, Xan Ziakis was seduced by erotic possibilities for the first time in his life.

Xan folded the letter with a dark forbidding smile that his opponents would have recognised as a certain sign of danger and threat. He would give his quarry a couple of days to stew and wonder and *then* he would get in touch…

CHAPTER TWO

Two ANXIOUS DAYS in which she never allowed her phone to stray from her pocket passed for Elvi and on the third day, at the point where she had almost given up hope entirely, it finally rang.

One of Xan Ziakis's staff invited her to a meeting late that afternoon. Distracted by what lay ahead of her, she pleaded a dental appointment with her employer to finish early and worked over her usual lunch break instead. She got through her working hours on autopilot while anxiously rehearsing speeches in the back of her brain, only to discard them again when she tried to picture herself saying such things to a stranger. She would have to be lucid and brief, she told herself, because Xan Ziakis was unlikely to give her more than ten minutes of his time.

Seated in the plush quiet waiting area on the top floor of Ziakis Finance, Elvi was a bundle of nerves. How likely was it that he would even consider dropping the theft charge? Very unlikely, she reckoned, because what would be in that for him? But he *could* be a really good person, a little voice whispered. What were the chances? her brain scoffed, unimpressed by such wishful thinking. Xan was a merciless financier renowned for his profit margins. Every single thing he did during his working day was focused on gaining an advantage…and what did she have to offer?

She plucked a piece of tapestry wool off a black-trousered knee and shed her jacket to reveal the long-sleeved blue tee below because she was too warm. It was a waste of time approaching the wretched man when she was already virtually drowning in a sense of defeat, she told herself furiously. He was a rich, privileged guy, who lived a life far beyond the imagination of other, more ordinary mortals. He would not understand where she was coming from unless he had a reformed alcoholic in his own family circle. He would not appreciate the challenges Sally Cartwright had already overcome in her efforts to rebuild her life, nor could he even begin to imagine the misery of the 'lost' years that Elvi and Daniel had lived through with their mother.

Stop it, stop with the negative inner talk, she urged herself just as the svelte receptionist uttered her name in the same low-pitched tone that everyone who worked on the top floor seemed to use. Elvi rose stiffly from her seat, full of apprehension but struggling to appear composed because she knew that that was necessary. She couldn't afford to get emotional with such a self-disciplined man.

In his office, Xan was on a high because he was *finally* getting to meet *her*. The woman he had wanted, the *only* woman he had wanted in years that he couldn't have, but now that her mother was no longer his employee, and that connection was at an end, he no longer had to consider that aspect. That was done, dusted, in the past as far as he was concerned. Now he could move forward freely. Admittedly she was still of much lower status than he or her predecessors in his life had been but did he really have to be so particular about the women he took to his bed? He straightened his jacket and leant back against his designer desk as the door opened.

The office was the size of a football pitch, probably supposed to intimidate, Elvi decided, inching in from the doorway like a mouse trying to evade a hungry cat before she threw back her shoulders, straightened her back and lifted her chin, determined not to appear either weak or too humble.

'I'm Elvi, Sally Cartwright's daughter,' she declared quietly, battling to stand her ground as Xan Ziakis angled up his arrogant dark head, his classic nose as high as his perfect cheekbones to look directly at her.

Behind her the door closed, locking them into uneasy silence. Involuntarily Elvi connected with dazzling amber-gold eyes screened by criminally long and distinctive lush black lashes. She had never been close enough to him to see those eyes before, nor had she realised quite how tall he was, while even his formal business suit failed to conceal the power in his wide shoulders and muscular torso, not to mention the virile strength of his long thighs as he stood braced against his desk. He was drop-dead beautiful and at that moment she wasn't at all surprised that for a little while she had succumbed to a pathetically juvenile crush on him. She'd been far from being a teenager, and that crush had mortified her pride.

'Xander Ziakis,' he matched, extending an elegant lean brown hand.

At least he had manners, Elvi conceded feebly as she advanced to shake that hand, finding his grasp warm and her own cold with nerves, goose flesh erupting beneath her top as nervous tension threatened again. That close to him she could hardly breathe as a faint tang of some exotic designer cologne infiltrated her nostrils.

'Take a seat, Elvi,' he instructed, angling his head in the direction of the chair in front of him.

'I don't think I would be comfortable sitting down while you're still standing,' Elvi confided, stepping back but avoiding the chair, wondering if he was always as domineering, deciding he very probably was when she caught the flash of surprise in his gaze before he cloaked it. She reckoned everyone did exactly what they were told in his radius.

Disconcertingly and with a gleam of humour lightening his dark eyes, for he was rarely challenged, Xan slid back behind his desk and waited for her to sit down as he had told her to do.

Outmanoeuvred, Elvi took a seat and rested her bag on her lap to hide her trembling hands.

'Would you like a drink? Tea? Coffee? Water?' Xan proffered politely.

'Some water if it's not too much trouble,' Elvi framed, watching as he pressed a button and gave an order to some employee. Thirty seconds later, a moisture-beaded tumbler of water was clutched between her restive hands and she sipped, wetting her dry lips.

Xan studied her in fascination, because she was much more controlled than he had expected and possibly ten times more attractive close up than he had forecast. In reality he had been prepared for disappointment, having only seen her so fleetingly in the past. But there she was in front of him with skin that had the natural lustre of a pearl, eyes as blue as the Greek sky, dainty features and white-blonde hair falling like a cloak to her waist. And then there were the fabulous hourglass curves with that tiny waist, the amazing feminine bounty at breast and hip she had hidden beneath that awful coat. Not overweight, *glorious*, Xan decided hungrily, wondering if it would even occur to her that he had been forced to sit down because her body made him hot as hell. He thought not, for there was nothing even slightly flirtatious or inviting about either her clothing or her attitude, and he wasn't accustomed to that lack of interest in the women he met. This one hadn't even bothered to put on make-up, he registered in mounting surprise.

'Why do you think I offered you this appointment?' Xan enquired with innate ruthlessness, because he doubted his reading of her character from her appearance and behaviour. He didn't trust women. He had *learned* not to trust women through the experience of growing up with several unpleasant stepmothers and the conviction had been rubber-stamped by his first love's change of heart the instant she realised his family fortune was gone.

'I don't know, which is why I am here,' Elvi said truthfully. 'Obviously you read my letter—'

Xan lounged back in his chair and lightly shifted an eloquent brown hand as if in dismissal of the letter. 'Why would I want to do anything for a woman who stole from me?' he asked bluntly.

In receipt of that acerbic enquiry, Elvi lost colour. 'Well, maybe not *want*—'

'That's the problem,' Xan interposed before she could even finish speaking. 'I don't want to help her because I believe that those who break the law should be punished—'

'Yes, *but*—' Elvi began afresh, thrown on the back foot because before her mother had been charged with theft she would have agreed with him on that score.

'There is no saving exception in my book,' Xan Ziakis sliced in again. 'I felt more sorry for you growing up with an alcoholic parent than I feel sorry for her.'

Elvi's hands tightened around the glass cradled between her hands and she forced herself to sip again; she wanted to slap him and shut him up because he wasn't allowing her to get in a word in her mother's defence. 'We don't need your compassion!' she heard herself snap back and then she bit her lip hard, knowing she shouldn't have responded in that tone for there was truth in that old adage about catching more flies with honey than vinegar.

'But *you* chose to *ask* for my compassion,' Xan reminded her with dogged purpose. 'And I have to wonder, what's in it for me?'

'You have your jade pot back?' Elvi suggested shakily.

'But I don't. It's police evidence at this moment in time,' Xan told her gently.

Elvi breathed in deep and slow, battling to think straight while he sat there as cool as a block of untouchable ice, and then she clashed with eyes that flamed over her like a fire and realised that his apparently glacial outlook had given her a mistaken impression of him. For a split second as her chest swelled on that breath, his gaze had dropped revealingly below her chin and she was shaken that he could be quite as predictable as most of the men she met. Her boobs were playing more of a starring role than *she* was, she thought bitterly.

'My mother *has* been punished,' Elvi argued, taking another tack in her growing desperation. 'She's been arrested and that was frightening for her and more than enough to teach most people a hard lesson. She has also lost her job and her good name—'

'*Elvi...*' Xan leant across his desk to interrupt her again.

'No, don't cut me off this time!' Elvi urged impatiently. 'Tell me why you can't drop the charges—'

'I've already answered that question,' Xan reminded her with finality.

Enormous blue eyes fixed on him hopefully. 'But don't you think that making a benevolent gesture would make you feel good?'

Xan could not believe how naïve she was and he almost laughed. 'I don't have a benevolent bone in my body,' he admitted without embarrassment. 'I'm a hard-hitter. That's who I am.'

'Well, I didn't come here to repeat the sob story I already put in my letter,' Elvi assured him with cring-ing dignity as she started rising from her seat. 'So, if that's your last word—'

'It's not. You don't listen very well, do you?' Xan shot back at her in exasperation. 'I asked you what would be in this benevolent gesture for me and I do *have* an option to offer you—'

Taken aback at the very point where she had felt that she was getting nowhere with him, Elvi sank slowly back into the chair. 'You...er...do?' she queried dubi-ously, her eyes openly bemused by the concept.

'It's simple and unscrupulous,' Xan warned her with-out hesitation. 'I want you. Give yourself to me and I will drop the charges.'

Elvi's lower lip parted company with the upper one as she stared back at him in complete astonishment, not quite willing to believe he had actually said those words to her. *Give yourself to me.* He meant sex. What else could he mean? *I want you.* The most enormous sense of shock engulfed her. It wasn't simply unscrupulous, it was filthy, and she was shattered that he could sit there behind his rule-the-world desk and dare to offer her such an offensive escape clause on her mother's be-half. What world did he live in? What kind of women was he accustomed to dealing with? It was a horrific suggestion no decent woman would accept.

'I finally appear to have silenced you,' Xan remarked with unhidden amusement.

And it was that glint of amusement in his extravagantly handsome face and the energy of it in his accented intonation that set free the tide of rage inside Elvi. She flew upright like a rocket and her hand jerked up and she flung the glass of water over him. 'How dare you?' she snapped at him furiously. 'I'm not a slut!'

Xan shook his dark head, water droplets rolling down his lean, dark, dangerous face. Never had he been attacked in such a way, but it didn't show because he did not move a single muscle. He gazed broodingly back at her, disturbed by her passionate nature but already wondering how that seeming flaw would play out between his sheets. Obviously he was bored with the identikit mistresses who had met his physical needs for years, but that rational, unemotional approach worked for him, he reminded himself, staving off the risks of more personal entanglements. 'I didn't suggest that you were, but there's a vacancy in my bed at present and I would be happy for you to fill it for a couple of months—'

'Well, I wouldn't be happy to fill it!' Elvi snarled back incredulously. 'A *vacancy*? Is that how you think of sex?'

'It is a need like hunger, an appetite that must be met,' Xan responded levelly, his hard, dark gaze locked to hers like a laser beam that made her body as hot and perspiring as if she were under a spotlight. 'If it makes you feel better, I wanted you the first time I saw you waiting in the foyer of my apartment block. I found out your name then and your connection to my maid. Doing anything about the attraction would've been inappropriate at that time—'

Elvi studied him in helpless wonderment. 'I don't believe this… I don't believe any of it!' she gasped. 'You don't even know me—'

Xan lounged back in his seat, damp but disciplined. 'I don't need to *know* you to want to have sex with you. I'm more about the physical than the cerebral with women,' he admitted smoothly.

'But you're trying to buy me with a bribe!' Elvi condemned furiously.

'And if the offer suits you, I'll drop the theft charge. That's how negotiations work in this world, Elvi. *You* give, *I* give. It really is that basic—'

'But it's blackmail!' Elvi accused heatedly, increasingly unnerved by his shattering level of inhuman self-control.

'No, it's not. You have a choice. Whether you choose to accept my offer or not is entirely up to you,' Xan pointed out with precision. 'Think it over for a week…'

'I'm not going to think it over!' Elvi assured him with blazing conviction. 'It's a filthy proposition and I'm not that sort of woman—'

'Presumably you enjoy sex like other women,' Xan interposed very drily. 'If you're afraid that I might be into something different like BDSM, you're wrong. I'm completely normal in the sex department—'

'I don't care! I'm not interested in what you do in the bedroom!' Elvi proclaimed, pacing his office carpet in a passion of disbelief at the direction their interview had gone in, her triangular face as red as a tomato. 'I couldn't imagine being some sort of sex slave—'

Xan laughed out loud, shocking her again, startling

her as he sprang up from behind his desk and extended a business card to her. 'The word you seek is mistress, *not* sex slave, which is rather melodramatic, if you don't mind me saying so—'

'Yes, I *do* mind!' Elvi gasped, snatching the card off him and backing away at speed from his proximity, her heart beating so fast she feared it might bounce right out of her tight chest. 'I mind every darned thing you've said since I arrived. I didn't like any of it and I wouldn't have come to this meeting if I'd known you were likely to suggest some immoral arrangement to me! Call me stupid but that idea didn't even cross my mind!'

Xan had never wanted to touch a woman as badly as he did at that moment. *Thee mou*…she excited him to the most extraordinary degree. Her amazing chest was heaving, her blue eyes were huge with anxiety and her opulent pink pouty mouth was yet another temptation that tugged at him as he pictured her lying in his bed. It was lust of the lowest possible order, he acknowledged grimly, but somehow, even though lust had never driven him to such a degree and he thoroughly distrusted the urge, he couldn't shake free of it. The harder she argued with him, the more he wanted to persuade her because, whatever else Elvi Cartwright was, she was neither boring nor insipid. A sex slave though, he savoured with unholy amusement, even while he wondered if that could possibly be a fantasy of hers… how did he know? But he very badly wanted to know about *her* fantasies. Yet he could not recall ever being so curious about any other woman and his innate caution cut in.

She was saying no, shrieking no, in fact, and possibly that was for the best, he reasoned flatly even as all the potential colour and enjoyment drained straight back out of his immediate future again. Was he so bored with his life that he had proposed such an innovative exchange of favours? It was out of character for him. He picked up women and dropped them again as easily as he worked seven days a week. He didn't normally *picture* them in that apartment bed, he merely joined them there to satisfy a natural desire for physical satisfaction.

'You have my phone number if you change your mind,' Xan Ziakis intoned, as if he could not quite credit that she had turned him down.

Elvi tossed her head, platinum-blonde hair spilling across her shoulders. She would have made a terrific Lady Godiva, Xan reflected abstractedly, wondering why he was even thinking that. He stalked across to the door and opened it for her, now determined to bring the unsettling meeting to a quick conclusion.

'Good luck,' he murmured graciously, feeling inordinately proud of himself for his restraint.

Blue eyes collided with his. 'You are the most hateful man I have ever met!' she hissed at him like a cat flexing her sharp claws and, turning on her heel, she sped off down the corridor.

Xan noted that she had left her jacket behind, lifted it and strode out of his office again.

'Elvi!' he called when he saw her standing at the lift, hugging her handbag as if it were a comforter.

Eyes flying wide, she spun and he handed her the jacket.

'Oh...thanks,' she mumbled in disconcertion, suddenly uncomfortably aware that every employee in the area had stilled to watch them.

That was the instant when Xan saw the tears glimmering in her eyes and wished he hadn't followed her. It made him feel like an ogre who kicked puppies, a complete bastard. But he was what he was and he had never been soft in heart or deed, he reasoned harshly. She needed to toughen up because the world was a thoroughly nasty place.

Still shell-shocked by that encounter with Xan, Elvi went home and found her mother in tears at the kitchen table. 'I don't know how I'm going to get work anywhere without a reference from my last job,' she confided chokily. 'And I can't tell the truth either. Nobody wants a light-fingered employee!'

Elvi paled. 'We'll think up something,' she said soothingly. 'Is Daniel at the restaurant?'

'Yes. Thank goodness he got that bar job. At least it gets him out of his room,' his mother remarked unhappily. 'He's so depressed, Elvi. He feels so guilty—'

Elvi nodded, trying not to think that, had she been of a different persuasion, she might have been able to make the whole nightmare go away. It would be indecent, though, for her to have sex with Xan Ziakis in return for him dropping the theft charge. Totally disgustingly indecent, she told herself squarely. Surely she didn't have to sink *that* low to help her family?

She lay awake half the night thinking about it. The irony was that before she had met Xan Ziakis he was the only man she had ever thought of having sex with. Well, in her dreams, her imagination, that was, because he was the first man she had ever been strongly attracted to. Of course, she had met very few men. Few men went into craft shops; customers who liked to knit, crochet and embroider were mostly of the female persuasion, although not exclusively. Throughout most of her teen years, while other young girls were flirting and dating, Elvi had been looking after her little brother and tucking her comatose mother into bed at night. She had missed out on a large chunk of her supposedly carefree youth, having to be responsible, having to be the adult for as long as Sally had been incapable of meeting that challenge.

By the way, I'm still a virgin, she tried to picture herself telling Xan Ziakis. Unexpectedly, her body shook with sudden laughter at the image. No doubt Xan had assumed that she was experienced when he'd made that crack about women enjoying sex as well. No doubt he also believed she would be mistress material with the sort of sexy tricks a more practised lover would provide. But she had no tricks, no clue, *nothing* to give in that department, and she was quite sure that that would have disillusioned him, maybe even put him off.

Although, how would that have helped them? He had only made that ridiculous offer because he found her attractive. For a split second, she cherished the knowledge of that startling truth. Xan Ziakis found *her* attractive as well. It was a fact that bolstered her ego even though she knew it shouldn't. Probably the boobs again, she thought wryly. As an adolescent, who had been tormented at school by the boys once she began developing way beyond what she had deemed an acceptable size, she had always loathed her large breasts and ample hips. Joel, her best mate since primary school, told her she looked lush and feminine, but then that was exactly the sort of comforting comment a friend was supposed to make, so she hadn't paid any heed to it.

The following morning, Joel sent her a text asking her to meet him at lunchtime. She smiled at the prospect, knowing she could tell her friend the truth about her mother and her brother, although she had no intention of mentioning Xan's proposition.

'How could a boy as smart as Daniel be that dumb?' Joel demanded, smoking while they sat outside a bar close to where she worked.

'Clever people don't always have common sense,' Elvi pointed out, leaning across the table to add, 'You're getting eyed up by that beautiful blonde over there. I think it's time I went back to work—'

'No!' Joel protested, closing an imprisoning hand over the one she had braced on the tabletop to rise. 'I'm not interested—'

'You haven't even looked yet,' Elvi rebuked as she met his brown eyes and wondered how his could be so different from Xan's, because they did not make her melt or heat up to even the smallest degree. Yet, Joel was tall and attractive with tousled dark curls. He was also an up-and-coming successful painter, already being singled out for his talent with portraits. But then Joel's life had gone much more smoothly than her own, she reflected ruefully, and sometimes she marvelled that he still stayed in touch with her because they now led such divergent lives.

'All I want to do right now is give you some cash to help out,' Joel told her ruefully. 'You earn a pittance and with Sally out of work—'

'No, thanks,' Elvi cut in hastily. 'Thanks for offering but no, thanks—'

'Don't you ever just want to walk away from the two of them and their problems?' her friend enquired ruefully. 'You could've been so much *more* without them holding you back—'

'You're talking about my mother and my brother,' Elvi reminded him tartly. 'I love them and they love me and you don't turn your back on that kind of love and support—'

'But you're always supporting *them*, not yourself!' Joel argued.

He didn't understand, he never *had* understood, Elvi reflected wryly, because his was not a close family. Elvi, however, knew that, no matter what happened to her, her mother and her brother would always be there for her just as she was for them. That made her feel warm and complete inside herself in a way she couldn't have described even to her longest-standing friend.

'I'm wasting my breath,' Joel recognised impatiently as Elvi slid back into her black jacket. 'For some bizarre reason you don't want the stuff other women want…the new clothes, the parties, the *fun*—'

'I'd give anything to own a dog,' she confided, and not for the first time.

'A dog would just be another burden,' Joel reproved.

Didn't stop her wanting one, Elvi reasoned wryly as she got off the bus to go home that evening. A dog to walk and cuddle when she felt lonely. A cat was a possibility but cats weren't necessarily cuddly, being more independent. As usual the lift was out of service and she had to climb flight after flight of stairs to the tenth floor, telling herself all the while that the exercise was keeping her fit even if she was wheezing like an old lady by the time she walked into the kitchen. That lighter mood didn't last once she saw her mother and brother standing there, clearly in the middle of a rare argument.

'What's wrong?' she asked tightly.

'Look, what I did wrecked everything for *all* of us,' Daniel declared forthrightly. 'Mum can't find work now, and you hardly earn anything. How are we going to live? Obviously I have to find a *permanent* job—'

'No, that's not what this is all about,' Elvi cut in hastily. 'That would make what Mum did pointless, Daniel. We *want* you to go to university and train to be a doctor—'

'I did this. This is *my* responsibility and I'm old enough to behave like a man,' her little but very tall baby brother announced. 'A man doesn't turn his back on his family and just go off and become a student without thinking about how *they* are going to survive!'

Elvi thought a very rude word inside her head, her shoulders slumping, and passed on by into the bedroom to sink down on her bed. Daniel was like a mule when he set his heart on anything and now he too was in full sacrificial mode, just like her mother. What now? If Daniel threw away his chance, it wouldn't come around again, and if he did that Sally Cartwright would self-destruct because her son going to medical school was the one thing she had in life to focus on and be proud of.

Xan Ziakis had won, Elvi reflected wretchedly, because her family was falling apart before her very eyes. From the kitchen she could hear the distressing noise of her mother and her brother having a major row as Sally tried to dissuade him from his plans and he fought back loudly. She pulled the business card out of her bag and reached for her phone. She didn't want to speak to a man she hated, a man who was forcing her into a choice that went against everything she had ever valued, so she texted him instead.

Rethink on mistress as you forecast. Need to discuss conditions of servitude.

Across London, Xan checked his phone and laughed out loud, something he didn't do very often and which spooked him with its unfamiliarity. He had won. He *always* won, he reminded himself with satisfaction. But even so there was a sweeter taste to this victory than most.

Meet you for dinner at eight...

And he gave her the address, telling her to ask for *his* table.

CHAPTER THREE

ELVI WENT INTO her slender wardrobe to withdraw a pair of black velour leggings and a black, rather glittery festive top she had received for Christmas the year before. The outfit would have to do because she didn't have anything else to wear.

'Where on earth are you going dressed like that?' Sally Cartwright demanded boldly as her daughter passed through the kitchen, wearing actual lip gloss and mascara to her mother's wonderment.

'I've got a date for dinner,' Elvi admitted, having reasoned that she had to make a start on her cover story.

'A...*date*?' her mother exclaimed in astonishment.

'Yes, he's handsome, he's rich, he can give me a good time, what's not to like?' she asked the older woman wryly. 'I'm twenty-two and I never go out. Isn't it time I got a life?'

'Of course, it is,' Sally agreed uneasily. 'I was only surprised, not questioning you.'

'I don't know if I'll be back tonight,' Elvi announced uncomfortably, her face flaming, but she had to work on her cover story.

'Elvi...?' her mother pronounced in a shaken tone, but she compressed her lips and said nothing more, accepting that her daughter was an adult woman.

Only Elvi felt nothing like an adult woman as she entered an exclusive restaurant, maddeningly conscious that she was underdressed, and where she was looked up and down in open dismissal before the mention of Xan's name produced a very different reaction and suddenly she was 'Madam...' and being escorted by the head waiter to the promised table where Xan was already seated, perusing the extensive wine list.

Xan leapt upright. He was a four-letter word of a man but someone some time had trained him well in courtesy, Elvi acknowledged, bending to set down her bag before deigning to take a seat in the chair pulled out for her occupation.

Xan was transfixed by his view of her. She was very poorly clothed, but the instant she bent down and he caught a glimpse of her rounded derriere outlined in clinging velour he became a spontaneous fan of clingy leggings that outlined the female form. A bottom as deliciously curvy and ripe as a peach met his attention and the stirring at his groin was even more immediate. He asked himself how he could possibly have reached thirty years of age without appreciating that he found curvaceous women more sexually appealing than their thinner cousins. Or was it only *her*? Something weird about her? That mane of long hair?

'Elvi,' he murmured in welcome. 'What would you like to drink?'

'I don't drink. Water, please,' she told him, settling

into her seat, seemingly unaware that he was riveted to his, locked there by the equally clingy glittery top that showcased her breasts. The smooth pale expanse of soft firm flesh and only the merest hint of cleavage sent the pulse below his belt to throbbing discomfort and a level of arousal that set his even white teeth on edge, because he was neither a horny teenager nor a sex-starved man and anything excessive in any personal field set off Xan's caution alarm.

She didn't drink. That didn't bother Xan at all because he had had the experience of several women who liked to drink a little too much and turned into public embarrassments. An alcoholic in the family, he recalled; naturally she was careful. He ordered wine for himself and ordered meals for both of them, as was his habit with companions.

Elvi sipped her water and watched food selections she hadn't ordered brought to the table with great pomp and ceremony. She wasn't that surprised by his failure to offer her a personal choice or a menu. He was a control freak. He was accustomed to commanding what other people did, even, it seemed, what they *ate*. He would probably be hell in bed, she found herself thinking ruefully, imagining what that innate selfishness would translate to in terms of sex with another person. But then what did she know about it? Maybe that was the norm for a rich man like him. A woman of her status was simply a new toy for him to play with, nothing more.

Elvi cleared her throat awkwardly. 'So, this arrangement…how long would it last exactly?'

'Three months,' Xan heard himself declare, although he had never before mentioned anything longer than two. He was being practical, he told himself, ensuring he could keep her until he got bored, and he *could* get bored the very first month, couldn't he? That had happened on a couple of occasions and could well happen with her.

Elvi studiously stared down at her water. 'And how often...er, would I...*see* you?'

'I doubt if there's a virile man in the world who would answer that question in advance,' Xan quipped, amusement flashing through him as he wondered how many one-night stands she had enjoyed. At her age, that was the norm, wasn't it? Or was it? He had no idea because he had never made use of that kind of freedom, reluctant to follow in the footsteps of a father who had been a notorious womaniser and playboy. He had never slept around, never been attracted by indiscriminate casual sex with strangers.

Elvi reddened, heat coursing through her as she met brilliant dark eyes alive with the kind of powerhouse energy he had kept in abeyance during that interview in his office. Stupid question, she conceded uneasily, insanely aware of the tightening of her nipples and the bizarre flush of warmth rising from her pelvis. Both sensations were unhappily familiar, echoes of what she had felt every time she'd seen Xan walk past her months earlier. She hadn't known attraction could make her feel like that about a man and she hadn't appreciated the yearning sense of vulnerability it infused her with.

'I will provide you with an apartment and a new wardrobe. You need clothes,' Xan intoned with a casualness that shot her straight back out of her reverie.

An apartment. Elvi swallowed hard, reminding herself that it would only be for a few months and that she could hardly act the mistress while sharing a bedroom with her adoptive mother.

'Why do I need *you* to buy *me* clothes?' she queried rather sourly.

'When I need a partner to attend a social engagement, you will be my companion,' Xan informed her, startling her afresh because she had assumed that being a mistress was a very discreet role in a back room some place where she would be hidden from public view.

'Not sure I would be up to that challenge,' Elvi admitted ruefully. 'You live in a very exclusive world.'

'You would merely be on my arm,' Xan told her as if she were a man bag. 'You wouldn't even need to speak. I would handle conversation—'

'Like you handled ordering my meal for me?' Elvi gently nudged her untouched plate away another few inches. 'If you had asked, I would've told you that I don't eat fish—'

'Fish is healthy,' Xan informed her smoothly.

'But you're not my doctor or my dietician and I am not so stupid that I require your guidance. I *hate* fish,' Elvi spelled out with emphatic cool.

Xan shrugged a broad shoulder, impervious to her reproof. 'So, order something else.'

'I'm really not hungry,' Elvi told him truthfully. 'As I said in my text, I'm only here to hear the conditions.'

'Of servitude,' Xan reminded her silkily. 'I *like* that word. It has a lovely medieval ring to it.' He removed something from an inside pocket and set it down beside her hand: it was a key with a label attached. 'The apartment key and the address. Do you require assistance to move in?'

'How soon will you withdraw the theft charge?' Elvi pressed anxiously. 'And no, no assistance required. I don't have much stuff.'

'The day you move in, the charge will be withdrawn,' Xan supplied. 'I will not do anything before that. You could still back out—'

Elvi tensed. 'And if I gave you my word of honour that I wouldn't?'

A cool smile curved his wide sensual lips. 'I wouldn't trust it. Women can be unpredictable—'

'As can men.' Elvi grasped the apartment key as though it were a stinging nettle and thrust it hurriedly into her bag. 'I'll move in tomorrow. What about my job?'

'You quit. When I want you, I naturally want you to be available,' Xan pointed out smoothly.

'I'll need to work a notice period,' she protested.

'No, you simply leave,' Xan contradicted arrogantly. 'From this moment on, you're my responsibility—'

Elvi froze as if he had struck her. 'Servitude is biting right now,' she conceded between gritted teeth. 'I don't like depending on anyone outside my family.'

'But now and first and foremost, you've got me and my demands to consider. I will deliver if you do,' Xan completed levelly. 'I will treat you like a princess.'

Yes, once upon a time, princesses had had to get into bed with strangers as well, Elvi thought mutinously, although at least they had been married off first. Not that she wanted to be married to him, which would probably be even worse than being *owned* by him, because that was how he was making her feel. Like a new possession, a *thing*, an object, rather than a person.

'I'm really not going to be very suitable for purpose,' she warned him tightly.

'Then you've been with the wrong men,' Xan assured her with unblemished confidence, his flawless cheekbones slashing taut to accentuate the brilliance of his stunning brown eyes and their black lashes.

Her face burning at that recollection, Elvi climbed into bed in the dark, striving not to wake her mother up.

'Elvi…?' the older woman whispered. 'Did you have a nice evening?'

Remembering her fib about having a date, Elvi grimaced. 'Yes.' She hesitated and then pressed ahead. 'I've been thinking of moving out and in with a…er…a *flatmate*,' she selected the final word abruptly.

Silence greeted her from her mother's direction and she wasn't surprised because she knew that her sudden announcement would shock Sally. Even more, though, did Elvi hate the necessity of telling lies because she knew that she could not possibly tell the truth.

'Anyone I know?' Sally prompted.

'No. A friend of Joel's but if I want to move in I have to move in tomorrow,' Elvi completed. 'I'm sorry it's such short notice—'

'No, don't apologise. You're twenty-two, Elvi, and naturally you would like some independence and freedom. I had those things at your age—why shouldn't you? Please don't sound so apologetic about it,' Sally Cartwright responded a shade shakily. 'You stayed with us all the years Daniel and I needed you, so, although I'll miss you, I'm certainly not about to try and make you change your mind.'

Relieved by that exchange, Elvi lay still until a tiny sniff alerted her to the reality that her mother was crying and she slid straight out of bed and wrapped her arms around the older woman as well as she could with the duvet separating them. 'I love you,' she framed, feeling ridiculously guilty about moving out even though she knew she didn't want to move but *had* to for Xan Ziakis's benefit.

'Things will settle down again. This is only a rough patch,' the older woman told her more cheerfully. 'I'll find work. Daniel will start classes and we'll all go back to normal again. We only have to be patient and strong.'

The next morning, Daniel accompanied Elvi to the Tube station with her single suitcase. 'You're moving in with a man, aren't you?' he shot unexpectedly at his sister, and when she glanced up with pink cheeks and a look of guilt, he laughed. 'Yeah, thought so. Mum's worried some smartass is taking advantage of you—'

'I'm not stupid,' Elvi declared, but saw no reason to add any further details when she was sure she would be moving back home again within a couple of months, if not sooner.

'Well, you *are* rushing into this too fast, but that's your business,' her sibling conceded, halting to pass her the case, which was too old to have handy wheels attached. 'Look after yourself, sis, and make sure you visit us when I'm not working.'

Tears were prickling in Elvi's eyes by the time she boarded the train and she gave herself an urgent reality check, reminding herself of the theft charge that would be dropped and the sheer guilt and strain that would drop away and allow her mother and brother to continue their lives without further harm. It *would* be worth it, she told herself urgently, absolutely worth anything she had to do to achieve that desirable result.

The apartment in an elegant building overlooking the Thames was much larger and fancier than she had dimly expected. She wandered around barefoot on opulent marble floors, viewing the beautiful and immaculate living area with its leather sofas and contemporary paintings. She walked out onto the balcony to take in the busy view of the river before entering a kitchen equipped with every necessity as well as a fully stocked fridge and freezer. She marvelled at the two separate opulent bathrooms she discovered off the very spacious bedroom, as well as a dressing room fitted with loads of closet space. It was a property prepared for the sort of woman who took a great deal of interest in her appearance, she reasoned with raised brows, noting the number of mirrors and racks for shoes and handbags. She was starting to unpack her case when the doorbell pinged.

A svelte older woman carrying garment bags greeted

her. 'I'm Sylvia. Mr Ziakis asked me to choose an outfit for you to wear tonight.'

So, it begins, Elvi acknowledged ruefully, her new life as an object. Xan hadn't bothered to tell her personally that he planned to take her somewhere that very evening and how had he even *known* she had moved in? Were there secret cameras installed? she wondered apprehensively.

'Nothing will be a perfect fit until I take your measurements,' Sylvia announced, unfurling a measuring tape. 'Could we take this into the bedroom? It would be more comfortable for you to try on the dresses I've brought for you to choose from.'

Elvi wasn't comfortable in any way having to strip down to her underwear for a complete stranger but she compressed her lips and did what she had to do, barely pausing to glance at her reflection in blue dress after blue dress.

'Only blue?' she queried.

'Mr Ziakis specified blue,' she was told as Sylvia whisked the tape over her figure and jotted down measurements on her tablet. 'Seems to be his new favourite colour, at least for you—'

'You've done this before for him with other women, haven't you?' Elvi commented.

'Every service that my company offers Mr Ziakis is completely confidential,' Sylvia countered with perfect diplomacy.

Elvi wasn't listening. Xander Ziakis was evidently a serial womaniser, given to keeping mistresses whom he placed in an apartment and dressing them from head to toe in *his* choice of colour and fashion. She was appalled and soon wondering how many other women had lived in the apartment before her and whether he had cared in any way about a single one of them. When he had said he was more about the physical than the cerebral, he hadn't been joking. Her attention strayed to the vast divan bed she had studiously ignored since her arrival and she breathed in deep, striving not to think about the sex aspect.

After all, thinking about it wasn't going to make it go away and dwelling on something she couldn't avoid would be foolish. She tried on the half-dozen dresses and vanished into one of the bathrooms to find the right size for the fancy lingerie Sylvia had placed on the bed. She chose the dress that fitted the best and hid the most, not being a fan of her own cleavage. Her back and arms and legs would be on show and that was quite enough, in her opinion. She had to practise walking in the very high heeled sandals and they pinched her toes horribly. It was a very great shame that wearing a designer outfit that probably cost hundreds if not *thousands* of pounds had never been on her bucket list, she conceded ruefully.

What on earth did Xan want with a young woman like her? For goodness' sake, she was a shop girl, or had been until she'd quit earlier that day in a very uncomfortable phone call to her employer. She was ordinary, not special, not a beauty, no great wit. What did Xan see in her that was so desirable he would go to such lengths to have her?

She looked in the mirror. Her *body*—what a lowering thought that was, she reflected unhappily. He didn't know her, wouldn't waste time even *trying* to get to know her; he only wanted to have sex with her, and the fancy apartment and the ridiculously big wardrobe Sylvia had insisted she would need were simply the luxury trappings that she was expected to be delighted to receive. She had no doubt that other women had enjoyed those benefits from sharing their bodies with a very, very rich man but, unfortunately for her, she wasn't one of them. She felt cheapened by living in an apartment Xan owned, wearing clothes and eating food provided by him. It felt too much like being paid for sex. But that was the arrangement she had agreed to, she reminded herself, and she did not see that she could do much about it.

For the first time in over a year, when a bout of flu had forced him to deviate from his routine, Xan finished at the office early. He acknowledged that Elvi roused an unusual sense of excitement that was new to his experience. It was nothing he couldn't handle though, he thought, choosing to be amused by his mood rather than disturbed by it. She was new, she was fresh, there was nothing odd about his interest. He was a normal guy, his libido inflamed by the prospect of a different woman. He texted her the time she would be picked up and smiled.

Elvi was disconcerted when the bell went shortly before eight and she was confronted with Dmitri on the doorstep. 'Ready?' he asked flatly, somehow radiating disapproval in waves.

Her complexion flaming, Elvi dug her key into the fancy clutch that matched her ridiculous shoes and preceded him into the lift he had already had waiting for her. 'What's your job with Xan?' she enquired stiffly.

'I'm the head of his security team. Does Sally know about this?' he framed.

'Of course not,' Elvi parried uncomfortably. 'I don't want her to know either.'

The older man released his breath impatiently and said nothing more, but the attitude he emanated had left her in no doubt that he had guessed exactly what her new role in his employer's life was and she was mortified by the deep sense of shame that engulfed her.

'What's wrong?' Xan heard himself demand as soon as he saw her, because instead of the smile, the warmth that he had somehow vaguely expected from her, she was flushed and stiff as a waxwork with her usual glow absent.

'Nothing,' Elvi responded tightly.

'I hate it when people lie to me,' Xan told her warningly.

'Well, if you must know, I feel like the slut I said I wasn't!' Elvi rounded on him helplessly, her emotions overpowering her innate practicality. 'Living in an apartment *you* own, wearing clothes *you* paid for!'

Never having been attacked on that score before, Xan tensed, slowly coming to terms with the truth that for the first time in his life he might just have chosen a woman with moral principles. He was utterly spooked by the suspicion. 'You're *not* a slut,' he breathed in a curt undertone of denial. 'We have an agreement—'

The reminder steadied Elvi as nothing else could have done. 'The theft charge?'

'Dropped. *Gone*,' Xan emphasised with relief, expecting that to improve her mood.

But Elvi said nothing, refusing to believe that assurance until she heard it from her mother herself. She knew Sally would have phoned her immediately with such news, not sat on it. Her hands merely tightened around her clutch.

'I have some jewellery for you to wear,' Xan continued.

'Don't want it,' she said mutinously.

'Nonetheless you *will* wear it as part of your role,' Xan contradicted, settling a wide shallow box on her lap without apology. 'You're being childish and difficult and that's not what I want from you.'

Possibly that was the wake-up call Elvi felt she needed at the moment. She *had* agreed to the mistress role and there was no room to wriggle out of the arrangement again. Gritting her teeth together, she opened the box on a diamond necklace and earrings that flashed like white fire as the streetlights illuminated the limo's interior. She pushed her hair over one shoulder and reached for the necklace but Xan got there before her.

'Allow me,' he breathed, tugging her round by the shoulder to put her back to him, so close to her that the sheer heat of his body hit her bare back like a burn inflicted by the sun and she froze as he bent over her to attach the necklace at her nape.

That close, he smelt amazing, a dynamite combination of clean, crisp masculinity, exotic cologne and an element that was uniquely his own but which reminded her of fresh air and the woods. The startling wonder of his scent filtered through her like an aphrodisiac, shocking her afresh. Her breath hitching in her dry throat, she shifted away again fast and fumbled for the earrings to attach them.

'You're very jumpy for a woman I have yet to touch,' Xan observed.

'This situation is new to me,' Elvi pointed out nervously.

'It's not a situation. It's a relationship like any other.' Xan surprised himself by saying the word he always avoided because he *knew* it wasn't a relationship, it was purely a sexual connection.

Now you're giving her mixed messages, he reproved himself immediately. No, he was simply trying to make her relax before she wrecked his good mood. He had set this up; he could hardly complain about her being different from the kind of women he was accustomed to when he had known that from the start. He was no softie with women but he was always rational, fair, he assured himself until he tried to apply that statement to the manner in which he had *acquired* Elvi, and the oddest sense of discomfiture assailed him for the first time ever in a woman's presence.

Elvi shot him an anxious glance, big blue eyes as easily read as a headline. There was a sort of strange innocence about her, almost as if she was expecting him to break out a whip and chains. Stubborn mouth quirking, he shelved that sudden unlikely suspicion, choosing instead to recall the moment she had looked back at him a couple of months back in the apartment foyer. She had wanted him then and he had known it, was way too experienced in that department with women to be mistaken. And now he had made it possible for her to *have* him and she ought to be pleased about that, shouldn't she? *He* was pleased. Why wasn't she? Why did women have to be so blasted irrational and change-able? And since when had he cared when one was? He was wasting way too much time speculating on her be-haviour and it was inappropriate with a sexual partner.

He took her to a very exclusive party in a London town house with a man playing jazz at a grand piano in the drawing room amid a crush of very well-dressed chattering guests. Xan was treated like a golden god from the moment he arrived, drinks brought, seats found, his every opinion sought. He did once say, 'This is Elvi,' but for the most part, she was studiously ig-nored, presumably because his habit of having a mis-tress as a partner at such engagements was well known and she was deemed to be beneath the notice of such wealthy people.

'Who is she?' she heard one woman whisper be-hind her seat.

'Not his usual type,' another remarked.

'Fabulous hair though. Dyed, of course—'

And Elvi had been horribly tempted to twist around and disabuse the women with a tart response, but she had resisted the urge, preferring to be ignored while she had to listen to boring financial discussions and Xan kept an unexpectedly possessive arm wrapped round her even while they were sitting down, as if he feared she might bolt for the door.

Perhaps he had ESP, she reflected ruefully, because

she was becoming increasingly apprehensive about the end of the evening. She had checked her phone repeatedly, even texting her mother to ask how she was, and if Xan *had* dropped the theft charge the fact hadn't yet been shared with the older woman. How was she supposed to trust him? How was she supposed to know that he had done what he had promised?

'That was a mind-numbing evening,' Xan commented, surprising her as he lounged back in a corner of the limousine. 'I hate it when people fuss over me like that and expect tips for free—'

'The price of success?' Elvi quipped.

As *she* was one of the benefits, Xan savoured, watching her with unashamed hunger. He had used his power to capture her and right at that moment he had not a single regret. She was a natural beauty and blue was definitely *her* colour, lighting up those eyes to brilliance. The wondrous curves were simply the icing on a very tempting cake and tonight she was finally *his*. He had been tempted to cut the party and stay in, had made himself go to convince himself that he was still in control of the need that made him ache with excitement in her radius. Not cool, not cool at all...but now he didn't have to be any longer.

Elvi was not unaware of the way Xan was watching her, could only compare the blaze of those slumberous amber eyes to a panther lazily eying his next meal. Her entire body felt hot and scratchy, her breasts heavy, the space between her thighs tingling and hollow. She knew it was how *he* made her feel and told herself she ought to be grateful for that in the circumstances. Suppose he had not appealed to her in any way? How could she possibly have made such an agreement?

And exactly how was she now supposed to tell him that there was no way she was sharing that bed with him tonight?

Nerves gripped her fast as he accompanied her into the lift and she knew she had to say something. She cleared her throat awkwardly. 'Look… I have something to say—'

'Say it,' Xan urged impatiently, his lean brown hands lifting to come down on her small shoulders and urge her closer even as the lift doors whirred back.

'We…er…*can't*. Not tonight anyway,' she warned him with hot cheeks.

Xan groaned out loud. 'Why didn't you tell me sooner?' he demanded, practically dragging her out of the lift and slotting his own key into the front door of the apartment.

'It was…difficult—'

'Surely you could have rearranged the pills or something? I would have sent you to the doctor, had I known,' Xan growled, pressing her into the apartment and leaning back against the door to close it, his entire brain preoccupied with what he *could* do, what he couldn't and the kind of frustration he had never experienced before engulfing him hard because he was literally *burning* for her.

As Elvi registered what Xan had taken from her declaration, her whole body lit up with embarrassment because her menstrual cycle was something she had never discussed with any man and the sudden realisation that his access to her was likely to include that kind of personal information appalled her.

'No, you misunderstood me,' she said swiftly. 'It's not *that*—'

'*Diavole*...you're driving me crazy here, *koukla mou*,' Xan growled, curving both his hands to her triangular face to gaze down into her beautiful but evasive eyes. 'What is it?'

But he didn't wait for her response. He fell for the enticement of those soft pink sultry lips, nibbled sexily along the bottom one, groaned out loud as she gasped into his mouth and bundled her right off her feet to kiss her.

The devastating urgency of that first plunging, ravaging kiss sent an earthquake of burning hunger travelling through Elvi right to the very heart of her. She hadn't thought, hadn't dreamt, hadn't even imagined that she was capable of feeling anything that powerful. But that hunger was like a seductive, sweet-talking infiltrator in her treacherous body, battling every thought, every other instinct and sweeping the floor with her. He blew her away with the sheer raw energy of his mouth on hers, unlocking her defences, connecting with her in a way she had never connected to a man before, making her want him and his body so badly, she felt shell-shocked by the experience, and that very small awareness reawakened her brain again and reminded her of what she had to do...what she had to say...

In a valiant effort, Elvi struggled out of Xan's powerful arms, sliding down the front of his lean, strong body, learning that there was not a shade of doubt that he was as ready for her and that bed as he could ever be, and embarrassment and regret washed over Elvi in a horrible wave.

'I'm so sorry,' she said jerkily, stepping back from Xan, much as if he were contagious. 'But I can't do this yet—'

Xan surfaced faster to study her in disbelief. *'Can't?'* he queried. 'But you *said*—'

'You didn't give me the chance to explain,' Elvi reminded him resolutely, struggling to rise above her chagrined regret over her wanton weakness of body and brain. 'My mother hasn't told me yet that the charge has been dropped and nothing, absolutely *nothing*, is happening between us until I receive that confirmation from her—'

Incredulous as only a young, handsome billionaire could be at meeting with the word no for the first time, Xan raked a slightly shaky hand through his tousled black hair. 'This is you joking...*right*?' he pressed hopefully.

'No, I'm only returning the same favour you gave me,' Elvi assured him without the smallest sense of triumph. 'You said you wouldn't act and drop the theft charge until I moved in here and I had to do that. Now I'm saying that when my *mother* tells me the charge has been dropped, I'm yours but *not* before it—'

A line of dark colour flashed over Xan's exotic cheekbones. 'That's outrageous!' he shot back at her angrily. 'The charge *has* been dropped! I don't break my promises. It's scarcely my fault if the police haven't yet got around to informing her—'

'It's nobody's fault,' Elvi cut in, trying to pour oil on troubled water a little late in the day, she sensed, registering the blaze of frustrated fury smouldering in Xan's amazingly eloquent gaze and the fierce clenched set of his strong jaw. 'But it's the way it is. It's my only safeguard in this arrangement—'

Xan was so outraged, he swung away from her and breathed in deep to muster self-discipline. He wanted to behave like a caveman, gather her up and throw her bodily on the bed and keep her there until she understood who she was dealing with. But he knew he couldn't behave like that, which infuriated him even more. *Her only safeguard*, he reflected in fuming disagreement. Did she really think he was about to break his word when she was standing there with a small fortune in diamonds around her neck and living in his apartment?

Or was it more payback time than safeguard? Payback for the manner in which he had forced her to immediately move in? That made better sense to him, integrating as it did the kind of cunning slyness he hated in her sex but had often experienced. There had been a stepmother who'd tried to seduce him to hit back at his father for his infidelity. There had been mistresses who tried to play games calculated to increase his interest in them, several who told him outrageous lies in an effort to charm more money or jewels out of him. So great was his ire at the suspicion that he had been played by Elvi, he couldn't even bring himself to look at her again or trust himself to speak.

'I'm sorry,' Elvi muttered in the pulsing silence, her

hands twisting nervously together in the tense atmosphere. 'I should have told you when I got into the car earlier but I didn't know how to say it. I didn't feel comfortable talking about having sex with you because you're a stranger. I don't suppose you understand but it would be a lot easier if you would allow me to get to know you first.'

Xan's lean brown hands clenched into fists. 'I don't get to know women I have sex with. That's not my style,' he admitted grittily, involuntarily forced out of silence by that naïve little speech of hers. 'Maybe I missed out on asking the one question I *should've* asked in my office last week…are you a prude? Because, to be brutally blunt, you sound like a hell of a prude and that's not going to work for me at all.'

Very pale now, Elvi chewed her lower lip and decided not to respond because silence was safer. Not a prude, a virgin, she almost said, and who could tell how he would react to a surprise like that? Perhaps he was already thinking of letting her go again but would that mean he would reinstate the theft charge? Could he even do that? She had no idea and she was scared and apprehensive, plunged into a relationship she had not the smallest idea how to handle with a man that said stuff that chilled her to the marrowbone.

Xan strode back out of the apartment, still maddeningly taut with an arousal unlike anything he had ever felt before and unnerved by it. *Let her go*, his intelligence told him, cut her free now before it gets even more messy. He wanted her but she could be a disaster waiting to blow up in his face.

He ignored his security team's open surprise at his almost immediate reappearance, climbed into his limousine and tried to think about walking away fast from Elvi Cartwright because she had taken him to a level of rage he had never felt before and that was disturbing.

Or merely normal? he reasoned, given his sexual frustration. The very last thing he had expected was to end the night with a cold shower. He was beginning to suspect that Elvi might not have even indulged in a one-night stand. Some nauseating romance with a long-term boyfriend struck him as the more likely base of her sexual experience, he decided cynically. She wanted him to get to *know* her? Was she a throwback to the Victorian era? Where did she get a weird idea like that when he had asked her to be his mistress?

Elvi got into the vast bed alone and shivered, still shaken by that confrontation and the kiss that had preceded it. When his mouth had crashed down on hers, she had been overwhelmed by his electrifying sensuality, her physical responses wildly out of her control, but she had pulled back, mustered her strength and finally said what had to be said. And not surprisingly, Xan had been furious because she should have made her position clear at the start of the evening, *not* at the end, she acknowledged guiltily.

Xan Ziakis wasn't accustomed to the word no. He was selfish, arrogant and obsessed with sex. Well, work and sex, she adjusted ruefully. He had expected to take her straight to bed and she had dealt clumsily with those expectations, probably because she *was* the prude he had labelled her. But the concept of sharing her body with someone she didn't even know properly had proved too much for Elvi to cope with on the spot. When she couldn't even imagine taking off her clothes for him, she was in trouble and way outside her comfort zone. Why, oh, why had she ever believed that she could give him what he wanted? That she could simply have sex as if it meant nothing?

And even more inexplicably, why was she just a little disappointed that he hadn't managed to persuade her to change her mind? He hadn't even *tried* to persuade her, had he? Had simply announced that she didn't suit him, rejecting her because she had dared to reject him. Was that it, then? Were they over before they had even begun?

CHAPTER FOUR

SALLY CARTWRIGHT PHONED her daughter mid-morning the next day. 'You'll never guess what's happened,' she burbled in an excited surge. 'The theft charge has been dropped. No explanation, nothing, just the assurance that the complaint has been withdrawn and the police have no further interest.'

'My goodness, that's wonderful news!' Elvi declared brightly, relief rolling through her in a rejuvenating wave of energy. It was done. Xan *had* kept his promise.

Elvi texted him a stiff apology for her lack of confidence, resisting the urge to remind him that he hadn't trusted her either. In truth she didn't know what she was wishing for. That he had ditched her and moved on? In which case she would be moving home again. Or was she stuck with the agreement she had made?

Xan was still in a temper with her when he read the text. He was done with her, *wasn't he*? Last night had been his warning. When you draped a woman in diamonds, threw in a new wardrobe and the use of a very expensive apartment, you expected something in return...*obviously*. It infuriated him that that conviction made *him* feel cheap. It infuriated him that he was tempted to walk out in the middle of his working day and stage a rendezvous with her because he still burned for her. After a sleepless night, the urge to possess Elvi's glorious body was as strong as ever, undaunted by the difficulty of dealing with her unrealistic expectations.

His thought processes were becoming disturbingly insidious and unfamiliar. Every man was entitled to *one* mistake, wasn't he? Why shouldn't he enjoy the mistake he had made and move on afterwards? He texted her that he would be with her that afternoon and endeavoured to get back into the meeting he was in. But he couldn't concentrate, not for wondering what she would be wearing, what she would look like naked, how she would look when he gave her pleasure. In a passion of rare indecision, Xan breathed in deep and slow and wondered what the hell had taken hold of him. He didn't like wanting Elvi as much as he did because such urges smacked of immoderation, indiscipline and chaos, every sin he meticulously avoided in life.

Even so, he stood up in the middle of the meeting and abruptly announced his departure. He would have Elvi one single time and then that would be it. *Once only*, as his mother lamented when she overindulged in chocolate. A treat was one thing, a habit quite another and he did not want a habit like Elvi who took his mind off his work.

Xan texted Elvi.

Coming for lunch.

Was she supposed to cook? Elvi wondered in panic. Or was lunch a euphemism for sex? Was she supposed to greet him in the rather risqué lingerie that had been delivered along with the most massive amount of clothing and accessories earlier that morning? Or was she simply supposed to drape herself somewhere and look inviting? I am *not* a prude, she told her reflection, and then pinched her cheeks because she looked so pale. Maybe she was a prude in comparison to him because *he* seemed to be astonishingly free of inhibitions and self-consciousness. Ironically his ability to be that way made her feel rather envious.

Xan didn't know what he was expecting but he *wasn't* expecting to be greeted by lunch or the shocking disarray of the living area, which ran counter to his every conviction of how an interior should be maintained. Something in the process of being knitted lay abandoned on one sofa and a box of sewing supplies sat on the rug. Books spilled across another seat and the coffee table was littered with random items. There was no organisation, no order. He averted his gaze from it all to focus on her, all anxious blue eyes above pink cheeks, glorious hair framing her face. And he had given her a new wardrobe and what was she wearing? An old denim skirt with a faded top and scuffed cowboy boots, he registered in stupefaction.

'I didn't know whether you'd be hungry or not,' Elvi admitted tightly, striving not to stare at him but, oh, it was difficult not to surrender to base and embarrassing promptings. Xan looked like her every fantasy in one devastating package from the black luxuriance of his hair to the flawless hard lines of his breathtakingly beautiful features, all set within the frame of an exquisitely tailored light grey suit, a white shirt and a crimson silk tie.

'I only have an hour,' Xan imparted, stunned by the food she had prepared because he had never had a mistress who tried to feed him before.

'Oh...'

'I'm only hungry for you,' Xan intoned huskily while wondering if he should draw up a list of rules to urge her in the right direction—tidy up, don't feed me, wear the clothes I give you—and then his attention locked onto the voluptuous pink lower lip she was chewing on and the throb at his groin overpowered every other thought and he simply reached for her.

He snatched her up into his arms and kissed her breathless and a sort of giddy, unfamiliar delight pierced Elvi, because Xan Ziakis could wreak havoc on her body with one extraordinary kiss. So, when the kisses piled up, she got lost in them, which in its own way was a relief because it stopped her overthinking stuff and held the nerves at bay. Her arms snaked round his neck as he carried her out of the kitchen and her momentary panic had subsided to be replaced by a helpless sense of anticipation. She was finally coming to terms with the truth that she wanted him too and that there was nothing one-sided about their chemistry.

Abandoned clothing festooned the single chair in the bedroom. Xan ignored the display, for once too caught up in the wonder of Elvi's response to notice. She tasted like strawberries and the soft damp welcome of her mouth inflamed him. He wanted that wondrous mouth of hers everywhere on him. In fact colourful images were tumbling through Xan's head and making control a rare challenge. *One time only*, he reminded himself doggedly, like a man trying to bargain with the devil, as he settled her down on the bed.

'I need a shower,' Xan confided, yanking loose his tie beneath her arrested gaze. 'Join me—'

The prospect of getting naked with him in a shower was a step too far too fast for Elvi and she gave him a tense smile. 'I'll just wait here.'

Xan was used to women who did exactly what he wanted when he wanted and he was disconcerted afresh by her reluctance. The instant one of the bathroom doors closed on him, Elvi leapt off the bed to buzz the blinds shut and undress at frantic speed. She had already had two showers that morning, one when she got up, the second after he texted her. She climbed back into the bed naked, every skin cell on high alert for his reappearance.

She wished she weren't so shy. Prudish, he had called it, but she was painfully aware that what was amiss with her was inexperience and a lack of confidence in her own body. At school the majority of her peers had been skinny and leggy and that had made her feel chunky and unfashionable, for the trendy clothing that had flattered their slimmer curves had done nothing for her very different shape. Nor could she escape the demeaning suspicion that the minute Xan saw her naked, he would realise that she wasn't quite the bombshell he had hoped.

But then what did any of that matter? she censured herself in exasperation. They had an agreement, not a relationship based on caring or commitment. It was only sex and it only seemed more of a challenge to her because sex was new to her. She had to assume that a womaniser would know what he was doing in the bedroom and by this evening she would probably be wondering what all the fuss was about. Her expectations were low. She might find Xan irresistibly attractive but the prospect of getting hot, sweaty and naked with a stranger still intimidated her.

The bathroom door opened and Xan emerged, towelling his hair dry; a naked bronzed muscular vision of masculinity in her shaken appraisal. No, Xan was definitely *not* shy. He seemed a little surprised by the dimness of the room and frowned as he crawled up lithely from the bottom of the bed, evidently equally surprised to find her waiting there for him. He reached up to stab the lights on.

'I like it dim—'

'I don't.' A slanting grin tilted Xan's wide sensual mouth. 'I lay awake half the night thinking about this moment—'

'Truthfully?' Elvi framed unevenly.

'You really do it for me,' Xan growled, yanking back the sheet she was cringing below. '*Thee mou*…what glorious breasts!'

Elvi just shut her eyes tight and lay there barely breathing, for an instant barely crediting that only a few minutes earlier she had believed she wanted him as much as he wanted her. And then he hauled her under him and crushed her ripe mouth under his and once again everything changed so fast that her head spun dizzily. She wondered what magic there was to his mouth on hers that made her crave more, her fingers skimming up his cheekbones into his silky cropped hair and holding him to her.

A kiss is only a kiss, she thought abstractedly, but it wasn't with Xan, it was fireworks and wild passion and the delving, curling intimacy of his tongue flicking inside her mouth, setting off a chain reaction that arrowed through her body with a piercing, burning sweetness that made her hips rise helplessly off the mattress.

He touched her breasts and she ached and quivered, the swollen, straining buds of her nipples shockingly responsive to the tug of his fingers and then the warm wet torment of his mouth, his tongue, his teeth…and her back arched, a sliding liquidity and heat rising in her pelvis because every touch felt as amazing as the hot, hard, muscular weight of him pinning her to the bed. He shifted back a little, muttering something in Greek, pausing to kiss her again with a hungry ferocity that made her heart beat stronger and faster than ever, excitement building as he stroked her thigh, parted her legs, finally touching her where she craved being touched. And at that point, everything became increasingly hazy for Elvi because she was out of control and pushed to a fever pitch by the intense sensitivity of her own body. Skilled fingers rubbed, delicately explored the sleek, silky depths of her, little tremors pulling at her, little sounds wrenched from her parted lips, the excitement blazing over her and soaring through her like leaping flames.

Burning all over, she writhed, yearning for more but too out of her mind to even recognise what more entailed. Xan's wide sensual mouth crashed down on hers again and it was as if she had stuck a finger in an electric socket because for an instant, with her heart hammering and her breath clawing for escape from her constricted lungs, that spellbinding kiss enthralled her. And then he slid over her, lifting her thighs, pinning them back. Somehow the weight of him and that intimate contact were what her body craved.

Xan plunged into her heated core with passionate force. Elvi jerked and twisted her head away at the fierce jolt of pain, no longer flying in a delicious play world of the physical, suddenly brought back down to earth with a crash. Tears stung her eyes and she closed them tight, sealing herself off in an instinctive need for privacy, recognising that what she had mindlessly craved felt more like a punishment than a pleasure. Mercifully the pain faded as fast as it had come and her tension disappeared with it. Different sensations began to coalesce within her as he changed his angle, tilted her up and an almost forgotten jab of excitement tightened like a band low in her belly.

And then he kissed her again, claiming her reddened lips with hungry need, and she reconnected with him, compelled by the convulsive little quivers travelling through her pelvis and the almost mystical push of elation beginning to grip her every nerve. Never had she been more aware of anything than the sleek, hard invasion of his body into hers, stretching her, rousing her with his dynamic drive. The peak of pleasure took her by surprise, throwing her up in a gasping breathless wave to the heights and then letting her fall, slowly, gently while the ripples of delight were still convulsing her.

Xan pulled back, convinced he had just enjoyed the best sex of his life and shocked by the wildness of it and the alarming awareness that he had lost control. And then *two* unexpected events drove all such ruminations from mind. He was about to head for the bathroom to dispose of the condom when he suddenly registered that he hadn't *used* one, a reckless omission that nothing could excuse and which froze him in his tracks. In that interim instant of inaction and disbelief he noticed the blood on the sheet.

'You're bleeding,' he noted jerkily. 'Did I hurt you?'

Raw mortification assailed Elvi and she squirmed away from him, yanking the top sheet over the embarrassing proof of her inexperience. 'No, it was my first time,' she muttered tightly, her face suffusing with chagrined heat.

CHAPTER FIVE

XAN COMPUTED THAT admission and he was so shocked by the revelation, he literally felt sick. His lethally accurate brain threw up the entirety of his dealings with Elvi Cartwright and shame engulfed him for the first time in his life because such a scenario, a sordid scenario in which he demanded sex from an innocent girl, appalled him. It had not once crossed his mind that at her age she could be literally *untouched*. No, not these days, when he was forever reading about young women treating sex as casually as young men and when he himself was offered sex as carelessly as a handshake at first meetings. He utterly recoiled from the image of himself as a violator of virgins. If he had known, he would have kept his distance, would never *ever* have suggested...

'Why the *hell* didn't you tell me that?' Xan demanded rawly, sliding off the bed in one powerful movement. 'Naturally I assumed that you had sexual experience—'

Shot from the heights of her first real orgasm to the depths of embarrassment and then held trapped there by the unexpectedly angry reaction of her first lover,

Elvi wrapped herself in the sheet and raised her knees to her chin, linking her arms round her trembling legs. 'But why would you assume that?' she asked shakily.

Xan raked an unsteady hand through his tousled black hair. 'Because that's the norm at your age. If I'd known you were a virgin, I would *never* have touched you and I would *never* have offered you the arrangement that I did!' he shot at her furiously.

Elvi was perplexed because Xan had not impressed her as a man with sincere moral principles and she shrugged a rounded shoulder in dismissal of that statement. 'It's a little late now for regrets,' she pointed out. 'I did warn you that I wasn't really suitable for what you had in mind but you weren't interested in hearing it.'

Xan was never interested in hearing anything that conflicted with his own needs and wants and he didn't require a stinging reminder from her that he had made an inexcusable mistake. Dark colour laced his high cheekbones and, with gritted teeth, he spun and strode towards the bathroom, only to freeze again and turn lithely back to her.

'Are you on the pill?'

Elvi shook her head. 'Why would I have been?'

'On any form of contraception?' Xan persisted tautly.

'No. I was planning to sort something out this week but the very tight timetable you imposed on me prevented me from doing anything in advance,' she said shortly.

'You should've told me you were a virgin!' Xan lashed back at her with unconcealed censure.

'Why?' Elvi countered. 'It was none of your business!'

'It became *my* business when you were planning to have a sexual relationship with me,' Xan contradicted with controlled savagery.

'As you well know, you were the one who planned to have a sexual relationship with me and I had to move in here barely twelve hours after agreeing, so my planning *anything* didn't come into it!'

Xan shuddered at the burn of being force-fed the truth on an unappetising plate. He and no one else had brought about this disaster. His arrogance, his ego had resulted in this mess and it was a lesson he had never expected to receive because for too many years he had been invincible, his every move lauded, his every deal a phenomenal success. It seemed he was not the man he had been raised to become, not the person he had believed himself to be. It was a pivotal moment for him, glancing round the spacious room where he had spent so many hours with forgettable women and inwardly cringing at how he had foolishly believed he had it made with that set-up, because that detached conveyor-belt system had now gone badly wrong for him. And he *still* didn't know how to fix it…

Elvi's clasped hands round her knees tightened, her knuckles showing white below her skin. She was a little ball of rigid tension in recognition of his. Presumably he was disappointed. That was why he was angry. Angry not with her, she sensed, but with himself for a poor choice of playmate.

'I'm not what you expected,' she said for him.

Xan swallowed hard. 'No,' he conceded, wondering

how the hell he was supposed to make amends. 'You surprised me. Very few people manage to do that.'

Let her go, Xan reasoned. It was the obvious answer to fixing what was wrong but he looked at her, all wrapped round herself as if she was trying to make herself small, and his chest tightened and he hauled in a long rasping breath, his broad chest expanding. He didn't want the obvious answer and he was *still* a selfish bastard, he acknowledged, because he still wanted her. Even when he could see the shininess of tears in her bright blue eyes. What did that say about him? That he was capable of wanting an unwilling woman? No way would he touch her again without an invitation from *her*, he told himself squarely, rationalising an irrational decision. He would make amends. He didn't know how but in some mysterious way he would manage that feat. He was very clever. He would work it out eventually.

'I think I'll eat that lunch you were kind enough to make me,' Xan said abruptly.

Astonishment flashed through Elvi and her lashes lowered on her anxious eyes. He was still imprinted on her eyelids, a spectacular bronzed man naked as a jaybird, standing there like a stone statue, his discomfiture obvious to her. What was the matter with him? The soft sounds of him dressing, the click of cuff links snapping closed, the sound of a zip penetrated her shell of silence. She had had sex for the very first time and *he* had disappointed *her* because he had denied the intimacy of the experience, pulling away as soon as he was done, and none of the pleasure he had given her had made up for that distance and reserve.

'What are you thinking about?' Xan prompted, more uncomfortable than he had ever been in his entire life with a woman.

'I'm lonely,' Elvi muttered truthfully. 'I'm used to having my family around—'

'I'm here,' Xan reminded her.

'But you're not cuddly,' Elvi told him apologetically.

Xan grimaced. 'No. Is that what you like?'

'It's not the kind of physical you're used to,' Elvi guessed wryly, wondering how she had given herself to such a man, wondering how she could look into those hard, dark but stunning eyes and want to give herself again, want to make him smile for once and hear him laugh.

'I hug my mother,' he declared in his own defence.

'Even you have to have one weakness,' Elvi quipped.

'Lunch,' Xan reminded her. 'Why don't you join me?'

Wrapping the sheet round herself with innate modesty, Elvi headed into the other bathroom and went for a very quick shower. In some ways, she was in shock. His possession had hurt more than she had been prepared for and then had come the pleasure that had also been more than she had expected. For the first time, she understood why Xan Ziakis was so hooked on sex. He was good at it too, she conceded ruefully, because he had turned a bad start into something truly amazing and then trashed that by moving away from her afterwards, as if, once he got his satisfaction, he was keen

to forget who had given it to him. It had made her feel
used, unappreciated. She should have anticipated that.
Sex was only sex for him. He didn't look to receive anything beyond that fleeting physical thrill.

He was still in the bedroom, his back turned to her
when she emerged breathless from hurrying out of the
fancy dressing room. She had worn something new
from what Sylvia had described as a basic 'capsule'
wardrobe, but which covered more garments than she
had ever owned in her entire life at one and the same
time. And apparently, even more clothes tailored to her
precise requirements would eventually arrive. The skirt
she had chosen was short and flirty, the top thin silk,
the sandals high-heeled. Did she look like a proper mistress now? she wondered unhappily. Would he actually
look at her again? For some reason, he seemed to be
avoiding looking. The strangeness of his behaviour was
starting to wear on her. She hated the knowledge that
she didn't know what was going on inside his head. But
why did she even *want* to know? That was a question
she couldn't answer.

'Lunch,' she murmured, thankful she had only made
a salad and not something that would have spoiled.

Xan swung round, immediately noticing the clothing, tensing because it gave her a much more sophisticated look than her own clothing did, reminding him
that right from the start he had tried to make her into
something she wasn't, ignoring the signs that she was
different, an individual, trying to make her over into the
kind of sleek, faceless sex object he was comfortable
with. That suspicion unnerved him because he wasn't

accustomed to examining his own motives or to see-ing how his stubborn determination to treat all his mis-tresses the same had ensured that he flatly refused to acknowledge that Elvi might be unique.

Xan was so tall, so dark he snarled up the breath in Elvi's dry throat. A jolt of wanton response curled warm and low in her pelvis, which amused her because had he tried to touch her again she probably would have screamed because she was sore, way too sore to desire further intimacy.

In a determined movement, she left the bedroom and went into the kitchen to serve the chicken salad. While she would have been happy to eat at the kitchen table, she reckoned Xan would baulk and she carried the plates out to the more formal dining area. He sank down into a chair within seconds of her taking a seat. For an instant, she allowed herself to look at him. The guy was insanely hot from those killer cheekbones to the shadow of stubble accentuating the fullness of his sensual lips. Heat mushroomed up inside her and she immediately dropped her head to eat.

Xan glanced around himself, disliking the famil-iarity of the room and the recollections of how he had spent his time there. He would sell the place, would never return to it, he decided at lightning speed. He couldn't wait to remove Elvi from surroundings which only reminded him of what he would prefer to forget. The answer of what to do next came to him and his cautious streak fired up. He would be breaking a habit, decimating his usual routine, but slavishly following that routine and indulging those habits had subjected him to several far from commendable discoveries about his own nature.

'Tomorrow, I am leaving early in the morning for Greece,' he murmured flatly. 'There is a wedding in my family and I must attend. I would like you to accompany me.'

Elvi was sharply disconcerted and a piece of chicken almost went down the wrong way because her throat tightened like all the rest of her in surprise. *'Me?'* she queried uncertainly.

'You see anyone else sitting here?' Xan said drily.

Elvi flushed and went back to eating.

'You have a passport?' he checked.

Elvi nodded. Her mother had spent her last bonus on equipping the three of them with passports. They had had a dream of travelling abroad for a few days, something cut price and last-minute and cheap. Of course, that prospect had died with Sally's dismissal, along with everything else. Like life as she *had* known it, Elvi conceded ruefully. Only a couple of days had passed since she had worked in the craft shop, going home each evening to her family. Xan had taken *everything*, she thought unhappily.

Xan had never been with such a quiet woman and it unsettled him. He had expected a modest amount of enthusiasm to greet the kind of invitation he had never given a woman before. Of course, she probably didn't appreciate that reality. But she had mentioned *wanting* to get to know him, hadn't she? What better opportunity could he offer her? It crossed his mind that possibly she no longer wanted to get to know him better, but he brushed off the suspicion with all the instinctive disdain of a man accustomed to being the number one, highly desirable target of every young woman in his radius.

'I'll send a car to pick you up at nine this evening,' Xan announced, rising lithely upright. 'It will be more convenient if you spend the night before we travel at my apartment.'

Elvi rose to follow him to the door, although she didn't know why she was offering him that courtesy when he had his own key to the apartment. He was already on his mobile phone, uttering what sounded like instructions to someone in another language. Greek? She had no idea, having only studied French at school.

For a split second, Xan hovered on the threshold and looked back at her, feeling weirdly uneasy about abandoning her when it was obvious that she was missing her family so much. Her glow wasn't back, he noted, thinking grimly that he had successfully killed that. An air of nervous uncertainty lay in her small restive movements. He hadn't discussed the pregnancy risk. It wasn't the moment, he told himself squarely, because she hadn't noticed that contraceptive mishap. Why worry her about something so unlikely? What were the chances after one encounter? Slim, to none, he reasoned, and he offered up his first inner prayer since childhood in support of that hope. Wasn't he already feeling guilty enough? Surely that ultimate axe would not also fall on him?

Elvi met Xan's dazzling amber eyes and it was as though a mental ping of recognition sounded somewhere deep within her own brain. He was upset about something. She didn't know how she knew that but somehow she did, belatedly recognising that nobody could be quite as detached from the rest of humanity as he liked to appear. And such beautiful eyes he had, lushly enclosed between black velvet lashes, such an amazing colour and surprisingly eloquent. Her body reacted with shocking intensity, her breasts tightening while a sensation of awareness purred between her thighs.

'H-how long will we be in Greece?' she asked abruptly, battling that awareness with fierce discomfiture.

'Five days,' Xan said in a roughened undertone, wondering how the hell he was going to keep his hands off her when she could turn him on so fast she made him feel like an animal.

Not that that was so very far from the truth concerning their single encounter, Xan reminded himself with gritted teeth as he strode into the lift, refusing to allow himself to linger, thoroughly distrusting, indeed loathing, the powerful sexual urges pulling at him. He had already fallen on Elvi once with all the refinement of a sex-starved teenager, so out of himself that he had forgotten protection and had failed to note that he had hurt her. Scarcely a stellar show of sophistication or skill. No way was he about to repeat that idiocy.

Determined to get every change made instantly, Xan contacted the concierge company to organise the removal of Elvi's possessions from the apartment and the sale of it. He was still issuing instructions when he climbed into the limousine and was absently aware of

Dmitri's frowning face. What the hell was up with his head of security? Dmitri Pallas had been with Xan for years. A former inspector in the Greek police force, he was very efficient in his field. But of recent, crucially the placing of Elvi's letter in the cause of Sally Cartwright, Dmitri's behaviour had been strange.

Already feeling unusually hassled, Xan shelved the acknowledgement as something else to deal with at a more opportune time. Maybe Dmitri had family problems or something. Maybe he knew more about that theft business than he had been willing to share. Whatever, Xan was in no mood to delve into anything that could verge on the personal. It was a direction he never went in with his staff because he valued his own privacy too highly. And the day when he blew his own cherished privacy sky-high was not a day when he felt prompted to break down barriers with others.

A woman in his apartment, even if it was only for *one* night, was a major departure from the norm for him. Should he have put her in a hotel? No, that would've been shabby, he decided, and his behaviour had been shabby enough for one day, hadn't it?

While Xan was contemplating the challenge of sharing his space for even one night, Elvi was on the way home for a visit, unable to sit alone in the empty apartment even though she knew she would either have to lie or evade the truth as the price of that family visit. The knowledge made her sad but the dropping of the theft charge was, in her opinion, a worthwhile return, regardless of the dishonesty it had involved her in.

She was startled when she got home to find her

mother actually turning out cupboards and packing the contents into boxes.

'What on earth are you doing?' she asked her mother from the kitchen doorway.

Sally smiled up at her daughter from her position on her knees on the floor.

'We're moving to Oxford in a few days...'

Elvi's brow furrowed, her eyes uncomprehending. 'I don't understand—'

Sally picked herself up. 'I'll make us a cup of tea and explain,' she said, visibly in a far better state of mind than she had been the last time Elvi actually saw her, with something of her usual bustling energy back in her step and voice.

'Dmitri Pallas...the head of Mr Ziakis's security team...is a good friend of mine,' Sally advanced with a slight deepening of colour. 'He's come to our rescue...'

Her brow furrowing, Elvi sank down at the table while her mother brewed the tea. 'You've never mentioned him before,' she pointed out uncomfortably.

'Didn't see the need because I used to see him every day at work,' Sally Cartwright told her wryly. 'And no, there's no romance there, nothing but friendship, and I don't know if there ever could be but I do like him very much.'

'Nothing wrong with that,' Elvi said gently, disconcerted by her mother's fluctuating colour and embarrassment. No romance, yeah, as if she was going to believe that with *that* look on the older woman's face! She thought of the man whom she had met so briefly, the warm concern she had seen in his eyes over that letter. She thought of Sally's lost years and of how in all the time since she'd lost her husband her mother had had not a single man in her life…and then she thought of how wonderful it would be if her parent could finally have something nice in her life, something for her rather than the children she adored.

'Well, Dmitri has a little house in Oxford because he has family living in the area,' Sally proffered. 'He knows how we're fixed financially and, now that I've lost my job…well, he's found me another one there with a connection of his. Waitressing, a step up from cleaning, I think—'

'Yes,' Elvi agreed.

'We're to stay in Dmitri's house initially and then, when we get on our feet again, we can move on to somewhere of our own. He doesn't live there…*ever*,' Sally added stiltedly. 'Mr Ziakis travels abroad a lot and Dmitri travels with him. Dmitri buys property as an investment for when he retires.'

'You'll be in Oxford for the beginning of Daniel's classes,' Elvi remarked approvingly.

'Yes…' Sally smiled suddenly, all her natural warmth on display as she hugged her daughter's shoulders where she sat. 'Isn't it amazing how life can just suddenly take a turn for the better?'

'Amazing,' Elvi agreed.

'My only concern is that I'm going to see less of you.' Sally sighed.

'Can't have everything,' Elvi quipped. 'And I can still visit.'

'Can I ask you just *one* question?' Sally prompted anxiously. 'Why can't we meet this boyfriend of yours?'

Elvi tried and failed to fit Xan Ziakis into the boyfriend category and reddened. 'It's…er…too soon,' she mumbled uncomfortably.

'So, it *has* been one of those "love at first sight" efforts, then,' Sally assumed, seeming to relax at that idea. 'He hasn't been around long—'

'And it could end as quickly as it started,' Elvi dared to add.

Sally grimaced as she made the tea. 'I won't wish *that* on you…but it would mean you could move to Oxford and join us.'

'Probably,' Elvi allowed, cupping her hands round the warm mug, her turmoil over Xan soothed by her mother's restored spirits.

And why did she even feel that she was in turmoil over him? she questioned with self-loathing. They had had sex and that was all. There was nothing more to them. They were not a couple in a relationship. And if she was learning things she would sooner not have known, well, that was part of growing up, she told herself impatiently. The first lesson had been that she could enjoy intimacy without the finer feelings getting involved, and she hadn't been proud of that until Xan's detachment in the aftermath had wounded her, teaching her that while she might *tell* herself that she expected nothing more, she was still somehow programmed to *want* more from the man than he was ever likely to give her.

Only a couple of minutes before nine, Elvi returned

to the apartment and was perplexed to find it stripped of everything she owned. Where was her stuff? It meant she couldn't change out of the jeans she had gone home in, even had she wanted to.

And why would she want to? she asked herself irritably. Pleasing Xan by wearing the clothes he had bought for her shouldn't be on her to-do list. In fact the sooner he got tired of her, she told herself, the better it would be for both of them. A trip to Greece in his company wasn't likely to change anything between them and they had nothing whatsoever in common beyond the fact that they had both been born human.

CHAPTER SIX

SHORTLY AFTER NINE, Elvi was wafted away from the apartment to Xan's penthouse.

There was nothing comfortable about that experience, primarily because Xan *wasn't* at the penthouse to greet her. Dmitri informed her with positive cheerfulness that his employer was attending a bankers' dinner at a private club, and left her to wander alone around the most amazing living space Elvi had ever seen.

It astonished her that here was only *one* massive bedroom, because her mother had never mentioned that fact, or that there was a gym. Of course, he had to make the effort to keep fit when he was in a desk job, she reasoned while a flood of spontaneous images of Xan's lean, muscular physique filled her memory to overflowing. Her face burned up and she registered that she had changed, he had changed her, whether she liked it or not.

The living area was all space and contemporary furniture, the bedroom simply empty by comparison until she peeked into the closets her mother had mentioned and discovered the marvels of Xan's need to classify everything into a category, and it made her wonder *why* he was that way. Her clothing was also to be discovered in a closet, but it hadn't been colour-coded. There was only one en-suite bathroom, and it contained a magnificent sunken bath that called to Elvi much like a siren's song after the day she had endured. Evidently Xan enjoyed a puritanical bathing experience because there were no perfumed lotions and nothing that made bubbles, but she sank into the warm depths of the water regardless, only then appreciating how very tired she was.

All that fretting about her first experience of sex had taken it out of her, not to mention the awkward aftermath when Xan had treated her much like a stranger to whom he had to be polite, she reflected wearily. In a minute she would get out of the bath and climb into the only bed available.

Taking his security team by surprise, Xan left the official dinner early. It felt very odd to him to picture someone waiting for him at the penthouse and he suppressed the observation, exasperated by the unusual thoughts interfering with his normally disciplined state of mind. He stalked into his bedroom, spotted a little pile of clothes on the floor and frowned. Well, she was here but *where*?

He walked round the entire apartment before deciding that she had to be in the bathroom and only then noticed that the door was slightly ajar. He pushed it quietly wide and saw her fast asleep in his bath and sunk low enough in the water for it to be dangerous. Jawline clenching, he reached for a large towel before reaching for her. She wakened, startled and apparently stricken to find herself in his arms, bright blue eyes filled with alarm. 'What? Where?' she framed in dismay.

'You fell asleep,' he told her as her torrent of hair dripped everywhere as if she were a mermaid dragged suddenly from the sea.

'What are you doing with me?'

'I was putting you in bed—'

'But I can't go to bed with *wet* hair!' she gasped.

Mouth compressing, Xan set her down again. 'Just wrap it in a towel and go to bed,' he urged.

'Have you any idea what it would look like in the morning if I did that?' Elvi exclaimed in receipt of that ill-advised male suggestion.

'Does it matter?' Xan traded from the doorway.

Elvi huffed and knotted the overly large towel round her ribcage to prevent it from falling and exposing her even more. Having found her naked in the bath, he had already seen it all anyway, she reminded herself rue-fully. She dug into her toiletries bag for a comb and met his brilliant dark eyes in the mirror. 'I'll dry it,' she muttered unevenly, disconcerted by the reality that he was still standing there.

'Don't fall asleep in the bath again. It's dangerous—'

'I'm not elderly or infirm. First taste of water I got would've wakened me!' Elvi told him with spirit. 'Tell me, do you always imagine the worst possible conse-quences from every event?'

'Pretty much.' Xan was studying her, noting the por-celain fairness of her skin below the lights, remember-ing how soft she had felt under him, the little sounds she had made, the dreamy look on her face when she climaxed. Hunger throbbed through him like a powerful drug, seriously disturbing him.

'Thought so,' Elvi confided cheerfully, finished combing and reaching for the dryer on the wall.

'There's something we have to discuss,' Xan told her tautly then.

'And what's that?' Elvi pressed, her hand falling back from the dryer.

'I failed to use a condom with you today—'

'*What?*' Elvi gasped in disbelief as she twisted around to look directly at him, heavy wet strands of hair snaking across her bare shoulders. 'You mean... we had unprotected *sex*?'

Lean, strong features set hard, Xan jerked his chin in confirmation.

'Are you crazy?' Elvi framed in horror. 'Why didn't you—?'

'I lost control... I forgot. I made a mistake. It's that simple,' Xan interposed in a tone of curt finality. 'Obviously I'm furious with myself, but I have regular health checks and there is no danger of—'

'But what if you've got me pregnant?' Elvi interrupted, her anxiety on that score overpowering her usual need to avoid any kind of intimate discussion.

'I think there is very little danger of that after *one* sexual encounter,' Xan informed her with impressive confidence, and some of her tension drained away because his unwavering assurance did have a soothing effect on her. 'It's most unlikely. I apologise, though, for causing the scare.'

'No, I should've thought about the risk too,' Elvi muttered uncomfortably, striving to be reasonable. 'I should've checked but I didn't even think about that… er…aspect.'

In the bedroom, Xan undressed for a shower, automatically putting everything in its designated space. Busy drying her mane of hair, Elvi didn't appear to notice him entering or leaving the shower and he slid into bed first, achingly aroused and knowing there was no possibility of relief. With a groan he turned over and punched a pillow, catching sight of her rustling through a drawer, emptying half of it in pursuit of what she wanted and then piling what remained back in and actually *forcing* the drawer closed on it. He tried to imagine living with that kind of disorder and almost shuddered, while covertly watching below his cloaking lashes as she crossed the room clad in the pyjamas from hell, which covered her from head and toe. She switched out the light on the far side of the bed and clambered in.

The bedding smelt vaguely of Xan, Elvi conceded sleepily, and it was an oddly comforting scent. She refused to lie awake fretting about the possibility of an unplanned pregnancy, dimly deciding that Xan probably knew the odds better than her. If it happened, that would be time enough to worry, she told herself. There was no advantage to agonising in advance, and in any case she would have the confirmation one way or another within a very short time.

He had given her something more to think about than the reality that she was sharing a bed with a man for the first time ever overnight, while she hoped he had got the message via the pyjamas that she was unavailable for anything more entertaining than sleep. Of course she knew there were other things that could be done that did not entail the final act that had left her body aching, but she was impossibly tired from all the stress of recent days.

'Night, Xan,' she mumbled, as if he were her roommate, and minutes later she was sound asleep.

Xan lay awake marvelling at her seeming indifference to his presence. Random thoughts bombarded him like shrapnel. Was it an act aimed at challenging him? He really didn't think so because there was nothing inviting or even slightly tantalising about those pyjamas. Obviously, she didn't like her new wardrobe and he would have to try harder in that department. He had never actually spent the whole night with a woman before but did Elvi know that? Did she even *care*?

And what had happened to *wanting* to get to know him? D for effort, Elvi, he mused, hugely irritated.

Elvi slept like a log and woke up in a surprisingly good mood. After all, yesterday she had crossed the sex bridge and now that apprehension was overcome, she reminded herself with determination. In addition, her mother and her brother were safe from prosecution and would soon be starting a new chapter in Oxford. Buoyant at how the worst of her fears had been vanquished, she bestowed a faint smile on Xan as he strolled out of the bathroom, immaculately dressed in his usual formal suit and looking spectacular as usual.

'I haven't even packed,' she exclaimed in sudden dismay.

It was the very first time she had smiled at him. Xan immediately forgave her for sleeping like the dead in his bed. 'It's very warm in Greece,' he pointed out. 'You'll need different clothing and I've taken care of it—'

'Oh, not *more* clothes!' Elvi complained in dismay, her nose wrinkling. 'I don't need anything more. Honestly, I can make do fine with what I've already got—'

'I will not be seen in public with a woman who is making do,' Xan declared with perceptible distaste.

'Of course, if you're going to be snobbish about it—'

'I'm not snobbish,' Xan asserted in a roughened undertone. 'But I do not wish you to be embarrassed by being inappropriately dressed.'

Elvi got out of bed, as inappropriately dressed as any woman Xan had ever seen and she exhibited zero embarrassment over that reality. The pyjamas were downright ugly, baggy and shapeless on her small form as she breezed past him into the bathroom. Having Elvi for the night hadn't proved much different from having one of his five-year-old nieces sleeping over. It was clean and innocent, not something that had much appeal for him. Belatedly he reminded himself that her stay and the trip were supposed to be all about her and *not* about him. He needed to ease his conscience and rise above the guilt and regret she had roused in him the day before. But there was no pressure on him to *enjoy* the process…

Having established that it was barely six in the morning—no, Xan had not been joking about that early start—Elvi dressed in haste and joined him for breakfast in the elegant dining room. She was unsettled by the realisation that she was excited about travelling abroad for the very first time. Xan, however, seemed rather downbeat and prone to wincing when she spoke, necessarily dragging his attention from the newspaper he was reading. 'Aren't you pleased that you're going to see your family today?' she pressed.

His high cheekbones pulled taut below his stunning amber eyes, his beautifully moulded mouth compressing. 'I'm not particularly close to my siblings.'

'But you're the eldest,' she said in surprise, adding a third spoon of sugar to her coffee beneath Xan's frowning gaze. 'Don't they turn to you for advice? I know Daniel does with me—'

'They do,' Xan confirmed. 'I look after them. That's my duty but that doesn't mean they're my best friends. I help them with problems—'

'How many siblings do you have?'

'Six,' Xan said succinctly. 'Four half-sisters, two half-brothers.'

'So...' Elvi rested inquisitive eyes on his lean, darkly handsome visage, momentarily reminding him of a baby bird seeking a titbit '...that means either your mother *or* your father had more than one marriage—'

'My father was a five times loser at the altar,' Xan supplied drily. 'Two models and two beauty queens followed my mother and all four wives were greedy to feather their own nests.'

'Oh...' Elvi said nothing more, understanding a little more about his background than she had previously because a multi-married father, a possibly betrayed mother and a bunch of half-siblings implied a fairly dysfunctional family history, compared with her own. But she was reluctantly impressed by Xan's assurance that he looked after his younger siblings, even though he didn't consider himself close to them. 'So, whose wedding are we attending?'

'Delphina, the youngest one. She's twenty. At an age when she ought to be out forging a career and a lively social life, she's tying herself down,' Xan declared with cynical disapproval. 'She and Takis will be in the divorce court within five years.'

Elvi winced. 'If they truly love each other they'll make it through,' she argued.

Xan rolled his eyes, unimpressed, and rustled his newspaper before dropping his head to give the printed word his full attention again. A shard of sunlight shone across the glossy blue-black strands of his hair, which he wore longer on top, shorn short at the sides. His wickedly long black lashes shielded his gaze from her, drawing her eyes down the straight blade of his nose to the faint dark shadow of stubble that shaded his golden skin even soon after shaving. Blinking in confusion, Elvi looked away, questioning her fascination, denying the licking little curl of heat uncoiling between her thighs, pressing them together to stop that betrayal in its tracks.

She had to be his mistress but that didn't mean she had to like it or blindly accept that she was attracted to him. She wasn't going to play that game to his rules, wasn't going to let sex seduce her into being disloyal to her own ideals. She didn't want sex *without* feelings involved and wasn't about to let her body mislead her. She was stronger than that...wasn't she? If she let herself sink without trace into that sexual chemistry, it would only encourage him to hang on to her longer. And she didn't want that, of course she didn't, she told herself firmly.

As Elvi drifted away from the table with all the precise direction of a dandelion seed blowing in the breeze, Xan watched her pause to look out of the window, almost trip over a chair and only then head towards the door. She lived inside her head more than she lived in the real world, he thought impatiently. Her nature was utterly alien to his and he couldn't understand why he had the most ridiculous urge to smooth her passage through every obstacle.

Returning to the bedroom, intending to make a start on that packing to be ready for their departure in an hour's time, Elvi was perplexed to find Sylvia already there with suitcases and an assistant.

'Tell me what you want to bring with you to Greece,' Sylvia urged helpfully, as if it was no big deal to be standing in someone else's bedroom working before seven in the morning.

Being rushed through the VIP channel at the airport only heightened Elvi's sense of anticipation, no matter how hard she tried to suppress it, and, stepping onto Xan's sleek private jet, she was unable to silence a small gasp of awe at the space in the cabin furnished with ivory leather seating and the kind of luxuries that even she, who had never flown before, knew were extravagances available only to the very wealthy. The svelte stewardess offered her an array of different coffees, a library of films, all the latest glossy magazines and even the option of a lie-down in the stateroom.

'Take a seat,' Xan instructed her tersely, wondering why she was still hovering in the middle of the aisle.

'It's my first flight,' she whispered, not wanting any of the smartly uniformed cabin crew around them to hear. 'I can't help staring—'

Xan closed a hand over hers and settled her down in the seat opposite his. 'Life's just full of firsts for you right now.'

Elvi dealt him a stonily unamused glance and lifted her chin.

'I'm not making fun of you… I'm *not*,' Xan insisted, working hard not to laugh at that look she had given him, which had washed off him like a feather trying to beat up a rock. 'But why haven't you flown before? For most people it's like catching a bus these days.'

'You really don't have a clue what my life has been like.'

'Then educate me.'

'You'd be bored,' Elvi told him repressively, having caught the gleam of amusement in his gaze at her earlier naïve admission.

His expectant silence nagged at her. 'Obviously we never had the money to go on holidays,' she admitted unwillingly.

'Then why have a passport?'

'Equally obviously people still like to live in hope.'

'Even with an alcoholic parent?'

'Sally went through a very tough time after my father died but she still adopted me,' Elvi proclaimed defensively.

'Adopted?' Xan shot her a startled glance. 'You were adopted?'

Elvi sighed. 'My mother was my father's first wife but she died when I was a baby. Sally adored my dad but she always believed that he only married her to get a mother for me. He was a junior surgeon working long hours and it was difficult for him to cope with a kid at the same time,' she told him. 'When he died, Sally worried that someone might try to take me away from her—'

'Presumably this adoption occurred before she took to the bottle?' Xan slotted in, his careless wording exasperating Elvi.

'Yes, but the point I'm trying to make is that, even in the midst of grieving for my dad, Sally was scared that I would be taken away from her because we weren't related by blood—'

A shapely black brow skated up. 'And presumably you feel that you owe her something for that devotion. Did you ever check the terms of your father's will?'

The insinuation that her adoptive mother could've had something to gain from adopting her set Elvi's teeth on edge but it struck her as typical of Xan's intensely cynical outlook on life. 'He didn't leave a will. He wasn't much older than you when he died from an aneurysm. Sally applied to adopt me because she loved me and wanted to keep me with her and Daniel.'

'Then it sucks to be you,' Xan could not resist saying, thinking about what he knew of alcoholic behaviour and how Elvi must've suffered throughout most of her childhood. How on earth, he marvelled, had she still contrived to form such an intense bond with her adoptive mother in spite of the woman's failings? Betrayed or cheated by anyone, Xan never forgot or forgave. He drew a line and if it was crossed, that was that.

'Well, it didn't, not always,' Elvi protested. 'There were good times even when things were tough and she was never a nasty drunk, never abusive or violent. We were lucky.'

Lucky? Xan swallowed back a derisive retort while he studied her animated face. She *loved* talking about her family, he noted, reckoning that he could use that to make her relax around him. Although, hadn't he *already* used it? She had sacrificed her freedom and her virginity to preserve her precious family and he had taken what she gave without a moment's hesitation. It was a sobering conclusion and he fell silent, irritated by the conscience that had come out of nowhere at him the day before to destroy his peace of mind. Elvi was as foreign to him as an alien would've been, he conceded grimly. That happy-clappy, positive attitude, that selfless streak of loyalty and love a mile wide. But no doubt his conscience would give up the fight and die again through lack of encouragement.

'So, where in Greece are we going exactly?'

'Thira, the island where I was born, not the most exciting destination if you're into partying,' Xan pronounced, but his hard, dark eyes and his intonation could not hide his fondness for the place, Elvi noted with interest as she learned that what Xan said did not always match what she read in his voice or expression. He was inherently deceptive, calculating too, and far too clever for his own good, she reminded herself warningly, but she could not help remembering the man who had thought to drag Sylvia out at dawn to help Elvi pack for a society wedding because Elvi had not had a clue what to wear or of how hot it would be in Greece. Occasionally, he could be thoughtful and he could identify potential problems in advance in a way she could not.

'And to celebrate the occasion of your very first flight...' Xan murmured as the steward approached them with a bottle of champagne. 'I know you don't usually imbibe but surely *one* glass—?'

Rather overwhelmed by the gesture he had made, Elvi nodded vigorous agreement, keen to prevent him from sharing *all* her secrets with the cabin staff. Xan paid no heed to hovering employees when he spoke, being apparently so accustomed to their presence that they might as well have been invisible. She clasped the moisture-beaded flute of champagne, bubbles bursting and tickling her nose as she sipped and politely smiled.

'It wouldn't have felt the same with orange juice,' Xan asserted.

She almost disagreed, tempted to say that it was the thought behind his gesture that mattered most, only such a comment seemed too revealing when she considered it and instead she said nothing. She sipped her drink while Xan told her about the island of Thira and his family home there. Only the family aspect didn't seem to be on his radar because, while he told her that his grandfather had built the house and his father had extended it, he mentioned neither his mother nor his siblings again. He told her about the private beach where he had learned to swim, the freedom of exploring the island as a boy and it all sounded idyllic, not what she had expected when he'd admitted to his father's five matrimonial forays.

'You can't possibly be getting tipsy on one glass,' Xan said abruptly when she giggled like a drain at only the mildest of jokes.

'It was topped up,' she reminded him, holding her breath to try and kill the giggles that had foamed out of her in a spontaneous tide.

Long brown fingers twitched the glass from between her fingers and set it aside. 'I want you sober,' he told her.

'I am,' she insisted, leaning forward, bright blue eyes locked to his lean, strong features, pale white-blonde hair rippling round her heart-shaped face.

Xan shifted in his seat opposite her, raw arousal humming through his big powerful body with almost painful intensity. 'Let's be frank,' he breathed in a driven undertone. 'I want you any way I can have you—'

'That can't be true,' Elvi responded uncomfortably. 'I'm no show-stopper—'

'You stop *me* in my tracks,' Xan reasoned.

Colour drenched her cheeks but the strangest little spark of energy danced through her veins, quickening her heartbeat and her breathing pattern. Nobody had *ever* wanted her like that. She fed herself excuses about how she rarely got the opportunity to even meet men, but Xan had only seen her a handful of times in passing and he hadn't forgotten her again. That made her feel important, special and infinitely less ordinary because she reckoned Xan could have any woman he wanted.

'Ditto,' she conceded in an awkward mutter when he appeared to be awaiting a response from her.

And Xan laughed and leapt upright without warning to simply lift her out of her seat and tumble her down on his lap as he sat down again. 'Thought you were never going to admit that,' he growled with unashamed satisfaction.

For once she didn't begrudge him that satisfaction. 'I don't lie,' she murmured with pride.

'All women lie,' Xan declared, lifting big brown hands to frame her face, brushing her hair back behind her small ears, his potent amber eyes hot and golden and bright with hunger.

'No, we don't—'

'What weight are you?' Xan shot back at her.

And she told him and he told her she couldn't possibly be that weight, standing up to set her down on her feet and lifting her again with a very funny fake grunt of effort that made her giggle helplessly. Xan mock-collapsed back into his seat still gripping her tight before hoisting her up on her knees to sit facing astride him, disconcerting her, killing her giggling fit.

'I wouldn't admit to being that heavy if I wasn't,' she pointed out more circumspectly, barely able to catch her breath that close to him, uneasy at the sudden intimacy, wondering how to remove herself back to her own seat without making a production out of it.

Xan stared down at her ripe pink lips and surrendered to the inevitable without an ounce of concern. He teased at that full lower lip, pressed them softly apart, darted, delved with enthusiasm and felt every inch of her tighten and quiver with response against him. His fingers trailed up a slim silky thigh to the heart of her, teasing fingers sliding below her knickers to locate the most sensitive spot and dallying there to make her moan feverishly into his mouth.

Elvi knew she ought to tell him to stop but she couldn't fight the seduction of sensation engulfing her in a shimmying surge of intense pleasure. She trembled over him, breath caught in her throat, her heart pounding inside her with electrifying anticipation. She squirmed as he stroked and teased and what she had believed she would never welcome again, she suddenly wanted with ferocious intensity. She buried her face against his shoulder, frantically breathing in the familiar scent of his skin, pressing her mouth against the strong brown column of his throat until his other hand caught into her hair to yank her head up. He drove her soft lips apart with a savage kiss of sizzling hunger at the same time as the tightening bands of tension in her pelvis sent her rocketing to her peak. Gasping, moaning, sobbing for breath, she came apart in his arms, shattered into so many pieces she barely recognised herself any more.

Xan settled her back into her seat and, although he was hugely aroused, his frustration was soothed by her explosive reaction to him. It was so honest, so *real*, like no connection he had ever had with a woman before and it excited him way beyond his experience. As Elvi focused on him in a daze of post-climactic bewilderment, as if she didn't quite know what had happened to her, Xan awarded her a dazzling smile of appreciation.

'Later, *moli mou*,' he savoured with growly masculine satisfaction.

CHAPTER SEVEN

NOTHING COULD HAVE prepared Elvi for the startling effect of Xan's mother, Ariadne, whose temperament was so very different from her only child's.

A helicopter had delivered Xan and Elvi to the huge sprawling white villa that overlooked a wooded cove on the island of Thira. As she climbed out a small woman accompanied by a pack of dogs stood up from a seat on the wide front terrace and came hurrying down the steps to eagerly greet them, dogs leaping and bouncing in concert. And from that moment, Elvi doubted that even Xan had managed to get a word in edgeways, for Ariadne talked in a constant stream, hopping confusingly from one topic to the next. She spoke fluent English, however, relieving Elvi's main fear that Xan would be the only person around who understood her, and the older woman was both friendly and welcoming.

On the way through the opulent house, Elvi received a stream of information. Ariadne's mother had been English and Ariadne did not normally live in the big villa, having her own home in the village by the harbour. But when Xan entertained the wider family, Ariadne always acted as his hostess.

'First wife seniority!' Ariadne joked. 'Xan doesn't like his stepmothers much but he accepts his brothers and sisters and, naturally, Delphina wanted her wedding staged here and her brother doing the service—'

'Her brother's a priest?'

'Lukas is a Greek Orthodox priest and Tobias, the other son, is gay. Not that I'm criticising, but Xan did turn out more conventional than his brothers,' Ariadne proclaimed with pride. 'And it goes without saying that he's the cleverest. Delphina's a dear, you'll love her. She and Takis fell in love at school, almost like Helios and me... Xan's father, you know. But of course, Helios and I didn't attend the same school. I was the village doctor's daughter and we met when he went fishing. Like Xan, Helios was gorgeous.' Ariadne loosed an extravagant sigh as if she was looking back in time before continuing briskly, 'But he was also weak and unreliable and quite unable to keep his trousers zipped. Not very good at making money either. By the time Helios passed he had even mortgaged this house. Xan rescued all of us from penury.'

'Xan's...' Elvi hesitated as the eyes of Xan's mother locked with fixed attention to her face. 'He's quite a character,' she pronounced lamely.

The older woman showed the way into a bedroom where confusion seemed to have broken out between two maids over Elvi's luggage. Ariadne smiled even wider and rested a supervisory hand on Elvi's arm to guide her away from the small domestic dispute they had interrupted. 'Do you *know* how many years I've been waiting for my son to bring a woman home with him?' she asked earnestly.

'Oh...' Elvi reddened. 'Xan and I are not...er, serious or anything like that,' she hastened to declare.

'Xan doesn't know *how* to do serious. Not after witnessing the sort of shenanigans he grew up with in this house...all those wives, the live-in lovers who didn't make it to the altar, the screaming dramas,' Ariadne told her with scorn. 'All Helios's children suffered but Xan was older and he endured the most.'

Elvi frowned. 'He lived with his father, not you, after...er...the divorce?'

'Helios refused to give up custody of his eldest son. I was distraught. Losing your husband to another woman and then losing your only child at almost the same time was a huge shock for me.' Ariadne paused in the sunlit corridor lined with magnificent paintings, her rounded but still attractive face full of remembered pain and regret. 'I was young and heartbroken but I was also selfish. I walked away to make a fresh start instead of staying on the island and accepting that I could only be a part-time mother to my son.'

Elvi was listening closely, deeply interested in what she was learning about Xan's childhood. 'Walked away?' she encouraged, impatient to hear more.

But Ariadne, who had paused on the threshold of a much larger and more magnificent bedroom than she had previously shown to Elvi, was no longer looking at her. She was studying her son and she addressed him in Greek, her attitude one of humour while Xan stood there, his tall, powerful figure rigid, his bronzed face impassive, responding to the older woman with a non-committal shrug that nonetheless telegraphed a temper on a short fuse to Elvi's increasingly observant eyes. Faint dark colour edged his killer cheekbones, a gleam of hot gold brightening his gaze.

'I will leave you with your...*friend.*' Xan's mother laughed in emphasis, standing back as Elvi's cases were brought in. 'Dinner is in an hour.'

Xan strode out onto the balcony that overlooked the sea. The Aegean Sea, almost as blue as Elvi's eyes, he brooded grimly, exasperated by his mother's infantile game-playing.

'So...' Elvi hovered uncertainly by the glass doors. 'What was that all about?'

Xan swung back, lithe as a jungle predator and as immaculate as he had been at dawn that morning, shirt still crisp and white, tie still straight. No, he badly needed a shave, she noted with relief, grateful he wasn't quite perfect when the linen sundress she had worn from travelling was as creased as though she had slept in it and bore a coffee stain.

'I haven't brought a woman to the island with me before.'

'I know. Your mother said.'

'To prevent her from reading too much into your visit, I said you were just a friend—'

'I said we weren't serious,' Elvi hastened to add.

'But Ariadne called my bluff,' Xan admitted, his beautiful stubborn mouth curling with annoyance. 'She put you in another room and naturally I countermanded that instruction.'

Elvi inwardly cringed and her cheeks reddened with embarrassment. In a household with other guests, all of them presumably Xan's relatives, staying in *his* room put her under the spotlight more than she would've liked, had she had a choice. And she didn't *have* a choice, she reminded herself ruefully.

'Ariadne's desperate for me to get married and produce grandchildren for her,' Xan revealed in an aggrieved undertone. 'But I'm nowhere near ready for that step.'

Elvi shrugged a stiff shoulder. 'Well, I imagine you'll do exactly as you like anyway and she knows that.'

Always throwing oil on troubled waters, that was Elvi, Xan noted, and it was a novel approach to a man quick to impatience and anger, but rather soothing to be around, if you needed to be handled as though you were an unstable explosive device. Was that how she saw him? To his own surprise, he asked her that question.

'Well, you're naturally intolerant,' Elvi pointed out almost apologetically, as if the unlovely trait of intolerance could not possibly be his own fault. 'You are very precise in your expectations and accustomed to other people meeting those expectations, either because you're paying them to do so or because you're used to people going out of their way to please you.'

'Both,' Xan agreed, impressed by her honesty and her tact. He didn't think he had ever been insulted or criticised so politely. 'Are you planning to go out of your way to please me any time soon?'

Elvi stiffened, her cheeks flushing, her mouth compressing. 'Probably not.'

Xan swung away to hide his smile because she would assume he was laughing at her and he wasn't. She was teaching him almost as much as he was teaching her and by the time she learned and accepted that sex was merely sex, he would probably be bored, he told himself stubbornly, striving to ignore the reality that simply the thought of getting her into the same bed at the end of the tedious evening ahead sent a throbbing, stabbing pulse of raw erotic craving through him. She would have an enjoyable holiday on Thira and then he would send her home. She would be restored to happy-clappy positivity, merely a little less innocent and the sordid aspects of their original arrangement would be tidily airbrushed over into something more acceptable.

Unaware of Xan's plans for her immediate future, Elvi smoothed down her dress, black, fitted with a lower neckline than she liked, but undeniably elegant.

'Wear your diamonds,' Xan advised, emerging from the bathroom in all his naked glory, so tall and bronzed with powerful pectorals and taut ropes of muscle visible across his flat abdomen.

With difficulty, Elvi dragged her eyes from that view, her body uncomfortably warm despite the air conditioning. 'They're not *my* diamonds—'

'I bought them for you.'

'I don't want them.'

'But you can *wear* them when I tell you to,' Xan cut in, flipping open the jewel case to extract the necklace and anchor it round her throat while she struggled to lift her hair out of his path.

She had sworn she would not do as she was told but here she was doing it like everyone else around Xan, Elvi reflected angrily. 'I'm leaving them behind when we part—'

Xan shrugged an indifferent shoulder. 'And when do you think that might be?'

'A week?' Elvi looked at him hopefully.

And without warning, Xan felt a surge of rage splinter through him. It was that hopeful look that implied that she could not wait to regain her freedom and escape him. A woman had never ever shown Xan that expression before.

'No chance,' he countered succinctly, his attention involuntarily lingering on the voluptuous display of her breasts in the dress. It wasn't so much that the neckline was too low as that she had rather more than could be easily contained.

'My face is at *this* level,' Elvi told him thinly, all too well aware of where his scrutiny had strayed.

'Obviously I'm going to look… I love your curves,' Xan retorted squarely. 'But I think you should change into another dress. I don't want anyone else looking.'

Thoroughly irritated by being asked to change when she was fully dressed, but disliking even more having her chest on display, Elvi stepped back into the built-in closet where her clothing had been hung to rifle through the selection for another option. She yanked out the blue dress she had worn for the party he had taken her to and dug out a different bra to go with it, disappearing into the bathroom for the exchange, tossing over her shoulder, 'I don't see why it should bother you if anyone did look!'

Xan compressed his wide sensual mouth while he thought about that. He didn't know why the idea bothered him, but it did. Her glorious hourglass shape was eye-catching and he didn't want to share it. Fortunately, she was not one of those women, and he had met quite a few, who deliberately exposed as much flesh as possible in the hope of attracting more male attention.

'Much better,' Xan pronounced when she reappeared, flushed and slightly tumbled, to settle exasperated eyes on him. 'I hope the swimwear you have isn't too revealing—'

Elvi rolled her eyes as she stepped through the doorway into the corridor ahead of him. Even the most modestly cut swimwear made her look like an old-style pin-up girl, a fact that had put her off swimming sessions at a young age. 'So, interestingly, you have a prudish streak too,' she remarked snidely.

Still insulted by her enthusiasm for leaving him to return to her workaday, poverty-stricken existence, Xan refused to rise to the bait.

Downstairs, a crowd of guests were enjoying pre-dinner drinks and Elvi was introduced to Xan's relations. The bride-to-be, Delphina, was a pretty brunette with a ridiculously shy version of Xan's eyes while her mother was a brassy blonde, who loosed a sarcastic laugh of disbelief when Elvi, asked what she did for a living, mentioned her most recent employment in a craft shop.

'You see, Callista,' Xan murmured in the mildest of tones. 'Some women do choose to *work* for a living.'

'I would just have ignored her,' Elvi whispered in reproof as they moved away.

'I'm not a fan of turning the other cheek,' Xan retorted crisply. 'Callista lives off the rich men she sleeps with and she had no business sneering at you. It's a wonder Delphina has turned out as well as she has.'

'Sleeping with rich men to get by sounds very *much* like work to me,' Elvi dared.

Xan froze and glanced down at her with a sudden frown.

'Oh, I wasn't getting at you,' Elvi said with mock innocence. 'After all, I did it to keep my mother out of prison and off drink, which is rather different.'

'Skase!' Xan shot down at her in a raw undertone.

'Meaning?'

'Shut up…drop the subject,' Xan bit out furiously as he leant down to her level.

'Well, you really can't go around with that "one rule for me but a different rule for everyone else" take on everything,' Elvi pointed out helplessly.

'I can do whatever I like—'

'And it's thoroughly bad for you,' Elvi told him firmly.

Xan swore under his breath, inflamed by her sheer nerve. Why didn't she worry about offending him, as other women did? He stood by watching his mother introduce Elvi to his remaining sisters, noticing how animated the conversation between them all became. Of course, he should've expected that, he told himself calmingly. His sisters all lived in the real world, unlike his former stepmother, Callista. One sister was an engineer with her own company, another was a doctor, the third a happy housewife with four children, two of which were very cute five-year-old female twins. Another and stronger generation of his family, he labelled with satisfaction, for not one of his siblings exhibited the money-grabbing greed of his former stepmothers. Yes, he had bought them all houses and financed their business projects, but essentially his brothers and sisters were independent, falling back on his wealth only in times of misfortune.

They sat down to dinner. By that stage it was clear to Xan that Elvi had gone down like a prize trophy with his family because his mother was pumping her about her love of dogs, while the wretched untrained little beasts formed begging round their feet, and his sisters were chattering to Elvi as though she were one of the family. It was her friendly gene, Xan decided, only becoming perversely annoyed when Elvi disappeared off to see his mother's latest craft project, which he knew would be an absolute disaster. Ariadne Ziakis might be the acclaimed author of several very weighty archaeology tomes and a professor in her university department, but she was not talented with her hands.

'I was doing the stitch wrong!' his mother proclaimed when she returned to the table to drink her coffee. 'And this wonderful girl showed me how to do it and it was *so* easy when you know how...'

Ne...yes, Elvi went down with the family like award-winning chocolate.

Tobias, always timid, confided in Elvi about his latest relationship breakdown, when he could barely bring himself to acknowledge that he was gay to Xan's face. Lukas pontificated happily about worldly indifference to the suffering of refugees and revealed that he had met the woman he hoped to marry. One sister revealed that she was pregnant again, another admitted to a serious boyfriend. Xan watched in silent astonishment while his family opened up to Elvi in a way they never did with him. Delphina related the entire story of her humdrum relationship with Takis in the kind of detail that would send most people to sleep, but Elvi listened as if she were hearing the most romantic story she had ever heard.

Maybe she genuinely did think that sort of stuff was romantic, Xan reflected in awe as not even a giggle escaped Elvi when she heard about Takis's marriage proposal: harbour restaurant, family party, roses at the table, bended knee, so conventional Xan's teeth hurt with saccharine overload just listening. Elvi was *nice*, he decided, in the most flexible interpretation of that overused word. People blossomed around her, drawn by her sincere interest, warmed by her kind and optimistic outlook on life. She was the absolute antithesis of him, Xan decided.

'She's adorable. Put a ring on her finger fast,' his mother urged as she said goodnight to him.

'She's far too kind and caring for you,' his eldest sister, the engineer, opined. 'You'll probably make her miserable.'

'Oh, I just love Elvi.' Delphina sighed blissfully, very much the lovestruck bride the night before her wedding.

'Elvi would make a good wife,' Lukas, the priest, told him staunchly. 'She's a godly woman.'

'She's a pet,' Tobias pronounced with starry eyes as Xan identified Elvi by his mother's side, down on her knees petting the scruffy dogs. 'Such a good listener.'

Chilled by that amount of family enthusiasm, Xan accepted the accolades without comment and reclaimed Elvi from the pet contingent with difficulty. On the upper landing, she paused to study a portrait. 'Is that your father?'

'Yes,' Xan confirmed, his attention locked to her rather than the painting. Her dress exposed her slender spine, where he already knew the soft, smooth skin felt like silk, and the fine fabric below her waist outlined the ripe, rounded swell of her bottom. His libido kicked in with lusty fervour and he coiled his hands into fists of restraint. Everything was going to be different *this* time, he assured himself. There would be no grabbing, no rushing, no cutting of sexual corners.

'When did he die?' she asked, still looking at the canvas.

'Nine years ago.'

'You do look very like him,' Elvi conceded as she moved on, her heart skipping a beat as Xan closed his hand over hers, engulfing her smaller fingers.

'Thankfully that resemblance is all we shared.' Xan thrust wide the door of his bedroom and she brushed against him, her face turning up, her eyes blindingly blue and bright above her soft full mouth, and that view cut through his self-discipline like a knife through butter.

Xan ran his fingertips lightly down the bare line of her spine and she trembled, suddenly fiercely aware of him, her body involuntarily awakening to his touch. He edged her back against the wall and stroked her hair back from her flushed face. 'Now tell me that you want me...'

Elvi dealt him a stubborn glance because only the champagne during the flight had forced that admission from her. 'You don't need the ego boost.'

'Why are you still fighting something so natural?' Xan demanded, as if she was being thoroughly unreasonable.

'It's not natural to me,' Elvi argued, struggling not to melt into the lean, powerful contours of his body as he penned her in by the wall. He was so warm and he smelt amazing, her nostrils flaring on the familiar scent of him. Her nipples prickled, swelling and tightening, and an edgy pulse beat between her thighs.

Xan could not credit how stubborn she could be. He could not fathom how a woman so seemingly soft and warm and eager to please those around her could then be so resistant when it came to pleasing him. 'You're only making this harder for yourself.'

Elvi was so tense as she fought her arousal that she was barely breathing, her small body stiff. 'I don't think so. This is who I am. If I changed that, I couldn't respect myself any longer.'

'Only you would care to think about such things,' Xan intoned thickly. 'This close to you, I can only think about how much I want you—'

He pushed closer, pressing her back against the wall,

and even through their clothes she could feel the hard, insistent length of him against her stomach. A jolt of hungry need took her by storm, drying her mouth, stealing her breath, sending her heart hammering. 'Xan...' she heard herself whisper almost pleadingly.

'Powerful, isn't it?' Xan husked, his hands bracing on either side of her head, his eyes a hot scorching gold enhanced by lush black lashes. 'So powerful you can't think of anything else.'

'You're teasing me,' Elvi said breathlessly, her fingers splaying across his shirt front, the heat of his muscled chest encouraging her hand to flex and the fingers to spread in something very like a caress.

Xan pulled her hand down to where he really needed her attention and her fingers traced his bold length through the fabric of his trousers, her shy fascination powerfully erotic. He wanted to rip off his clothes there and then and teach her everything she didn't know and, gripped by that image, he shed his jacket where he stood and yanked off his tie, unbuttoning his shirt with one hand, unzipping with the other.

It was as though Elvi's heartbeat had extended to thump through her entire body. She felt giddy, over-excited despite her nerves. Recognising Xan's feverish eagerness for her touch removed her fear of doing the wrong thing. That he could crave her caresses as much as she craved his was a revelation and a tremendous equaliser. She pushed down his boxers and found him, she glided her fingers up and down before she got down on her knees. He shuddered as she found him with her mouth and he arched his hips, groaning something hoarse in Greek. She swirled her tongue, tantalising, teasing while she stroked and cupped and savoured him. His hand tightened in her hair and then he yanked her back up to him, kissing her as though his life depended on that connection.

He cannoned off the corner of a dresser as he hauled her bodily over to the bed, stood her up, struggling with the backless dress and its complicated closure. There was a ripping sound as he simply lost patience and tore the fragile fabric down the middle. She looked up at him in shock.

'I can't wait...' Xan confided fiercely, flipping her round to unfasten the bra that anchored at her waist. 'What a strange contraption,' he muttered, his hands rising to mould the full swell of her breasts, tugging at her straining nipples and then ravishing her mouth with his again, his tongue plunging deep, extracting a startled cry of urgency from her.

They landed on the bed with a bounce and she had no idea how they had got there from the door. Xan ripped off his shirt and flung it aside, yanking off what remained of his clothing at the same time, his impatience unconcealed. He crawled up the bed like a lethal predator, golden eyes ablaze as he repositioned her to his satisfaction.

'No, not this time,' he censured when she tried to inch beneath the sheet. 'No barriers, no boundaries, *moli mou*. You're a work of art and I want to look at you.'

He was all male power and muscle sheathed in sun-kissed skin from his wide shoulders to his lean hips and strong thighs. The thrusting, potent proof of his arousal made damp heat rise at the heart of her.

'I promise to drive you out of your mind with pleasure,' Xan breathed with raw sensuality.

Sliding down the bed and parting her thighs to feast on her with his mouth, he took her entirely by surprise. She gasped, yanked unavailingly at his black hair, and then finally surrendered to wild sensation. He teased her with his skill, and her frantic tension grew and grew while the hollow ache between her legs became unbearable. She tossed and she turned and then she writhed, lost in the excitement until she soared to a glorious peak and the world splintered into a multicoloured shower of fireworks.

Xan grinned down at her bemused face and sank into her with one powerful thrust. His groan of sheer unalloyed pleasure made her feel even hotter. This time her body craved him and she was much more relaxed and there wasn't even a hint of discomfort, only the wonderful rolling tide of exquisite sensation as his every movement sent smouldering pleasure winging through her.

'Don't stop,' she gasped at the height of another peak, every nerve straining greedily for more.

And Xan laughed with pure unashamed enjoyment, pulling back from her briefly to flip her over onto her knees to continue, driving deeper into her receptive body with every cry he wrenched from her until finally Elvi reached the highest summit of rapturous excitement and a seething rush of convulsive delight sent paroxysms of electrifying pleasure travelling through her exhausted length.

'Please don't make me move until tomorrow,' she mumbled, face down on the bed.

'I thought you were into cuddling.'

'Are you hot and sweaty?' she asked prosaically.

'You want me to shower first?'

Elvi turned back over and laughed with helpless appreciation. 'Only joking!'

Xan closed an arm round her and pulled her close. It wasn't a hug or a cuddle but it was more of a connection than he had offered before and it soothed her racing thoughts and the anxiety she was holding at bay.

'You used a condom, didn't you?' she checked worriedly.

'Of course. Are you still worrying about that?' he said in surprise.

'Worrying comes naturally to me,' she admitted.

'Worrying is a waste of energy that can be better employed. I want to have you again,' Xan confided, pressing a kiss to a sensitive pulse point below her ear, making her squirm.

'Already?' she gasped, huge blue eyes lifting to his lean, darkly handsome face, instantly rejoicing in the sleek dark beauty of him laced with the wilder elements of his tousled hair and stubble.

Xan nodded very seriously. 'I've got a major backlog of Elvi hunger to clear. I'm going to be very demanding, *moli mou...*'

A little flame of anticipation kindled wickedly low in her pelvis at that news. For the first time Elvi acknowledged just how much she revelled in Xan Ziakis, clothed or unclothed. It didn't matter how much he infuriated her, it didn't stop her craving him with every fibre of her being. It was only physical attraction, nothing more serious, she told herself with determination, telling herself to move with the times and stop judging herself for a situation she couldn't change. After all, their arrangement wouldn't last for ever and the real world would reclaim her soon enough.

Before she'd met Xan, she had sunk into a rut and stopped thinking about her own future, she acknowledged ruefully. Perhaps Joel had had a point when he'd criticised her for her absorption in her family. When Xan moved on, she decided that she would change her attitude. She would seek a more challenging job or even training that would enable her to be more ambitious. Her mother and brother were finding their own feet now and would no longer need to rely on her to the same extent.

When Xan emerged from the bathroom, Elvi was fast asleep. He had to fight the temptation to wake her while he studied her with brooding disquiet. Sex had never been so intense for him and his voracious desire to have her again disturbed him. He wasn't treating her the way he normally treated a mistress. He didn't know what it was about her that got to him deep down where he had sworn never to let a woman go again.

And inexplicably and unnervingly, she made him keep on changing his mind. What had happened to his determination not to touch her until she invited him to do so? What had happened to his decision to let her go free in five days?

Even worse, Elvi made him want more and he liked that even less.

Was it the fact that he was her first lover? Did he somehow feel responsible for her now? He reminded himself that he had wronged her and that he had deliberately set out to redress that damage. But that didn't explain why he hadn't just let her go or why he was tempted to put his arms around her when she was asleep and there was no chance of sex. *Thee mou*…that urge was freaking him out! He was even more unsettled by the tangle of clothing untidily littering the bedroom floor. That wasn't like him either. He was quick to remove the evidence of his lack of patience and control, but throughout the exercise he was acknowledging that he should not allow any woman to affect him the way she did and he was urging himself to walk away fast.

Elvi drifted slowly out of a deep sleep to greet the dawn. Light was filtering through the curtains and she was too warm. She muttered a complaint and the sheet was tossed back, Xan's fingers returning to the place which made her writhe and heat up even more. A slight gasp escaped her as he shifted against her, all power and potency and temptation and then he was where she needed him to be, sinking into her welcoming body with urgent force. But then the tempo changed to sensually slow and her tension ramped up accordingly, heart hammering with frantic longing, her body gripped by fierce, needy impatience. She pushed back against him, wanting, needing, and with a husky sound of appreciation, he speeded up, delivering what her body was programmed to crave in a heart-stopping, blood-stirring storm of sensation that peaked and then left her floating.

'I ordered breakfast in bed for you,' Xan murmured lazily. 'I have some work to catch up on before I have to walk Delphina into the church.'

'It'll take me all my time to get ready for the wedding,' Elvi sighed, feeling like a hot sweaty mess even while her whole body purred with little aftershocks of pleasure.

Xan strode out of the shower and she watched him dress, her brow furrowing while she ate. He seemed very preoccupied, his dark classic profile taut, his stunning eyes veiled. Something had changed, she grasped on a level she didn't quite understand: there was something different about Xan. A distance she hadn't noticed the night before? The first hint that their arrangement was already heading towards its natural end? Was he getting bored with her? It was what she wanted, what she *needed*. She had to pick herself back up and get her life back on track. Unfortunately, that did not clarify why her skin chilled and her tummy succumbed to a nauseous lurch at the thought of their parting.

There was no way she was becoming attached to Xan, she reasoned with firm conviction. She wasn't that foolish or that quick to allow her feelings to control her. At heart she was sensible and practical and a stranger to the kind of dangerous emotions that were likely to upset her. For goodness' sake, she had only been with him a few days, long enough to learn that sexual pleasure was a lot more seductive than she had ever dreamt but nowhere near long enough to start thinking too warmly of a man she disliked.

And she *did* dislike him, she *thoroughly* disliked

him, Elvi reminded herself with satisfaction. Xan was immoral and unscrupulous and he expected the whole world to revolve around him and his needs and wants. All he cared about was making money and maintaining a stress-free sex life. They weren't even *in* a relationship. Everything Xan did and said spelled out that message because he didn't want her to misinterpret an intimacy that was not destined to last.

The sooner it was over between them, the better it would be for her, she told herself staunchly. She had changed as well. She would never be so naïve or trusting again. But that made her stronger rather than weaker... didn't it?

Two hours later, Elvi was garbed in an elegant dark green dress and accompanying Xan's eldest sister, Hana, and her family to the village church. A former monastery, the large church sat at the heart of a very picturesque little village overlooking the harbour. The pews were packed, even though Hana had said that Delphina had wanted a very small wedding attended only by relatives. Elvi's attention was fully engaged taking in the wonderful painted ceiling and icons that made the candlelit church interior so colourful and warm. And then beside her, Hana said something abrupt in Greek and turned her head to look at the woman smilingly taking what appeared to be the last available seat in the row in front of them.

Hana's husband put his finger to his lips to silence the speech that was visibly brimming on his wife's lips as her dark eyes hardened with annoyance.

It wasn't the time or the place to ask who the woman

was. She was certainly eye-catching, Elvi conceded admiringly, and evidently not bound by the tradition that suggested that only brides should wear white at a wedding. The brunette in the shimmering white dress was very tall, very slim and graceful and she had the face of an angel with big dark eyes, flawless features and a sultry pink mouth.

Elvi watched a sort of selective shimmy take place amongst the guests, heads turning as much as they dared, all eyes skimming in the direction of the late arrival, a low buzz of comment following. Clearly, whoever the woman was, her attendance was unexpected and food for a good gossip.

Xan dealt with the sudden appearance of the only woman who had ever broken his heart without batting a single eyelash. His first reaction was irritation, because even though Angie would have received an invite, being the bridegroom's cousin, she should have stayed away because Xan's family universally loathed her. His second reaction was that, although he despised her, she had worn well in their years apart.

When he received a lingering look of invitation from her, his inventive brain projected an image he very much liked. Two birds...*one* stone. Revenge and the freedom to move on in one perfect little package, he decided with ice-cold logic. Sometimes doing the right thing could mean doing it by nefarious means. It would be the wisest move he had ever made and would certainly kill at source his family's ridiculous conviction that he was ready to settle down.

CHAPTER EIGHT

'I'M SO SORRY about Angie showing up,' Delphina said, as though it were her fault that Xan's ex-girlfriend had decided to attend her wedding. 'Takis's mother insisted that it was only courtesy to send her an invitation but *nobody* expected her to actually come.'

'Why are you worrying about it?' Elvi asked gently. 'I'm not one bit bothered.'

It was a complete lie but Elvi had already heard enough about Angie Sarantos from Xan's worried family to last her a lifetime, and Delphina's embarrassment made her feel guilty because every bride had the right to enjoy her wedding day free of all such concerns.

Apparently, Xan had met Angie when he was twenty-one and had asked her to marry him. Angie, however, had ditched him once it became clear that the Ziakis family was in serious debt following the death of Xan's father. Within months she had married another man and moved to Switzerland to live and she was now a childless widow. Ariadne, Xan's adoring mother, was convinced that Angie was broke and on the prowl for a wealthy second husband. But Xan was no fool, Elvi reflected wryly. She just couldn't see him falling for the charms of an obvious gold-digger.

But if that was true, what *was* he playing at? He had not neglected Elvi in any way. He had sat beside her throughout the wedding breakfast staged back at the villa and had made very polite conversation, much as though they were chance-met strangers, rather than lovers. But once they were freed from their table and able to mingle, Xan had continually drifted in Angie's direction, pausing to chat with the other woman at every opportunity, laughing and joking with her as if she were his long-lost best friend. Old friends catching up and able to relive fond memories now that their parting was well behind them?

Maybe so, but Elvi had also noticed the cool distance of Xan's altered attitude towards herself and, whatever else that change denoted, she was convinced that he had decided that they were over. Why else would he behave in such a way? Besides, Angie Sarantos was absolutely stunning and Elvi knew she couldn't hold a candle to her.

How any man could travel so fast from wanting her passionately only hours earlier to flirting madly with his ex, she had no idea. But then she wasn't a transitory sort of person, was she? What she *did* feel, she felt deeply and the sentiment stayed with her. Xan, however, had only felt lust for her, nothing profound or more lasting.

Bearing those realities in mind, why did she currently feel as if she had been punched in the stomach? Why was she in shock? Why was she *hurt*? Where had those responses come from? In truth she hurt as much as if Xan had taken a hammer to her heart and smashed it to pieces and she hated herself for that anguished sense of rejection and disillusionment, when instead she knew she should've been celebrating the prospect of returning to her own life, the life he had so ruthlessly yanked her out of.

Clearly, beneath the surface show of her hostility, she had contrived to become more emotionally attached to Xan than she had been prepared to acknowledge. That shamed her and put her on her mettle to appear untouched by the little drama of the flirtation that every other wedding guest appeared to find a source of fascination. You couldn't fall in love with anyone that quickly, she reasoned angrily with herself; it just wasn't possible. Possibly her pride was hurt, that foolish part of her that had unwisely revelled in Xan's seemingly overwhelming desire for her ordinary self. Pride cometh before a fall, she reminded herself studiously, trying to keep a smile pinned to her lips, struggling to stop her gaze tracking Xan or Angie round the room.

For that reason, it was a surprise when Xan appeared at her side and suggested they dance. Elvi gave him a pained glance and shook her head. 'No, thanks,' she said quietly.

She was pale, her eyes shadowed and for a split second Xan's resolve almost faltered, but the growing conviction that he was finally doing what he should've done some days earlier held him fast. He *had* to let her go: nothing else was acceptable and dragging out the process would be unnecessarily cruel.

'Go off and enjoy yourself... I'm quite tired,' Elvi insisted, not wanting his company if he was only putting on a show for the sake of appearances.

'If you're sure...' Xan straightened back to his full height, avoiding a meaningful look from his brother, the priest, that warned him that Lukas was in the mood to preach. Aware of his family's censorious appraisals, Xan decided it was time for a break to take care of some work and when the event was at an end he would speak to Elvi about her departure.

Alone again, Elvi walked outside onto the terrace and sat down, ostensibly to take in the panoramic view of the island and the sea. But she couldn't see anything but Xan inside her head, sleek, darkly beautiful Xan with his dazzling eyes laughing with her, smiling with her, filling her with feelings that felt so natural to her that she had not even realised that she was falling for him.

Angie Sarantos strolled out with a champagne goblet cradled nonchalantly in one slender hand. 'He's bored with you,' she murmured softly.

Elvi clenched her teeth hard. 'Are you speaking to me?'

'I imagine you hate my guts,' Angie remarked. 'But Xan and I have something special. I didn't know how special it was until I lost it. Point is, I made a mistake nine years ago and I know it.'

Elvi was reluctant to engage with the brunette in any way. 'It's none of my business—'

'It's not,' Angie agreed. 'But I won't let anyone come between me and Xan.'

Elvi's phone vibrated with a text and she pulled it out as an excuse and stood up. 'Excuse me, I have to take this—'

Stepping back into the cool air-conditioned interior, Elvi read the text from her mother and a wave of dizziness ran over her, perspiration beading her upper lip. Her brother, Daniel, had been injured in a car accident and he was in hospital. Suddenly, Elvi was desperate to get home and be with her family.

'Are you all right?' Hana asked her worriedly. 'You're as white as a sheet. Sit down for a moment—'

'No, I need to speak to Xan,' Elvi broke in apologetically. 'Do you know where he is?'

Minutes later, Elvi entered Xan's office on the ground floor. He was standing by the window, talking in French on the phone. Some words she vaguely recognised from school but most were incomprehensible as she hovered just over the threshold staring at him. For probably the *last* time, she reasoned numbly.

'I want to go home,' she declared shakily. 'My brother's in hospital.'

And from that point on, everything moved on oiled wheels. In fact, she had the feeling that Xan couldn't get her off the island of Thira fast enough because he could not have been more helpful. He insisted that she travel back on his private jet, instructed the staff to pack for her while also informing her that he had organised accommodation in London for her and that he would place money in her bank account.

'But I don't need accommodation or money!'

'Of course, you do,' Xan overruled without hesitation. 'It's my fault that you don't have employment to return to and you need support to get back on your feet again. The apartment you originally moved into is up for sale at present, so naturally I will provide somewhere else for you to stay.'

And at that point Elvi simply stopped arguing because arguing with Xan was exhausting. He would regroup and address the topic from another angle, usually one she hadn't yet thought of. What did strike her like a blow was his eagerness to speed her on her way and ease her passage with his wealth.

'You don't need to feel guilty that we're over,' Elvi told him abruptly, the reproof literally leaping straight from her brain onto her tongue. 'We didn't suit. We're like oil and water—'

Xan froze, his lean, powerful physique pulling taut, and his magnificent eyes flashed pure gold. 'I'm not feeling guilty. Why would I feel guilty?'

Her stomach already rolling with nausea, Elvi decided not to mention Angie. Why go there when she didn't have to and her family emergency had given Xan a ready excuse to move her back *out* of his life again as fast as he had dragged her into it?

'Look after yourself,' Xan urged grimly. 'And if you ever need anything, call me—'

Elvi dealt him a rueful grimace. 'Like that's going to happen,' she derided with newly learned cynicism. 'Goodbye, Xan.'

'Daniel's going to be fine. Your mother says he looks like he's been beaten up and he's sprained his ankle but that's all, so you don't need to worry,' Dmitri declared, letting her know that he too was in regular contact with her parent as he accompanied her out to the helicopter waiting in the grounds of the villa. 'I hope you know you're very welcome to move to Oxford with your family—'

Elvi smiled warmly at the older man. 'Thanks. I'm going to tell Mum the truth when I get back, well... *almost* the truth,' she adjusted with a slight wince. 'I won't tell her anything that upsets her.'

At noon the next day, after a sleepless flight on Xan's opulent jet and a harried arrival at yet another very fancy apartment, where she left her luggage stacked, Elvi went straight to the hospital and met her mother in the waiting area. Her eyes were burning in her head from exhaustion and the battle to stay in control of her emotions. *It's over.* The phrase kept on crashing into her head like an alarm bell shrilling and lacing her every thought with far too much drama. No, no, I'm *not* in love with him, this is a crush, a long-overdue crush and it *is* manageable, she told herself firmly.

'You were with Mr Ziakis...in *Greece*?' Sally Cartwright repeated in disbelief. 'What on earth—?'

'I went to see him after you were arrested and...then we had dinner and somehow we ended up getting involved,' Elvi admitted starkly. 'It was crazy and it all happened terribly fast...of course, it was never going to last—'

'But that's why he dropped the theft charge, I imagine.' Her mother wrapped her arms round her trembling daughter and muttered soothing things, seeing far more than Elvi would ever have admitted in the hollowness of the younger woman's eyes and her drawn pallor.

The lies swept away, Elvi hoped she would feel better but her mood remained flat as a pancake. As Dmitri had forecast, Daniel was fine, his face badly bruised and swollen and his ankle sprained. Her sibling would be returning home with them on crutches.

Two weeks dragged past. Dmitri hired a van and moved Sally's family to his terraced house in Oxford. The property was beautifully renovated and a vast improvement on their previous home. Elvi finally got her own bedroom while her mother enthused about the freedom of having a garden again. Elvi, however, had more pressing things on her mind because her period was late. In a sombre mood, she went out to buy a pregnancy test, anxiously counting days on her fingers, striving to be optimistic as she recalled Xan's lack of concern over that contraceptive mishap.

Thinking about Xan only upset her and she tried not to do it but late at night, lying sleepless in bed, there was nothing else to think about. Xan hadn't had to say the words in the end but he had found her wanting and he had dumped her like an old shoe within days of taking her to bed for the first time. Her self-esteem at rock-bottom, Elvi threw herself into organising their new home with her mother and looking up training courses online in an attempt to find something that truly interested her rather than settling for the first job available. Unhappily, the pregnancy scare hit her like an express train just when she was trying to move beyond heartbreak.

She sat in the bathroom clutching the wand before she even went downstairs to breakfast. Her brain was running at a thousand knots a minute. How *could* she be pregnant? How could a single oversight result in such a life-changing event? Yes, she knew the facts of life, but her hazy recollection of that first time with Xan seemed more about passion than anything else. The confirmation of a positive test came up and, in a panic, she re-read the instructions all over again. She felt sick and dizzy, overwhelmed by fear of the unknown. She was pregnant, she acknowledged in shock; she was actually going to have Xan's baby.

She dragged in a steadying breath of oxygen. Naturally she knew there were alternatives but the idea of surrendering her baby to adoption had no appeal for her and she couldn't bring herself to consider a termination. She would have to tell Xan because he had the right to know: this was his child too. Before she could lose her nerve, she pulled out her phone to text him.

I need to see you. Something to tell you.

Xan read the text in the middle of a meeting. *Elvi.*

Meet for lunch?

His intelligence warned him that lunch was a very bad idea. Going cold turkey to kill an obsession was a basic ground rule. His hunger for Elvi was persistent, there in the morning when he awoke, there at night when he tried to shut down his thoughts and sleep. Somehow

Elvi and her glorious curves had become an obsession, rarely out of his mind. What the hell would she want to see him about? Probably some problem relating to her family, he reasoned grimly, recalling that he *had* urged her to contact him at any time and could hardly complain if she had decided to take him up on the invitation.

Can't make it to lunch in time. Living in Oxford now.

Xan froze. She wasn't even occupying the apartment he had bought her? What the hell was she doing in Oxford? He asked her to meet him that afternoon at her apartment, the one she *wasn't* using, he clarified with controlled sarcasm.

It was ages before she assented with a grudging OK and promised to text him once she had worked out what time she would be there.

Elvi wouldn't allow herself to dress up for her meeting with Xan. He was the father of her unborn child, *not* a lover, *not* someone she wanted to impress, not anything really. In jeans and a purple filmy top, her hair confined in a long braid that snaked down her slender spine, she caught the train and battled every intimate memory that tried to sneak back into her mind. But she had forgotten nothing about Xan from the way he liked to check stocks and shares and eat in silence over breakfast to the provocative blaze of his stunning golden eyes when he was hungry for her.

Had he reconciled with Angie Sarantos? Or had that flirtation simply been a symptom of his restive boredom in Elvi's company? She allowed herself to think along those lines because it was realistic thinking and naturally she was curious. It was also best not to dwell in advance on Xan's likely horror at the news that she had conceived because she was well aware that he had not seriously entertained that possibility.

She texted Xan as soon as she arrived at the apartment and anxiously paced the living area while she waited. The shrill of the doorbell took her by surprise because she had assumed he would have a key for the second apartment as he had had for the first.

'Don't you have a key?' she asked as she pulled open the door and fell back a step.

'No, this apartment is in your name. I have no right of entry here,' Xan told her quietly.

'Are you saying you *bought* it for me? An *apartment*?' Elvi gasped incredulously as she went into instant retreat, intimidated by the height of him towering over her that close. Nor could she believe what she was hearing. He had moved her out of the other apartment to put her into a new one but she had no idea why. In any case, why on earth would he buy her an apartment?

Xan jerked a casual shoulder, dismissing the guilty conscience that had powered the purchase. 'I wanted you to be secure—'

'But you don't buy someone you barely know an apartment!' Elvi bleated, so disconcerted by what he had told her that she could think of nothing else. 'Obviously I assumed you'd rented it for me and I planned to let you know that I was back living with my family, only I hadn't got around to it yet....'

Xan wasn't listening although his attention was locked to her. He noticed that she had gone back to wearing her own clothing, tacitly rejecting the new wardrobe he had also given her, but just at that moment he didn't care. Indeed, given even the most minimal encouragement, he would have carted her off to the bedroom, unbraided her beautiful hair and laid her out like a banquet for his delectation. One look at her flushed face, evasive blue eyes and the curves no top in creation could have concealed and he was painfully aroused and...*and* obsessed again? He froze and then swung round to close the door behind him, utilising that moment to suppress his baser urges.

'You'd better come in,' Elvi muttered belatedly. 'I've got something to tell you—'

Xan moved warily to the threshold of the living area and lodged there, carefully maintaining his distance. 'So, tell me... I sent my limo round the block. I wasn't expecting to be here for long.'

'I'm... I'm pregnant,' Elvi announced in a hoarse undertone.

Deprived of speech and reaction for possibly the very first time in his life, Xan stared back at her in unconcealed shock, his strong features tightening and paling as the gravity of her admission sank in on him.

'I wouldn't have got in touch with you again for anything less serious,' Elvi added defensively. 'You thought we didn't have anything to worry about but we *do*...'

'Yes, clearly,' Xan agreed, struggling to come to terms with her announcement at the same time as he came up with a solution. It was the way he worked. He saw a problem and he immediately set out to fix it and fast. A baby, the kind of little entity he had imagined would enliven his middle age, rather than his wild-oats-sowing years. Bang went his perfectly planned future! But thinking on his feet was second nature to Xan and flexibility was a key skill. There *had* to be a resolution that would cover their situation.

'I don't want a termination and I don't want to put my child up for adoption either,' Elvi declared, deciding to lay all that out for him upfront before he got any ideas.

'I suppose the odds of conception were more promising than I was prepared to contemplate,' Xan commented reflectively, stalking deeper into the room as he pulled out his phone to let his driver know that he would be a while. 'I am one of seven children, after all.'

Her knees wobbling as her extreme tension faded, Elvi dropped down like a stone into a leather seat and clasped her hands tightly together on her knees. 'What are we going to do?'

'We're adults. We'll deal with it,' Xan asserted without hesitation.

Elvi resisted the urge to admit that she didn't feel much like an adult at that moment because she was in unfamiliar territory and apprehensive of a future as a single parent. Both admissions, however, sounded defeatist to her. Even worse, all the angst in the air was preventing her from taking any pleasure at all in her conception. Instead of feeling excited at the prospect of becoming a mother for the first time, she felt guilty, as though her body had done something it shouldn't have done.

Xan was thinking at top speed and already acknowledging that there *was* no magical solution to their plight. A child would be born, *his* child, *his* responsibility. But regardless of the support he gave to his child's mother, he would only be an occasional parent, who received scheduled visits. He would never be fully involved because he and Elvi would be leading separate lives.

And that would be where the problems started, he conceded reluctantly. He was very much aware of the consequences children suffered after a relationship breakdown when parents led separate lives. It had most often been Xan, as the eldest, who had been required to deal with his siblings when any of them had gone off the rails as adolescents. His father had been a useless parent, his priority always to move on selfishly to the next new woman in his life, leaving the children of his past relationships to sink or swim alongside their resentful, embittered mothers.

Xan knew he could walk away and be a parent from a safe distance, leaving Elvi to deal with the burden of childcare. But if he did that, he would be no better than the father he had despised. In any case, he *wanted* his child to have everything he and his siblings had been denied: stability and security and parents who watched over them. If he didn't want a parade of stepfathers or stepmothers disrupting his child's life he had to be tough and accept that he had only one sensible option open to him, he reasoned tautly. And unpalatable as the prospect of marriage might appear, there was, nevertheless, nothing more attractive to Xan in that moment of hard realism than the concept of having the right of unrestricted access to Elvi. For that benefit, he acknowledged, he was willing to make considerable sacrifices.

'We should get married,' Xan breathed harshly, shaken by the inescapable conviction that marriage offered a security for his child that he could not achieve by any other means.

'Don't be silly,' Elvi mumbled straight away, thinking he was trying to lighten the atmosphere with an ill-judged joke.

Xan settled hard dark golden eyes on her. 'Marriage is still the best framework in which to raise a child.'

'But you don't *want* to marry me!' Elvi countered impatiently. 'So why talk about it?'

'Let's not get into personal feelings,' Xan advised very drily, noticing her bra through the filmy top, his body tensing like a schoolboy's in response and decimating his pride. He swung away from that alluring view before continuing, 'More importantly, we now have a child's future to consider and we must do the best we can to ensure that our child enjoys the best possible start in life.'

Disconcerted by that unexpectedly serious assessment, Elvi glanced away from him uncomfortably. 'People don't get married just because they're parents these days. I'm amazed to hear you talking like this.'

'Elvi…' Xan exhaled in an impatient hiss. 'I'm talking like this because I *know* what I'm talking about! Children thrive only when they feel secure. In all the years I was growing up I never felt secure because there was nothing stable about my home life. It was constant upheaval and change and I had no control over it. A new wife or lover would move in, turn the house on Thira upside down with different rules and then it would happen again…and *again*,' he told her in a roughened undertone, loathing the need to speak about such personal experiences.

'What you're really telling me is that even your father's many marriages didn't give you or your brothers and sisters security,' Elvi pointed out ruefully. 'So, how could us marrying possibly be the answer?'

Xan threw his arrogant dark head high, his jawline clenching. 'Unlike my father, I'm willing to make the effort for it to work.'

'But you said to leave personal feelings out of this and that doesn't work either because a marriage is based on two people living together,' Elvi argued. 'And I *couldn't* live with you.'

Xan stiffened in astonishment at that claim, a winged ebony brow climbing. 'What do you mean? You *couldn't* live with me? Why not?'

The look of outrage in his stunning golden gaze failed to intimidate Elvi, who believed that any talk of Xan marrying her was total nonsense. 'Xan, have you forgotten how you behaved at your sister's wedding?' she asked tightly. 'You got bored with me within forty-eight hours and wasted no time in switching your interest to Angie. You're volatile—'

Xan gritted his even white teeth, incensed by the condemnation. He had had good reason to behave as he had but he was not prepared to share those reasons with her. 'I am *not* volatile,' he breathed, anger lacing his dark deep drawl with warning.

Elvi was tempted to tell him that possibly he bore more of a resemblance to his womanising father than he liked to think, but she resisted the urge because infuriating Xan would only create more problems. He couldn't really be serious about his suggestion that she marry him, she reasoned in bewilderment.

'You're just not the faithful type,' she said, unable to prevent that belief from leaping straight off her tongue. 'And I couldn't cope with that.'

Dark colour laced Xan's killer cheekbones. He was in a rage and battling to contain it. Women had been angling for a marriage proposal from him since he'd made his first billion. He knew that the lifestyle he could offer was his biggest attraction. He had always assumed that when he finally proposed he would be trodden on by his choice of bride in her haste to get him to the altar before he could change his mind. He had never once envisaged rejection. After all, Angie had been a different case, ditching him at a time when he appeared to be a poor financial bet. That Elvi could summarily dismiss him in the husband stakes as volatile and likely to be unfaithful incensed him.

'It may surprise you to know that I have *never* been unfaithful to a sexual partner,' Xan grated. 'My lovers don't overlap. I like clarity and candour in my personal life.'

Elvi coloured uncomfortably, wondering whether she could believe him. To be fair, he had been blunt with her from the outset about the limits of their arrangement. He had not told her any lies or broken any promises. But even so, his behaviour with his first love at his sister's wedding had *hurt* Elvi and continued to nag at her like a sore tooth. Perhaps she was too rigid in her outlook, not having had any former loves in her own past, she conceded ruefully.

Evidently, Xan had not seen Angie Sarantos since their breakup and naturally he had been curious. Furthermore, his familiarity with the other woman had only underlined the fact that they must once have been very close. Equally, there had been no sin in his enjoying Angie's company. There had been no stolen kisses, indeed nothing that Elvi could label an actual betrayal of trust. True, Angie had cherished a strong desire to win Xan back but Elvi could hardly blame him for the brunette's aspirations.

Elvi released her breath on a slow hiss. 'I was judging you and I shouldn't have been,' she admitted stiffly. 'The trouble is I still don't know you well enough to know if I can trust you.'

'You can surely trust that I want to do the best I can for our child,' Xan argued in a driven undertone. '*Thee mou*, Elvi…asking you to marry me was a major act of trust for me! And how else can we share our child? We *need* that framework… I'm not very good at sharing but if you're my wife, I will adapt.'

I'm not very good at sharing. That careless admission sliced through Elvi's thoughts like a blade and released a sudden flood of apprehension. Xan's father, Helios, had not wanted to share his child either. Although he had ditched his first wife, he had insisted on retaining custody of their son. How could she have forgotten that she was dealing with a man raised almost exclusively by his father?

And what if she too became superfluous to Xan's requirements? What if the way she chose to raise their child failed to meet his expectations? What if he decided that he wasn't seeing enough of his child? How many rights would she have as an unmarried mother on a low income? And how the heck would she ever contrive to fight such a very wealthy and powerful man?

Sheer panic at the threat of such future developments stirred nausea in Elvi's tummy and turned her entire skin surface clammy. Wives had more legal rights than single mothers, didn't they? Surely a wife could not be brushed aside in the same way? Out of pride and hurt, Ariadne had simply chosen not to fight her ex-husband for custody of her son, but Elvi knew that she would have fought to the death before surrendering her own flesh and blood. If such a battle ever became necessary, she decided that she *would* be safer and stronger as Xan's wife.

Xan scanned Elvi's troubled blue eyes and the hands she was unconsciously twisting together on her lap. Guilt sliced through him. In using Angie as an excuse to extract himself from his affair with Elvi, he had done much more damage than he had ever intended. The consequences were only hitting him now. Elvi was wary, distrustful and reluctant to even *reach* for the security of a wedding ring. Angie would've grabbed the ring and laughed all the way to the divorce court and a fat financial settlement. But then, he conceded wryly, Angie and Elvi had barely a thought in common. He had only appreciated that contrast when Angie had sworn viciously at him when he'd told her that he wasn't interested in reliving their past after his sister's wedding. Angie had been enraged, not hurt. She was hard as nails, bitter over the choices she had made and as much a stranger to the softer, more feminine emotions as a rock.

With difficulty, Elvi dragged herself out of the freezing grip of extreme apprehension and drew in a slow, steadying breath before looking across at Xan. There was a brooding, distant look already etched on his lean, breathtakingly handsome features and she imagined manipulative wheels were already turning at speed in that dynamic brain of his because Xan was programmed to fight and win. If Plan A failed to deliver, he would waste no time in moving on to Plan B and heaven only knew what Plan B might entail.

'If you honestly believe that marriage would be the best option for our child,' she muttered shakily before she could lose her nerve, 'I agree.'

Xan studied her in astonishment because she had performed a one-hundred-and-eighty-degree turnaround in the space of minutes. 'You'll marry me?' he pressed with a frown.

'If that's what you want,' Elvi stated more firmly.

What had changed her mind? Xan scanned her with questioning dark golden eyes and then tossed pointless curiosity on the back burner. She would marry him and he would have both her and his child. For the moment that was enough, he told himself stubbornly. Did it really matter that she would want much more from him than any other woman ever had? Elvi would want him to change and cuddling would be the least of it. Ultimately, Elvi would want love and that worried him because he really didn't think he could give her love. He could be loyal and faithful but the thought of loving anyone, when everyone he had ever loved in life had either let him down or abandoned him, sent menacing cold chills running through Xan.

'The first thing we will do is visit a doctor to have your pregnancy confirmed,' Xan decreed. 'You'll come home with me to the penthouse tonight—'

'No. I'll stay with my family until we get married,' Elvi interrupted tightly, shying away from the thought of returning to that intimate setting with him. 'And if I agree to see a doctor, it has to be alone.'

'Let's not quibble about the details, *moli mou*,' Xan urged softly, his spectacular golden eyes gleaming like priceless ingots as he appraised her, already trying to picture her swollen with his child. The image shocked him by turning him on hard and fast, something primal in him reacting to that concept with spontaneous vigour.

'I guess not,' Elvi muttered uncertainly, meeting the blaze of his scrutiny and stilling like a mouse suddenly scenting a predator stalking her. Colour banished her pallor, heat curling between her thighs in a wanton surge that embarrassed her. 'But there's something I should explain to you *before* you meet my family.'

Xan hadn't even thought of meeting Elvi's family. He had merely vaguely assumed that they would attend the wedding. Her mother, his former maid, he thought now with a faint shudder, and a thief into the bargain.

'It's time you knew the truth about the theft,' Elvi told him with determination.

CHAPTER NINE

XAN LISTENED IN stunned silence while Elvi told him the story about her kid brother's accidental removal of the brush pot from his penthouse apartment. Anger sparked, flared and climbed to an extraordinary height inside him.

'So, let me get this straight,' Xan urged with lethal derision. 'I was cast as the baddie in this scenario right from the start. You couldn't trust me with the truth, your mother couldn't and even my own head of security, who clearly worked out the truth from the beginning, couldn't trust me to do the right thing!'

'It wasn't like that, Xan—'

'It was *exactly* like that,' Xan retorted crushingly, his volatile temper flaring like a comet over the lowering awareness that everybody but him had known what was going on. 'You *all* presupposed that I would visit my wrath on your little brother and would refuse to believe his version of what happened.'

'We didn't want to take the risk that you would react the wrong way,' Elvi admitted heavily.

'*Diavole*...well, I'm reacting very much in the wrong

way now!' Xan slung at her in a raw undertone. 'You all conspired to keep the truth from me.'

'No, that's untrue!' Elvi argued, leaping upright. 'My mother worked it out when the police found the brush pot in our home and she immediately owned up to protect Daniel. There was no discussion, no conspiracy and Dmitri simply *guessed* what had happened because he was there that day. I *had* to tell you before the wedding, Xan. I'm sorry you're annoyed but I couldn't let you go on believing that my mother is a thief.'

Still furious, Xan released his breath in a measured hiss even as he reflected that that word, 'annoyed', barely covered his reaction. Even as he controlled his scorching anger, however, he was understanding another, even less palatable side to what he had belatedly learned: he had taken his rage over the theft out on a complete innocent. Although no actual crime had been committed, he had intimidated Elvi into becoming his mistress. There was no escaping that harsh fact. His unjust treatment of her bit deeper than ever. His conscience would never be clear on that score because, not only had he railroaded a virgin into his bed, he had also been careless enough of her well-being to get her pregnant.

Xan's long brown fingers curled into potent fists of frustration. It was another dark day for him, he acknowledged bitterly. Was there to be no end to the constant revelations of his sins, his oversights, his *mistakes*? Had some greater force thrown Elvi into his path simply to trip him up and teach him that he was as fallible as every other human being? Cocooned by wealth and arrogance, he had believed he was untouchable and far too clever to be seduced by temptation. But one fatal moment of weakness had overwhelmed him with the kind of messy consequences he had successfully avoided all his life.

Elvi was that weakness and his inability to resist Elvi had directly led to the conception of his first child and would soon be followed by a shotgun marriage. Without warning, Xan was viewing life through a changed lens and feelings he had suppressed for years were surging to the fore and destabilising him. He didn't do self-doubt and castigation but Elvi's arrival had changed everything, transforming him into a man he barely recognised.

'You have my promise that in the future I will treat your family with every respect,' he ground out flatly.

'I appreciate that,' Elvi admitted quietly.

Xan gazed at her, hunger rising spontaneously from the ashes of his anger. He didn't understand how she could *do* that to him, make him flip from rage to a sexual craving so deep and strong it made him ache. He wanted to take her home with him and possess her over and over again until that ferocious, uncontrollable need was finally sated. And all that desire meant was that once again he was selfishly in the wrong because the unwitting object of his desire was pregnant and fragile.

Elvi met Xan's dark brooding gaze and butterflies leapt and danced in her tummy, emotions and responses she struggled to contain assailing her, making her feel hot and foolish and giddy. 'If it's any consolation, I'm sorry I didn't feel able to tell you the truth sooner.'

Possibly Xan didn't appreciate how daunting his reputation was or how frightening the amount of power he wielded could be, Elvi reflected ruefully. But the clenched set of his hard, dark face disturbed her, making her appreciate that Xan's emotions ran deep, much deeper than she had ever suspected. It was not that she had ever believed him to be shallow, but she had mistakenly assumed that his self-discipline kept his emotions fully in check. She could see, however, that he was still angry and upset, papering over the cracks to put her at ease, but still upset by her clear belief that he could not have been trusted to treat her little brother with understanding and compassion. And try as she might, that suspicion only made her want to hold him close and hug him, a response which would've been no more welcome to him, she conceded unhappily.

'You are sure that you want to go through with this?' Sally Cartwright prompted worriedly, her attention locked to her daughter's pale profile as she sat staring out of the window of the limousine. 'You *can* change your mind at the very last moment. I won't be upset.'

'I'm not having second thoughts. I'm just nervous.' Elvi forced a smile and tugged at the sleeves of her dress with restive fingers. It was a dream creation. Intricate embroidered lace sheathed her arms and ornamented the bodice, the classic shape moulding her figure while the slim skirt lent her an elegant tailored look.

'I've said it before and I'll say it again. Falling pregnant isn't a good enough reason to get married,' her mother continued. 'We would manage—'

'Xan wants this baby too,' Elvi reminded the older woman.

'He's a very reserved man, the exact opposite of the kind of man I always thought you would choose,' Sally admitted bluntly.

'Somehow we work,' Elvi parried uncomfortably, wishing her mother noticed a little less, knowing her subdued mood had encouraged Sally's last-ditch attempt to get her daughter to reconsider her plans.

In the two weeks since she had agreed to marry Xan, she had been very busy. Xan had come down to Oxford to meet her mother and her brother. He had been smoothly polite and pleasant but Elvi had recognised his discomfiture even if nobody else had. Everyone in her family had assumed the worst of him and he knew it.

He had hired a wedding planner to take charge of their big day. He had arranged for her to visit a designer salon, where she had fallen in love with her dress and where the staff had taken great care to ensure it was a perfect fit. He would've preferred her to move into the penthouse with him, but he had accepted her decision to stay with her family without argument. He had even accompanied her to the doctor to have her pregnancy confirmed and, since he had taken that time out of his day for her benefit, she had allowed him to join her for the consultation. In fact, in every way possible Xan had been supportive, reasonable and considerate of her needs. So why were her spirits low on her wedding day?

Possibly being forced to consider her future had also forced her to be more honest with herself. Once she had recognised Xan's emotional depth and his sheer determination to do what he believed to be right, she had finally acknowledged that she had fallen in love with him. He worked very hard at hiding his true nature behind a cold, indifferent façade and she wondered why he was that way, why he had felt the need to suggest that he had enjoyed an idyllic childhood when clearly, from the number of marriages his father had had, it must have been anything but idyllic. But Xan had only allowed her the glimpse of that harsh truth when he discussed what he wanted for his own child and admitted that he had never felt secure when he was a boy.

And ironically the reason she loved Xan was also why she was unhappy. In marrying her because she was pregnant, he was doing what he believed he *had* to do for their child's benefit. He didn't love her, wouldn't miss her if she was gone, wasn't marrying her for the *right* reasons, so how could she celebrate her wedding day? Even worse, he had not laid a finger on her since she had left the island, had stolen not so much as a single kiss, which scarcely suggested that she was the most sexually desirable of brides.

They arrived at the London church and she walked down the aisle on her brother's arm, wondering if her friend, Joel, was in the church. Joel had been acting oddly with her from the day he received the wedding invitation, phoning her up to demand to know when she had met Xan and why she hadn't mentioned that she was seeing someone. His apparent annoyance had been unfair when he had been up in Scotland and out of contact for weeks while he worked on a portrait commission. Elvi supposed that Joel's reaction was proof that some people really didn't like surprises.

Meeting Xan's mother, Ariadne's beaming smile as she reached the end of the aisle, Elvi went pink. Xan's family had greeted her with open arms and she was very grateful for that, even if she recognised that their hostility would not have made a dime of difference to Xan, who ruthlessly walked his own path. She finally let her attention focus on the tall Greek man awaiting her at the altar, the fine dark grey suit outlining his broad shoulders and lean, powerful physique, a ripple of compelling awareness shimmying through her before she even connected with his dazzling amber-gold eyes and the lush black lashes that so effectively framed them. Her tummy shifted and her heartbeat quickened as her mouth ran dry, liquid heat snaking wantonly up through her pelvis.

She wanted Xan, wanted him as she had never known she could want any man and it still unnerved her, that needy wanting, that treacherous hunger that transcended all barriers and had nothing to do with her brain. Her colour heightened, her legs weak, she swayed a little and he rested a steadying hand against the shallow indentation of her spine, the heat of his light hold leaving her insanely aware of his masculinity. Not cool, so not cool, she castigated her disobedient body as the ceremony began.

Xan threaded a slender platinum ring onto her finger, his touch sure, his responses firmer and clearer than her own, no hint of nervous tension in *his* demeanour. He was her husband now, she registered in awe, turning away from the altar with her hand resting on his arm. It was done now: they were married. *Because* she had conceived, not for any other reason, she reminded herself wretchedly, feeling like a ball and chain foisted on him, telling herself off for that fanciful thought. After all, they were both equally responsible for the contraceptive oversight that had led to conception.

All Xan's family had made a special effort to attend their wedding, even Delphina and Takis, who had cut short their honeymoon to spend a few days in London. On the steps, Elvi smiled and smiled until her face hurt with the effort of putting on a good show. Joel had come to the wedding, she noted with relief, seeing her best friend in the crowd, his mobile face unusually stiff and expressionless. Disapproving? Like her own family, he probably assumed she was rushing into marriage too quickly but then she hadn't told Joel that she was pregnant. Just then she wondered if Xan's family were aware of her condition and she asked Xan once they were in the limo travelling to the hotel for the reception.

His lean, darkly handsome features tensed. 'I saw no reason to mention it. The baby's our business.'

Relieved, Elvi nodded agreement, wondering if his family would have been as welcoming had they known the truth or whether she would have been downgraded to the level of a calculating hussy, who had entrapped Xan. Whatever, it scarcely mattered, she conceded ruefully, because they would realise that she was pregnant soon enough.

After the meal was served they circulated. She saw her mother chatting to Dmitri and noted Xan staring.

'What's going on there?' he asked drily.

'Nothing as yet, but give them time,' Elvi said lightly. 'I shouldn't imagine Dmitri went to the trouble of offering my mother his house and setting her up with a job for no good reason.'

'You don't mind?' Xan queried.

'Mum's been on her own a long time. Does it bother you?'

Xan ignored the question, deep within his own thoughts. He blamed Dmitri for not sharing his doubts with him concerning Sally Cartwright's guilt. Had he known there were grounds for doubt, would he still have offered Elvi that iniquitous arrangement? He knew he was splitting hairs and was grimly amused by the fact. After all, no honourable man would have offered Elvi the option Xan had.

Joel signalled her from across the room and she left Xan's side with a warm welcoming smile. 'Thought you weren't sure you could come,' she greeted her old friend. 'I'm so glad you could make it after all.'

Joel dealt her a comprehensive appraisal, taking in the diamonds glittering in her ears and outlining her slender throat. 'You look amazing,' he told her thinly, curving an arm to her spine to guide her out to the bar, which was quieter. 'I'm glad sour grapes didn't keep me away—'

'Sour grapes?' she queried, not getting his meaning as he drew her into a secluded corner.

Joel sighed. 'You never did work it out, did you? You didn't notice what was right in front of you. I wanted you to turn to me when you were ready for a relationship but obviously I missed the boat—'

Elvi turned pale in shock and frowned at him in dismay. 'You don't mean that—'

Joel studied her in frustration. 'I always wanted you, even when we were at school…that's how far back it goes for me,' he admitted ruefully. 'When you didn't pick up on my signals, I told myself that it was because you were still immature and too wrapped up in your family but I've *always* loved you—'

Her tender heart was pierced by the vulnerable look in his eyes. 'I'm so sorry, Joel. I didn't realise—'

'You don't come to a wedding to tell the bride *that*,' Xan intoned harshly from behind Elvi and she spun round in consternation, disconcerted by his arrival.

'There's no harm in telling her,' Joel argued defiantly. 'After all, when you mess up, I want her to know I'm here *waiting* for her—'

Elvi froze in disbelief as Xan pressed her back out of the way with one arm and punched Joel with the other. Stunned by Xan's behaviour, she staggered back as Dmitri appeared out of nowhere to band his arms round Joel and restrain him when he tried to throw himself at Xan. There was a tough exchange of words between the men, but when Elvi went to Joel's side to apologise for the bridegroom's behaviour and check that her friend was all right, he told her angrily to leave him alone and he stalked out.

'What on earth did you think you were doing?' Elvi demanded of Xan.

Xan didn't have an answer for Elvi. Thumping the pretty boy with the dimples and curls had been instinctive and if his security team hadn't prevented further violence Xan would have enjoyed hitting him again. *And* again. How *dared* the little twerp? Who the hell was he anyway? Who had invited him? What sort of relationship did he have with Elvi? Xan wanted answers too.

'Who is he?' Xan bit out in a raw undertone.

'Joel is my best friend…and you *hit* him!' she condemned.

'Your best friend is a *man*?' Xan countered in disbelief. 'Well, that ends now. I'm not putting up with that kind of nonsense. You're my wife…you're *mine*. You don't let other men come onto you like that!'

Elvi was fit to be tied but she was conscious that people were watching them and she chose discretion, walking away and heading fast for the cloakroom.

Xan was tempted to yank her back because he was determined to hear the entire history of her involvement with Joel with no detail overlooked. Her best friend? How was he supposed to react to a crazy announcement like that? The sneaky little bastard had been telling Elvi that he loved her, trying to tempt her away when any decent man would have accepted the reality that she was newly married. Pregnant into the bargain, Xan recalled with sudden immense satisfaction.

CHAPTER TEN

ELVI BOARDED XAN'S private jet with a sense of liberation because the strain of the day and the pressure of being the centre of attention as bride and groom were now safely behind them. Being forced to act as though nothing was wrong between her and Xan after that incident with Joel had stressed her out. His aggressive reaction to Joel's declaration had shaken her and she knew she had to confront him. Violence would never ever be acceptable to Elvi.

'You still haven't told me where we're going,' she reminded Xan gently once they were airborne.

'The South of France. I have a house there that I rarely use. I did think of taking you back to the island, but my family wouldn't have given us much peace on Thira,' he told her wryly.

'I like your family,' Elvi protested.

'We need alone time,' Xan countered smoothly. 'That's your cue to start telling me about Joel...'

Elvi tensed and stirred her coffee. 'There's not much to say. We've been friends since primary school. He was so into art even then that he didn't fit in with the boys but I got on great with him. He's now making quite a name for himself as a portrait painter.'

'If you're that close, you should've told me about him,' Xan informed her disapprovingly.

'You should've told me about Angie,' Elvi countered without hesitation. 'She's much more relevant to this conversation than any we could have about Joel. Joel and I have only ever been friends. He's the big brother I never had.'

'Only it's obvious that he cherishes *far* from brotherly feelings for you,' Xan derided, his lean, strong face revealing not an ounce of discomfiture at her reference to his former girlfriend.

'He said he does but I still find that hard to believe,' Elvi confided, shaking her head in amazement. 'I have to admit that I didn't notice anything different in the way he treated me—'

Xan's wide sensual mouth quirked at that admission. 'You're not vain and you wouldn't have been looking for it. I saw how shocked you were. If I hadn't I would have been wondering if you had been involved in some relationship with him behind my back.'

Elvi's temper stirred at that insinuation and she lifted her chin and gave him a defiant look, her cheeks reddening. 'Surely you could hardly have wondered that when you became my first lover?' she dared. 'Please don't try to use *that* as an excuse for the violence you employed.'

'I'm not looking for an excuse. I'm not sorry I hit him,' Xan asserted immediately, springing upright to tower over her, the fine fabric of his tailored suit pulling against his strong muscular thighs and wide taut shoulders, distracting her when she least wanted to be distracted.

'There was absolutely no need or excuse for violence,' Elvi declared.

His lean bronzed features were taut and hard as he helped himself to a drink at the integral bar. 'He crossed a line,' he spelt out coldly. 'You're my wife. It was our wedding day. No man would listen in silence when another man threw a challenge of that nature at him.'

'Joel did *not* challenge you!' Elvi proclaimed in heated disagreement.

An ebony brow skated up. 'It *wasn't* a challenge when Joel said he would be waiting to catch you *when* I messed up?'

Elvi stiffened and flushed. 'That was just one of those silly things a man says when he's trying to save face. You should've ignored it—'

'Consider me punching Joel as one of those silly things a man does when he's angry,' Xan advised lethally. 'Your compassion for him is misplaced—'

'No, it's not!' Elvi protested. 'I felt horribly guilty when he said he loved me because I felt that I should've noticed something. I wished I'd told him about you, for a start, but I didn't tell him about you because of the way our relationship started...*the arrangement*...we agreed.'

A faint line of colour scored Xan's killer cheekbones, the distaste with which she whispered those two explanatory words hitting him hard. 'Even when I wish I could, I *can't* change the past, Elvi,' he breathed in a driven undertone.

'No, but you can ensure you don't plough in and punch one of my friends again over something you overheard in a private conversation. Joel went too far but you went in fists flying and there was no need for it,' she told him stiffly.

'There was every need. Now he knows his boundaries but, since the violence upset you so much, I can assure you that it won't happen again,' Xan conceded grimly.

Only a little soothed, Elvi threw her head high. 'And you said I was *yours*,' she reminded him doggedly. 'I'm not. Putting a ring on my finger doesn't transform me into property.'

'You are mine,' Xan delivered in contradiction. 'Mine in a way no other woman has ever been.'

'Angie?' Elvi queried helplessly.

Xan compressed his lips. 'I didn't marry Angie or conceive a child with her.'

'But you didn't *intend* to do either of those things with me,' Elvi pointed out flatly.

Xan merely shrugged a dismissive big shoulder. 'Angie was my first love. We met at university. I fell hard for her,' he admitted harshly, his lean, strong face grim. 'I knew she was a material girl but it still didn't occur to me that if my prospects appeared to go downhill, she would choose money over me. There were rumours even before my father's death that his company was in trouble. Angie left me the same day the accountant confirmed that the family fortune was gone. She already had another man in her sights and within months she had married him and moved abroad.'

'You had a lucky escape,' Elvi told him staunchly. 'In the light of her behaviour why on earth did you make such a fuss of her at your sister's wedding?'

His spectacular bone structure pulled taut, amber-gold eyes shielded by his black lashes. 'I *had* to let you go. I was very much in the wrong dragging you into my bed in the first place and the only possible recompense I could make, after I discovered the extent of your innocence, was to let you return to your life,' he framed grittily. 'I *should* have let you go free that first day but I still wanted you too much. On Thira, wanting you, *needing* you to that extent freaked me out. Flirting with Angie gave me an escape route and forced me to set you free and I didn't have to tell you any lies—'

Elvi was stunned, listening in shaken silence to that unexpected confession because she had not appreciated how deep Xan's guilt over making her his mistress went. 'You make everything so complicated. You were behaving like one of those men who deliberately treats a woman badly to ensure that she breaks things off and saves him the trouble of doing it,' she mumbled in bemusement.

To be fair to her, her brain was working on more than one thought train. She was still thinking about Xan's surprising admission that needing her to such an extent had seriously worried him, which suggested to her that Xan had been feeling something more than lust for her, something strong enough to ignite his fear of a deeper commitment.

'But I've got you now,' Xan pointed out with unashamed satisfaction as he closed a powerful hand over hers and tugged her up out of her seat. 'I won't be treating you badly because I definitely don't want you to leave me—'

'You're sure of that?' Elvi checked. 'No more Angies or major affairs lurking in your past?'

'Not one. She burned me too badly. I protected myself after that,' Xan confessed huskily, his attention locking to Elvi's ripe pink mouth with smouldering intensity. That fast, he was aroused and aching for her.

He leant down to taste her in an exploratory foray that was supposed to be teasing, but which swiftly turned into a breathtakingly sensual assault. He plucked at the inviting fullness of her lower lip, traced the sealed line of her mouth with the teasing tip of his tongue and then plunged deep between her lips with the kind of hunger that made her tremble in his arms. A nagging hollow sensation deep down inside forced her to clamp her thighs tightly together.

'Were you jealous of Joel?' Elvi asked hopefully.

Xan drew back from her frowning. 'Of course not. I've never been the jealous type and since you won't be *seeing* him again—'

It was Elvi's turn to freeze. 'I beg your pardon?' she interrupted.

Xan shrugged. 'You can't see him again until he's got over you. If you keep on seeing him, you'll be encouraging him to continue wanting what he can't have. That would be cruel—'

'I can see him if I want to.'

'Not if I have anything to do with it,' Xan sliced in squarely. 'And why would you *want* to see him? He doesn't want to be your friend, he wants to be your lover.'

Elvi reddened uncomfortably, unable to escape the maddening reality that Xan was making valid points.

'He'll get over it eventually,' Xan forecast carelessly. 'If he had *really* loved you, he would have taken the risk and told you how he felt about you. But if you want my opinion—'

'I don't,' Elvi told him cuttingly.

'He knew if he told you how he felt about you he'd be plunging himself into a serious relationship and he wasn't ready for that. He kept you on ice for the future, encouraged by the fact that you weren't putting yourself out there for other men. He missed his chance.'

'You walked away from me too,' Elvi reminded him tightly.

'No, I *made* you walk away from me and it cost me. I've gone through a month of hell without you,' Xan murmured hoarsely, startling her with that grated confession. 'I haven't even looked at another woman since the day you came into my office—'

Elvi shook free of her disconcertion and treated him to an unimpressed appraisal. *'Angie?'*

'I was faking it,' Xan said drily.

Elvi settled down into her seat. 'You fake it well,' she responded, stamping on the nugget of hurt that even thinking about that day recreated.

'I wanted you to believe I'd moved on.'

Purely because he had a guilty conscience about her? Or had he had other more personal reasons? Elvi speculated, not quite convinced that conscience could have driven Xan into creating a false picture when the more obvious solution would've been to let her go immediately. Had a desire for more sex been his sole motivator? There was so much she wanted to ask but Xan had that distant look back in his eyes again, suggesting that he had already given up enough in explanations for one day.

An SUV whisked them from the airport to the villa in the South of France. It was rural, which surprised her, a picturesque stone property surrounded by rolling lavender fields. A housekeeper greeted them. Xan went off for a shower while Elvi wandered round the cool interior, impressed by the clever mix of contemporary and antique that came together to create a relaxed atmosphere.

'Why did you buy this place if you hardly ever use it?' she asked him as he was getting dressed in lightweight chinos and a cotton shirt.

'I thought it would do me good to take holidays, but every time I came here I ended up working, so eventually I stopped coming,' he admitted wryly.

'I won't let you work while I'm here,' Elvi told him playfully.

Xan rested vibrant amber-gold eyes on her animated face. 'I don't want to work when you're around. You're bad for me.'

Elvi smiled at that very serious admission and, drawn by the glow of that encouraging teasing smile, he stalked across the room and grabbed her up into his arms, settling down again on the side of the bed with her cradled across his hard, muscular thighs.

'Sorry, I shouldn't have grabbed you like that, not when you're pregnant,' Xan breathed tautly. 'I need to be more careful—'

'The doctor told you I was perfectly healthy and strong,' Elvi reminded him.

Very deliberately, Xan splayed long brown fingers across her lower stomach. 'As far as I'm concerned, you're glass and breakable now,' he contradicted, smoothing her flesh gently. 'That's our child in there and we won't be taking any unnecessary risks.'

Warmth stole into Elvi, his concern banishing her fears. 'You really want this baby,' she murmured.

'As much as I want you, *moli mou*.' Xan lifted her up again and set her down on her feet with careful hands. 'Even if it was an unexpected development, it feels right now. Let's go downstairs and get dinner.'

Elvi gazed up into brilliant amber eyes and her heart skipped a beat. His fingers engulfed hers as he tugged her towards the stairs. He wanted their baby and he wanted her. It was sufficient to power a healthy start for any marriage, she told herself soothingly. Shame pierced her when she recalled *why* she had agreed to marry him, because she suspected she had fretted herself into an unreasonable state of paranoia when she worried that Xan might try to take her child from her.

Dinner was served out on the candlelit terrace. It was a light meal because neither of them was especially hungry. Over coffee, Xan studied her with hooded dark eyes, his lean bronzed face sombre. 'Why did you suddenly change your mind and decide to marry me?' he asked, sharply disconcerting her. 'I mean, you were saying no and so set against the idea and me and then, all of a sudden, you—'

It was now or never, Elvi registered, and, although she quailed at the prospect of telling him the unlovely truth, she also felt that she had to be honest. 'I was in a panic that day. I'd just found out I was pregnant,' she reminded him carefully in her own defence. 'I was very conscious that your father took you from your mother and I was scared that if we didn't get married, you might try to take our child from me at some time in the future.'

Xan frowned, staring at her in patent disbelief.

'I told myself that wives have more rights than unmarried mums and that your mother may not have fought for you but I would fight to hold on to any child of mine. I thought I'd be safer as a wife from that threat.' Her voice ran out of steam, her apprehension rising at the look of angry disbelief growing on his lean dark features.

'You can't be serious...' Xan intoned in a driven undertone.

'I'm not thinking that way any longer,' Elvi admitted ruefully. 'But unfortunately that *is* how I was thinking that day when I agreed—'

'I can't believe this,' Xan grated with a shake of his handsome dark head as he rose upright to stare across the table at her. 'I can't believe you actually thought that I would *do* that to you and my child after what I went through myself as a boy.'

'Yes, you did say you never felt secure—'

'It was a lot worse than that!' Xan objected, swinging away from her, suddenly short of breath and desperate to be alone. 'I'm going out for a drive—'

Elvi leapt out of her seat. 'Not without me, you're not!' she exclaimed.

'I'm not in the mood for company right now, Elvi,' Xan admitted harshly as he belatedly recognised that the mess of emotions he was experiencing all boiled down to that awful, ego-zapping word *hurt*, and the shock of that recognition hit him even harder.

What had he thought? That somewhere deep down inside Elvi had come to care for him? *Care* for the male who had virtually blackmailed her into his bed, into her first experience of sex and landed her into unplanned motherhood at the same time? Naturally, caring had had nothing to do with her decision to marry him. Knowing nothing good of him, she had decided to protect herself in advance from any further wrong he might choose to inflict on her. How could he blame her for that?

Elvi planted herself in his path to the front door. 'No, Xan, you shouldn't be driving anywhere when you're upset—'

Stormy amber-gold eyes locked to her. 'I'm *not* upset! Now move away from the door.'

'No.' Elvi stood her ground and when he tried to lift her to shift her to one side she swarmed up his lean, powerful body like a monkey climbing a tree and clung, her arms wrapping round his neck. 'Please talk to me, *please* don't walk away...don't hide things—'

His strong jawline setting hard like granite, Xan wrapped his arms round her to secure her and he carried her upstairs, where he lowered her down onto the bed. Or at least he *tried* to lower her, but Elvi was clinging like a limpet and when he tried to loosen her grip, she dropped her head and kissed him instead.

'No, Elvi,' he began doggedly.

Elvi threw her weight against him to unbalance him and he backed down on the bed to ensure that he didn't lose his balance. 'You don't mean no,' she told him with all the conviction of a woman who had come into contact with the noticeable bulge in his trousers. 'I won't let you leave me when you're upset.'

Xan groaned out loud and momentarily closed his eyes, trying to deny everything he was feeling. Meanwhile, Elvi hugged him tight and peppered his face with soothing kisses.

'*Thee mou*…what are you trying to do to me?' Xan ground out, engulfed by warm clingy woman and finding it surprisingly pleasant.

'Make you talk. I've explained myself as best as I can. I *had* to be honest. I won't lie to you,' Elvi stated. 'I was all over the place emotionally the day you asked me to marry you. I was still getting over the pain of you flirting with Angie and I didn't feel I could trust you at all. I was scared, confused and then I thought about how your father had taken you away from your mother and it petrified me.'

'I would never *do* that to you,' Xan intoned grimly. 'I had a hellish childhood living with my father.'

'Yes, I gathered that, but only recently. Initially you made your childhood sound idyllic.'

Xan groaned again, lush black lashes lifting on sombre amber-gold eyes. 'I always lie about it for my mother's sake. I don't like to hurt her. I don't want to make her feel guilty for not fighting for me because she really didn't have much choice,' he said grimly. 'My father replaced her with another woman and then insisted on keeping me as well. My grandparents persuaded Mum to go back to university to finish her Masters in the USA. She needed to get away from the island and she needed a new future to focus on. I have never blamed her for cutting her losses and running. She was still only a girl—'

Still perched on top of his big powerful body, Elvi ran gentle fingertips across the tightness of his wide sensual mouth as she bent over him. 'So, Ariadne went to America—?'

'And wrote and sold her first archaeology textbook. It was a bestseller—'

'While you were doing what?' she queried.

'Getting used to my first stepmother, Hana and Lukas's mother. That broke up when I was six and Dad moved another woman in. She didn't last but she gave birth to Tobias before she left. Wife number three came next and so it went on throughout my childhood and adolescence. Helios couldn't be faithful for five minutes and on a couple of occasions, between women, he even drifted back to Mum, causing her great distress,' he confided bitterly. 'He was a liar and a cheat and he pretty much ruined her life. She focused on her career and I saw very little of her until I reached my teens.'

'That must've been very difficult for you and your mother.'

'I'm very fond of her. She has a huge heart. She coped with losing me by burying herself in her stud-

ies and travelling round the world to work on archaeo-
logical digs—'

'What was it like for you growing up in such an unsettled household?' Elvi pressed, helplessly curious.

'Imagine what it's like to come home from school
and discover your bedroom has been taken off you and
given to a new step-sibling instead,' Xan urged. 'Nothing was permanent, nothing was private, nothing in
the house on Thira truly belonged to me. I was at the
mercy of Dad's latest wife or lover. It made me a loner,
who didn't trust anyone. I always thought my father
married my mother too young and that's why he made
such a mess but now I think he was just an easily bored
womaniser.'

Elvi was drinking in every word, finally understanding how the boy had grown into a man with a colour-coded wardrobe and a powerful need for privacy.
Deprived of order, control and security as a child, Xan
had made order, control and security his first goals as
an adult.

'Being a womaniser entails messy, dramatic relationships so I went the mistress route instead,' Xan confided. 'I suppose it was sleazy—'

'It *was* sleazy,' Elvi told him.

Xan shrugged a shoulder. 'It worked for me until
you burst onto my horizon and then I blew it… I didn't
want you in the same apartment where I'd been with
other women. I didn't want to treat you the same way…'

As the silence dragged unbroken, Elvi stroked his
lips apart with a tender fingertip and bent down to kiss
him. 'If you talk, you get rewarded…and the more you

talk, the bigger the reward gets,' she whispered encouragingly.

Xan arched his hips up beneath her, letting her know that his erection had not subsided. 'Tell me more, *moli mou*—'

'No, you bring out a side of me I don't know,' Elvi mumbled, suddenly embarrassed by her forward behaviour.

'You do the same to me. Unnerving, isn't it?' Xan prompted. 'I want you more than I've ever wanted a woman in my life—'

'Angie?' Elvi challenged shamefacedly.

'Angie was never a challenge. You were… Will you quit bringing her up?' he demanded impatiently.

Elvi nodded seriously. 'OK.'

'I thought you and I were just about good sex until I tried to make myself give you up. I felt huge guilt about depriving you of your virginity, but I still couldn't bring myself to let you go or admit that what I had with you was different from anything I'd ever had with a woman,' Xan told her, reaching up to untie the narrow shoulder straps of her sundress and tug her bodice down inch by dangerous inch.

'Stop it…we're talking!' Elvi protested.

'Can't we play at the same time?' Xan questioned, giving the dress a rough yank to free her full breasts, and then groaning out loud as her bountiful pale curves filled his hands to overflowing. 'I mean…let's be honest…at this moment… I will tell you *anything* you want to know—'

Her breath caught in her throat as he rubbed her

swollen nipples between finger and thumb, sending a flash of heat shooting through her. 'Why were you trying to run away earlier?' she demanded shakily.

'I was…' Xan flung his tousled dark head back and breathed in deep and slow. 'When you told me you'd only married me because you were scared I might try to take our child away from you, I was…' Again he hesitated.

'You were…*what*?' Elvi prompted in frustration.

'Hurt… OK? I was *hurt*!' Xan finally got that word out and grimaced. 'Because by the time I got to our wedding today I knew I wanted and needed you round the clock and that somehow you had made me fall passionately in love with you, which explains why I continue to screw everything up. Passion and logic don't work well together and the way *you* make me feel often leaves me feeling like I'm clinging to sanity by my fingernails alone.'

Elvi gazed down at him in awed incredulity. 'You love me…*seriously*?'

'Serious as a heart attack.' Xan flipped over, carrying her with him, reversing their positions at the same time as he endeavoured to remove her dress. 'I think I started falling for you the minute I saw you, which is why I was so eaten up with guilt when I first took you to bed. Suddenly I was seeing every wrong thing I'd done and said to you in horrible Technicolor and I didn't know how to sort it out and start again.'

'You were hurt when you believed I'd married you just to safeguard my position.' Elvi smoothed gentle fingertips along his strong jaw while with her other hand she ran down the side zip on her dress to facilitate his manoeuvres. 'And I told myself I was agreeing for that reason, but I suspect that I was really giving myself a good reason to do what I secretly wanted to do because I love you. Do you deserve my love?' she asked for herself. 'No, you probably don't, but you can work at deserving it for the rest of our lives—'

Xan laughed out loud. 'I like it when you're blunt like that—'

'And, no, you don't get any time off for good behaviour,' she told him sternly. 'And after sex, you will always, *always* hold me close.'

'It's not just sex with you...it's much more than that,' Xan muttered awkwardly.

Elvi fluttered her eyelashes. 'Souls meeting?'

Xan laughed again, reaching down to kiss her at the same time as he unzipped his chinos. 'Our bodies are definitely going to meet,' he intoned against her reddened mouth with unconcealed hunger. 'On a collision course right now to that meeting—'

Being both a little frantic to make love again, they never did make it back downstairs for the dessert course and they lay talking lazily in bed until almost dawn. By that stage, they were involved in negotiations with Xan agreeing to take weekends and holidays off and Elvi agreeing not to drop clothes on the floor.

'I love you so much, *agape mou*,' Xan murmured, experiencing contentment for the first time ever, his beautiful eyes locked tenderly to Elvi's smiling, happy face. 'I'll buy you a dog once we've got used to being parents.'

Blissfully relaxed, Elvi let her arms tighten round his long, lean body, gentle fingers smoothing over his satin-smooth back. Xan liked to plan everything, cautiously moving from one checkpoint to the next. Yet without any preparation at all, he had plunged into their marriage and the promise of fatherhood with his whole heart, freely accepting those changes and loving her into the bargain.

'I love you too,' she whispered, happily convinced she had found a very special man.

Five years later, Elvi sat on the sand of the cove below the house on Thira and watched her daughter, Molly, patiently build a sandcastle with all the devotion to detail that Xan had already taught her. The little plastic flag had to go in exactly the right place, the moat had to fill with water, the shells that denoted windows had to sit in exact lines, and then disaster came along on two sturdy toddler legs. With a shout of delight, Molly's little brother, Ajax, flung himself at the castle, for he delighted as much in smashing things down as his sister delighted in building them.

But the split second before Ajax made contact and destroyed his sister's creation, a pair of arms stretched out and grabbed him back. 'No,' Xan told his son firmly.

Ajax wailed and screeched and struggled to escape his father's hold while Molly plonked herself defensively in front of the castle and told her brother off.

'When did you get back?' Elvi asked her husband, battling to be heard over Ajax's enraged yells.

'Ten minutes ago. The Athens meeting didn't last

as long as I expected,' Xan told her with a lazy smile, quite unbothered by his son's vociferous complaints.

'Oh, let him wreck it,' Molly groaned in exasperation as her brother's sobbing reached an ear-splitting peak. 'The sea will take it tonight anyway.'

'Are you sure?' Elvi asked her daughter.

'He's a baby,' her daughter pointed out pityingly, anchoring herself to her father's side. 'I'll make another one tomorrow.'

Xan lowered Ajax back to the sand. The toddler hovered, tears sprinkling his chubby cheeks, his platinum-pale curls blowing in the breeze. He stretched out a chubby fist to bat at a tower and then overbalanced and fell on top of the castle, getting sand on his face, which he hated.

'It's really not his day,' Elvi pronounced as she rescued the little boy and brushed him free of sand while he watched her with the huge amber-gold eyes he had inherited from his father.

Their children were an endearing mix of their parents. Molly had black hair and blue eyes and a love of order. Ajax was two and he loved to make a mess. He was usually much quieter than Molly, except when he got overtired.

'He's ready for bed,' Elvi pronounced, gathering up the clutter around her and stuffing it into bags while Xan hoisted his son onto his shoulder. Holding Molly's hand, Xan led the way up the steep steps back to the house.

They'd had two children in five years and life was busy. Elvi had had an easy pregnancy with Molly and terrible morning sickness while carrying Ajax. She reckoned that their family was now complete. Their dog, a terrier mix called Bones, romped along in their wake, his frantic energy keeping his wiry little body fit in spite of a calorie intake that would have powered an elephant.

Their nanny whisked the children away for supper and bedtime and, having spent the entire day with her son and daughter, Elvi was grateful to have time for Xan. Xan might have given up his seven-days-a-week schedule but he was still very much in demand, flying round the world to make speeches and give advice. In the early days of their marriage she had travelled with him, but Molly's birth had intervened and their home base was now a very comfortable town house in London, convenient for Xan's office in the City. They spent holidays on Thira, finding the more laid-back lifestyle there perfect for raising their young family. When they wanted alone time as a couple, they flew to the South of France and left the grandparents in charge of their household.

Ariadne was an adoring grandmother but not as regularly available as Dmitri and Sally, who had, after a lengthy and very discreet relationship, married the year before at around the same time as Dmitri had taken early retirement. They now owned a house on the island and were regular visitors, just as Xan's siblings were. Family parties were regular events on Thira, and Elvi had become accustomed to hosting everything from barbecues to christenings. She loved the fact that their children were growing up with their cousins and enjoyed a wide circle of relatives, unlike herself.

Daniel had graduated in medicine and was now entering hospital training where his working hours would be very much longer. Elvi was grateful that her brother was based at a London hospital where she hoped to see more of him.

'You do appreciate that I have been away from you for an entire week,' Xan murmured, cornering her on the landing to extract a very hungry kiss from her willingly parted lips.

Her heart singing, Elvi gave him a sparkling smile.

'I *did* have this fantasy where you were waiting on the front step to greet me,' Xan told her as he walked her down to their bedroom.

'Like a Victorian servant?' Elvi asked with intense amusement dancing in her eyes.

'And then I had to go find you on the beach and you're covered in sand and windblown and…absolutely *gorgeous*,' Xan emphasised huskily, backing her down on the bed. 'And now you're going to get sand all over the bed—'

'Of course, if you're that fastidious I could go and have a shower first,' Elvi proffered, knowing he wouldn't have the patience to wait even three minutes.

Xan was undressing where he stood and nothing got hung up or carefully draped. Indeed, his tie, shoes and socks went flying. Of course, she knew he would tidy it all up afterwards and complain about the unfortunate effect she had on him. Confident that she was entirely the centre of his attention, Elvi shimmied seductively out of her sundress, skimmed off the last garments with panache and knelt on the bed, veiled in the hair he wouldn't let her cut. And as he studied her, she studied him, her breath catching in her throat as the long, taut muscular lines of his beautiful body emerged.

The hunger never died, she thought dreamily, turning her face up for his kiss, rejoicing in the fact that the whole world stopped for her when Xan was with her. It was the kind of happiness she had never hoped to find and *he* had given it to her, *he* had made her feel secure and adored and more precious than the diamonds he was continually gifting her.

'I love you,' she said softly. 'You never know your luck—I might wait on the front step for you the next time—'

'No, I like this…just you and me, *hara mou*,' Xan insisted, gathering her into his arms with a deep sigh of satisfaction, because coming home to his family, slipping back into the warm and happy atmosphere Elvi created for them, was the greatest pleasure of his life. 'Loving each other and living happily ever after… I didn't think I'd ever have that, but you gave it to me.'

* * * * *

PRINCESS'S
NINE-MONTH
SECRET

KATE HEWITT

To Laurie,
thank you for being such a fantastic editor!
Warmest wishes, K.

CHAPTER ONE

IN THE END it was surprisingly easy to escape. Abdul, the royal bodyguard posted by the hotel suite's door, dozed off around ten o'clock, his head nodding onto his chest, and Halina Amari, Princess of Abkar, slipped by him on her tiptoes, holding her breath.

She'd never done anything like this before, never once tried to escape whatever narrow confines she'd been put in—although she'd certainly tested the boundaries and stretched her wings as much as she could, which was very little indeed. But tonight she wanted to fly.

This might be her last chance. The world was closing in, getting smaller and smaller thanks to her father—and Prince Zayed al bin Nur, her fiancé. The realisation of how close she'd come to being even more of a prisoner than she already was made her heart leap into her throat. And as for Olivia...

But she couldn't think about Olivia, not now, during her one bid for an evening's freedom. Halina hurried down the hall of the elegant luxury hotel in Rome towards the lift. Abdul stirred and she pressed herself against the wall. She could hardly believe it had been so easy, but why not? The door to their suite had been locked from the inside, the guard posted outside as a matter of form. Her mother had been trying to keep people out, not in.

No one had expected her to escape. She could barely believe it herself.

The doors whooshed open and Halina stepped into the lift, her heart pounding, her palms slick. What was she *doing*? She'd spent every one of her twenty-two years hidden behind high walls—the palace, the convent school in Italy and then the palace again. Waiting, always waiting, for the fiancé she'd never met to regain his throne and become a suitable suitor. Waiting for her life to begin, or at least something to happen.

Three days ago, Zayed al bin Nur had mistakenly kidnapped Olivia Taylor, her sisters' governess and her school friend, thinking she was Halina herself.

Rumour was he'd married Olivia out in the desert before realising his grievous error. Zayed had sent a message to her father, assuring him that he had not in any way harmed Olivia, for which Halina was heartily relieved. But the whole episode had made her realise how precarious her own position was. How limited her own freedom. And it had infuriated her father, Sultan Hassan, who had sent Halina to Italy with her mother, away from Zayed's clutches.

Halina was glad for the escape; she'd never wanted to marry Zayed, a man she'd never even met, and she certainly didn't want to be kidnapped—although she doubted her fiancé was fool enough to try the same trick twice. But the walls around her were closing in.

After this, her father would make sure she was even more restricted, more guarded, than she already was. And that was something Halina could not stand. After twenty-two years of waiting, she wanted to live…even if just for a night.

The lift doors opened and from the hotel's opulent ballroom she heard the tinkling sound of piano music and crystal, the low murmur of cultured voices. When she and her mother had arrived that afternoon, she'd seen the notice in the hotel's lobby about the private party, a charity function hosted by some CEO, a glittering event for all of Italy's richest and finest. Her mother had given Halina a sympathetic smile.

'One day, such parties will be for you,' she'd said, steering Halina towards the lift. 'When you are wed. But as for tonight, a quiet night in while we wait for your father's further instructions.'

Halina had never been to a proper party. Since she'd turned eighteen she'd attended a few dire state functions, endless banquets with fussy old dignitaries, but never a *party*. She'd never worn a cocktail dress, flirted or drunk champagne. And that was what she wanted to do tonight—to be normal just for a little while, a young woman having fun, enjoying life.

Of course, there were a few obstacles to be overcome. She'd managed the first—escaping her room. She'd pleaded a headache and hidden in her room until her mother had gone to have a bath before making her getaway.

The second obstacle was clothes. She didn't have anything appropriate to wear. Fortunately the hotel had an upscale boutique, and after hurrying across the lobby Halina slipped into the elegant shop and picked the first suitable dress she saw—a knee-length sheath in black satin, simple, stark and very sexy. She found sheer stockings and high heels as well, and charged it all to her hotel room. She'd think about the repercussions later. Hopefully her mother would never look at the bill.

Holding the elegant bag with its embossed silver logo and thick cord handles, Halina snuck into the bathroom off the hotel's foyer and changed in a stall, her hands shaking as she stuffed her plain shift dress into the bag from the boutique. Was she really doing this? Was she *crazy*?

She'd always enjoyed pranks and dares, and had forever got into good-natured trouble at school. But this... this was something else entirely. If her mother discovered her...if her father found out... Halina trembled to think of their disappointment and wrath. Her parents were both genial, but they'd never had to deal with such direct defiance from her or her sisters. Still, she had to try. She'd just have to live with the potential consequences, whatever they were.

The door to the bathroom opened and Halina held her breath, one hand on the latch of her stall, fingers near to trembling. She couldn't be discovered now, not when her evening was just about to begin.

She heard the click of heels and from beneath the stall she saw the stiletto-shod feet of two women as they stood in front of the bank of sinks.

'Did you see him?' one of the women asked in Italian, in which Halina was fluent, as the other unzipped her make-up bag. Halina peered through the crack in the stall's door and saw the women, sleek and elegant, their lips pursed and eyes narrowed as they gazed at their glossy reflections.

'Falcone? Yes, he's just arrived,' the other woman answered with a toss of her head. 'The man's *cold*. Sexy as anything, but with a heart of ice. He's finished with his latest mistress, you know. Gave her the usual diamond bracelet as a payoff and now he's completely blanking her. She was crying her eyes out by the buffet.'

'That French supermodel? She didn't last more than a week.'

'They never do.' The other woman capped her lipstick in one decisive movement. 'Would you fancy him?'

'Everyone fancies him. But would I *go* for him?' The woman tilted her head, considering. 'He must be fabulous in bed, based on everything I've heard, but I don't think I could warm up to someone that cold. One of his mistresses said that afterwards he always asks the woman to leave. And I mean, *right* afterwards. He's booting them out only seconds later.'

'There could be worse things.'

'And he insists on no personal questions at all. No asking, no answering, nothing. He just doesn't care.'

'But as long as you know that...'

'So it really would just be sex,' the woman finished with a sigh. 'And apparently that *is* amazing. That supermodel said she's been ruined for life, and it's only been a week.'

Halina's head whirled at the kind of gossip she'd never heard before. Whoever Falcone was, he sounded both appalling—and intriguing. Fabulous sex? She'd never even been kissed.

'Oh, well,' the first woman said as she zipped her bag up. 'Someone said he's already looking for his next mistress tonight—he doesn't like to have long in between paramours.'

'Mere minutes, it seems,' the other woman quipped. 'Well, it won't be me.' She sounded glum rather than determined.

With a swish of skirts and a click of heels the two women left the bathroom. Halina exhaled a huge sigh of relief. She was alone again—and it was time to make her own exit. She stuffed the bag with her own shift dress behind the toilet, hoping it would stay hidden for the evening until she was ready to return to her suite.

She hadn't quite figured out how she was going to return—would Abdul, her guard, still be asleep? And, if he wasn't, could she make something up about having taken a walk, gone for some fresh air? She'd just have to and hope Abdul—and her mother—bought her lie. This was her one night to shine, or at least twinkle a little.

Halina stepped out of the stall, her eyes widening at the sight of her reflection. The dress hugged her curvy figure, leaving little to the imagination. She'd never, ever worn something so flagrantly sexy. She'd never worn a dress so beautiful, so bare. She felt practically naked. The sheer stocking made her legs look long and slim, as did the sparkly black heels. She had no jewellery or make-up, and she'd have to leave her hair down, tumbled about her shoulders. She wouldn't look nearly as sophisticated as the women she'd just been spying on, but it would have to do.

One night. An hour, even. All she wanted to do was circulate among people, drink champagne, chat and maybe, *maybe*, flirt a little. And then she'd creep back to her bed. But for an hour—or two—she'd have fun. She'd live.

With her head held high, Halina walked out of the bathroom. She wasn't used to the heels and she stumbled for the first few steps before she got the hang of it, swinging her hips, sashaying a little. It buoyed her confidence, as did the admiring look from the man behind the concierge desk. She didn't even think he recognised her from when they'd checked in earlier in the day.

She followed the signs for the party and then paused as she saw a man on the door checking a guest list. She hadn't thought of that. The prospect of being turned away before she'd even put a toe inside the opulent ballroom made everything inside her shrivel with dismay and disappointment. She couldn't let that happen.

A couple glided past her, pausing in front of the man. Halina watched, nibbling her lip as they gave their names and he ticked them off his list. Another couple came by, and Halina watched as they followed the same procedure before going in.

Could she sweet talk her way in? She had a flair for the dramatic, but only in the safety of home or school. She'd never tried to charm a stranger, but she supposed she'd have to try.

Just then the man with the guest list caught her eye. He raised his eyebrows, managing to look both inquiring and a bit disdainful. 'May I help you, miss?'

Halina opened her mouth, her heart beating hard. 'Well…' she began, trying desperately to think of some credible reason why her name wasn't on the list but why she should still be allowed entrance to the party. 'As a matter of fact…'

The man's polite smile started to turn cool. 'Are you a guest tonight, miss…?'

Halina stared at him wretchedly. It was going to be over before it had even begun. Then she heard a voice from behind her, low and dark and rich.

'Yes, she is,' the man said. 'She's with me.'

Rico Falcone was looking for a woman, and he knew from the tightening in his gut that he'd found her. A startled gasp escaped the woman in question, her rosy lips parting as she whirled around to face him, dark hair flying about her shoulders in luxuriant waves and curls.

He'd caught a glimpse of her as he'd walked down the hall and his attention had been snagged immediately. A lush, curvy figure poured into a tight silk dress. Long, tumbling dark hair that she'd left loose and wild, like an open invitation. When she turned he saw dark-brown eyes widen, the colour of mahogany extravagantly fringed with soot-dark lashes.

'I…' she began in a breathy voice.

'Cara,' Rico purred, sliding a hand around her waist and enjoying the feel of his hip bumping hers. 'It was so good of you to wait for me.'

'I… I…' she stuttered again, looking shocked. Was she playing the innocent or was she just slow? She was obviously a gate crasher, so Rico would have expected her to play her part in this charade with a bit more alacrity. Never mind. He didn't bed women for their brains.

'Very good, Signor Falcone,' the man said, and ticked his name off the list, officious little nobody that he was. Rico moved into the room, his arm still around the woman's waist. She didn't resist, he noticed.

'Champagne, I think,' he murmured, and snapped his fingers. A waiter hurried forward and Rico plucked two glasses from the proffered tray before handing one to his next mistress. He'd already decided on that, although he didn't think she'd last too long. They never did. 'So. You obviously don't have an invitation to this party, but what is your name?' It was just about the only information he required of her.

'H— Lina,' she said, her fingers clenched tight around the stem of her glass.

'Lina?' He arched an eyebrow. 'You sounded as if you were going to say something else.'

She smiled sweetly, her eyes flashing dark fire, intriguing him. 'Lina will do for you.' So she had some spirit. He liked that, as long as she didn't start getting notions, thinking she could control him. Make him care. A few of the women he'd bedded had made that error, and it had been very tedious indeed. He'd had to make short work of them, when he would have enjoyed their attentions for a little bit longer.

'Lina,' he repeated, letting the syllables slide around in his mouth. 'And why were you so desperate to attend a party that you weren't invited to?'

She cocked her head, her smile teasing, her eyes alight, although he sensed a surprising nervousness underneath. 'What girl doesn't want to have fun?'

'Right answer,' he murmured, and clinked her glass. Her smile deepened, revealing a delightful dimple in one cheek, and she took a sip of her champagne.

'Oh, it's delicious!' she exclaimed, and he couldn't help but laugh.

'You almost sound as if you haven't tasted champagne before.'

She gave him a haughty look. 'Of course I have,' she said, and then, as if to prove the point, she drained her glass.

'Time for another, I think,' Rico said, and summoned a waiter with one imperious gesture. This woman, this Lina, was fascinating. Gate-crasher, definitely. Gold-digger as well, he was quite sure. He didn't mind, though; as long as women were upfront about what they wanted—as he was about what he didn't—the arrangement was usually satisfactory. He felt the tingle through his body of attraction and, yes, desire as he looked at her. Tonight, he hoped, was going to be very satisfactory.

She was certainly lovely, and unabashedly sexual with her tight dress and tumbled hair. She hadn't bothered with make-up or jewellery, as if she had no need for extra frippery for what was, after all, a very basic transaction. She'd come to this party looking for fun, and quite possibly a protector. Rico intended it to be him, at least for a short while.

He took another flute of champagne from the proffered tray and handed it to her. *'Cin cin,'* he murmured, and she smiled.

'Cin cin.' They'd been speaking Italian, and hers was flawless, although Rico suspected it was not her first language. He wondered what was. There was a faintly exotic cast to her features, her slightly tilted eyes and golden skin. He had no intention of or interest in asking her such questions or learning more about her. He'd long ago found that women started expecting things, emotional things, when he asked them even the most basic of questions. So he didn't. And he made sure they didn't ask any of him, either.

'Lina,' he said. 'This party bores me. Do you want to go upstairs?'

Surprise flashed through her eyes and her tongue darted out to moisten her lips, causing another painful arrow of desire to knife through him. 'Upstairs?'

'Yes, upstairs. I have the penthouse suite.' He let his mouth curve in a lazy smile. 'I think it would be a great deal more comfortable up there, and the champagne is of a far better vintage.'

'I don't even know your name,' she protested, her cheeks flushing. She looked uncertain but also excited. Perhaps he'd been a bit too abrupt. He was getting tired of the same old niceties.

'Rico,' he said, although he was quite sure she knew who he was. Everyone here did. 'I'm the CEO of Falcone Enterprises.'

'Falcone…' Recognition flashed in her eyes.

'You've heard of me, then.'

'Yes, in the bathroom just now.' Lina bit her lip, looking both guilty and amused. 'Two women were talking about you.'

'Were they?' Rico arched an eyebrow. 'Women's gossip in a bathroom—I can imagine what they said, and I assure you, it's all true.'

Her eyes rounded. 'All of it?'

Rico didn't even hesitate. 'All of it,' he drawled, and Lina let out a hiccuping laugh. She had, he noticed, already finished her second glass of champagne.

'They said you were cold. A heart of ice...'

'Pejorative, but essentially true.'

'Oh?' Lina tilted her head, her eyes sparkling, a small smile curving her lush mouth. 'How are you so cold, then?'

Rico took a sip of champagne, considering. 'I'm matter-of-fact,' he stated, deciding as always that bold honesty was by far the best policy. 'I don't dress up what is essentially a physical and very satisfying transaction.' He met her curious and impish gaze with a direct challenge in his own eyes, and he watched with pleasure as colour flared in her cheeks and her lips parted soundlessly.

'Do you mean...?' she began, and Rico cut her off.

'Yes,' he said. 'I do mean.'

She shook her head slowly, her pupils dilated, her cheeks still wonderfully pink. 'They said something else in the bathroom.'

'Did they?' Although he affected a bored drawl he realised he was interested. He wanted to know what Lina had heard, what preconceptions she might have of him.

'They said...they said...' She licked her lips, making his libido take a little leap. 'They said you were fabulous at sex.' She let out a little laugh, seeming almost incredulous that she'd admitted such a thing. Rico's mouth curved into a wicked smile.

'Also true.'

She laughed again, shaking her head, seeming embarrassed, almost shy. Was it an act, a rather obvious and unneeded attempt to snag his interest? A woman didn't pour herself into a sexy dress and try to gate-crash the party of the year without having some brash confidence and bold hopes.

'So?' Rico demanded in a low, sensual voice. He was tired of chitchat, of waiting. 'Shall we go upstairs?'

'Upstairs…'

'To my suite. A bottle of champagne is waiting.' It always was.

'I… I don't…'

Annoyance flickered through him. He didn't have time for this. Rico stretched out one hand and slid his fingers through hers, enjoying the shower of sparks that fired through him at that slight touch. He'd made the right choice, he was sure of it. 'Well?' he murmured. 'Are you coming…or not?'

CHAPTER TWO

HALINA COULDN'T THINK. From the moment Rico Falcone had rescued her from the box-ticking bouncer, she'd been ensnared. Bound body and mind by the sensual charisma of the man standing in front of her, so arrogant and self-assured and so very, very attractive.

She had limited experience of the opposite sex, and she had no experience whatsoever of the kind of man who stood in front of her now, one dark slash of an eyebrow arched, his mobile mouth curved into a smile of supreme self-confidence, his body radiating pure, muscular, sensual power.

'Are you coming with me?' he asked, and there was a note of challenge in his voice, as well as a hint of impatience. Halina hesitated. She shouldn't go with him, of course, this man whom she knew, from both gossip and his own gorgeous mouth, was a cold womaniser. A man who was fabulous at sex.

Not that she had any intention of having sex with him, of course. Her virginity was a point of honour, as well as a prized asset. As a princess of a desert kingdom, her chastity was of utmost importance. She'd never even *touched* a man before tonight.

But why did this have to be about sex? All she wanted was to drink champagne, perhaps even be kissed...

It was hard to resist such a beguiling invitation. And he was quite the most perfect specimen of a man she'd ever seen—dark hair cut close, silvery grey eyes that flashed like sunlight on metal as he remained with his hand outstretched, fingertips gliding along hers, his tall and powerfully built body encased in a top-end tuxedo, the crisp white shirt and black fitted jacket the perfect foil for his dark hair and grey eyes, his swarthy skin.

From the corner of her eye Halina saw the two women she'd glimpsed in the bathroom shooting her speculative and frankly envious glances. No matter what they'd said to each other, they wanted this man...this man who, improbably, *impossibly*, seemed to want her.

'Yes,' she said, flinging the word out the way a knight would fling down a gauntlet. It felt like a challenge, a dare, completely reckless but also brave. 'Yes, I will.'

'Excellent.' His fingers tightened on hers, causing a fizz of fireworks to go off in her belly. She was already feeling light-headed from two glasses of hastily drunk champagne, imbibed to steel her nerves. Now she felt utterly overwhelmed by the sheer, lunatic magic of the situation—she, the innocent Princess in her ivory tower being lured upstairs by the most magnetically sexual man in the world, never mind this room. *And he wanted her.*

Taking a deep breath, Halina followed Rico down the hall, away from the party, determined not to panic or even doubt herself. A little bit of flirting, another glass of champagne, maybe a kiss...and then she'd leave. Of course she would. And she wouldn't think about her mother, or Abdul, the sleepy bodyguard, and certainly not her father the Sultan who would be both furious and heartbroken to know she'd dared to go this far, never mind what she might get up to once they were in Rico's suite.

One night. One adventure. That was all she wanted, all she was asking for. Surely it wasn't too much?

Rico stabbed the button for the lifts and the doors whooshed open. Still holding her by the hand, he drew her inside, then the doors closed and they were alone, soaring upwards.

'So what made you decide to crash the party tonight?' he asked in a lazy voice. Halina tried not to blush. So it had been obvious that she hadn't had an invitation.

'An impulse decision.'

'Some of the best decisions are borne from impulse.'

'Are yours?' she asked. She was so nervous and hyper-aware of him that she wondered if he could see the hectic, urgent thud of her heart from beneath her dress. She resisted the urge to wipe her damp palms down its sides.

'My impulses are borne of instinct,' Rico answered. 'So they're always right.'

She laughed, incredulous and a little bit amused by his arrogance, despite her nerves. 'Is there anything you're insecure about?'

Something dark flashed across his face, so quickly that Halina almost missed it. She couldn't decipher what it was. Then his expression evened out and he smiled, his lips curving, showing a flash of very white, very straight teeth. 'No,' he answered. 'There isn't.'

The doors opened straight into the penthouse suite of the hotel, the one her mother had demanded but which the concierge had regretfully informed her was already booked. What kind of man was Rico Falcone, that the hotel had turned away even a queen?

'So, where's this wonderful champagne?' Halina asked as she stepped into the suite, her heels clicking the black marble floor. The space stretched on into the darkness, the only light coming from the floor-to-ceiling windows overlooking the city.

Rico threw her a darkly amused glance. 'Are you quite certain you want another glass?'

Surely he wasn't going to treat her like a child? Halina lifted her chin. 'Why wouldn't I?'

'I don't want you drunk when I make love to you.'

Everything inside her trembled, her internal organs reduced to a plateful of jelly. 'Who says you're going to—to make love to me?' Halina demanded with far more bravado than actual courage. An image slid through her mind like a sensuous snake—body entwined with body, candlelight gleaming off satin sheets—and a current of desire zinged through her, twanging all her senses, every nerve.

'I do,' Rico replied baldly as he retrieved a bottle of champagne chilling in a silver ice-bucket by a pair of white leather sofas. 'Why else would you have come up here with me?'

Nerves clamoured in her belly. Was she in over her head? The answer was obvious—of course she was. Yet she didn't want to leave. Not so soon, not yet. 'For the champagne, of course,' Halina quipped as she strolled through the sweeping living area of the suite towards the floor-to-ceiling windows that overlooked the Eternal City, its ancient, crumbling buildings now awash with moonlight.

'At least on that I can oblige.' With a satisfying pop he pulled the cork from the bottle and then filled two glasses right to the brim before handing one to Halina. She took a sip, relishing the crisp taste of bubbles on her tongue, and definitely needing the Dutch courage. *What now?*

'You really shouldn't be quite so arrogant,' she said as she lowered the glass. Her palms were slick and her heart thudded but she managed to hold his sardonic gaze. Just.

'Oh? Why shouldn't I?'

His utter, unapologetic confidence stunned her. She admired it too, because although she knew she could seem confident to her school friends or sisters, playing to familiar crowds with her trademark drama and humour, when it came to the real world she had nothing on this man. Nothing at all.

'It's not a particularly appealing trait,' she said at last.

'I disagree.'

His self-assurance was like a brick wall, high and wide, impossible to cross or find a chink in. Still, for some perverse reason, she tried. 'So you think it's an asset? Being so ridiculously self-assured?'

He shrugged, as if the answer was so apparent the question should not have even been asked. 'Of course.'

'Why? How?'

'Because there is a basis for it. I am the way I am because I know what I'm doing and, more importantly, I know what I want and I go after it.' His eyes flashed, a glint of silver like moonlight flashing off the blade of a knife. 'And do you know what I want right now, Lina?'

She swallowed. Hard. Excitement licked along her veins like the most dangerous fire. 'What?'

'You.'

Before she could form the words for a semi-coherent reply he'd crossed the room, swallowing up the space in a couple of strides, and plucked the champagne flute from her nerveless fingers. She opened her mouth to protest—she hadn't finished her drink—but then his hands were on his shoulders, warm and so very sure, and he was kissing her.

Her very first kiss, and it felt like diving head-first into ice-cold water, a shock to her entire system. She stiffened underneath the onslaught of his persuasive mouth, the sudden intimacy of it, even as heat exploded in her centre and stars shot from behind her eyes. Her knees buckled and she felt Rico smile against her mouth as he gauged her obvious and overwhelming response to him.

She clutched at the slippery, satiny lapels of his tuxedo jacket, lost in the sensation of his mouth on hers. Were all kisses like this? Did you always feel as if you were drowning, caught up in a whirlpool of pleasure, every sense singing? She'd never experienced anything like it, and all she knew was that she wanted more. Much more.

Her mouth opened under his and she stood on her tip-toes, straining to reach more of him. Feel more of him. Her breasts pressed against his chest and created even more arrows of sensations sizzling through her, making her whole being burn.

Rico slid his hands from her shoulders to her waist, anchoring her against him so her hips nudged his and she felt the hard throb of his arousal against her, shock-ing her to her core and thrilling her too. Even she, in her innocence, knew what *that* was. As much as it thrilled her, it also made a ripple of terror go through her. What was she *doing*? And did she want to stop?

Rico spread his fingers across her hip, each lean digit creating a burn even through her dress as if he were branding her by his touch. She was so achingly conscious of every part of him, from the hard planes of his chest and thighs to the sure movement of his mouth and the delightful press of his hands. He was everywhere on her, yet she still wanted more, a delicious and insistent ache of need starting at her centre and spreading outwards, right to her fingertips.

She felt so much, she was afraid she might combust, burst into flames right in front of him. How did people experience this and *live*?

Then, quite suddenly, Rico tore his mouth from hers and took a step away, raking his hands through his hair before dropping them to his sides. Colour blazed along his blade-like cheekbones and his breathing was ragged. He was, it seemed, as affected as she was, or almost, and that was an incredible thought.

Halina's knees wobbled and she grabbed onto a nearby table to steady herself. She felt the absence of him like a physical thing, everything in her all at once turning empty, cold and aching. For a little while she'd felt so gloriously alive. She couldn't let it end so quickly. She couldn't let it end at all.

Because she knew then, no matter how inexperienced and nervous she was, she wanted more. Needed it. She wasn't done with Rico…and she prayed he wasn't done with her.

Rico gazed at Lina thoughtfully, trying to ignore the hectic thud of his own heart. He'd been far more affected by her clumsy kisses than he liked to admit, even to himself. Even in love-making, in the highest heights of his pleasure, he kept his control. To lose it would be another form of weakness, one he despised. He would not be a slave to any emotion, whether it was love or its poorer but equally powerful cousin, lust. He'd decided that a long time ago, when he'd watched someone walk away from him and felt his heart break. *Never again.* Never again would he allow someone to break something inside him. He wouldn't even allow himself to be affected…at all. Never would he give in to the weakest emotion of them all, the torment of love.

And as for Lina… He let his gaze sweep over her, noting her flushed cheeks and swollen lips, her ink-dark, wavy hair falling in tumbling waves over her shoulders.

Her breath shuddered through her, and artlessly she pressed one hand to her pounding heart. She was just as affected as he was, and she wasn't even trying to hide it. He didn't think it had even *occurred* to her to hide it, to hide anything, and that made her very different from the women he usually bedded.

Those women were beautiful and hard in a sharply glittering way, as determined to get his money as much as they were eager to get into his bed. He gave them pleasure, of that he was certain, but they didn't respond as Lina just had—trembling and eager, unrestrained and artless, seeming to crave him just for him…which was an intoxicant in and of itself.

'What is it?' she asked, her voice a breathy whisper. 'Why are you looking at me like that?'

'How am I looking at you?'

'As if I'm a puzzle you're trying to solve.'

He laughed; he couldn't help himself. She was absolutely right and he wasn't used to that kind of perception, especially from a potential bed partner. 'Yes,' he said. 'That is how I'm looking at you. You intrigue me, Lina.' More than she should. He didn't want to be interested in the women he bedded, beyond their capabilities in that particular department.

Yet something about Lina, her utterly unrestrained response, made him pause. And then wonder. Because, he realised, she seemed the one thing he felt he'd never been, at least not since he'd been nine years old and realised that promises could be broken and dreams shattered. Easily.

What had given him pause just now was that Lina seemed innocent. And innocence was a quality in his bed partners he definitely did not want. He'd had enough dreams broken not to want to break anyone else's, which was why he was so upfront about his relationships, if he could even call the sexual transactions he enjoyed such a thing.

'I don't think I'm that complicated, really,' she said on a laugh, but the sound wobbled and she bit her lip, increasing Rico's curiosity…and his unease. Why was she acting as if this was all so *new* to her?

'Tell me what you were doing tonight at the party,' he said abruptly. Her eyes widened in surprise at the sudden change of subject.

'Trying to get into it,' she answered with a shrug. 'I didn't have an invitation, as you realised.'

'Do you do that often? Try to crash parties you aren't invited to?'

'Not…that often,' Halina said, keeping his gaze, but clearly with effort.

'But why that party?' Rico pressed. 'And why did you want to get into it so badly?'

A frown crinkled her forehead and something flashed in her eyes, something like unease. She was hiding something. But what? He'd already assumed she was a gold-digging mistress-in-expectation. What could she possibly be hiding that would bother him?

'Why not that party?' she challenged. 'It looked fun.'

'Were you hoping to meet someone in particular?'

She shrugged. 'I was hoping to have fun.'

Rico swung away from her, annoyed as much with himself for pressing the point as he was with her for her non-answers. What did he care why she'd shown up tonight or what her motives were? What did he care at all? He never had before. And he wouldn't now.

She was here in his suite for a reason. When she'd kissed him, as clumsily as she had, it had been with a genuine, eager desire. She was willing and so was he. That was all that mattered, surely?

And yet…it was almost as if she'd never been kissed before. She'd been so unrestrained, so open, and it had been that seeming innocence that had enflamed him. Yet surely she couldn't be as innocent as all that? Surely she wouldn't be in his suite now if she was?

'I've drunk all my champagne.'

Rico turned to see Lina clutching her glass, a determined tilt to her chin. She held it out and after a second's pause he reached for the bottle and poured her another glass, the fizz foaming over the top and onto her hand. She laughed and licked off the droplets, a move that seemed as thoughtless and uncomplicated as everything else she did. If it had been another woman, the kind of woman he was used to, he would have thought it a planned part of an attempt to ensnare him. Not that he could ever be ensnared.

'Cin cin,' she said again, a note of defiant bravado in her voice, and she lifted her glass to drink. Rico watched her, noting the sinuous movement of her throat as she swallowed, wondering yet again what was making him hesitate.

'Cin cin,' he answered automatically, even though he'd discarded his glass already. Slowly Lina lowered her glass, her eyes wide and dark above the rim as she stared at him.

'I… I should probably go now,' she said, and that surprised him even more. Was she playing hard to get? Or did she really mean it? And should he let her, considering how uneasy this whole exchange was making him feel? He felt strangely reluctant to watch her walk away, which was irritating and alarming in itself.

'Do you want to go?' he asked starkly.

She paused, her tongue darting out to dab a drop of champagne sparkling on her lips. Her gaze was wondering and transfixed as she slowly, so slowly, shook her head. 'No...no, I don't. But I probably should.'

'Should? Why?'

'Because you're a dangerous man, Rico Falcone.' She set the glass on a side table. 'And you're way out of my league.'

More honesty that took him by surprise. He wasn't used to such unvarnished truth. 'I'm not so dangerous if you know what to expect.'

'Which is?'

'A wonderful time and then a farewell.' He was absolute about that. He would never be left again, never watch someone walk away, leaving his heart in pieces. No, he would watch whomever it was walk away, a smile on his face because he was in control. He was always in control.

'Ah.' She nodded slowly. 'Just like the women said.'

'Those women in the bathroom?'

'The very same.'

He walked towards her, a long, loose-limbed, lazy stroll. 'Forewarned is forearmed, or so they say.'

'They said you kicked women out of your bed in rather indecent haste.'

'I suppose it depends on whom you ask.'

He stood in front of her so he could feel the heat coming off her, the desire. Her body trembled. He felt as if they were both on the edge of a glorious precipice; all it would take was for one of them to take that first tumbling step.

'I really should go.' Her voice was soft.

'Don't play games with me, Lina.' He met her gaze; her lids were half-lowered in dark challenge. 'I abhor any kind of dishonesty. If you want to go, go.' He swept one arm towards the lift. She didn't move, and if she had he didn't know what he would have done. Stopped her? Persuaded her to stay in any way that he could? Maybe. Probably.

But Lina stayed still, her gaze darting from the lift back to him. 'This is madness,' she whispered.

'Why?'

'Because…because I don't even know you. And you don't know me.'

'We know enough.'

'For you, maybe.' She closed her eyes briefly. He had the sense that she was battling with herself, and he wondered why it was such a momentous decision. She'd come to the party. She'd come upstairs. Was she going to cling to some outdated remnant of morality now? Still, it felt bizarrely important not to push her. This would be a decision she'd make on her own, though God help them both if she walked away now.

Then Lina opened her eyes. Stared him straight in the face. Took a deep breath and spoke. 'I'm staying.'

CHAPTER THREE

HALINA WASN'T SO innocent that she didn't know what she was agreeing to. Her heart tumbled in her chest and excitement zinged through her veins because, no matter how crazy this was, how nervous she felt, she wanted this. A lifetime of humble obedience and duty to her royal family and it had all shattered to broken pieces with Prince Zayed's foolish, desperate act. She would not marry him now; she might not marry anyone. So why not take one night? One night for herself, for pleasure? She'd deal with the consequences later. Maybe she'd be lucky and there wouldn't be any.

'Are you sure?' Rico's dark gaze searched hers, his voice a rumble in his chest. Halina had the feeling it was not a question he asked often. Did he know how innocent she was? Had he any idea that he was her first kiss, her first everything? Halina had no intention of telling him. She had a gut instinct that such lack of experience would horrify and perhaps even repel him. She wasn't like his usual women. Even in her inexperience, she knew that.

'Yes, I'm sure.' The words trembled through her and part of her, quite a large part, wondered what on earth she was doing. Losing her innocence, her prized virginity, to a man who had made it clear he had no expectations, no desires, beyond sex. Fabulous sex.

But perhaps that was better. This didn't have to be complicated. There would be no entanglements. And after a lifetime of waiting she wanted, *needed*, something finally to happen. To be the author of her own destiny, if only for an evening. Even if it ultimately led to heartbreak, or at least disappointment.

'Lina.' Rico's voice was rough. 'If you're sure, come here.' Her eyes widened but then she obeyed, walking towards him on trembling legs so she was standing before him. 'Take off your dress.'

Her heart was thudding so hard it hurt. Was he really going to ask her to do that right *now*? She swallowed hard and Rico's gaze seemed to burn into hers, his eyes like molten silver as he waited for her to obey his command.

'Well?' One eyebrow lifted arrogantly. This was a test, a dare; if she didn't do it, he would call her bluff. Accuse her of inexperience, and maybe even send her away. Taking a deep breath, her gaze never leaving his, Halina reached behind her and tugged the zip down her dress.

As the dress slithered off her shoulders, leaving her bare to the waist—her breasts encased in a serviceable white bra rather than the sexy lingerie she would have preferred—Halina could hardly credit she was doing this. Was it the champagne that lent the recklessness to the moment, or was it the urgency she felt? Or was it the man himself, Rico Falcone, his body radiating the most powerful sexual charisma Halina had ever experienced?

The dress pooled around her waist and Halina lifted her chin, resisting the impulse to cover herself. 'Well?' she demanded, and thankfully her voice didn't waver. 'Take off your shirt.'

With a low husk of laughter, Rico undid his tie and then the studs of his tuxedo shirt, tossing them aside heedlessly so they clattered onto the marble floor. He shrugged out of his jacket and shirt so his chest was bare and magnificent, his skin gleaming like bronze satin stretched over powerful muscles, the dark hair sprinkling his impressive chest veeing down to the waistband of his black trousers.

'Touch me,' he said softly, and it felt more like a plea than a command, surprising her, because for a moment Rico Falcone didn't seem arrogant. Gently she placed her hand on his chest, the dark, crisp hairs a sensual abrasion against her palm. His skin was warm, the muscles hard and flexed, and she felt the steady thud of his heart beneath her palm.

Rico encircled her wrist with his fingers, holding her hand there, against him. Neither of them spoke; the only sound was the ragged draw and tear of their breathing. Halina had never felt so close to a human being before, connected in a way that felt both intimate and intense.

Rico's fingers tightened on her wrist, and then he drew her slowly towards him so her hips and breasts pressed against him. The feel of his body in such close contact with hers made a thrill run through her, as if a live wire ran right through her centre and Rico's touch was the electric current.

He dipped his head, his mouth hovering over hers, their breaths mingled, everything suspended. Halina's eyes fluttered closed, waiting for his kiss, but then she opened them again when he remained where he was, his lips barely brushing hers.

'Rico...?'

Whatever he saw in her questioning gaze seemed to satisfy him, for in one swift movement he drew her even more closely to him, his hands on her hips, shrugging her dress down to her ankles as his mouth plundered hers with soft yet determined persuasion.

Halina brought her hands up to his head, her fingers threaded through his short, dark hair, her nails grazing his skull as she surrendered herself, body and soul, to that one endless kiss that demanded everything from her.

Her mind was a blur of sensation as Rico backed her towards the corridor that led to the suite's bedrooms; she stepped out of her dress, stumbling slightly in her unfamiliar heels, and when she did he swept her up in his arms as if she were an armful of feathers and, with her curled against his chest, he strode into the bedroom.

The room was swathed in shadows and moonlight as Rico laid her on the bed. She was dressed only in her stockings and plain bra and pants, and she felt shy but not uncertain as she lay sprawled on the black silken sheets for his thorough inspection.

And inspect he did, standing above her as he slowly unbuckled his trousers and then shucked them off so he wore nothing but a pair of navy silk boxer shorts that did little to hide the impressive evidence of his masculinity.

'You are very beautiful.' The words were stark and sincerer because of it. Rico was not a man to flatter; he was merely stating a fact. And Lina could tell by the silver blaze of his eyes that he meant every simple word.

'Thank you,' she whispered. Rico stretched out alongside her, the sinewy muscles of his body rippling with the easy movement. Halina held her breath as he hooked his fingers around the edge of her tights and tugged them downwards.

Her breath came out in a restless shudder as the tips of his fingers brushed against her sensitive core, igniting sensations she'd barely felt before. He tugged the tights lower, down her thighs, leaving fiery trails of sensation wherever his fingers brushed until he'd got rid of them completely and tossed them aside.

He loomed above her, his hands braced by her shoulders and his knees on either side of her hips. She felt caged by his body, but it felt protective rather than threatening, thrilling in a way she could barely articulate even to herself. She had no idea what he was going to do next.

Then he lowered his mouth and pressed a kiss to her navel, his tongue flicking inside her belly button and making her cry out in surprised pleasure. The cry turned to a moan as his mouth moved lower. Surely he wasn't going to…?

But he was. His breath fanned hotly on her underwear before he hooked his finger through the top of it and slid it down her legs so it went the way of her tights. She was bare and exposed before him, and it made her both tense and strain in expectation, incredulous and waiting, a little bit embarrassed and yet so eager.

Her body arched off the bed as he pressed his mouth to her centre, the feeling so intimately invasive that her mind blurred into nothing but sensation. His tongue flicked among her folds, seeming to know exactly what touch and pressure would make her writhe mindlessly, her body attuned to the exquisite pressure building within her.

'Rico.' His name was a moan, a plea. Her hips bucked with the restless ache inside her that she desperately needed to be assuaged. *'Rico.'*

He lifted his head, laughing softly, and then he slid his hands under her bottom, lifting her up so he had even greater access to her most intimate self. She felt too crazed with desire and need now to feel embarrassed or exposed, wanting only more from him.

And he gave it, his mouth plundering her centre until she felt as if she were shattering inside, breaking apart into glittering pieces, her hips arching under his knowing touch as her cries rent the still, taut air.

She'd never known anything like it, had never had such an experience so intimate, so intense, so over-whelming.

Rico rolled on top of her, braced on his forearms, his breathing ragged. 'Is it safe?' he demanded in a ragged voice and Halina blinked up at him, still dazed by an experience she could only describe as completely life-changing.

Safe? What, she wondered hazily, was safe about this? She was risking everything, including her very soul, by being here with him. It wasn't remotely safe. But she sensed that if she said as much Rico would exercise the incredible self-control she instinctively knew he had and roll off her, tell her to go. Their night would be over, and she couldn't bear the thought.

'Yes, it's safe.'

With a grim smile of satisfaction curving his features, Rico nodded, then Halina gasped as she felt him start to slide inside her. Her fingernails pierced his shoulders as she braced herself for what felt like a complete onslaught, an invasion of everything she was.

Before she could accept the discomfort and adjust to it, Rico stopped. His expression was one of complete and utter astonishment.

'You are a *virgin*?'

She couldn't be. Rico gritted his teeth, sweat breaking out on his brow as he held himself above Lina, calling on every shred of self-control he had to keep himself from sinking inside her velvety depths as he longed to do.

Lina looked up at him, her face pale, her eyes defiant. 'What does it matter if I am?'

Matter? He didn't deflower virgins. He didn't cor-rupt innocents. Having been heartbreakingly naive once himself, he had no desire to rip away the veil of innocence from someone else. Yet here he was, poised to do just that. If he was being completely honest with himself, he'd ignored every neon warning sign that had been flashing at him tonight, every obvious example of the evidence of her innocence and inexperience. Her total naivety.

'It matters,' he gritted out and, though it felt like the worst form of torture, he started to withdraw from her welcoming, silken entrance.

'*No.*' Lina hooked her legs around his hips, pulling him back inside her. Her expression was fierce, her eyes bright with determination. 'You can't ruin me without fulfilling your side of the bargain.'

He let out a choked laugh, every muscle straining as they engaged in this absurd, exquisite push and pull. 'My side of the bargain?'

'You said you were going to make love to me, Rico,' she stated fiercely. 'So do it.' And with that she wrapped her legs more tightly around his waist and pulled him deeper into her, wincing as she did so, but not hesitating for a second.

Rico muttered a curse as he sank deep inside her, his mind going hazy with the incredible feel of her body wrapped around his. His instinct was still to withdraw, to roll away from her and send her from the room. A *virgin*. A disaster.

Yet the tightly held shreds of his control were disintegrating under the welcoming heat of her body, and with a groan he surrendered to her, knowing she was the victor as their bodies began to move in that ancient, harmonious rhythm.

The least he could do for her was bring her back to that dazzling precipice, even as he climbed towards its heights. Rico watched in satisfaction as her face softened with pleasure, her eyes unfocused, pupils dilated, her breath coming out in a shuddery rush as her body convulsed around his. Then, and only then, did he find his own satisfaction, releasing himself inside her with a final groan of surrender.

For several moments afterwards his mind blurred and blanked as the last aftershocks of his climax pulsed through him. He rolled off her onto his back, one arm thrown over his eyes. Regret lanced him, a sword he threw himself on with bitterness—because he *knew* better. Of course he did.

He'd lost his self-control, he'd thrown it away with both hands, and for what? A single moment of pleasure? A damning *need*? He hated the thought. He didn't need anyone. He wouldn't let himself.

'Why,' he gritted out, his arm still over his eyes, 'did you come up to my hotel suite if you are—were—a virgin?'

She shifted next to him, pulling a sheet across her body. 'What does one thing have to do with the other?'

'You knew what I intended. I made it very clear, for a *reason*.'

'Yes.' She sounded calm and a little resigned, but not particularly regretful. Rico removed his arm from his eyes and turned to stare at her. Her face was rosy and flushed, her lips swollen, her eyes bright. She looked… She almost looked happy. He didn't understand it at all.

'Did you intend for this to happen?' he asked incredulously. 'Was that why you were waiting outside the party? Were you waiting for me?'

'Not for you in particular.'

His ego took a surprised bruising at that honest statement. 'So any man would have done?'

She bit her lip, her gaze sliding away from his. 'That sounds awful.'

'But that's what you're saying?' He felt outraged, even though he knew it was ridiculous. He'd had that very attitude countless times. He *preferred* that attitude…in himself. And one thing he was not was a hypocrite. Yet here he was, feeling offended by her honesty.

'No, that's not what I am saying.' Lina's eyes flashed and she scrambled up to a sitting position, her lush breasts on glorious display. She had the most amazing figure— curvy and womanly and round. Just looking at her made Rico ache all over again. Virgin or not, Lina still enflamed him.

She pulled the sheet up, wrapping it around herself as she glared at him, her chin tilted at a defiant angle. 'What does it matter to you?' she demanded. 'According to those women back in the bathroom, you should be showing me the door right about now.'

'Is that what you want?' Rico hurled back at her. He didn't even know why he was so angry, only that he was.

'It's what I *expected*. And wasn't that what this was all about? You warned me, Rico, about how little I could expect from you. Now it seems I'm getting more than I bargained for.' And she didn't sound very happy about it.

Rico stared at her in fury, wondering why he didn't just let her go. She was acting exactly the way he should want, but something compelled him to keep her here. He wanted answers. He also wanted her.

'It's different,' he ground out. 'Since you're a virgin.'

Lina rolled her eyes. 'That's my business, not yours.'

'You should have told me.'

'Why?'

'Because I never would have slept with you then!'

'And that's exactly why I didn't tell you.'

She was impossible. Rico rolled up to a sitting position and yanked on his trousers. A sudden thought occurred to him, terrible and profound. 'You said it was safe.' From behind him Lina didn't say a word and slowly Rico turned around. 'I asked you if you were on birth control…'

Her eyes widened a fraction and she hitched the sheet higher. 'That wasn't actually what you asked.'

'I asked if it was safe!'

'Which could mean something completely different.'

Cold dread swirled in his stomach, along with an anger fiercer than he'd ever felt before. 'Most women, when in the intimate situation we were in, would know precisely what that meant.' He took a deep breath and let it out slowly. 'Are you saying you're not on birth control?' Why would she be, if she was a virgin? Unless she'd taken it with the express purpose of losing her virginity tonight. The thought seemed so bizarre he didn't know what to do with it. 'Tell me you're on birth control.'

Lina shrugged, her ink-dark hair sliding about her shoulders. 'Fine. I'm on birth control.'

'You're lying.'

'You asked me to tell you—'

Rico swore loudly and viciously. 'I didn't mean for you to *lie*.' He raked a hand through his hair, his fingers pulling on the short strands, frustration now matching his fury and confusion. 'Lina, I don't understand you.'

'You don't need to.'

He knew she was right, and that infuriated him all the more. He should just send her away. By this point in an evening, usually he would already be in the shower, expecting his bed partner, whoever she was, to be finding her own way out. What was so different now?

'If you're not on birth control, you could be pregnant.' Lina lifted her chin another notch and said nothing. 'Damn it, Lina, that's a rather major issue, don't you think?'

A muscle flinched in her cheek. 'It's not your concern.'

'It is very much my concern,' Rico returned in a low, dangerous voice, certainty thrumming inside him. He would *never* abandon his own child, as he had once been abandoned. He would die first. 'If you are pregnant with my child, it is my paramount concern.'

Her face paled and she blinked slowly, seeming to absorb that statement. Rico shook his head, impatient as well as furious. 'Did it not even occur to you that you could become pregnant?'

'Not exactly.' She bit her lip. 'I wasn't thinking about that just then.'

'Then why on earth did you say it was safe? Did you lie on purpose?'

'I... I didn't understand what you meant.' Colour crept into her face and she looked away.

Rico stared at her incredulously. 'What did you think I meant, then?'

'I don't know.' Her voice rose in agitation. 'I wasn't thinking at all, to be honest.'

'Neither was I,' Rico returned grimly, hating that it was true. What a mess. And he had no one to blame but himself. He should have realised how naive she was. She'd given him plenty of clues.

Sitting in his bed, wrapped in his sheet, her hair everywhere, her eyes wide and her face pale, she looked very young and incredibly vulnerable. How could he have thought for a moment that she was experienced, a woman of the world? She was anything but.

'How old are you?' he asked abruptly and she gave him a look of scorn.

'Twenty-two, so you have no worries on that score.'

'Still—'

'I'm not your problem, Rico.'

'But you could be—' His words were cut off by a sudden buzzing. Lina looked at him questioningly.

'It's the lift,' he explained tersely. 'The doors lock automatically, since it opens right into the suite.' The buzzing sounded again, insistent. Whoever was in the lift wanted to get in. Who the hell was trying to find him now?

CHAPTER FOUR

HALINA WATCHED IN misery as Rico grabbed his shirt and strode from the room. She slid from the bed, still clutching the sheet to her, and reached for her dress. She needed to get out of here as soon as possible, before her mother or Abdul missed her. Before she broke down completely and burst into tears in front of Rico, appalling him even further.

How could she have been so *stupid*?

Hurriedly Halina snatched her underwear and yanked it on before wriggling into her dress. She managed to get the zip halfway up and decided that would have to do. She couldn't find her bra, so she just left it. She had to get out of here—now.

She needed to absorb everything that had happened tonight, everything she'd let happen, because she'd been so befuddled, besotted and bewitched by Rico Falcone. Those women had been right—he was fabulous at sex.

Too bad that didn't do much for her now, when she was facing a terrifyingly uncertain future. She looked back on the last few hours, blurred as they were, and marvelled that she'd been so reckless, with scarcely a thought for her future, her self. How could she have jeopardised everything for a single night's pleasure?

'What the hell are you doing?'

Halina's head jerked up at the sound of Rico's furious voice, and then her mouth dropped open in shock as the royal bodyguard, Abdul, strode into the bedroom. She'd thought things were bad enough but they'd just become a million times worse.

'Come now, Your Highness,' Abdul said in Arabic. He bowed his head so he didn't have to look upon her near-nakedness.

'Abdul…' Halina licked her lips, her mouth dry, her mind whirling. 'How did you…?'

'Please, Your Highness. Come now. Your mother is waiting.'

The balled tights she'd been clutching in one fist fell to the floor. 'Does my mother know…?' she began. Abdul's terse nod was all the confirmation she needed, and far more than she wanted. Any hope of creeping back into her hotel suite with no one the wiser crumbled to ash. Not only did she have to deal with the loss of her virginity and a possible pregnancy, but her parents' fury and disappointment. She swayed on her feet, sick with both fear and shame.

Rico stood in the doorway, looking furious. 'Who is this, Lina?' he demanded. His face was flushed, his shirt unbuttoned, his eyes blazing.

'I have to go,' Halina said numbly. She had to go now, before she passed out, or was sick, or burst into tears. She felt close to doing all three. With trembling fingers, she struggled with the rest of the zip. Rico muttered a curse and then crossed the room to her and did it up himself.

'Do not touch her again,' Abdul ordered in English, his voice flat and lethal, and Rico whirled on the man as if he'd been waiting for the chance to attack.

'*Excuse* me?'

'Please, Rico, just let me go.' Spots danced before her

eyes and a pressure was building in her chest. She needed to get out of here *now*.

Rico glanced furiously at Abdul, who was waiting by the door, his arms crossed, his face studiously blank. 'Who is he? What is he to you?' he demanded.

'No one,' Halina answered quietly. 'No one like that. He's one of my guards.'

'Guards?'

'We must go now.' Abdul stepped forward, six-foot-four of solid muscle, but he paled in comparison with Rico in all his glittering fury, who looked as if he was seriously contemplating throwing a punch at the body-guard.

'We aren't finished here, Lina,' Rico insisted in a voice that throbbed with angry intensity.

'We have to be,' Halina whispered, and she slipped by him towards the lift. As she stabbed the button she saw out of the corner of her eye Abdul block Rico's way. Rico looked mutinous, his fists clenched, his whole body taut with rage.

Thankfully the doors of the lift opened before he did something precipitous, and Halina stepped inside with a shuddery sigh of both relief and regret, Abdul following quickly... The doors closed as Rico strode to face them, fury and disbelief etched on every rugged line of his face. Then she saw him no more.

All the courage and defiance Halina had felt earlier in the evening, all the excitement from being with Rico, had all gone, leaving her flattened and empty. She was terrified too, yet she knew she deserved everything she was going to get, which she couldn't bear to think about yet.

She glanced at Abdul, who was stony-faced and silent. 'How did you find me?' she whispered.

'It was not so difficult, Your Highness.'

'But how did you know I was gone?'

'I check all the rooms of the suite throughout the night.'

And she'd thought she was being so clever. She hadn't realised Abdul was so thorough, never mind that he'd dozed off for a few minutes.

He must have seen she was gone and then looked for her downstairs. The bouncer at the party could have identified her, as well as Rico, and how he'd seen them leave together. No, it had not been so difficult. And she was even more foolish than she'd realised.

'My mother…?' she began, but Abdul just shook his head. It was not his place to say what her mother thought.

Soon enough they were walking down the hallway to their hotel suite, and Halina's heart began to thud in an entirely new and unpleasant way at the prospect of facing her mother. What would Aliya Amar think of her daughter's flagrant disobedience? What would happen?

She didn't have to wait long to find out. As soon as Abdul swiped the key card, her mother threw open the door. She stood with her shoulders thrown back, her face flushed with both fury and fear, her eyes narrowed to dark slits.

'Leave us,' she commanded Abdul, and he did so.

Halina closed the door behind her, her fingers trembling on the knob. She'd never seen her mother look so angry. Her mother was always carefree and charming, her light laughter tinkling through the rooms of the royal palace of Abkar. Yet now she looked like a woman possessed by rage. Halina shrank back. She couldn't help it.

'I cannot believe you have been so stupid,' Aliya stated in a cold, restrained voice. 'So utterly reckless. We leave

Abkar for one night—one night!—and you manage to completely disgrace yourself. How completely, I can see from the state of your dress.' She raked Halina with one up-and-down glance, taking in her rumpled dress, her lack of stockings, her tumbled hair and still-swollen lips. Halina felt as if the truth of her evening was written all over her, and she bowed her head.

'I'm sorry, Mama,' she whispered as tears gathered in her eyes. She couldn't even blame her mother for being so angry. She knew she deserved it, and more. From the moment she'd escaped her bedroom she'd acted foolishly, without a thought to her future. Now that it was all over, she couldn't believe she'd been so completely stupid.

'I always knew you were impulsive,' Aliya continued. 'Ever since you were a little girl, going after whatever you fancied. Doing whatever you liked.'

'That's not fair!' Halina protested, even though she knew it was unwise to argue. She'd been spoiled a little, yes. She could acknowledge that. But her life had been so restricted, with so little opportunity for fun or excitement. Halina knew it didn't justify her actions, but at least it explained them a little.

'Fair?' Aliya repeated, her voice ringing out. 'You want to talk to me about fair?' She whirled away from Halina, pacing the sumptuous carpet of the suite's living area. Then she stopped, her back to Halina, her shoulders slumping. 'Heaven help us both, Halina,' she whispered. 'What am I going to tell your father? He is going to be devastated. Heartbroken. This affects everything. All our plans…the political alliances that are so important…'

Halina swallowed, blinking back more tears. She hated the thought of disappointing her father so badly. She didn't even understand why she'd done it. Had Rico

Falcone really possessed that kind of hold on her? In the heat of the moment, he had. Even now she could recall a flicker of that intoxicating pleasure, the way it had blurred her mind and emboldened her actions.

Aliya turned slowly to face her. 'Who was this man? Why did you meet him? Was it planned?'

'I...' Halina stared at her helplessly. What answer could she give? 'It wasn't planned. I... I was scared,' she finally whispered.

'Scared? Did this man scare you?'

'No, not like that. I...' Her mind whirled. 'Olivia's kidnapping frightened me. It made me realise how little I've experienced, how little chance I've had to have fun...'

'Fun?' Her mother looked incredulous. 'This was about having *fun*?'

It made her sound so silly, so shallow, and in truth Halina knew she'd been both. 'I just wanted to go to a party,' she said. Aliya shook her head slowly. 'To see something of life, to feel...alive.'

'You are such a child, Halina. Do you have any idea what is at stake?'

'I never meant things to go so far.' Yet she'd chosen her fate. Halina knew she couldn't pretend otherwise. Rico had given her the opportunity to walk away and she hadn't taken it.

'How far did you go, Halina?' Aliya demanded in a low voice. 'As far as I fear, judging by the look of you?'

Halina said nothing. Her throat was too tight to speak. Her mother whirled around again, her fingers pressed to her temples.

'I cannot even believe...' she began in a throaty whisper. 'Could you be pregnant? Is that a possibility?'

'No.' The denial, the lie, was instinctive, and Halina

desperately wanted to believe it. She *couldn't* be pregnant. She just couldn't. Aliya turned around slowly.

'Because if you were,' she said, 'we would have to get rid of it. I know how heartless that sounds, but as a royal family we cannot endure the scandal. It would shame us all, and ruin your sisters' potential matches.'

Halina kept her mother's gaze even as she quailed inwardly at Aliya's total ruthlessness. Get rid of her child? No matter how much she'd wrecked her future, Halina knew she would never want that. But she hated the thought that what she'd done might affect her three younger sisters, who were still in the schoolroom and even more innocent than she was—or, rather, had been.

'There's no chance,' she said firmly, willing herself to believe it along with her mother. Inside her everything shook. Her future felt more uncertain than ever. She had no idea what was going to happen to her now.

Rico stared at the hazy landscape of Rome's buildings in the muggy summer heat, unable to concentrate on the property deal laid out on his desk. All he needed to do was review a few simple terms and scrawl his signature. Yet his brain had stalled, as it had many times over the last two months, ever since Lina had left his hotel suite in a cloud of confusion and shame.

It hadn't been difficult to find out who she was—Princess Halina of Abkar, known to be a spoiled pet of her father, a guest of the hotel where the party had been held and presently engaged to Prince Zayed al bin Nur of Kalidar. The fact that he'd deflowered a virgin promised to another man was like a stone in Rico's gut.

He might be considered cold and ruthless—he'd been called emotionless and even cruel—but he was a man of honour, and in lying to him Halina had made him violate his own personal code of morality. It was one he'd lived by staunchly since his days in the orphanage, determined to rise above the desperation and poverty, to be better than those around him, because that had felt like all he'd had. He didn't lie, steal or cheat. He never would. But in taking Halina to his bed he felt he'd done all three. It was something he could not forgive himself.

But, regardless of whether or not he could forgive her for lying to him, he needed to know where she was... and if she was pregnant. Because no matter what he felt for Halina he would take care of his child. His blood. That was a certainty. The very idea that he might be put in the position his mother had been in, a stranger to his own child, was anathema to him. His mother might not have cared about her own child, but he did. He would. Absolutely.

The day after Halina had left his suite Rico had hired a private investigator to discover where she was and what she was doing, determined to find her, and more importantly to discover if she was pregnant.

The possibility that she might be carrying his child and marry someone else burned inside him. He would never allow such a travesty; it would be even worse than her simply being pregnant. But as the days slipped by with no answer he knew he might have to; it might have already happened.

The thought of another man raising his child, passing him off as his own, made his fists clench and brought bile to the back of his throat. *Never.* But he'd had no word from the investigator who had flown to Abkar to ferret out information.

All he knew was that Halina had returned to Abkar the day after their encounter and hadn't been seen since, although she was believed to be residing in the royal palace. Attempts to get any information or gain entrance to the palace had been fruitless, so he had no idea if she'd married al bin Nur as planned or if she was pregnant.

Rico turned away from the window, pacing the confines of his luxurious office. For the last eight weeks he'd lived in a torment of ignorance and uncertainty, unable to focus on anything until he knew the outcome of his one night with Halina.

He'd told himself it was unlikely she was pregnant, that in all likelihood he'd never see her again and never needed to. His own history made that hope a faint one. His mother had been a waitress, his father a worker on Salerno's docks. They'd had one night together and he'd been the unwanted result. His mother had dumped him with his father when he'd been two weeks old and walked away, never to return. He'd been a mistake, a terrible inconvenience, and he'd never been able to forget it. He would not allow his own child to suffer a similar fate.

'Signor Falcone?' The crackle of his intercom had him turning. He reached over and pressed a button.

'Yes?'

'A Signor Andretti to see you, *signor*,' his assistant said, and Rico's heart leapt with fierce hope. Andretti was the private investigator he'd hired a month ago. 'Send him in.'

Moments later the neatly dressed man, slim and anonymous-looking, stepped into Rico's office.

'Well?' Rico demanded tersely. 'Is there news?'

'The marriage to al bin Nur has been called off. Apparently the Princess refused to marry him, and so he is remaining married to the governess he kidnapped.'

Rico had heard already, through the investigator, how Halina's fiancé had kidnapped the wrong woman and married her in so much haste that he hadn't ascertained her name first. A fool's mistake, one he would never make. He dismissed them both; they were irrelevant to him now that he knew Halina had called off the marriage. 'And the Princess?'

'I believe she is currently staying in a royal residence in the north of Abkar, a remote location.'

'Are you sure?'

Andretti shrugged. 'I bribed a maid in the palace, who told me the Princess had left about a month ago. It seems the Princess is going to stay in the north for some time…' Andretti paused meaningfully. 'At least nine months.'

Nine months. Shock iced through him, followed by a fiery rage. She must be pregnant and she hadn't told him. Hadn't even tried to tell him. Instead she'd gone into hiding…*hiding from him?* He took a deep breath, steadying himself.

'Thank you.' As his head cleared a new emotion took the place of that first lick of anger, something that took him by surprise. Hope. Joy. If Halina was pregnant…he was going to be a father. He was going to have a child. One he would keep by his side, for whom he would fight to the death Someone he would never, ever leave. Not as he'd been left.

'Do you have the location of the palace?'

Andretti withdrew a folded piece of paper from his pocket. 'Right here, *signor.*'

It took Rico only a few hours to make the necessary arrangements. By nightfall he was on a plane to Abkar's capital city, where the following morning he picked up the all-terrain SUV he'd bought over the phone. The palace where Halina was staying was three hundred miles north of the city through inhospitable desert, a landscape of huge, craggy boulders and endless sand. She really must have wanted to get away from him.

Of course, she could have been banished there but, judging from all the gossip Rico had heard through the private investigator about how the Sultan spoiled his four daughters, Rico doubted it. This was a choice Halina had made. A decision to hide from him.

He drove the first hundred miles before the sun got too hot, his body taut with suppressed energy, his mind focused with grim purpose on the task ahead.

When the sun reached its zenith he stopped the Jeep and sheltered under a rock from the worst of the midday heat. Along with the SUV he'd arranged for provisions to survive in the desert for a week. He always made sure to be prepared in every situation, even one as extraordinary as this.

As for when he arrived at the palace... His mouth curved grimly. He would be prepared then, as well.

He stopped again for the night and then drove as soon as the first pearly-grey light of dawn lightened the sky. The sun had risen and bathed the desert in a fierce orange glow by the time he arrived at the palace, a remote outpost that looked as if it had been hewn from the boulders strewn about the undulating dunes.

Rico parked the SUV far enough away that he wouldn't be noticed and grabbed a pair of binoculars. From this distance the palace's walls looked smooth and windowless; the place truly was a fortress, and the nearest town of any description was over a hundred miles away. Halina had chosen as remote a place as possible to hide from him, but it was no place for a young pregnant woman. The sooner he got Halina out of there, the better.

As the mother of his child she belonged with him— by his side, in his bed. As the mother of his child, she would raise that child with him, so he or she would never know a day without love, would never feel abandoned, an inconvenience to be discarded. A child needed both mother and father, and Halina would be there for their child and for Rico...as his wife.

CHAPTER FIVE

HALINA GAZED OUT of the window of her bedroom at the endless desert and suppressed a dispirited sigh. She'd been at Mansiyy Rimal, the Palace of Forgotten Sands, for nearly a month and it had been the longest month of her life. The prospect of spending several more months here filled her with despair, but it was better than contemplating what might come after that.

The week after her night with Rico was a blur of misery and fear. Her father, always so genial and cheerful, had become a complete stranger, cold and frightening in his fury, and Halina had shrunk before him, afraid of a man who had had only cause to spoil and indulge her until now.

He'd forced her to take a pregnancy test as soon as possible, and when it had come up positive the bottom had dropped out of Halina's stomach—and her world. She'd waited, barricaded in her bedroom, forbidden even to see her younger sisters, on whom she was now considered a bad influence, while her father negotiated on her behalf. He wanted her to marry Prince Zayed after all, now that she was spoiled goods and unsuitable for any other man. And Prince Zayed had seemed willing to go ahead, although reluctant.

Halina had used her last remnant of strength to resist

such a fate, especially when she'd seen how Zayed and Olivia had fallen in love with each other. She'd thought she could bear a loveless marriage, but not when her husband so obviously cared for someone else.

Her steadfast refusal was the straw that had broken the remaining remnant of her father's terse goodwill. Halina still couldn't bear to think of the torturous aftermath, those days of despair and fear. Eventually, in cold fury, her father had sent her here to this remote outpost in the cruellest stretch of desert, with only a few stony-faced staff for company, to remain until she gave birth.

After that she had no idea what would happen to her or her child, and that was something that filled her with terror. The Sultan had warned her that he would take her child away from her, but Halina tried to believe that once his grandchild was born he would relent. Her father loved her. At least, he had once. Surely he couldn't be so cruel, despite how she'd disappointed him? Yet he'd already shown just how cruel he could be.

Escape was an impossibility—she was constantly watched by the palace staff, and in any case there was three hundred miles of inhospitable desert between her and the nearest civilisation. She was well and truly trapped.

Halina turned from the window, surveying the spartan room that was to be her bedchamber for the coming months. The palace was a barren place both inside and out, without any modern conveniences or amusements. All she had were a few books, some drawing materials and endless time.

Halina pressed one hand to her still-flat stomach, trying to fight the nausea that had become her constant companion a few weeks ago. She felt lonelier than she'd ever imagined feeling, and far more grown up. She looked back on her evening with Rico and wanted to take her old, girlish self by the shoulders and give her a hard shake. What on earth had she been thinking? Why had she gambled her future away for a single, reckless encounter? The sex, fabulous as it had felt at the time, most certainly had not been worth it.

Restlessly Halina plucked a sketchbook from the table and a few charcoal pencils. She'd always enjoyed sketching, and now she had endless hours to hone her skill. Not that there was much to draw but craggy rocks and sand dunes.

A sudden commotion from outside her room had Halina stilling, the charcoal barely touched to the paper.

'You cannot, sir!' Ammar, one of the palace staff, exclaimed, then the door was thrown open so hard it rocked on its hinges, swinging back and hitting the wall.

Rico Falcone stood there, dressed in desert camouflage fatigues, his sharp cheekbones flushed, his eyes glittering. Halina's mouth dropped open and she found she couldn't speak.

'You,' he said in a low, authoritative voice, 'Are coming with me.'

Ammar burst in behind him. 'You cannot take the Princess!'

'The Princess is pregnant with my child,' Rico returned evenly, the words vibrating with taut anger. 'She is coming with me.' His tone left no room for disagreement.

For a second Ammar looked uncertain. He wasn't trained to defend the palace; it was remote, as forgotten as its name, and he was nothing more than a steward, meant to fetch and carry. Sultan Hassan had never anticipated anyone looking for Halina, much less finding her. She was here with a skeleton staff who were more used to cooking and gardening than wielding arms or defending the ancient stone walls.

'Halina.' Rico stretched out one hand. 'Come now.'

Halina would have resented his commanding tone if she'd felt she had any choice. But when the alternative to going with Rico was mouldering in this palace, and then in all likelihood having her baby taken away from her, she knew what she'd choose. What she had to choose. Wordlessly she rose from where she sat and crossed the room to take his hand.

The feel of his warm, dry palm encasing hers sent a shower of untimely sparks through Halina's arm and then her whole body. Quite suddenly, and with overwhelming force, she remembered just how much she'd been attracted to Rico. How he'd overpowered her senses, her reason, everything. And how completely dangerous that had been.

He pulled her towards him and then started down the steep, turreted stairs while Ammar made useless noises of protest.

'Wait—what about my things?'

'I will buy you whatever you need.'

A shiver of apprehension rippled over her skin. What exactly was she agreeing to?

'What am I to tell the Sultan?' Ammar demanded, sounding both furious and wretched.

Rico turned, his hand still encasing hers. 'You may tell the Sultan,' he said in a low, sure voice, 'That Princess Halina is with the father of her child, where she belongs, and where she will stay.'

Ammar's mouth opened silently and Halina had no time to ask questions or reconsider her choice as Rico led her out of the palace with sure, confident strides.

'How on earth did you get here?' she demanded as he strode through the courtyard and then out the front gates.

'I bought an SUV.'

'And how did you get Ammar to open the gates?'

'I told him who I was.'

'You mean—?'

'A billionaire with considerable power and the father of your child.' He turned back to subject her to a dark glance. 'He saw reason quite quickly. Why did you not tell me, Halina?'

'Not *tell* you?' Halina repeated in disbelief. 'As if—'

He cut her off with a slash of his hand. 'Now is not the time. We need to get back to Rome.'

'Rome,' Halina repeated faintly. 'You're taking me to *Rome*?'

Rico gave her another scathing look. 'Of course. Where else would we go?'

'I… I don't know.' She felt dizzy with everything that had happened so quickly. She didn't even know what questions to ask, what answers she was ready to hear. Why had Rico taken her? What was he going to do with her?

They'd reached Rico's SUV parked a short distance from the palace behind a cluster of craggy rocks.

'You know,' Halina said shakily as Rico opened the passenger door and she climbed in, 'Ammar will radio my father and he'll send out guards to find us. To take me back.' Her father would be furious that after everything she'd been kidnapped after all. And Halina knew he wouldn't leave her alone once her baby was born. He'd take away her child and then marry her to whomever he could find that was politically suitable and willing to take damaged goods.

'I am not worried about your father,' Rico dismissed.

'Maybe you should be,' Halina tossed back. She couldn't believe she'd forgotten how impossibly arrogant he was. 'Considering he is a head of state and he will send out trained soldiers who know this terrain far better than you do.'

'True, which is why I will not be traversing it,' Rico informed her shortly. He swung into the driver's side and then pulled away, choking clouds of sand and dust rising as the tyres peeled through the desert. Halina pressed back against the seat, every movement jolting right through her bones.

'Where are we going, then?'

'North, to Kalidar. I have a helicopter waiting at the border.'

'A helicopter?' Halina stared at him in disbelief. 'How did you arrange such a thing? How did you even find me?'

'I told you that if you were pregnant you would be my paramount concern.'

'Yes, but...' Halina shook her head slowly. Rico's steadfast determination shocked, humbled and terrified her all at once. What else was this man, this stranger, capable of? The father of her child. 'Where will we go after Kalidar?' she asked numbly.

'I told you, Rome. I have a private jet waiting to take us there in its capital city, Arjah.' Rico's face was set in grim lines as he navigated the rocky terrain. 'We should be at the helicopter within the hour.'

Halina lapsed into silence, still dazed by the day's events. To think only moments ago she'd been contemplating how bored she would be, stuck in a desert palace for the better part of a year. Now she didn't know what to feel.

The jolting movements of the SUV eventually lulled her into an uneasy doze, only to wake when it stopped as Rico cut the engine. The sun was hot and bright above, creating a dazzling sparkle on the undulating sand dunes.

In front of them was a helicopter bearing Kalidar's military insignia.

'How...?' Halina began, but then merely shook her head. Should she really be surprised at the extent of Rico's power? He was a billionaire, ruthless, arrogant and used to being obeyed. She had no doubt that he could get whatever he wanted...including her.

Rico helped her climb into the helicopter and then settled into a seat, putting on her headgear to muffle the powerful sound of the machine's blades as it started up into the sky.

Halina watched the desert drop away with fascinated disbelief, part of her still blessedly numb as she wondered what on earth her future held now—and how afraid she should be.

Rico stared straight ahead as the helicopter moved over the harsh and rugged landscape, a mixture of exultation and anger rushing through him. He'd done it. He'd found Halina. He'd brought her with him. Yet despite the triumph he felt at having accomplished that he couldn't let go of his anger that she would have hidden her pregnancy from him, his own child. Considering the nature of his origins and childhood, the possibility was even more repugnant to him. She would have turned him into a liar, the worst sort of man, without him even knowing.

He glanced at Halina who was sitting still, her hands in her lap, her gaze resting on the horizon yet seeming to be turned inward. Her face was pale, her figure slenderer than when he'd last seen her. In fact, now that he was looking at her properly, she seemed entirely different from the innocent yet knowing siren who had tempted him in Rome wearing a sexy dress and stiletto heels, everything about her lush and wanton.

Now she was wearing a drab tunic and loose trousers in a nondescript beige, both garments hanging on her gaunt frame. Her hair, once loose and wild, was now secured in a simple ponytail low down on her neck. She was as far a cry from the woman he'd made love to as was possible. But despite what she'd done Rico felt an inconvenient shaft of desire as he remembered the feel of her body against his, the silken slide of her limbs and the honeyed sweetness of her mouth. He looked away, determined not to give in to that unwanted emotion right now.

The next time he slept with Halina, it would be as her husband, their relationship made permanent for the sake of their child and the security he intended his son or daughter to know. The next time he slept with Halina, he wouldn't lose control. Even now the memory of how far he'd gone, how lost in her he'd been, made him grit his teeth with regret and shame. Never again.

The helicopter started to descend, and moments later they touched down in a remote and barren location where he'd arranged for another SUV to pick them up and take them to Arjah, from where they would fly to Rome.

Halina looked startled as she gazed around at the landscape, as inhospitable as at the Palace of Forgotten Sands.

'Where are we?' she asked as she took Rico's proffered hand and stepped out of the helicopter. The wind was kicking up, blowing sand everywhere, and she lifted one slender hand to shield her eyes from the dust.

'We're about a hundred miles from Arjah.'

Her eyes widened. 'So far?'

'Such measures were necessary.' He hadn't been sure how Sultan Hassan would respond, and he wanted to deal with the head of state on his own terms, back in Italy with Halina as his wife, not during some ill-advised skirmish in the desert.

Halina's lips trembled and she pressed them together. 'I see.' Her face was pale, and she swayed slightly where she stood. Rico realised, with an uncomfortable jolt, that she was tired. Exhausted, by the looks of it. And, of course, pregnant.

'Not too much longer now,' Rico said, even though it would be another three or four hours at least jolting across the desert in the SUV until they reached Arjah.

'Okay,' Halina murmured, and headed towards the car. She fell asleep curled up on the back seat, her dark hair spread over the seat. Rico had dismissed the driver, who had joined the helicopter pilot in a safe return to Abkar. It was just the two of them as the night fell, stars twinkling in an endless sky, until the wind started up again and obliterated nearly everything.

After another hour of painstakingly inching across the rugged sands Rico was forced to stop. He glanced back at Halina, who had risen sleepily as she'd felt the vehicle come to a halt.

'Are we there…?'

'No.' Rico's voice was terse. This wasn't part of his plan. This was out of his control, and he didn't like it. 'It looks like a sandstorm is brewing.' He'd known it was a possibility, but he'd hoped they could afford being caught in the crosswinds. 'We'll have to spend the night here.'

'Here? Where?' Halina pushed her hair out of her face as she looked around. There was nothing to see but dust and dark. 'But…where are we?'

'In the middle of nowhere,' Rico said with a humourless laugh. 'About fifty miles from Arjah.' Spending the night in the middle of a sandstorm was not a good idea, but he didn't have any others. It was too dangerous to keep driving.

'But it's a sandstorm,' Halina said, and she sounded

genuinely afraid. 'Rico, do you know how dangerous these are? People can be swallowed up in an instant— *consumed!*'

'I know.' Grimly he reached for a kerchief and tied it around his nose and mouth. 'Stay in the car and cover your face when I open the door.'

'What are you doing?'

'Going out to make us a shelter.'

'But shouldn't we stay in the car?'

'No, because it will be buried by the sand, and then we'll never get out.'

'Oh.' She swallowed, her fragile throat working, her face pale, eyes wide. 'All right.' Setting her chin with a determined courage that strangely touched Rico's hardened heart, she lifted her tunic to cover her mouth and nose.

Taking a deep breath, Rico opened the door. The wind and sand hit him full in the face, making his eyes sting and cutting off his vision. Despite the covering of his mouth and nose, the sand worked its way in, filling his mouth with grit and choking him.

Quickly Rico closed the door behind him and hunched his shoulders against the unforgiving onslaught. He gathered provisions from the back of the SUV—a tent, water, food and blankets. As swiftly as he could, his head bowed against the relentless wind and sand, he erected a tent against the partial shelter of a massive boulder. It wasn't much, but it would help a little against the wildness of the wind and sand.

Then he battled his way back to the car which was already becoming covered in sand and grit. He wrenched open the door and reached for Halina; she grabbed onto his hand with both of hers.

With his arm around her shoulders, their heads tucked

low, he led her to their shelter, pulling the flap closed behind them and taping it shut to keep out the blowing sands.

Halina fell onto the floor of the tent on her hands and knees, coughing.

'Are you all right?' Rico knelt next to her, one hand on her back as she shuddered and coughed.

'Yes,' she finally gasped out. "Although I feel as if I've swallowed half of the Sahara.' She looked up blinking, her hair tangled about her sand-dusted face.

'Here.' He reached for one of the plastic gallon containers of water he'd arranged to have packed in the SUV. Fortunately they would not suffer through the storm, as long as they could stay safe through the worst of the wind.

Rico poured a tin cup full of water and handed it to her. 'Slowly,' he advised, and she nodded and took a few careful sips. He held her gaze as she drank; he'd forgotten how lovely and dark her eyes were, how thick and full her lashes. Something stirred inside him, something half-forgotten and ever-insistent.

'Thank you,' she murmured as she lowered the cup. Rico dabbed the corner of a cloth in the remaining water and then gently wiped the sand from her face. Halina sucked in a shocked breath, staying completely still as he swept the cloth along her forehead and cheekbones, her dark, wide gaze tracking his.

What he'd intended to be expedient and practical suddenly felt erotic and charged. Desire throbbed through him as he continued to wipe the sand away, conscious of Halina's soft skin beneath his fingers, the pulse hammering in her throat, every hitched breath she drew.

'Rico…' His name was a whisper, whether plea or protest he didn't know. He dropped the cloth, not wanting the distraction of desire at this point, as insistent as it was. He needed to focus on their future…their child.

'You should eat,' he said roughly. 'You need to keep up your strength. You look as if you have wasted away to little more than skin and bone.'

'I've had morning sickness. All day sickness, really.' She smiled wanly but her eyes were dark and troubled. 'You're angry. Why?'

He was, but he disliked how she made this about his unruly emotion rather than her deliberate actions. 'Eat,' he said as he yanked out some pita bread and dried meat. 'Then we'll talk.'

Halina took the bread and nibbled on it, barely swallowing a mouthful. 'What are we going to talk about?'

'We could begin,' Rico said, an edge entering his voice, 'with why you dared to attempt to hide your pregnancy from me. Going all the way to that godforsaken place to keep it from me, even.' His eyes flashed fire and the pita bread dropped from Halina's fingers.

'Is that what you think…?'

'It's what I know.' He picked up the bread and pushed it towards her. 'But first, eat. There will be time enough to discuss the past…as well as our future.'

CHAPTER SIX

HALINA STARED AT Rico in disbelief, although why she should be surprised by his high-handed manner she had no idea. It was par for the course. Still, she struggled to find a suitable reply. Her mind was spinning and her stomach seethed. She was not at her best for an all-out confrontation.

'Eat,' Rico said again, and because she knew she needed the sustenance, she nibbled the pita once more. 'You look terrible,' he remarked after a moment and she let out a huff of humourless laughter.

'Why, thank you very much.'

'Why have you not been taking care of yourself?'

She lowered the bit of bread and eyed him with disbelief. 'Seriously? You're going to ask me that?'

'What else am I supposed to ask?'

She shook her head. 'God only knows. You blame me for everything, even being a virgin.'

'You should have told me.'

'Not that again. Are we going to revisit that particular argument now?'

'No,' Rico answered tightly. 'We are not.'

Which made Halina's stomach clench unpleasantly because she didn't think she wanted to talk about the other matters that might be on Rico's agenda. The courage that had been buoying her briefly, sparked by his sheer pig-headedness, trickled away.

She glanced at him from under her lashes, taking in the obdurate set of his jaw, the sharp cheekbones, the hard eyes. She'd forgotten how intimidating he was, especially when he wasn't trying to get her into bed.

The memory of just how easily she'd tumbled into that bed made her cringe with shame. She'd had nearly two months of public and private shame to deal with—her father's icy fury, her mother's heartbroken disappointment, her own inner torment. Even the lowliest of the palace staff had sensed her humiliation. No one had remained unscathed by her actions, least of all herself. When she thought of what she'd almost had to do…

She tossed the bread aside, her stomach too unsettled even to think of food. Rico frowned.

'I said you should eat.'

'I know, but I don't feel up to it. And I don't think you want me retching in this small space.' She wrapped her arms around her knees, feeling lonelier even than she had when she'd been at the Palace of Forgotten Sands, and the days had been endless and empty. Now she was in a tiny, enclosed space with a man who seemed to be taking up all the air and energy and she felt even more alone…and afraid. The relief that she'd been rescued was replaced by a greater fear. 'Frying pan and fire' came alarmingly to mind.

'Try the meat,' Rico said gruffly, handing her a strip of meat that looked as tough as leather. Halina couldn't tell if he was trying to be kind or just insistent. She took it reluctantly, because she really was feeling wobbly inside. Even though she didn't like Rico's methods or manner, she knew he was right. She'd lost nearly a stone since the nausea had hit. For her baby's sake, she needed to eat.

'Has your morning sickness been very bad?' he asked after a moment as she worried the salted meat with her teeth.

'Yes.' Halina swallowed. 'For the last month or so I've barely been able to keep anything down.' She managed a wry smile, her tone tart. 'Which is why I look so terrible.'

Rico, of course, did not look remotely abashed by her reminder. 'You need to take better care of yourself. Why hasn't your doctor prescribed something for the nausea?'

Halina stared at him, torn between fury and an exhausted exasperation. 'I haven't seen a doctor.' Not one she wanted to remember, anyway. The one doctor she'd seen... But, no. She didn't want to think about that.

'What?' Rico's mouth dropped open in outrage before he snapped it shut, his eyes narrowing. 'Why on earth not?'

She shook her head wearily. 'You have no idea.'

'Then enlighten me.'

Halina sat back, wondering whether she had the strength or will to explain to Rico about the last two months, and then no doubt be subjected to his scorn and condemnation—or maybe just his disbelief.

'Lina.' His voice was rough, urgent. '*Ha*lina. Tell me what you mean.'

'I was called Lina as a child,' she said inconsequentially. 'I didn't lie when I told you that's what my name was.'

'That is hardly my concern now.'

'But it was before.' She was splitting hairs, but she was too emotionally fragile to battle all this out now. 'Rico, I'm tired and it's raging out there. Can't we leave this for a little while?' Maybe another day she'd have the strength to admit everything she'd endured. As for now, she just wanted to sleep, if she could.

The wind had picked up even more and was battering

the sides of the tent, howling around them, a relentless monster eager for prey.

Rico gave a terse nod. 'Very well. As you say, now is not the time or the place—but I will have answers, Halina. Of that there is no doubt.'

'Fine.'

He unrolled two sleeping bags and shook them out. With an entirely different kind of queasy feeling, Halina realised how close they'd be sleeping to each other— shoulder to shoulder, thigh to thigh. Not that anything was going to happen in the middle of a sandstorm, and with her feeling like a plate of left-over pudding. But still... She was aware of him. Even now.

She adjusted the shapeless tunic and trousers she wore, as if they could offer her more coverage. As if Rico would even be tempted. She knew she looked terrible and he'd already told her so. Feeling silly for even considering such a possibility, Halina scooted into the sleeping bag and drew it up to her chin.

Rico eyed her for a moment, his mouth compressed, a look of cool amusement on his features.

'Are you worried for your virtue?' he drawled. 'Because, I assure you, it's not in any danger.'

'I don't have any virtue left to lose,' Halina retorted. 'You made sure of that.'

Rico's face darkened. 'Are you going to blame me for that now? Because—'

'No, Rico, I'm not. I should have told you. Trust me, I know. I wish I had, because then—' She cut off that unfortunate thought before she could give it voice. She would not regret her baby. It had already cost her too much, innocent life that it was. 'I just want to go to sleep,' she said. And then, pointedly, she turned away from him on her side and closed her eyes.

Sleep, however, felt impossible. Her stomach seethed, as did her mind. What was she doing here? And what was going to happen? Her life was in chaos, and the only sure thing was the baby nestled in her womb. But even that little one's life was being thrown up in the air like a set of dice... Rico was entirely in control, as he always was. Whether she was in a fortress or a tent, Halina acknowledged starkly, she was still imprisoned, her fate at the whim of another, and in this case a complete stranger.

Next to her she heard Rico moving around and then sliding into his sleeping bag. The rustle of fabric in the darkness felt intimate, and Halina inched a little bit away, not that there was much room.

Inconvenient memories were sliding through her mind in an all too vivid montage. The feel of Rico's body on hers. In hers. The way she'd given herself to him, utterly and overwhelmingly. It had felt as if she hadn't even had a choice, but of course she had. She'd just made the wrong one.

Then, even though it only hurt, Halina let herself think that treacherous *what if?* What if she hadn't been so stupid as to sacrifice her entire future for a single night with Rico Falcone? Where would she be now? Would Zayed al bin Nur have stayed married to her friend Olivia? Halina hoped so. She knew they were in love, and it would have been even worse to be married to a man who loved another than to be where she was now, pregnant and shackled to a man who regarded her with contempt and disdain.

So if Zayed stayed married to Olivia and she hadn't been pregnant...right now she might be free, the future stretched out in front of her, shining and brimming with possibility.

Of course, realistically her father would have arranged

another marriage to another suitable stranger, but Halina didn't want to think about that now. She had enough to deal with, sleeping next to *this* unsuitable stranger.

'Stop wriggling around,' Rico said irritably, his voice sounding loud in the enclosed space.

'I'm not wriggling,' Halina returned indignantly. 'I'm barely moving.' She'd been staying completely still, as if Rico might forget she was there.

Rico just sighed as if she were simply too tedious to deal with. It was going to be a long night. It was going to be a long life. What had Rico meant, 'their future'? She shuddered to think.

Eventually, simply because she was so utterly exhausted, Halina fell into a restless doze, only to wake suddenly, her body on high alert.

'What...?' she began, blinking in the darkness. Outside the wind was shrieking, and the sides of the tent sagged inwards from the weight of both the wind and the sand, and Halina felt as if she was being entombed. Perhaps she was.

A shudder of terror went through her and she whimpered out loud. The storm raged all around them, seemingly ready to consume their tent in its ravenous maw. Heaven help them both, was this going to be the end of them both?

'It will pass.' Rico's voice was low and steady, a thrum of comfort.

'How do you know?' Halina asked in a high, faltering voice. 'We could be buried alive.' She started to tremble, her teeth chattering with pure, unadulterated fear.

Then, to her shock, she felt Rico's hands on her shoulders and he pulled her against him, fitting her body next to his so she could feel the hard, warm press of his chest, his powerful thighs.

She stayed rigid with shock for a few seconds, then Rico began to rub comforting circles over her back with the palm of his hand, and Halina started to relax.

It felt so good to be held. It felt so safe. Until this moment she hadn't realised how much she craved both the comfort and security of another person's touch. She closed her eyes as she snuggled into him, telling herself this didn't count. Extraordinary measures for extraordinary circumstances—that was all this was. In the morning she would be back to keeping her distance and composure—and regaining her strength.

Rico continued to rub Halina's back as he felt her melt into him and he tried not to react. Even in her gaunt state she was pliant, warm and womanly. He desired her even now, with the storm raging all around them and their lives at stake.

'Have you never been in a sandstorm before?' he asked, trying to distract himself from his own demanding need.

'No, I've only seen them from a distance. From the safety of a palace.' She let out a choked laugh, her breathing fanning his neck. 'I've led a very restricted life, Rico.'

A very privileged life. Her upbringing was a world away from his on the docks of Salerno, a mother who hadn't wanted him at all and a father...

But why the hell was he thinking about his father now?

Seeing Halina, knowing she was carrying his child, had opened a need in him and, worse, a vulnerability that he struggled to contain. Control was paramount. He would provide for his child, he would love him or her, his own flesh and blood, he would make a stable family that his child could trust in absolutely. But he would not give in to this inconvenient and shaming need; he would never allow himself to be weak.

To make the point to himself, he inched a little bit away from Halina's soft, tempting body. Outside the wind howled and the tent continued to be battered mercilessly.

'Have you ever been in a sandstorm?' Halina asked, moving closer to him again, one fine-boned hand resting on his chest. Resigned, Rico put his arms more securely around her, telling himself he was doing it for her sake, not his own.

'No, I have not.'

'Then you don't know if it will pass.'

'I checked the weather before I set out on this journey. The high winds were only meant to last a few hours.'

'Somehow I don't think sandstorms bow down to weather reports,' Halina returned. 'They are entirely unpredictable, coming out of nowhere, sometimes lasting for days.' Her voice hitched. 'What if we're stuck out here for that long? What if we're buried alive?'

'We won't be.'

'You don't know that, Rico. You don't control nature, as much as you might like to.'

Of course he didn't, but he prided himself on living a life where he always maintained control. Where he was always totally prepared. Where nothing ever surprised him, because then he wouldn't betray himself, his doubt or his need. Yet, just as Halina had said, he could not control a sandstorm, and he feared this was just the beginning of all the things he would not be able to control.

His arms tightened around Halina. 'I admit, the storm is stronger than I anticipated, but I brought the necessary equipment and food, and we are well positioned to wait it out. We'll be safe, Halina. I will make sure of it.'

Halina relaxed a fraction. 'I'm sorry,' she murmured. 'I don't mean to overreact.'

Rico couldn't keep a wry smile from touching his lips as he stroked her hair. No matter his promises, they were in a life-threatening situation. He'd hardly call it over-reacting. 'You're forgiven,' he said, and Halina let out a little huff of laughter.

'Even when you're being kind, you're arrogant, do you know that?'

'It isn't arrogance when I'm right.'

She just laughed again, her lips brushing his neck, sending gooseflesh rippling along his skin. Desire arrowed through his body and he knew Halina felt it too by the way she tensed in his arms, shifting a little so she was looking up at him, her hair cascading down her back in an inky blue-black river that Rico could just make out in the darkness of the tent.

His mind blurred and he started to lower his head to claim her mouth with his own. He could imagine the kiss, the rightness of it. He could already taste it, like a drink of clean, sweet water. He heard Halina's quick, indrawn breath as she waited for him to close the space between their mouths and it shocked him into clarity. He lifted his head.

He could not complicate their relationship with sex. Not yet. Not until he'd made it very clear what he expected of Halina and their marriage. Of their life together, or lack of it. Until then, he'd keep his distance, for both their sakes.

He heard Halina draw another shuddering breath and knew she'd felt his withdrawal. She moved a little bit away from him, or tried to. Rico stilled her, keeping her close, although he wasn't sure why. Surely it was better to let her go, give them both a little distance? Still, he stayed where he was, and made sure she did as well.

'Go to sleep,' he said gruffly. Halina did not reply, but after a few endless moments he felt her body start to relax again, and then he heard the deep, even breaths of sleep as the storm continued to rage.

When he awoke the tent was hot and airless, awash in a greyish morning light, and the world was still. Halina was still snuggled in his arms and now he could see her properly—the luxurious spill of her hair, her lush lips slightly parted, her thick, spiky lashes fanning onto her cheeks.

He brushed a tendril of hair from her face and her eyes fluttered open. For a taut second they simply stared at one another, their bodies pressed close together, Rico's already responding.

Halina moved away first, wriggling away from him as her face turned fiery. 'The storm has stopped,' she muttered as she scooted across the tent, putting as much space between them as she could, considering the limitations of their environment.

'So it has.'

She peered out, as if she could see right through the dark canvas. 'Are we going to be able to get out?'

'I should think so.'

It took some doing, but after Rico had torn the tape from the entrance to the tent he managed to dig them out.

'Only half-buried,' he said with a smile, and then reached for Halina's hand to help her out.

Outside they both stretched and blinked in the glare of the morning sunlight, the landscape made even more strange by the ravages of the storm. Drifts of sand were piled on either side of the tent and the SUV was completely buried, no more than a large hump in the sand.

New dunes had formed, turning the once-flat stretch into a newly undulating lunar-like landscape.

'Goodness,' Halina murmured. Her arms were wrapped around herself, her face pale as she looked around. 'I'm amazed we're still here.'

'Yes.' Rico eyed the buried SUV. It would take him several hours to dig it out. 'We need to get going. Why don't you refresh yourself? Eat and drink something? I'll start digging out the car.'

'Why are we going to Rome, Rico?'

'Because that is where both my business and home are.' He rolled up his sleeves and started scooping the sand away from the car with his hands. Unfortunately he had not thought to pack a spade in his desert provisions.

'And what will we do when we get to Rome?' Halina pressed. Rico gritted his teeth. He didn't want to have this conversation, not until they were safely back in Rome, in his domain. But Halina seemed determined to discover his intentions, and Rico decided she might as well know them. It wasn't as if she could escape, anyway.

'We're going to Rome,' he said clearly, his gaze on the sand-covered car, 'because that is where we are going to live. Where my child is going to be born…and where you are going to marry me.'

CHAPTER SEVEN

HALINA STARED AT Rico in dawning realisation—and horror.

'Marry you?' she squeaked. *That's* what you have in mind?'

'Yes.'

'But...but we don't know each other! And we don't even like each other.'

'I believe those statements are contradictory. And, in any case, you were prepared to marry more of a stranger to you than I am mere weeks ago.'

Halina flushed, not needing the reminder. 'I was prepared to do that out of duty,' she began, but fell silent when Rico gave a decisive shake of his head.

'And you will marry me out of duty as well. Duty to our unborn child.'

'We don't have to be married for our—'

'Yes.' Rico cut her off. 'We do. It is important to me, of paramount importance, that my child grows up in a stable and loving home.'

'Loving?' Halina repeated incredulously. 'But you don't love me.'

'I will love my child,' Rico stated flatly, his voice thrumming with certainly. 'But now is not the time to discuss this. We have more important matters to attend to.' He nodded towards the tent. 'Eat, drink and refresh yourself. We leave in an hour.'

Biting her lip, preferring not to argue with him when he was in such an intractable mood, Halina wordlessly turned and went back into the tent.

She choked down some more pita bread and dried meat, knowing she needed the sustenance, then washed her face with a sparing amount of water and rinsed out her mouth. With her hair tidied and her clothes straightened, she was as presentable as she was going to be, but she didn't feel at all ready for whatever lay ahead.

Marriage. She shouldn't have been surprised, she realised. Rico moved people about like pawns on his personal chessboard. Why should she, why should marriage, be any different?

Because he was the classic commitment-phobe who never kept a woman for more than a night. But with a sinking sensation Halina acknowledged that marriage to Rico Falcone was most likely not going to look or feel like a normal marriage. Not that she knew what that felt like. If she married Rico, she would just be exchanging one expedient union for another. One stranger for another. A loving, normal marriage had never been within her grasp, no matter how much she might have wanted it. Her life had never been her own.

Halina rolled up the sleeping bags and repacked their provisions in the canvas rucksack Rico had brought. Then, taking a deep breath, she went in search of her rescuer and captor.

He was hard at work digging out the SUV; he had shucked off his shirt and his tawny skin gleamed like polished bronze under the unforgiving glare of the desert sun. Halina blinked, trying not to let her gaze move slowly over his perfectly sculpted pectoral muscles, the six-pack definition of his taut abdomen. She failed and, even worse, Rico turned and caught her staring openly at his incredible physique.

His mouth quirked and something like satisfaction flashed in his eyes. He jerked his head in a nod towards their vehicle. 'I should be finished in another half hour.'

'Can I help…?'

'No, of course not. You're pregnant.'

'Pregnant, not an invalid.'

'Even so.' Rico turned back to the car. 'I do not wish you to tax yourself.'

With a sigh Halina wondered if Rico intended to wrap her in cotton wool for the next seven months. Then, with a jolt, she wondered why she was thinking this way. Was she just going to roll over and do whatever he said, including binding her life to his for ever? Would Rico let her do anything else?

Her choices, as ever, were limited. She'd never known what freedom felt like save, perhaps, for her one night with Rico. And look what had happened then.

Her mind in a ferment of indecision and uncertainty, Halina turned back to the tent. 'I'll pack up our things.'

Half an hour later the vehicle was clear and Rico had thrown their things into the back. His expression was grim and determined as he slid into the driver's seat. 'We have another two hours' drive to Arjah.'

'What if my father's soldiers are there? What if we're found?'

'We won't be.'

And if they were? Her father must have discovered her absence by now and most likely would have sent soldiers out to find her. And what then? Rico wouldn't give her up without a fight, but even he was no match against trained soldiers and weapons. Halina leaned her head back against the seat and closed her eyes. It was too much to think about on top of everything else.

'Any soldiers your father sent out would have been caught in the sandstorm, the same as we were,' Rico said. 'We have some time.'

Halina just nodded, not trusting herself to speak. In such a scenario she didn't even know what she'd prefer. To stay with Rico, or be rescued by her father? Both options seemed abysmal in their own way.

A bumpy few hours passed as they jolted along, the rough desert track gradually becoming a tarmac road, and then the low mud-brick buildings and handful of skyscrapers came into view—Arjah, the capital city of Kalidar.

Halina felt herself getting more and more tense as Rico drove through the city, his expression harsh and grim, his fingers tight on the steering wheel. They made it to the airport without notice, and Rico drove directly to a private plane waiting in its own bay.

Halina's breath came out in a shudder of relief that they had not been caught or detained. So she would prefer to stay with Rico. Her own reaction had betrayed her. That was why she'd left with him in the first place, she supposed—because she'd rather risk her future with this man than face the continuing wrath of her father, her baby taken away, her body given to a man she'd never even met.

Rico gave a grimly satisfied nod. 'It is just as I had arranged.' He parked the SUV and strode out to meet the plane's crew who were waiting for them on the tarmac. Halina followed, feeling exhausted and emotionally overwhelmed. If she got on that plane, it would take her all the way to Rome. And then where would she be? What would she do? What would Rico do?

'Come. There is no time to delay.' Rico beckoned her forward. 'You will be more comfortable on the plane.'

Halina hesitated, even though she knew there was no point. No choice. What was she going to do? Make a sprint for the airport? She had no money, no clothes, nothing. No resources at all, and no friends to help. For a second she thought of Olivia and Prince Zayed, who might be currently residing in the royal palace at Arjah. She could seek sanctuary with them perhaps, but did she want to do that—be the unexpected and undoubtedly unwelcome guest of her former fiancé and his new bride? She'd be putting them into an impossible position as well as herself, and that was assuming she could even get to the royal palace from here, which she probably couldn't.

'Halina.' Rico's voice was touched with impatience. 'Everyone is waiting.' On leaden legs Halina walked slowly towards him and as he took her arm she climbed the steps to the plane.

She'd been on Abkar's royal jet many times before, going to and from school, but it felt different now, walking into Rico's own plane. She glanced around at the sumptuous leather sofas and low coffee tables. Several crew members were waiting attentively, their faces carefully bland. Did they know who she was, that she was pregnant with their employer's child?

Rico strode in behind her and gestured for her to sit down. 'After take-off you can shower and rest. The flight will take approximately six hours.'

Numbly Halina nodded. She felt dazed, unable to process everything that had happened to her. Everything that was going to happen. *Marriage.*

She swallowed hard and looked out at the bright blue sky, the glare of the sun making the tarmac shimmer. The plane began to taxi down the runway and then they were taking off into the sky, away from all she had known.

As soon as they'd reached cruising altitude, Rico rose. 'I'll show you the bedroom.'

Halina followed him, aching with exhaustion, too tired even to think. The bedroom was even more luxurious than the living area, with a king-sized bed on its own dais, built in wardrobes and a huge flat-screen TV.

She gazed around at the adjoining bathroom, complete with a glassed-in shower and marble tub, the furnishings and amenities the height of luxury.

'This is amazing,' she murmured. 'I've never been on such a plane.'

'Not even the royal jet?' Rico returned with a quirk of his eyebrow.

Halina shook her head. 'Not even then.'

He stared at her for a moment, and Halina gazed back, uncertain how to navigate this moment. How to navigate every moment. She couldn't discern what he was thinking, what feelings, what fears or desires, lurked beneath his hard, metallic gaze, if any. Rico Falcone was a completely closed book and she had no idea what its pages held.

'When you're rested and refreshed,' Rico said implacably, 'we'll talk.'

Halina nodded and Rico walked back out to the main cabin, closing the door behind him. She sank onto the bed with a sigh of relief, glad to be alone for a few moments, away from the intensity of Rico's presence. She was desperate to wash, and also to think. To figure out what her next steps were...because Rico certainly knew his.

She spent far longer than necessary in the bath, luxuriating in the hot water and fragrant bubbles. The Palace of Forgotten Sands was forgotten in more ways than one; there had been no updating of its interior in over a hundred years, which meant her washing facilities, along with everything else, had been depressingly basic. A long, lovely soak went a good way to restoring her strength and spirit.

There were clothes in her size in one of the wardrobes, and Halina wondered if Rico had had them chosen specially for her. Or did he simply have a woman's wardrobe on hand for whatever mistress was his flavour of the week?

Pushing the thought out of her mind, she dressed in a pale-blue shift dress that, despite being her usual size, hung off her currently gaunt frame. She'd lost more weight than she'd realised in the last few weeks. Twisting her hair up into a loose bun, Halina squared her shoulders and then went to meet her fate.

Rico was sprawled on one of the sofas, a laptop in front of him, his forehead furrowed in a frown. He looked as sexy and as self-assured as ever, having changed into a knit shirt in charcoal-grey and dark trousers, both garments fitting his body to perfection and emphasising his incredible physique.

He looked up as soon as she entered, and then snapped his fingers. A staff member sprang forward.

'Sparkling water, orange juice and a full breakfast for both of us,' he ordered. 'And I'll have coffee as well.'

'Very good, sir.'

Halina watched as the man hurried to carry out his employer's orders. 'Are all your staff terrified of you?' she asked as she sat down opposite Rico, tucking her legs to the side to avoid his own long outstretched ones. She was determined not to be caught on the back foot, as she had been ever since Rico had stormed into her room at the palace. Now she would regain some control and all her composure. She knew she needed both for whatever lay ahead.

'Why should they be terrified of me?'

'Because you shout at them.'

'I didn't shout.' He looked mildly annoyed by her observation. 'I gave an order. There is a difference.'

'Is there? You don't seem to use "please" or "thank you" the way most people do.'

His mouth compressed. 'I do not like to waste time with useless fripperies, but I can be as polite as the next person.'

Halina looked away, wondering why she was baiting him over such a trivial matter at such a tense and crucial moment. Maybe because she felt so raw, chafing under his endless orders. He fully intended to command her life, and the truth was she didn't think there was anything she could do about it, except perhaps face it head on.

'So.' She squared her shoulders and met his narrowed look directly. 'What do you mean, you're going to marry me in Rome?' Rico regarded Halina and the way she was bracing herself, as if for bad news.

'Exactly that,' he informed her crisply.

'I have to say, your proposal could use some work.'

'I imagine it's a sight better than your last fiancé's,' Rico remarked with a touch of acid, nettled, even though he knew he shouldn't be. 'As I've heard it, you never even met him.'

'No,' Halina said slowly. 'I didn't. Not until a few weeks ago, anyway.'

Rico drew up short at that. He'd known the marriage had been called off, but he hadn't realised Halina had actually seen al bin Nur. 'You saw Prince Zayed recently? Since we…?'

'Yes, *since we*.' Her smile was tinged with wry sorrow. 'When my father found out I was pregnant, he tried to reopen marriage negotiations with Prince Zayed.' Fury flashed through Rico, a lightning strike of emotion he quickly suppressed. So his fears that another man might raise his child had been justified, making him realise how right he'd been to take drastic measures in finding Halina.

'And?' he asked, biting the word off and spitting it out.

'And I refused him, because I didn't want to marry a man who loved another.'

'Who does the Prince love? The governess he kidnapped by accident?' Contempt dripped from every word; how could a man be so unprepared, so foolish, as to abduct the wrong woman and, even worse, fall in love with her? Weakness twice over.

'Yes.' Halina's eyes flashed darkly. 'They fell in love with each other out in the desert, and I wanted them to be happy. And,' she added, flinging out the word, 'I didn't want to bind myself to someone who could never love me.' There was a challenge in her words, in her eyes, as if daring him to disagree, to disabuse her of such a notion—and so he would, without compunction.

'You were willing to do so before, it seems.'

'I knew Prince Zayed didn't love me before,' Halina clarified, 'but he could have grown to love me in time, as we'd come to know one another. To go into a situation knowing it will never happen…that the man you have bound yourself to for ever will never feel even the smallest affection for you…that is truly hopeless. It is total despair.'

Her words hammered through him, echoing emptily. Rico's mouth twisted. 'And yet here we are,' he observed.

She gave a small, strained smile, the knowledge of

their situation clouding and darkening her eyes. 'Yes. Here we are.'

He regarded her closely, trying to gauge her mood. Acceptance, resignation, or something else? 'I take it then you have no objections to our marriage?' he said after a moment, making it not quite a question.

'If you mean will I resist then, no, I won't.' She turned her head to look out of the window, acting as condemned as a prisoner in the dock.

'You will want for nothing,' Rico informed her, his tone harsher than he'd intended. 'I can promise you that.'

She turned back to stare at him, her expression bleak. 'No, you can't, Rico. You can't promise me anything. You don't know me, and you cannot presume to know either what is in my head or my heart. But if you meant I will live in comfortable circumstances...' She glanced around the plane, appearing deliberately unimpressed despite her earlier comments about the jet's luxury. 'Then, yes, I believe that.'

Rico stared at her, trying to suppress the ever-deepening twinge of annoyance her words caused. He shouldn't care what she thought or felt, only that she wasn't going to protest their inevitable marriage. Yet somehow her attitude of resignation rankled, as if he were marching her towards a noose rather than down an aisle.

'I'm glad to hear you will not attempt some pointless protest.'

She let out a huff of humourless laughter. 'Exactly. It would be pointless. My life has never been my own. I suppose it doesn't matter much whether it is you or my father who is pulling the strings.'

'I think it would matter at least a little,' Rico returned. 'As my wife you will certainly have some freedom and autonomy. More, I think, than you would have had otherwise, should you have married Prince Zayed or stayed in your father's home.'

Halina's eyes flashed dark fire. 'Prison is prison, no matter how gilded the cage.'

Although it wasn't an avenue of discussion he really wanted to explore, Rico could not keep from asking, 'What is the alternative, Halina? You are carrying my child. What would you propose, if not marriage?' He thought of the way she'd hidden from him. 'Would you really want to live the rest of your life out in the desert to escape me?'

She was silent for a long moment, gazing out of the window at the azure sky, her expression thoughtful and a little sad. Rico felt himself getting tenser and tenser. *What was she thinking?* And why did he want to know so badly?

'When I was a little girl,' Halina began slowly, 'I had this daydream. I wanted to live in Paris, in one of those tall, old houses, like Madeleine in the children's story. Do you know those books?' Wordlessly Rico shook his head. 'I had them as a child, given to me by my French godmother. I loved them.' She lapsed into silence and Rico waited, having no idea where she was going with this.

'I pictured it all in my head,' she continued in a dreamy, faraway voice. 'I used to decorate it in my imagination. I'd live on the top floor, and there would be vines climbing outside and big French windows that opened onto a balcony with wrought-iron railings. I'd grow flowers and herbs in pots and I'd sit outside and sip my coffee and look at the world bustling below.' She smiled, caught in the memory, and Rico stared at her, bewildered. He had no idea what to say. What to think.

'And there was a piano in the living room,' Halina continued. 'A grand piano that I played on. I'd give music lessons as well, and I'd have a tin of sweets on top of the piano to hand out to children when they were good. And when I wasn't working I'd go outside and wander through the Tuileries Gardens—they were mentioned in the Madeleine books as well—and sketch.' She glanced up at him, a hint of a smile in her eyes. 'Do you know, I've never actually been to Paris? This is all just in my dreams.'

'Perhaps you'll visit there one day,' Rico said gruffly. 'With me.'

'Perhaps.' Halina turned back to the window. 'The thing is,' she said softly, 'I always knew I'd never live that dream. I'd never even have the chance. I've never had any say in my life, Rico. That's why I went to the party that night in Rome. The night I met you.' She drew a shuddering breath. 'I just wanted one evening to myself, to make my own choices.' She let out a hollow laugh. 'And look what a disaster that was. Perhaps my father was right all along in restricting my life so much. Maybe I'm not capable of making my own choices, or at least wise ones. But I've always wanted the chance. I still do.'

Her words resonated uncomfortably inside him, because in a strange way he could relate to them. His childhood had been entirely different to Halina's; she'd been cossetted, protected, privileged. He'd grown up first on the docks and then in the orphanage, both places of nothing more than grim survival. And yet he'd felt as trapped and restricted as she had, and his only choice had been to fight his way out. To be seen as cold, arrogant, ruthless. Because at least then he was in control. At least then he couldn't be hurt.

What was Halina's choice?

She didn't need one, Rico reminded himself. He would provide for her, protect her, give her every luxury she could possibly want. All this nonsense about an apartment in Paris was just a childish dream, meant to be discarded and forgotten upon adulthood.

Their breakfasts arrived, putting an end to any more whimsical conversation.

'You need to eat,' Rico reminded her as he watched Halina push the eggs around her plate. 'Keep up your strength.'

'I know.' She took a tiny bite of dry toast. 'I've just been feeling so ill.'

Which reminded him that she hadn't yet seen a doctor. 'As soon as we arrive in Rome, I want you to be checked over. I'm sure something can be prescribed for your nausea.'

'Hopefully,' Halina murmured, her gaze downcast. She took another bite of toast. Rico regarded her in growing frustration, unsure why he felt so dissatisfied.

He'd found her, he'd got her on the plane and they were now only mere hours from Rome. She'd already agreed to marry him. He was getting everything he wanted, and still he felt disgruntled and annoyed. *Hurt.*

The word popped into his head and he suppressed it immediately. He wasn't hurt. He never felt hurt. He'd never allowed himself to feel such a thing, not since his father had walked away from him while he'd watched. If he was bothered by Halina's lukewarm response to the idea of their marriage, then he knew just how to rev up her enthusiasm.

In bed.

CHAPTER EIGHT

HALINA TOOK A deep breath as she gazed at her pale reflection in the mirror the morning after her arrival in Rome. The last twenty-four hours had been a whirlwind of activity and movement: a limousine had met them at the airport and taken them to Rico's penthouse apartment in a sleekly elegant modern building near the Spanish Steps.

Halina had stepped into the sprawling luxury, too tired to be dazzled or impressed by the striking minimalist architecture and hand-crafted pieces of furniture. She'd felt as if she were a tiny boat being tossed on an endless stormy sea and Rico was the one controlling the wind and the waves.

As soon as they'd arrived he had shown her to the guest bedroom and practically ordered her to rest. For once Halina had been glad to obey. She was so tired she was swaying on her feet.

'Will you tell my father where I am?' she'd asked as she stood on the threshold of her bedroom. 'So at least he won't worry?'

Rico had given a terse nod, his expression flinty. 'I think he already knows, but I will inform him of our plans at a suitable time.'

'And when will that be?'

Rico had shrugged. 'When I decide it is.'

Of course. He decided everything. She'd turned into the bedroom and closed the door in Rico's face. At least she had control over that.

Six hours of sleep later, Halina was feeling refreshed physically even as her emotions remained wrung out. She lay in bed and relived the last twenty-four hours—the escape from the palace, the terrifying sandstorm, the flight to Rome. It all felt incredible, almost as if it had happened to someone else, scenes out of an action film or a melodrama. Until she'd met Rico Falcone, her life had been quiet, contained and definitely dull. Now, she acknowledged wryly, it was merely contained.

By the time she awoke from her nap, dusk was falling over the city. Rico knocked on her door, telling her she needed to eat, which seemed to be his constant refrain. Halina went out and managed to choke down some soup before retreating to bed before Rico could ask her any more questions or give her any more orders.

'I have made an appointment for you to see a doctor tomorrow morning,' he informed her as she headed for her bedroom. 'You need to start taking better care of yourself.'

She didn't trust herself to answer in a civil manner, so she merely nodded. Alone in bed that night, misery rushed over her. She'd thought being locked away in a palace in the remote desert of Abkar had been bad enough, but amazingly this actually felt worse. She was so alone. Rico was a hostile stranger who seemed intent on blaming her for everything, yet still intended her to marry him. What would her life be like with Rico? What would her child's life be like?

For a few seconds Halina imagined resisting. Running away, carving some kind of life for herself. But where would she go, and what would she do? She had no money, no clothes even, and her life skills were, she knew, pitiable. She could speak three languages, play two instruments and make sparkling conversation when required. They were not exactly qualifications for making her own way in the world.

She hated feeling so trapped. Yet her one bid to escape her gilded shackles had resulted in her ruin, so she hardly trusted herself to try again, even if she could have worked up the courage or the means.

'Halina?' Rico knocked on the door of her bedroom, startling her out of her gloomy thoughts. 'We leave in twenty minutes for the doctor.'

'All right.' She turned away from her wan reflection and opened the door. Rico stood there, looking both glorious and impatient, dressed in a pin-striped suit in deep navy, his eyes glinting like metal, his jaw freshly shaven and his hair spiky and slightly damp from the shower. He smelled of sandalwood, and the scent of him hit Halina like a fist squeezing her heart. She remembered his hands on her body all over again, the honeyed persuasion of his kiss.

With effort she yanked her gaze away from him and walked past him into the living room. 'I'm ready.'

'I sent out for some things I thought you might like to eat.' Halina turned, surprised to see a flash of uncertainty on Rico's rugged features. She didn't think she'd ever seen him look that way before.

'Thank you.'

'There are some pastries and fresh fruit, and also ginger tea. I read that ginger helps with nausea.'

Surprise rippled through her. 'You've been reading up on it?'

He shrugged. 'I want to know as much as I can. Information is vital.'

'Thank you,' Halina said again. She felt strangely touched by his concern, although another part of her acknowledged how little it was in the larger scheme of things. But maybe she'd just have to get used to little, at least in terms of affection or concern. Rico hardly seemed likely to offer anything else.

Rome was shimmering under a haze of heat as they stepped outside Rico's apartment. He held open the door of the limousine and she slid inside, edging to the far side as Rico sat next to her, seeming to take up all the space and air. Heat emanated from his powerful body and strength radiated from every taut muscle. The sheer power of his charisma left her breathless. She'd forgotten how overwhelming he was, and she was reminded again and again of that fact every time she went near him. It was no wonder she hadn't been able to resist him back at that party.

'So, do you live in Rome all the time?' she asked as the limo pulled smoothly into the traffic. 'I don't actually know that much about you.' Or anything, really, except that he was rich, ruthless and arrogant. *And fabulous in bed.*

'Most of the time.' Rico swiped his phone and slid it into his pocket, giving her his full attention, which felt like stepping into a spotlight. 'I travel for business to my various concerns and properties, most of which are in Europe.'

'Your penthouse isn't really suitable for a baby,' Halina said impulsively. 'Would I live there?'

Rico stared at her for a moment, his expression unfathomable. 'Of course we will need to work out the details, but I would most likely buy a house in Rome suitable for a family.'

For a second Halina let herself imagine it—a happy home, a place she could decorate and fill with music and art, books and laughter. A place of her own, of their own, where she and Rico could learn to live and maybe even love together. But of course it wouldn't be like that. How it would be, she didn't yet know.

'And when will we marry?' she asked eventually. The silence between them had become strained, tense, as it always seemed to.

Rico looked out of the window. 'Let's concentrate on today and making sure you and our child are both healthy. After that we can focus on the wedding.'

The doctor's office was upscale and comfortable, with a staff member fluttering around them making sure they had everything they needed, including fresh juice and coffee.

Halina's nerves started to jangle as she stepped into the examining room with Rico right behind her. The doctor smiled at her and introduced herself.

'My name is Maria Loretto. Signor Falcone has engaged me to be your obstetrician.'

Halina nodded and shook her hand. 'Thank you.'

'So the first thing we need to do is ascertain how far along you are.' Maria gestured for her to sit on the examining table, and nervously Halina perched on its end. 'If you know the date of your last period...'

'We know the date of conception,' Rico interjected flatly. Halina closed her eyes. Did he have to control this too?

Maria glanced up. 'If you're sure of it...'

'I'm sure. It was June twenty-fifth.'

Colour scorched Halina's cheeks and she stayed silent while Maria calculated her due date. 'So you are just over ten weeks along,' she said cheerfully. 'And your due date is March nineteenth.'

Halina let out a shaky laugh and instinctively pressed

one hand against her still-flat middle. Somehow just those words made it feel so much more real. For the last two months she'd been merely existing, feeling wretched and uncertain and afraid, barely able to contemplate what was ahead of her. But now the reality, the good reality, of her situation hit her with encouraging force. A baby. A child.

'Now we can check the heartbeat,' Maria continued. 'You're just far enough along perhaps to hear it with a Doppler. Would you mind lying down?'

Halina lay back on the examining table, feeling weirdly vulnerable as Maria lifted her top. She switched on the Doppler and then pressed the wand onto Halina's stomach, hard enough to make her flinch.

'You're hurting her.' The words seemed to burst out of Rico; he looked tense, almost angry, his jaw clenched. Unfazed, the doctor gave him a reassuring smile.

'Halina is fine, Signor Falcone, and babies are remarkably resilient.'

Rico still looked unhappy about it and Halina reached out one hand, almost but not quite touching him. 'I'm fine, Rico.'

He nodded once and then they heard it, the most amazing sound Halina had ever listened to. It sounded like a cross between the whooshing of waves and the galloping of a horse. Their baby's heartbeat.

'There it is,' Maria said with satisfaction. 'Nice and strong.'

'That's amazing.' Halina felt near to tears, but when she turned to look at Rico, instinctively wanting to share this moment with him, he'd turned away as if he wasn't affected at all.

The sound seemed to fill the room, rushing and strong, the sound of hope. Rico clenched his jaw, forcing the sudden and unexpected rush of emotion back. It was just a sound, yet it filled him with joy and terror in equal measures. Their child. A human being that they had created, that he would be responsible for. That he would love.

He glanced at Halina out of the corner of his eye and saw how moved she looked, her eyes bright with tears. No matter how much he wanted to keep things on a businesslike level between them, this was an emotional business for them both. How could it be otherwise?

'Halina's been feeling very nauseous,' he told the obstetrician, his voice terser than he meant it to be. 'As you can see, she hasn't been taking care of herself.' Halina sucked in a quick breath and belatedly Rico realised how that sounded. But he was *worried*, damn it, and he didn't like being worried.

'I can prescribe something for the nausea,' Maria said. 'But first I'd advise fresh air, plenty of rest and lots of good, wholesome food. Have you been able to have all those recently, Halina?'

Was there a knowledgeable glint in the doctor's eye? Rico hadn't informed her of their circumstances, and he didn't like the thought of her knowing.

'Not exactly,' Halina murmured.

'But she will now,' Rico said firmly. Taking care of Halina would be his priority. Taking care of his unborn child.

'Then I'd suggest you come back to me in a week or two, Halina,' Maria said. 'And we'll discuss medication then. You do look a bit run down.'

She smiled sympathetically and Halina nodded and rose from the table, pulling down her shirt. 'All right. Thank you.' Her head was bowed, her dark hair swinging in front of her face. Rico had no idea what she was thinking. Feeling.

Why did he care?

Because of their baby. For the sake of his child, he needed to care about Halina. About her moods as well as her health. It was all part of the same package. Satisfied with his reasoning, he took her arm as he thanked the doctor and then escorted her out of the building into the waiting limo.

'What now?' Halina asked listlessly as she stared out of the window at the city streaming by. Rico wished she didn't sound so damned downtrodden. When he'd met her, he'd been as intrigued by her humour and spirit as he had been by her lush, curvy body. Now both were gone and he wanted to bring back the Halina he'd only just come to know—bring back the sparkle in her eyes, the impish smile to her mouth and, yes, the curves on the woman whose body had made his palms itch to touch her.

But bringing a smile to her face felt like the most important thing right now.

'What would you like to do now?' Rico asked, seeming to surprise them both. She turned to him, her eyes widening, jaw dropping in shock.

'You're asking me what I want?'

'Why shouldn't I?'

'Because you're King of the World, Maker of All Decisions Ever?'

'That is a slight exaggeration.' His mouth twitched; he was heartened to see even that little display of spirit. 'But only slight.'

'Of course.'

'Perhaps I should put that on my business card. It's quite catchy, as a title.'

Her mouth curved just a little. 'You're joking with me.'

'Shouldn't I?'

'No, it's just...' Her smile faded. 'I don't know you,

Rico, at all. And yet you're the father of my child and soon you're likely to be my husband.'

'There's no likely about it,' Rico couldn't keep from saying, his voice hardening, that moment of levity vanishing like morning mist.

Halina sighed and turned back to the window. 'Exactly.'

Frustration boiled within him. Why could he never get this right? He wasn't used to feeling wrong-footed, unsure, wanting something he couldn't have. 'So what is it you'd like to do today?'

She shrugged, her face still to the window. 'I don't care.'

He found he hated her apathy. 'I'm giving you a choice, Halina—'

'Oh, that's right.' She whirled to face him, a sudden and surprising fury lighting her eyes and twisting her features. 'You're *giving* me a choice. I suppose I should trip all over myself to say thank you for that unimaginable kindness.' He opened his mouth to speak but found he had nothing to say. 'And tomorrow, perhaps, you won't give me a choice. Tomorrow I'll be informed of our plans without any discussion and expected to fall in line immediately *or else.*'

'You are talking about something that hasn't happened yet.'

'You don't get it, do you?' She shook her head in weary despair. 'You never will. I tried to explain before, but you're so used to ordering the universe you can't imagine what it feels like to be the one ordered about. And as privileged as my life has been—and I'm not stupid... I know it has—it's also always been ordered and arranged by someone else. So if you want to know what I want today, Rico, I'll tell you. I want my freedom, and that is something you'll never give me.' She broke off, breathing heavily, turning back to the window as she struggled to compose herself.

Rico sat back, stunned speechless by her outburst. Yes, he understood her life had been restricted and that she resented that, but he hadn't realised how bitterly she chafed against it, against *him*. How she now saw him as her captor, her commander. And he suddenly felt sympathy for her that was both overwhelming and inconvenient.

'Actually,' he said after a moment, keeping his voice mild, 'I do know what that feels like.'

Halina let out a huff of disbelieving laughter, her face still turned firmly towards the window. 'Yeah, right.'

'As you said yourself just a few moments ago, you don't actually know me. So how can you say whether I've felt something or not?'

She stayed silent for a long moment and then she turned towards him. Her face was still flushed, but that moment of furious rebellion had left her, and bizarrely Rico found he missed it. 'Tell me, then.'

But did he actually want to tell her? This was all becoming a bit too…intimate. Rico hesitated, debating the pros and cons of admitting something of his past to her. Then he decided he could tell her. He just wouldn't get emotional about it.

'Well?' Halina lifted her chin, a challenge in her dark gaze. 'Are you going to tell me or not?'

CHAPTER NINE

HALINA SAW THE indecision flicker in Rico's silvery eyes and knew he was regretting admitting even as little as he had to her. He didn't want her to know him. Didn't want to be known.

'For all my childhood, I had little control,' he said at last, his voice toneless. 'Over anything.'

'Most children have little control,' Halina answered with a shrug, determined not to trip all over herself in eager gratitude now that he was sharing something with her. 'Isn't that the nature of childhood?'

'I suppose it is.' His jaw was tight, his eyes flinty. Perhaps she shouldn't have been so dismissive simply because she was frustrated and feeling trapped. She did want to know more about the man she was going to marry, and if Rico was willing to open up even a little she wanted and needed to encourage that.

'How was your childhood different, Rico?' she asked in a gentler tone. 'What was it like?' She really did want to know, and she was sorry for her flippancy.

His lips compressed, his gaze turning distant. 'As it happens,' he remarked in a cool, matter-of-fact tone, 'I never knew my mother. She was a waitress who had a fling with my father. She didn't want the baby—me—and so she left me with my father when I was two weeks old.'

'Oh.' The word was a soft gasp of sorrow. She had assumed, she realised, that Rico was from as great a world of privilege as her own. He certainly acted as if he had always been entitled, had always expected obedience, or even obeisance. She'd had no idea that he'd been born in such lowly, unfortunate circumstances.

'Yes, oh.' His mouth twisted with wry grimness. 'My father worked on the docks, and I don't think he was best pleased to have a baby foisted on him, even his own.'

'Oh,' Halina said again, helplessly. 'That must have been... What did he do?'

'He kept me, to his credit.' Rico flicked his gaze away for a second before he turned resolutely back to face her, his face bland. 'Raised me himself, with help from some kindly neighbours who looked after me when I was small.' His lips thinned. 'It could have been worse.'

'So you never knew your mother at all? You grew up with your father?'

'Until I was nine.' Rico shrugged, as if to dismiss the matter. 'Then I ended up in an orphanage in Salerno. A convent, run by nuns who didn't like children very much, as far as I could tell. That's where I really grew up. I left when I was sixteen and never looked back.'

Sadness clutched at Halina's heart. It sounded like a truly miserable childhood—not a childhood at all. 'Oh, Rico, that sounds horrible. So lonely—'

'I've never been lonely.' He cut across her. 'I've never needed to feel lonely, because long ago I learned to depend only on myself.' He paused, adding a certain emphasis to the words, making her realise that he wasn't just talking about his childhood. He was talking about now, about not needing anyone now. Not needing her.

'But the real reason I told you all this,' Rico resumed,

'is to explain that I do know how you feel when you say you're trapped and want freedom.'

Halina flushed and looked down. It sounded as if Rico's life had been far more restricted than hers had ever been. She felt ashamed, a spoilt princess whingeing for even more than she already had. 'I'm sorry for doubting you. I never would have guessed... How did you get to where you are now?'

'Determination, hard work and a little bit of luck. Perhaps more than a little bit.' His eyes flashed with fire. 'I bought my first property when I was nineteen, a run-down warehouse near the docks, and turned it into a gym. I sold it for twenty times what I paid for it when I was twenty-one and then never looked back.'

Halina shook her head slowly. 'That is truly amazing, Rico. You're an inspiration.'

He gave a nod of acknowledgement and thanks. 'So, now I shall ask you again. What would you like to do this afternoon?'

Halina stared at him thoughtfully, wondering what she could suggest that Rico would agree to, that could be fun for them both. Because now that he'd shared something of his life, that surprising insight into a difficult childhood, she realised she wanted to spend time with him. To get to know him, to crack open the door into his mind, if not his heart, and gain another tantalising glimpse.

If they were going to be married, she needed to know this man. Understand him and hopefully even like him.

'What do you recommend?' she asked. 'I spent all my secondary schooling in Italy, but I've never actually seen any sights.'

'That's tragic.'

'Have you?' she challenged and his lips twitched.

'I'm too busy to sightsee.'

'Of course you are. But today…?'

He glanced out of the window, his expression as thoughtful as her own. 'We could see the Colosseum. That's something I've always wanted to visit.'

Halina's heart leapt with excitement and a strange hope. This was new, doing something together just for fun. Not sex, not squabbling, just simple pleasure, spending time with each other. 'All right,' she said. 'Let's see that.'

Rico insisted on lunch first, so they ate in the private garden of an elegant bistro only steps from the Colosseum. The food was fresh and delicious, a refreshing breeze ruffling the leaves of the plane trees that offered some much-needed shade.

Halina sat back as they waited for their food, feeling surprisingly happy for the first time in months. Maybe even longer. Her heart was light, anticipation burgeoning inside her.

'You're smiling,' Rico noted as he twirled his wine glass between long, lean fingers.

'I am, actually,' she admitted as her smile widened. 'This is very nice, Rico. Thank you.'

'You're welcome.' He tilted his head, his silvery, heavy-lidded gaze sweeping over her in assessment, considering. 'You're quite easily pleased, you know.'

'Do you really think so?' Halina took a sip of her sparkling water. 'I suppose, after the last few months, I am.'

Rico's eyes narrowed. 'What does that mean exactly?'

Halina bit her lip and looked away. 'It doesn't really matter.' She didn't want to drag up all those painful memories, only to have Rico question and doubt her and definitely spoil the fun but fragile mood that had begun to develop between them.

'And I think it does.' He leaned forward, as intent as

a predator on its prey, and just as lethal. 'You have never told me about the time between your visits to Rome. Why you didn't see a doctor. How you ended up in that remote palace.'

'I thought you believed I'd gone there to escape from you,' Halina returned. She'd meant to sound light but a note of bitterness crept in. How could he have made so many assumptions? But how could she be surprised that he had?

'It was the first thought that came to my mind,' Rico acknowledged. 'But perhaps that is because of my experience, not yours. Now I'd like to hear in your own words how you came to be at that palace.' He paused, gazing down into the glinting ruby depths of his wine. 'How did your family take the news of your pregnancy?'

'Not well.' The two words scraped Halina's throat and she took another sip of water. 'Not well at all, to be perfectly frank.'

Rico frowned. 'I thought your father doted on you.'

She laughed, the sound rather grim. 'Where did you hear that?'

'I hired a private investigator to find you. He found that the general sense was that your father doted on you, and that you were rather spoiled.' His gaze, when she dared to meet it, was steady and clear, without judgement or pity. 'Is that true?'

'It *was* true,' Halina said after a moment, when she trusted her voice to be as steady as his gaze. 'But it all changed when I ruined myself.'

Rico's eyebrows drew together in a straight line, his frown turning into a scowl so that he looked quite ferocious. 'Tell me what happened.'

'What I should have expected would happen,' Halina answered with a shrug. Even now she couldn't believe how stupid, how utterly naive, she'd been, and in so many ways. About Rico, about her father, about life. 'My parents were beyond furious with me. When the negotiations with Prince Zayed broke down, my father had been hoping to marry me to someone else, someone he deemed suitable, who would afford us another political alliance. My disgrace precluded that.'

'Surely in this day and age a woman's virginity is not a prerequisite, even for a royal marriage?'

'In my country, in my culture, it is. And I knew that.' She shook her head. 'All along I knew that, and yet still I acted as if the consequences wouldn't apply to me.' She tried for a twisted smile. 'I suppose you truly did sweep me away, Rico.'

'It was mutual,' Rico said after a brief pause. 'If I'd had any sense myself, any ability to think straight, I would have realised how innocent you were. And I wouldn't have touched you.'

'Was it that obvious?'

'In hindsight, yes. So what did your father do?'

'He was livid with me, first of all. Utterly enraged, as well as disappointed. I'm not sure which felt worse.' She shook her head, the memories assailing her like hammer blows. 'And when he found out I was pregnant...'

'How did he find out, as a matter of interest?'

'He made me take a pregnancy test,' Halina said simply. 'At the earliest opportunity. And then he tried to have Prince Zayed marry me, spoiled goods that I was, because he didn't think anyone else would have me. And when that didn't work out...' She gulped, not wanting to go on, closing her eyes against the harshness of the memory that still hurt her even now.

'What?' Rico demanded roughly. 'Whatever it is, tell

me, Halina. Surely it can't be worse than another man claiming my child?'

She saw how the skin around his lips had gone white, his eyes hard and metallic. He was angry, but with her father, not with her. Would he be even angrier when she told him the whole truth?

'You have to understand,' Halina said slowly. 'My father is a good man. A loving man.' She had to believe that, because if she didn't what did she have? A father who had never actually truly loved her? 'But,' she continued painfully, 'he was in very difficult circumstances...'

'It sounds as if you were in very difficult circumstances,' Rico interjected shortly.

Yes, she had been, but the circumstances had been of her own making. And she supposed she wanted to explain her father's actions—absolve him, even—because she still loved him and wanted to believe he loved her. Otherwise, what was love, that he could be doting one minute and damning the next? How did you trust it, if it could so easily turn into something else? What was love, if you couldn't forgive a mistake, an insult, an open wound?

'Halina,' Rico said, and it sounded like a warning.

'He tried,' Halina confessed in a low voice, 'To make me have an abortion.'

Rico stared at Halina, her pale face, her pain-filled eyes, and felt a whole new kind of fury sweep through him—a tidal wave of anger and indignation and, beneath those, a deep, soul-reaching pain.

'He tried?' he repeated in a growl. 'What do you mean by that?'

'He insisted, and he wouldn't listen to me at all. My mother agreed with him, and they took me to a discreet doctor. Forced me.' She blinked rapidly but a tear fell anyway, glistening on her cheek like a diamond. Rico's fists clenched on the table. 'I fought the whole way, tooth and nail.' She stared at him, her eyes huge. 'You have to believe that, Rico. I would never want to get rid of my child. I begged and pleaded, I cried and fought. I did.' She let out a choked cry, one trembling fist pressed to her mouth.

'I do believe it,' he said in a low voice. It was impossible not to when he could feel her desperation and grief like a tangible thing, a shroud covering her. 'So, what happened then?'

'The doctor refused to perform the operation,' Halina whispered. 'Because I was fighting against it so much. My father was furious, but in the midst of it all I think he saw where his own anger had led him, and he was ashamed.' She swiped at the tear still glistening on her cheek. 'I have to believe that.'

And Rico understood that too, because he'd felt the same about his own father for many years, trying to excuse the inexcusable, to give a good reason for cruelty towards a child. Towards him. You could twist the truth into knots to try to make it an acceptable shape, but it all came apart eventually, and he'd had to acknowledge the hard, unvarnished reality. His father just hadn't cared.

'So he sent you to the Palace of Forgotten Sands,' Rico said flatly. 'He banished you.'

Halina nodded, swallowing hard in an attempt to restore her shaky composure. 'Yes, I was meant to remain there until the baby was born.'

'And afterwards?'

'I... I don't know.' Halina bit her lip. 'My father said he would take my baby away from me, but I hoped... I hoped in time he would change his mind and let me keep him or her.' She pressed one hand to her belly. 'I can't believe he would have been so cruel to me or his own grandchild.'

Rico sat back, his mind whirling with all the revelations Halina had just levelled at him. He'd misjudged her badly, assuming she'd been acting on her own selfish whims, going to a remote location to keep his child from him. It had been a stupid assumption, founded on his own unfortunate experience and the ensuing prejudices he still had about mothers and fathers, about family, about love.

Because he'd never experienced a mother's love, a father's trust. Because he'd assumed Halina would act in as selfish and capricious a manner as his own mother had done. He'd been wrong. So very wrong.

'I'm sorry you went through all that,' he said finally. 'And I'm sorry I assumed...' He paused, realising how much he'd assumed. How much it must have hurt her, considering her true experience. 'I'm sorry,' he said again.

Halina nodded, pale-faced and spent now. 'That's why I didn't see an obstetrician,' she explained quietly. 'I wasn't given the chance.'

'I understand.' Rico spoke tautly, trying to control the raging anger he felt towards Halina's father. The man had no right to assume control over Halina's life, over their child's life. The thought that Halina might have been forced to terminate her pregnancy—end the life of his child—made Rico grind his teeth together. But his rage served no purpose now, not when Halina was looking at him so warily, as if afraid his anger might be directed at her. And why shouldn't she be afraid? Since snatching her from the desert palace, he'd assumed the worst of her at nearly every turn. Guilt, an unfamiliar emotion, lanced through him.

From the depths of his soul, a barren landscape until now, Rico summoned a smile. 'Let's put such unpleasant things behind us, Halina. The future will be different now—for you and for our baby, who will never know a day without the love of his or her mother and father. That is my promise.'

Halina nodded, but she didn't look much convinced, something which made guilt rush through Rico all over again. He could see now how arrogant and inconsiderate he'd been—announcing his dictates, never giving her a choice—and he vowed to do better in the future. He would provide for Halina, he would make her smile, he would see her blossom, so she could rediscover her old spirit and joy.

He just would do it without engaging any of his own emotions. Because even now, when his heart was nearly rent in two by Halina's sorrowful story, Rico steeled himself not to care. That was one place he could not go, and one thing he would never, ever give his bride-to-be. His heart. Even now, having shared and been entrusted with so much, he couldn't risk that much.

They spent the rest of lunch talking about inconsequential matters, then strolled through the sunshine to the Colosseum.

'Photographs don't do it justice!' Halina exclaimed as they walked through an archway, one of eighty. Although partially ruined, the Colosseum was still a magnificent and awe-inspiring structure with its high walls and many archways, the expanse of the old arena.

They roamed through its many corridors, reading each other bits from the guidebook—how it had been built by three different emperors and then had fallen to ruin a few hundred years later, much of its stone used to build other structures in Rome.

'It's horrible and beautiful all at once, isn't it?' Halina said as they stood on the viewing platform that overlooked what had once been the main arena. 'The architecture is so impressive, and yet so many people and animals suffered and died here terribly. It's awful to think about.'

Rico nodded. 'Beautiful things can be used for evil,' he said, feeling strangely sombre after their walk around the ancient archways and corridors. He felt as if he was sharing more than a mere tourist attraction with Halina; the way they'd talked together, reflecting on what they'd learned in the guidebook, was something he'd never done with a woman before, or really with anyone.

He didn't have friends, not beyond business colleagues, and women had been no more than mistresses, mere objects of sexual desire and fulfillment. Strolling in the sunshine on a summer's afternoon, sharing ideas, talking and listening, was all incredibly novel. And, he realised with a pang of unease, quite pleasant, which he hadn't expected at all.

He'd been viewing this afternoon as an expedient means to an end, a way to improve Halina's mood, gain her trust. But somewhere along the way it had turned into something else, something deeper and more meaningful, and he really didn't know how to feel about that because, the truth was, he didn't want to *feel* at all.

Halina glanced down at the guidebook. 'It says we shouldn't miss the museum in the inner walls of the top floor,' she remarked. 'It's dedicated to Eros.'

'Eros?'

'The god of love.'

'I know who Eros is,' Rico returned. 'I just don't know why they'd have a museum dedicated to him in a place that was used for torture and death.'

'Maybe that's why, to bring some light and hope to a place that has been the stage for so much darkness.' Halina's smile was teasing and playful, but her eyes looked serious and Rico felt a twinge of alarm, a deepening sense of unease.

Love did not bring light to the darkness; it wasn't the hope held out in a broken and damaged world. No, love was nothing but risk and pain, loss and weakness. He knew that because he'd made the grievous mistake of loving his father. A broken childhood might not be the best reason to avoid love, but it was Rico's, and it had affected him to the depths of his soul. It had made him determined not just to avoid love but revile it and all it meant. Because the alternative was unthinkable. Unbearable.

As he took Halina's arm and led her towards the stairs, Rico sincerely hoped that she wasn't holding out for some remnant of love from him. Surely she knew him better than that, even if their acquaintance had been limited so far?

If she didn't know it, he reflected grimly, he would certainly tell her as soon as possible, gently but firmly. He didn't want to hurt Halina any more than he already had, but the last thing he needed or wanted was a wife who was looking for that damnable emotion—love.

CHAPTER TEN

HALINA GAZED AT her reflection in the mirror, noting the colour in her cheeks, the new sparkle in her eyes. It had been two weeks since she'd arrived in Rome with Rico and the nausea was finally abating, thanks to plenty of rest, healthy food and fresh air, as well as simple time. She was nearly at the end of her first trimester, and her pregnancy—her baby—was becoming more real with every passing day.

The last two weeks had been surprisingly unpressured. Rico had been focused on restoring her health, and Halina had appreciated the chance to take long naps and baths, or simply sit out in the sun on the huge terrace off Rico's apartment. He'd hired a cook to make fresh, nourishing meals and had cancelled all his social engagements so he could be home as much as possible in the evenings after work.

He was acting every inch the loving, considerate husband except…he wasn't. After that first shocking conversation when he'd told her about his childhood, Rico had buttoned up, sharing no personal details, inviting no intimate conversations. Halina had missed it, had tried several times to engage him again, but any questions about his childhood, his feelings, his very self, had been firmly and sometimes brusquely shot down. Halina had a suspicion he regretted sharing as much as he had with her, and this was his way of retrenching.

That had been most apparent when they'd visited the museum dedicated to Eros at the Colosseum. They'd strolled through the galleries of frescoes and sculpture, terracotta vases and bas-reliefs, while Halina had read from the guidebook.

'The ancient poets describe Eros as an invincible force that can bring happiness but also destroy it.'

Rico had snorted, his hands shoved deep in his pockets. 'The latter is certainly true.'

Halina had glanced at him over the edge of the guidebook. 'You sound as if you've been in love,' she'd remarked, trying not to feel an inconvenient twinge of jealousy at the thought. Was that why he kept to mistresses, none of whom lasted longer than a week? To keep his heart from being broken again?

'Not *in* love,' Rico had corrected, then had refused to say anything more.

'I've never been in love,' Halina had remarked with an insouciant shrug. 'Never even close. Never had the chance.'

'Consider yourself fortunate, then.'

'What have you got against it?' She tried to keep her voice light, to disguise the hurt and, yes, the yearning she knew she felt. She might never have been in love but she wanted to be one day. And if she married Rico, *when* she married him, it seemed likely that she wouldn't be.

'You heard what the ancient poets said.' Rico paused to study a statue of Eros stringing his bow. 'It can destroy happiness. Who wants to tangle with that? And what about the whole concept of love being an arrow that hits you?' He nodded towards the marble figure.

'Something that is alleged to bring joy actually brings pain. That sounds about right.'

Halina stopped where she was and lowered the guidebook. 'Who hurt you, Rico?' she asked quietly. He jerked as if shot by the aforementioned arrow, his eyes narrowed.

'No one.'

'That can't be true, not with the way you're talking.'

He shrugged one powerful shoulder. 'It was a long time ago.'

'How long ago?'

'I don't want to talk about it, Halina.' His tone couldn't have been more repressive, and Halina didn't have the courage to press any more. But she wondered. Oh, how she wondered. What kind of woman had captured Rico's heart and made him as cold and closed-off as he was?

Because that was what she'd discovered over the last two weeks, pleasant as they had been. Rico had no interest in getting to know her, or being known himself. No desire to have a conversation that probed more deeply than the weather or the latest films. There was no need to deepen their relationship now that they were going to be married.

Tonight's party would be his way of introducing her to Roman society as his wife-to-be, and Halina quailed at the thought. She'd only been to one party before, and look how that had turned out. How was she going to be able to manage with everyone's eyes on her, and Rico remaining so solicitous yet so cold?

'Halina?' He knocked on the door of her bedroom. 'The limo is here.'

'All right.' Taking a deep breath, Halina gave her reflection one last inspecting glance. Yesterday Rico had taken her to the prestigious Via dei Condotti to shop in the city's most exclusive boutiques. She'd emerged from the various shops with half a dozen gold-corded bags filled with everything imaginable—lingerie, day dresses, casual clothes, evening gowns.

'I'm not sure what the point of all this is,' she'd told Rico. 'I'm going to start getting bigger soon and nothing will fit.'

He'd merely shrugged. 'You can wear them again after the baby is born. And you have a responsibility to look the part as my wife.'

A remark that had made her want to ask what their marriage was going to look like, what Rico expected from her in all sorts of ways. But she'd held her tongue because she wasn't ready for that conversation. Two weeks of rest had helped her a great deal in recovering both physically and emotionally from the last couple of harrowing months, but she didn't think she had the strength yet to tackle that emotional, explosive subject.

'I'm ready,' she called and, reaching for her gauzy wrap, she turned to the door. She took a deep breath and opened it to find Rico standing there, looking as devastatingly sexy and charismatic in his tuxedo as he had when she'd first laid eyes on him.

'Bella,' Rico murmured, his pupils flaring as his gaze travelled from the top of her head to the tips of her toes. He made no effort to disguise the heat simmering in the silvery depths of his eyes. *'Molta bella.'*

Pleasure coiled within her like a tightly wound spring. She'd taken care with her appearance, styling her hair in a complicated up-do and applying make-up that was both subtle and effective, emphasising her lush mouth and dark eyes. As for the dress…

She'd chosen to wear one Rico hadn't seen during their shopping trip, an emerald-green full-length evening gown with a halter top and a plunging neckline. It was quite the most daring and sexy thing she'd even worn, and when Rico looked at her with so much unabashed desire she felt heady and powerful. She felt the way she had that fateful night two and a half months ago, and realised afresh how and why it had led her to abandon all common sense.

Rico stretched out one hand and drew her by the fingertips towards the living room and onto the terrace. The night was sultry and warm, the terrace lit only by a sliver of moon and the wash of lights from the buildings spread out before them in a living, breathing map.

'I want to give you this,' Rico said, and withdrew a small black velvet box from the inside pocket of his tuxedo jacket.

Halina's heart stuttered in her chest. 'Is that…?'

'Yes,' he replied as he opened it and showed her its contents. 'It is.'

Halina gazed down at the exquisite solitaire diamond that was big enough to reach to her knuckle. It glittered and sparkled in the darkness, its many facets catching the moonlight. 'It's beautiful,' she whispered. 'And huge.'

'Try it on.'

Wordlessly she held out her hand, unable to keep her fingers from trembling as Rico slid the massive ring onto her finger. It felt heavy, so much so that her hand faltered and Rico caught it up in his own, drawing her even more closely to him.

Their hips nudged and heat flared. This was the closest she'd been to him since the night of the sandstorm, when amidst the fear and uncertainty she'd almost lost her head. Again. Now dizzying sensation spiralled through her, and he was barely touching her.

'Now everyone will know you are mine,' Rico said as

he placed his hands on her bare shoulders and drew her even closer towards him. The brush of his lips against her was like an electric shock, twanging all the way through her as he deepened the kiss, turning it into a brand.

Halina swayed as Rico moved his mouth with firm, sure possession over hers, plundering its depths, taking control in this as he did in everything.

He broke the kiss first while stars danced behind her eyes and her knees nearly buckled. Blinking away the haze of desire, she saw his smugly satisfied smile.

'We will have a good marriage, Halina.'

'There's more to a marriage than that,' she returned shakily, and Rico's smile vanished, replaced by a wintry look.

'Not for us.'

She'd known it, of course she had, but it still hurt to have him spell it out so plainly. 'Why not, Rico?'

'What exactly are you asking me?'

'I guess I'm asking you what kind of marriage we will have,' Halina said slowly. Her heart had started beating with painful thuds. 'Because we've never even discussed it.' She held up her hand, heavy with the glittering ring. 'I don't even know when we're getting married.'

'In one month's time.'

'Have you told my father?'

'We'll send him an invitation.'

Halina cringed inwardly at his coolly dismissive tone. Despite the agonising way her father had hurt her, she still missed him and the rest of her family. She hated the thought of them not knowing how she was, or even where she was, but Rico had assured her Sultan Hassan knew she was with him—and that, Rico had said flatly, was all he needed to know.

Now she lowered her hand and gazed down at the ring.

'In one month,' she repeated slowly. 'And what about our marriage? What will it be like?' She hesitated, then dared to ask the question pulsing through her heart. 'I know you don't love me now, but would you ever, perhaps in time?'

She felt Rico stiffen as the seconds ticked on. 'I am not interested in love, Halina. It's an ephemeral emotion. It counts for nothing.'

Pain thudded through her. 'Yet you've said you would love our child.'

'That is different.'

'It's specifically romantic love you're talking about, then?'

A hesitation, telling, painful. 'Yes.'

Halina drew a deep breath. 'So you're telling me you'll never love me?'

'I'm telling you I will provide for you, protect you, seek your happiness above my own. What is love compared to all that?'

She stared at him sorrowfully, unsure of her answer but knowing with a leaden certainty that his wasn't enough.

Rico glanced across at Halina's thoughtful profile, wishing he could see into her mind, even as he acknowledged that he most likely didn't want to know what thoughts lingered there.

He'd planned for the ring—and the kiss—to seal the deal between them and bring her pleasure. What woman didn't like a nice piece of jewellery? And the ring he'd chosen was magnificent. But since the moment he'd slid it onto her finger Halina had cradled her hand as if it was too heavy, as if the ring were a burden or even a wound rather than a symbol of their forthcoming union.

His stomach cramped as he remembered how she'd

asked about the nature of their marriage, about whether he would ever come to love her. He'd been postponing such a conversation while Halina regained her strength; her health along with their child's was his main priority. But when asked so directly, he'd had to tell her the truth. He just hoped she could learn to live with it.

'So what is this party for?' she asked as the limo slid through Rome's traffic, the buildings blurring outside the car. She turned to him, looking so achingly lovely he longed to draw her towards him and kiss her lush, plump mouth. He could kiss away all her concerns and worries about the nature of their marriage; he was sure of it. What they would have together in bed would be far better than any tedious notions of love or affection.

He'd waited to reignite their physical relationship because he'd wanted her to feel better physically with her nausea and also because he'd wanted to gain her trust. But now he wondered if kissing away her concerns would be the most expedient option.

'Rico...?' Halina prompted, a frown crinkling her brow. Her eyes still looked sad, just as they had when she'd asked him earlier about their marriage.

'It's a charity event,' he replied. 'For street orphans.'

'Is that a charity you support?'

'Yes.' To the tune of millions of pounds, not that he would tell her as much. It was a charity that cut far too close to the bone, so he kept the amount of his giving secret. Few people knew the nature of his childhood, and no one knew about his father's rejection of him. He did not want to advertise his private shame, or cause people to pity him.

'And what will people there expect of me?' Halina asked, sounding nervous.

'The usual thing at parties. To chat and socialise.' He

smiled, wanting to lighten the mood and lift that sadness from her eyes. 'You surely know which fork to use with which course and other such matters?'

'Yes,' Halina allowed. 'But the socialising bit might be beyond me.' Rico looked at her in surprise and she let out a shaky laugh. 'Sometimes I think you have a completely skewed view of my life.'

'Oh?' He frowned, curious and a bit discomfited. He'd assumed, as she was a princess, she'd gone to plenty of parties, dozens of social occasions. 'Enlighten me, then.'

Halina shrugged. 'Before I met you, I'd been to exactly two parties, and they weren't parties the way you probably think of parties. They were diplomatic events at the palace—all I had to do was show up, bow my head and appear modest and subservient. I've never socialised beyond the schoolroom, and before the night I met you I'd never even worn a cocktail dress. This...' she gestured to the gorgeous gown that encased her lush body in a satiny sheath '...is the first evening gown I've ever worn.'

Rico's frown deepened as his wife-to-be surprised him yet again. Yes, he'd known Halina had had a sheltered and even restricted life behind the palace walls, but more and more she showed him just how small it had really been. And he wanted to make it bigger. 'What did you wear to the diplomatic events if not evening gowns?' he asked.

'Traditional dress. Very conservative.'

Something else he hadn't actively considered. 'Is this...these clothes, this lifestyle...difficult for you?'

She laughed, the sound crystalline and musical. 'Difficult? No, definitely not. I love these clothes. I love the freedom of going out to a party.' For a second something sad flickered across her face. 'Believe it or not, I have more freedom here with you in Rome than I did before in Abkar.' *But that's not saying all that much.*

Rico could practically see the thought bubble appearing over her head.

'Then I hope you enjoy tonight,' he said sincerely. 'It's your chance to shine.'

And shine she did as they stepped into the elegant ballroom of one of the city's best hotels. Halina was easily the most gorgeous woman in the room, looking like a brilliant green flame in her emerald evening gown. Rico steeled himself not to mind the curious and lustful looks slid her way by just about every male guest. The women looked too, just as intrigued by the woman on his arm. Rico waited until they'd attracted a decent-sized crowd before delivering the bombshell he knew would explode in the entire room.

'Please let me introduce Princess Halina of Abkar,' he said smoothly, his arm linked with Halina's. 'My fiancée.'

Murmurs of shock and surprise rippled through the room as Halina stiffened beside him. Rico pulled her a little closer, determined to stake his claim in every way possible. 'We will be married next month.'

'So soon?' a woman asked with acid sweetness. Rico didn't recognise her, but he certainly knew the tone. He held her gaze, putting iron into his own.

'Yes. Neither of us wish to wait.'

The woman's eyes narrowed and her mouth curved into a speculative smile. Halina put a protective hand over her belly and, from the ensuing ripple of murmurs that spread out through the crowd, Rico knew that just about everyone had seen that revealing action and judged it accurately.

'Let me get you some champagne,' he told Halina, and she gave him a wan smile.

'You mean sparkling water.'

Several people heard, adding fuel to the fires of speculation. Rico knew by the time the evening was at an end everyone there would know Halina was pregnant. Well, so be it. Halina's pregnancy would be physically apparent soon enough, and he would never be ashamed to claim his child.

He asked a waiter for a glass of sparkling water, then he began to move through the crowd, Halina pressed to his side.

As the hours wound down and the conversation and speculation swirled, Halina became quieter and quieter. At first she'd tried to enter into the various conversations, smiling and nodding, shyly offering her own opinions, but as time passed Rico sensed her withdrawing into herself.

After a five-course meal where they were seated on opposite sides of a table for twelve, she excused herself, disappearing for over twenty minutes before, both impatient and alarmed, Rico went to find her.

He strode down the hotel's opulent corridors, annoyed that he'd been compelled to leave the event to find his errant wife-to-be, even as he fought a growing sense of worry that something was really wrong with her. What if she was ill? What if, God forbid, something had happened to their child?

He asked the attentive staff of the hotel if they'd seen her, and finally tracked her down to the opulent women's powder room down one endless corridor. Not hesitating for a second, Rico rapped on the door.

'Halina? Halina, are you in there?' There was no reply, so he cracked open the door a bit and called again. 'Halina, please answer me if you're in there. Tell me you're all right.'

Two women came to the door, sidling past him with amused glances. 'So attentive,' one of them drawled, and the other gave an unpleasant cackle of laughter. Rico glared at them both.

'Is Princess Halina in the powder room?' he demanded.

One woman, looking spiteful now, shrugged a bony shoulder. 'Why don't you see for yourself?' she called as she walked off with the other woman, their angular bodies and raucous laughter reminding Rico of a pair of glossy, pecking crows.

He pushed open the door to the powder room and strode inside. The place looked empty—a row of gold-plated sinks, a plush settee and several opulent wood-panelled stalls. The room was completely silent, save for the drip of a tap and a sudden, revealing sniff from behind one of the stall doors.

'Halina,' Rico called, his voice rough and urgent. Another sniff sounded. 'Open the door,' he demanded. 'Tell me what's going on.'

After an endless moment Halina unlocked the door and stepped out into the bathroom. Rico gaped at her, taking in her dishevelled hair and tear-stained face, his heart lurching at the sight of her obvious distress.

'Halina,' he said and reached for her. 'What has happened? What's wrong?'

CHAPTER ELEVEN

RICO'S STRONG, WARM hands encased Halina's icy ones as he drew her towards him, his brow furrowed, his expression somewhere between thunderous and terrified.

'Why have you been crying? Has something happened? Is it the baby...?'

'No, it's not the baby.' Halina pulled her hands from his to dash at the tears on her face. She felt embarrassed for falling apart so completely. This evening had been an utter failure, and it was all her fault. She couldn't handle a party. She couldn't handle being Rico's fiancée. 'At least,' she amended, taking a steadying breath, 'it was, in a manner of speaking.'

'What do you mean?' Rico's gaze swept over her, as if looking for open wounds or broken bones. 'Are you hurt?'

Halina let out a shaky laugh, torn between wry amusement and deep, abiding sorrow. 'Yes, Rico,' she managed tartly, 'I am hurt. But you won't find any visible wounds so you can stop looking at me as if you want to take me to the hospital's emergency department.'

'I don't understand.'

'No.' She sighed. 'You wouldn't.' She moved past him to study her reflection. She was even more of a wreck than she'd realised, her supposedly waterproof mascara giving her panda eyes, and her once elegantly styled hair falling about her shoulders in tangled ringlets.

'What is that supposed to mean?' Rico asked, his tone gruff.

Halina sighed and attempted to dab at her mascara even as she recognised a lost cause when she saw one. 'My *feelings* are hurt, Rico,' she said, deciding she needed to speak as plainly as she could. 'Feelings. You know those things you try not to have?'

Rico's mouth thinned. Clearly he didn't appreciate her pathetic attempt at humour. 'Why were your feelings hurt?'

She hesitated, her gaze still on her unhappy reflection. 'It doesn't matter.'

'Yes, it does.' Rico spoke with a force that surprised. 'Who hurt you? Did someone say something, do something? Because if they did it to you, then they did it to me.'

A feeling bloomed in Halina's chest, a mixture of surprise and warmth. It spread through her like sunshine or honey, warming her right down to the tips of her fingers and toes. 'Do you mean that?'

'Of course I do.'

Was that what marriage was? Maybe not love, but something just as fundamental? The question was, could it be enough?

'So what happened, Halina? Tell me.'

'Not here.' She glanced around the bathroom. 'Someone's liable to come in, and I can't cope with another snide remark.'

His frown of concern deepened into a positive scowl. 'So someone did say something to you. One of those women?'

'Not *to* me,' Halina clarified, and felt the tightening

of tears in her throat. The snippy, bitchy comments she'd overheard while in the bathroom stall had wounded her deeply, more than she cared to admit to Rico, because even though he wanted to know she knew he wouldn't understand. Not completely.

'Tell me,' he demanded. 'Tell me what they said.'

'Why, so you can punch them?' She let out a hiccupping laugh. 'I will tell you, but can we please go somewhere private?'

'Fine.' He slid his phone out of his pocket and quickly texted a message. 'The limo will meet us out front in five minutes.'

'We're leaving?'

'Do you really want to go back in to the party?'

'No, but I thought you would. This charity is important to you.'

He shrugged. 'Your well-being matters more.'

Which both touched her and made her feel guilty. She really had failed him this evening. Feeling miserable on so many levels, Halina followed Rico out of the bathroom. He took her arm as he strode away from the party so that Halina had to take quick, mincing steps in her tightly fitted evening gown and tottering heels to keep up with him.

'Rico, wait! I can't walk so fast. These shoes are killing me.'

'Sorry.' He glanced at her, contrite. 'I just wanted to get you away from here.'

The limo was waiting for them outside the hotel, and Rico opened the door before ushering Halina inside. She slipped into the luxurious leather interior with a sigh of relief. Every part of her ached.

'Are you in pain?' Rico asked, catching her wince, and Halina managed a laugh.

'No, I'm just not used to these stilettos. They kill my feet.'

'Take them off, then.' Before she could do so he reached down, undid the straps of her shoes and slipped them off her feet. Halina let out a gusty sigh of relief, then gave a little gasp of surprise when Rico took her feet and drew them up to his lap. When his thumbs began to massage powerful circles on their soles she wriggled with pleasure and couldn't keep a moan of delight from escaping her.

'Oh, my goodness, that feels fantastic.'

Rico laughed softly. 'I can tell.'

He reached over and tucked one of the throw pillows adorning the limo's seats behind her head. 'There. Now tell me what happened at the party.'

Halina's eyes fluttered closed as she surrendered to Rico's tender ministrations, his fingers continuing to work their magic on her aching feet. 'It wasn't such a big deal. I'm sorry I made it so.'

'That's for me to say, not you. What happened, Halina?'

She sighed and then wriggled again with pleasure as Rico's hands moved up to her ankles, his thumbs tracing the delicate bones.

'I was in one of the bathroom stalls and some women came in. They started talking about me—and you.'

His fingers stilled for only a second before he continued with the slow, rhythmic circles. 'And what did they say?'

'They knew I was pregnant. I don't know how…'

'You put your hand on your belly during our engagement announcement and then you asked for sparkling water.'

'Oh.' Now she felt stupid. 'Well, that explains it, then,' she said with an attempt at a laugh.

'I don't mind people knowing, Halina,' Rico said, his voice low and sure. 'I will never mind. You're going to be my wife and you're carrying my child.'

'Are you sorry?' Halina blurted, opening her eyes. In the darkness of the car she couldn't make out his expression.

'Sorry...?'

'That you slept with me. That I became pregnant. That I...that I ruined your life.'

'Halina.' Rico leaned forward so his gaze met hers and she could see how fiercely his silvery eyes glittered. 'You have not ruined my life.'

'But to be suddenly burdened with a wife and baby you didn't want... And you had all those mistresses...' A sudden, horrible thought occurred to her, one that now seemed appallingly obvious. 'Are you...are you going to keep on with them...after we marry?'

'What?' Rico's brows drew together in a ferocious frown. 'Of course not. Do you honestly think I would?'

'You didn't ask for this, Rico.'

'Neither did you. And, in any case, I believe I will be wholly satisfied in that department by my wife.' His hand slid from her ankle to her knee, his fingers splayed across her tender skin as his gaze remained hot and intent on hers. 'Perhaps I should remind you how good we are together, *bella*. How explosive.'

Halina's breath came out in a shuddery rush and the sensitive skin of her knee tingled. His fingers felt warm and very sure as they started to slide upwards. 'You've barely touched me in two weeks,' she whispered. 'Not since you saw me again.'

'I wanted you to rest.' His smile turned wolfish, his eyes filled with heat. 'To regain your strength.'

'Plus I looked like a worn-out dishrag.'

'You have always been beautiful to me. Never doubt that.' With his gaze still fastened on hers, he moved his hand to her inner thigh, his warm palm sliding upwards in a sure, fluid movement. Halina shuddered, every nerve on over-sensitised alert as his fingers skimmed along her skin.

'We're so good together, Halina,' Rico murmured as he continued to stroke her thigh. 'We always have been.'

'You mean the one time.'

'I am looking forward to many others. You have ruined me for other women.'

'That's what someone said about you.' Her breath came out in jerks and bursts as his fingers crept even closer to her feminine centre. If he touched her there, she thought she might melt—or explode.

'What do you mean?' One finger skimmed the lace of her underwear, making her shudder. Halina slid a little lower down on the seat.

'In the bathroom…that first night…some supermodel you'd slept with… The women said she'd been ruined for life by you, because you're so…' His fingers were becoming more insistent, more daring, sliding beneath her underwear, skimming her tantalised flesh and then going even deeper, with sure, knowing strokes. Pleasure swirled inside her, obscuring her senses so she could barely think, much less speak. 'They said…they said you were so good,' she half-moaned as her body arched upwards. 'At sex.' With a little cry she gave herself up to the pleasure crashing over her and felt herself go liquid and boneless.

As the last shudders of her climax rippled through her, Rico leaned over and pressed a hard kiss to her mouth. 'Which I've just proved, I think.'

She opened her eyes, dazed and more than a little embarrassed to be slouched on the seat, her elegant gown rucked up halfway to her hips, her wanton pleasure so very evident.

She struggled up to sitting, pushing her hair out of her face. 'I must look a mess,' she muttered.

'You look beautiful.' Rico touched her chin with his fingertips. 'Do you know how enflaming it is to see you come apart under my touch? Do you know what it does to me?' Wordlessly Halina shook her head, shocked by the admission, by the blatant need she saw in his eyes and felt in the tautness of his body. 'When we get back to the apartment,' Rico said, his voice roughening, 'I'll show you.'

Desire thrummed through Rico, a slow burn that threatened to ignite into a full conflagration. Seeing Halina respond to his touch, her face and body both suffused with pleasure, had been a severe test of his self-control. He'd wanted to take her right there on the seat of his limo, in the kind of helpless display of overwhelming need that he never gave into.

So he didn't. He wanted her—heaven help them both how much he did—but he still clung to his self-control, if only by his fingertips.

The limo pulled up to his building and without a word Rico emerged from the back, holding Halina's hand as he drew her along.

'My shoes,' she protested, and he saw she was barefoot.

'They don't matter. Forget them.' His self-control only extended so far.

With a little laugh Halina did, following him into the darkened foyer of the building and then into the lift. That was how far his self-control went; as soon as the doors closed, he pulled her into his arms, plundering her mouth as he backed her up against the wall.

She gasped, driving her hands through his hair as she surrendered to his touch, wrapping her arms around him and pulling him even closer.

It still wasn't enough. He yanked her dress up to her waist, needing to feel her against him.

'Rico…' His name was a soft protest and he stilled, shocked by his own urgent actions.

'Do you want me?' he demanded, unable to keep from saying the words. Voicing his fear. 'Do you want me as much as I want you?'

'You know I do.'

The doors to his apartment opened and with a sound nearing a growl Rico swept Halina up into his arms and strode to his bedroom. 'Then show me.'

'I already have,' she protested breathlessly as he peeled her dress off her and laid her on the bed. 'How could you doubt it, Rico? I've been putty in your hands since the moment I first laid eyes on you.'

'Good.' He pulled off his tie and tuxedo shirt, studs flying everywhere and clattering to the floor. 'That's how I want it to be.'

The self-control he'd been so determined, so *desperate* to hold onto was in shreds. All he could think of, all he could feel, was his need for her. Shucking off the rest of his clothes, Rico pulled Halina into his arms. The feel of her golden, silken skin against his was an exquisite torture.

'I've been dreaming of this,' he muttered against her skin, wanting to touch and taste her all at once. 'Dreaming of this ever since you walked out of my hotel suite all those weeks ago.'

'So have I,' Halina whispered, her body arching under his touch. 'Even if I tried to keep myself from it.'

Just as he had, because such need was weakness. But now he didn't care. Now he simply wanted—and took.

When he slid inside her velvety depths he felt a crashing sense of relief, almost as if a burden had been lifted. This felt right and true, the home he'd never had. Then she arched up to meet him, matching his thrusts, and he stopped thinking at all.

Later, when his heart rate had started to slow and he felt himself come back to his senses, Rico reviewed his actions as dispassionately as he could. Yes, he'd lost control. Completely. But so had Halina. The fact was they shared an incredible chemistry, and that was no bad thing. So as long as he kept the loss of control in the realm of the bedroom, he would be satisfied. He wouldn't be in danger of losing anything to Halina…such as the heart he'd always acted as if he didn't have.

Next to him Halina stirred sleepily. 'That was a nice way to end the evening.'

'Perhaps the evening is just beginning.' Rico rolled over to face her. 'But we never finished our conversation. What did those women say?'

'It really doesn't matter…'

He hated the thought of her being hurt. 'I think it does.'

With a sigh Halina rolled onto her back. 'They just said they couldn't believe you'd finally been snared—that was the word I think they used. And the fact that I was pregnant and a princess could be the only reason you'd ever marry me, because you were obviously way out of my league.'

Rico stiffened, a new fury starting to boil through

him. How dared those insipid, catty women say such things about his chosen bride?

'I don't know why you seem angry,' Halina remarked lightly as she rolled back to face him. 'It's all true.'

'What? No, it isn't.'

'Come on, Rico.' Despite her light tone, pain flashed in her eyes. 'Let's be honest. I know there are a lot of things we can't have in our marriage, but surely truth isn't one of them?'

'It's not true,' he insisted stubbornly.

'It is,' Halina returned, her tone just as stubborn. 'You know it is. You never would have married me if I hadn't been pregnant, and the fact that I'm royal no doubt has something to do with it too.'

'What are you saying? That if you'd been a nobody I wouldn't have married you?'

'Would you have?'

'I would always,' Rico said flatly, fighting back a tidal wave of fury, 'marry the mother of my child.'

'So I guess you didn't get a woman pregnant before.'

'No, I always took precautions, for a reason.'

She nodded slowly. 'And I'd told you it was safe. I'm sorry.'

He shook his head, annoyed and exasperated by the whole conversation. He didn't want to tread over this old ground yet again. He didn't want to be reminded of how he used to be, either. He was different now—just not *that* different.

'My point,' Halina said after a moment, 'Is that my pregnancy is what precipitated your proposal. How's that for an alliteration?' She gave him a teasing smile but Rico didn't have it in him to respond in kind.

His fury was fading, replaced by a far more alarming confusion as he realised that Halina was right, at least in part. He never would have married her if she hadn't been pregnant. He never even would have seen her again. It was blindingly obvious, but it didn't sit well with him. At all.

'I should go back to my own bed,' Halina said, starting to rise. Rico stayed her with one hand.

'You'll sleep here.'

Even in the darkness of the room he saw the surprise flash across her face. 'I thought you never slept with a woman—'

'You're going to be my wife,' Rico interjected fiercely. 'And we'll sleep together from now on. It's time,' he added, drawing her towards him so she was nestled snugly against his chest, 'That we started to plan the wedding.'

CHAPTER TWELVE

'THIS DRESS IS very discreet.' The sales assistant gave Halina a knowing smile as she gestured to a gorgeous dress of ivory satin with a convenient empire waist to hide Halina's small but growing bump. She was fifteen weeks pregnant and only just starting to show.

It had been three weeks since she and Rico had reconsummated their relationship, three weeks of virtually living as man and wife, even if they weren't going to say the vows for another fortnight. Three happy, hopeful yet so uncertain weeks, and with every passing day Halina felt more and more anxious.

She had spent every night in Rico's bed, as well as in his arms. He was a tender and attentive lover, awakening her body to sensations and desires she'd never experienced before.

As she'd grown in experience, she had also grown in confidence, daring to touch and explore his body as he did hers. It had brought an intense intimacy that left Halina breathless with longing for Rico to feel the same as she did...even as she forced herself to acknowledge that he didn't, he couldn't, not when he'd gone through a woman a week for most of his adult life. Sex was just a physical exercise for him, not the emotional, soul-shattering experience it had become for her.

As for out of bed… Rico was attentive then, too. Solicitous to her every need and comfort—often coming home with some treat she'd been craving, accompanying her to her doctor appointments and helping with the planning of their wedding which, according to the city's tabloids and gossip magazines, was going to be the event of the year.

Halina wasn't sure how she felt about that; in the weeks since that first, awful party they'd gone out on several social occasions and she'd managed to hold her head up high, despite several women's sneering looks and whispering comments.

'They're just jealous,' Rico said blandly, and Halina had laughed.

'That's a rather arrogant comment, you know.'

'But it's true.' And she knew it was.

As the wedding loomed closer, she veered between excitement and a growing terror. Excitement because part of her was looking forward to being part of a family again, to starting a new life with Rico. She'd enjoyed these last few weeks with him, more than she'd ever expected to, but the terror came from the creeping fear that it wasn't enough and it never would be.

His care, his solicitude, his thorough attentiveness in bed—none of it would be enough, because he didn't love her. He'd made that very clear in a thousand painful ways. He would never love her, and she had to accept that, learn to live with it, because she had no choice. As much freedom as she felt she had now, she still lived under the worst restriction of all.

'Would you like to try it on?' the assistant asked, and Halina nodded, needing a distraction from her circling and increasingly unhappy thoughts. She also needed a wedding dress; the church and reception hall had been booked, the meal planned, the champagne ordered and the guests, all six hundred of them, invited. Although she'd been looking for a while, she hadn't yet found a dress she liked—and it was getting late.

Halina went into the dressing room and slipped into the empire-waist dress. The bodice shimmered with crystal jet and diamanté, and the skirt fell in a drop of exquisite ivory satin, swirling around her ankles. It was simple and elegant and, as the assistant said, very discreet.

Halina tried to picture herself walking down the aisle in the huge church and inwardly trembled. She'd be walking alone; her father had refused to attend the wedding, or let her mother or sisters attend. Their absence made her relationship with Rico feel even lonelier and more lacking. He was all she had in the world, and he didn't love her.

'What does *signorina* think?' the assistant called, and Halina gazed at her pale face, her wide dark eyes.

'It's fine,' she called back tonelessly. 'Perfect. I'll take it.'

Her fingers shook as she fumbled with the hook-and-eye fasteners at the back of the dress. What was wrong with her? She'd been happy these last three weeks; she really had. There had been so much to enjoy, and yet…

Marriage. A loveless marriage. For ever. She closed her eyes and leaned her forehead against the cool mirror. Why did it matter so much? Why did it make her ache so?

'*Signorina?*' The assistant peeked through the curtain and Halina jerked back, embarrassed to be caught looking as if she were about to fall apart.

'I'll be straight out.'

The woman smiled sympathetically. 'Everyone gets cold feet, no? It is normal.'

It wasn't her cold feet she was worried about but Rico's icy heart. Quickly she slipped out of the dress and handed it to the assistant. 'Thank you.'

'You are sure...?'

'Yes.' She was sure about the dress, if nothing else at this moment.

Halina dressed quickly, as Rico was planning to meet her for lunch at a new upscale restaurant off the Via dei Condotti and she didn't want him sensing that she was worried or upset. He would just harangue her, demanding to know what was wrong and how he could fix it. Touching at times, but he couldn't fix this. He wouldn't want to.

'Did you find a dress?' Rico asked when she walked into the restaurant fifteen minutes later. He stood up as she came to the table and kissed her cheek.

'Yes, I have found one.' Halina sat down and smiled. 'I think it's very pretty.'

Rico scanned her face, a slight frown settling between his brows. 'What's wrong?'

He was so irritatingly perceptive, Halina reflected. A strange quality for man who claimed to have no use for feelings. 'Nothing's wrong,' she said and picked up her menu. Now that thankfully her nausea had gone, she found she was ravenous.

'Something's wrong, Halina. I can tell.'

Halina looked up from the menu, her eyebrows raised. 'How can you tell?'

Rico shrugged, seeming slightly discomfited by the question. 'I just can. There's something about you...it's like a sixth sense, I suppose. We're attuned to each other.'

Which could have been heartening, but wasn't. She didn't want to be *attuned*. She wanted to be loved. The realisation solidified inside her, although she'd been trying to talk herself out of it for weeks. Why did she care if Rico loved her or not, when he promised her so much else?

The answer came suddenly in a tidal wave of amazement and despair.

She loved him. She'd gone and fallen in love with him, even though she'd known it was foolish, the stupidest thing she could ever do. Yet she'd still done it. Her heart hadn't been able to resist because Rico was gentle, kind and fiercely protective, because he made her laugh and ache and sing.

This was love, then, that ephemeral emotion Rico dismissed out of hand. And it was so much more than that, because Halina knew what it meant. It meant she would love him no matter what; it meant she would love him even if he didn't love her back.

She'd wondered what love felt like, if she'd really know when it was missing or whether she'd found it, and now here was her proof. She loved Rico, and it filled her with both joy and despair because she knew, no matter what she felt, that he utterly refused to love her back.

'Well?' Rico demanded. 'Has something happened? Has someone said something? Tell me.'

'I don't want to, Rico,' Halina said wearily. She knew he wouldn't let it drop, just as she knew he'd hate to hear what was really troubling her—the realisation that thudded through her, a wonder and fear.

Rico's frown deepened. 'Why don't you want to?'

'Because there's no point, and it will just annoy you.' As much as it hurt her to say it. 'You don't have to be such a bull dog about everything, you know? I'm allowed to have some thoughts I can keep to myself.' Because it would horrify him to know she'd fallen in love with him. That much she knew.

'I'm hardly asking you to tell me your every thought,' Rico protested. 'But, if something is troubling you, I want to fix it.'

'Trust me, you can't fix this.'

That, of course, did nothing to appease him. 'There must be something I can do,' Rico insisted, and Halina almost smiled. Her husband-to-be hated the thought that he was not all-powerful.

'There isn't,' she informed him firmly. 'Shall we order?'

Rico looked unconvinced but he beckoned the hovering waiter over and they ordered their meals.

'You are happy with the dress?' Rico asked once the waiter had left them alone.

'Yes, it's very nice.' Although now she could barely remember what it looked like. It wasn't the way she had wanted to buy her wedding dress, alone and anonymous in a boutique. If she'd been at home, her sisters would have surrounded her, jabbering excitedly, and her mother would have been there to offer benevolent and wise advice. Even her father would have wanted to see the dress, and offer an opinion.

Sudden tears stung her eyes and she blinked them back rapidly, but not before Rico noticed.

'Halina,' he said, his voice low and urgent as he leaned forward. 'You must tell me what is wrong. I can't stand to see you so obviously unhappy.'

'I just miss my family,' Halina said, which was the truth, if not all of it. 'I wish they could be here for the wedding.'

Rico sat back, his lips pressed together. 'You are right, in that there is nothing I can do about that.'

'I know.' She sniffed and took a sip of sparkling water. 'I'm sorry. I'll be better in a moment.' She managed a wobbly smile. 'It's all these pregnancy hormones making me emotional.' But it was so much more.

'You don't need to be sorry.' Rico was subjecting her to one of his thorough, considering glances. 'But there's something else, isn't there?'

'Oh, Rico.' Halina let out a shuddery laugh as she rolled her eyes. 'What if there was?'

'Then I want to know.'

She stared at him for a moment, knowing he wouldn't let it go. Well, fine. She'd asked for honesty from him once; now he could have it from her, at least some of it.

'All right.' She took a deep, steadying breath. 'The truth is, I'm sad because I know you don't love me, and from what you've said you'll probably never love me. I'm trying to come to terms with it, but it's hard. I know I was willing to marry a virtual stranger, but a cold, loveless union is not what I've ever wanted for my life.'

Rico stared at Halina, trying not to let his emotions show on his face. His utter horror at what she'd just stated with such stark, bleak honesty. He must not have done a very good job because Halina let out a huff of humourless laughter.

'You don't have to look quite so appalled. Consider the bright side—I do know what I'm getting into.' She looked away, blinking rapidly, appalling him further. 'You made sure of that.'

'Yes, but I… I didn't realise you wanted…love quite so much.'

'Is it so surprising? Isn't it what most people want?' She turned back to give him a direct, challenging look. 'Perhaps you're the strange one, Rico, not me.'

'Perhaps.' He knew, on some level, she'd wanted love.

She'd said as much, but he'd been sure he could convince her otherwise.

What *was* love anyway? Nothing more than a feeling, as ephemeral as the morning mist. Halina could learn to live without it, just as he had. Everything would be better that way. Happier, even. He just had to convince her of it.

Rico eyed her carefully. 'Halina,' he began, choosing each word with delicate precision, 'Just because we do not love each other...we can still be happy together.'

'Can we?' Tears shimmered in her eyes and she blinked them back resolutely. 'I know all this emotion is appalling you, Rico. I'm sorry.'

'For heaven's sake, you don't need to be sorry.' Did she think he was that intransigent, that hard and unyielding? Perhaps once he had been, but now... He *had* changed, at least a little. Just not too much. 'You can't help the way you feel.'

'Just as you can't help the way you don't.' She forced a smile. 'So there we are.'

'It doesn't have to be all gloom and despair,' Rico persisted, trying to keep the impatience and urgency from his voice. 'What is love anyway, Halina? A feeling? A warm glow in your heart?'

She flinched at the scorn he'd unintentionally and instinctively put into those words. 'Maybe that's a sign of it, Rico, but it's not all love is.' Her lip curled, and now she was as contemptuous as he was. 'Love is so much more than that, which you should know, since you've loved someone before.'

He felt himself go still. 'What makes you say that?'

'You said it before,' she answered with a shrug, her pain-filled gaze sliding away from his. 'You told me it was a long time ago, but she obviously hurt you very badly if you can't bear the thought of letting yourself love someone years later.'

'She?' Rico repeated blankly, and Halina turned back to him with a frown.

'The woman, whoever she was.'

'There was no woman, Halina.' Perhaps it would have been easier, safer, to pretend there had been, but it didn't feel fair to Halina and he didn't want her to labour under the misapprehension that he'd loved another woman but wouldn't love her. 'I told you before, I've never been in love with anyone.'

'Then who was it who broke your heart?' Halina asked in a whisper. Rico flinched at the phrase.

Broke his heart. So trite, so real. 'It was my father,' he said after a tense pause. 'He hurt me very badly when I was a child and I never forgot it.'

'What did he do?'

'He didn't love me back,' Rico said simply. Even that felt like admitting way too much. Halina stared at him, her gaze both searching and yearning.

'And that's why you don't want to love anyone? Because of something that happened when you were a child?'

'It taught me a valuable lesson,' Rico said shortly.

'Which was?'

'That love isn't real. Whether it's a warm glow or not, that doesn't matter. It doesn't last. It doesn't change things, and you can't count on it or trust it. Frankly, we're both better off without it, Halina.'

'Of course you would think that.'

'Yes, I would,' Rico returned, his voice gaining force. He felt a deep-seated need, bordering on a compulsion, to prove this to her. To liberate her from such childish notions, as well as cement the foundation of their own future happiness. 'Think about it, Halina. You want me to love you. What does that even mean? What would it look like, practically?'

She flushed, looking as if she resented the question. 'If I have to spell it out to you...'

He reached across the table to cover her hand with his own. 'Humour me. Please.'

'Fine.' She pulled her hand away and folded her arms. 'It would mean I was the most important thing to you. That you couldn't bear to be away from me. That I made the sun shine more brightly and the sky look more blue. That I complete you.' She shook her head. 'How many clichés do I have to pull out of the book, Rico? Love just *is*. Either you love someone or you don't, and if you don't, then whatever you feel—whether it's affection or duty or something in between—is eventually going to fade and pale. At some point in the future it's not going to be enough, and that's what I don't want to have happen. I don't want to look up from my dinner or roll over in bed and see that knowledge in your eyes.'

'I swear to you,' Rico said in a low voice that thrummed with sincerity, 'that would never happen.'

'You can't make that promise.'

He put his hands flat on the table, a sudden fury coursing through him. 'And you think love is the failsafe guarantee, Halina? That, if I loved you, that feeling would never fade? Because, I can assure you, it would. Love is a guarantee of absolutely nothing. Haven't you learned that yourself? Look at your own father. You thought he loved you but he would have killed your own baby if he could have, and now he won't even come to your wedding. Is that love?'

Her face crumpled and he regretted his harsh words.

He'd been so caught up in the moment, in his own memories. He reached for her hands. 'Halina…'

'Maybe you're right, Rico,' Halina said, her expression composed now, although her voice trembled. 'Love can fade, or at least seem as if it does. But I choose to believe, and to hope. People make mistakes, they do unloving things, but at the core of their being the love remains. And I choose to believe that my father still loves me, and eventually he'll realise the mistakes he made. *That's* the difference. Someone who loves you can still let you down. They're only human. But because you love them, and they love you, you keep going. You forgive and you grow stronger, and you move on. Together. You asked me what love is. Well, that's my definition.'

Rico stared at her, humbled by her brave honesty and also by the gaping emptiness he felt in himself. Had he ever felt that, either to give or to receive? Did he even know what love was?

'So we're right back at the beginning,' Halina said with an attempt at a laugh. She shook her head sadly. 'There's no solution, is there, Rico? We're going to get married, but you will never love me. I just have to live with it.'

'I might not love you,' Rico said, 'but, as I told you before, I will protect and provide for you. Always. I will be loyal and faithful, and I will do anything in my power to make you happy. Isn't that enough?'

Her mouth curved in a sorrowful smile as she answered. 'I suppose it will have to be.'

CHAPTER THIRTEEN

A WEEK BEFORE the wedding Halina woke up in the middle of the night with terrible stomach cramps. It had been a week since her all-too-honest conversation with Rico, a week of learning to live without love and finding a way to be happy. At times she'd felt she was on the verge of finding it: when she and Rico could laugh together, when he reached for her in bed. But then memories would rush through her, or he would roll away, and she feared she'd always be searching for that ever-elusive feeling.

Now she lay in bed, blinking up at the ceiling as her stomach cramped, muscles contracting painfully. She was only four months along, and in the last few days she'd felt the first flutters of movement, which had filled her with joy. Now she feared something was wrong.

Quietly she slid from the bed and went to the bathroom, hoping that the issue was merely a spicy meal that had disagreed with her. But when she saw the rusty streak of blood on the toilet paper she knew otherwise.

Her soft scream had Rico bolting upright in bed. 'Halina?'

She came out of the bathroom, her whole body trembling. 'I'm bleeding,' she whispered. Her body throbbed with terror as her stomach continued to cramp. 'Rico, I'm bleeding.'

Rico's eyes widened as he got her full meaning. 'I'll take you to the hospital,' he said, already getting out of bed. 'To the emergency department, right now.'

Halina watched, fear hammering through her, as Rico pulled on a shirt and trousers. He was in the middle of buttoning his shirt when he saw that she hadn't moved from the doorway of the bathroom.

'Halina, we need to go.'

'I'm scared.' The two words fell softly into the stillness. She wrapped her arms around herself. 'I don't want to lose this baby. I can't. Not after everything…'

'You won't.' Rico took her by the shoulders and stared into her eyes, his expression both grim and comforting. 'You won't. The doctors will figure out what's going on. They'll help you and they will help our baby.'

She nodded, wanting to believe him, needing to. Her teeth chattered; she felt icy cold.

'Come on,' Rico said gently, steering her towards the bureau. 'Let's get you dressed.' Halina felt like a child as she stood there and let Rico tenderly strip her night-gown from her body. He found one of her new maternity tops and loose trousers and helped her shrug them on.

'I'm sorry,' she choked. 'I feel frozen…'

'Shh.' Rico brushed a kiss against her forehead. 'It's all right…it's going to be all right.'

He took her hand and together they walked out to his car, a luxury sports model that he used in his down time with a private parking space. Halina slid into the passenger seat and wrapped her arms around herself. Even though it was a balmy evening at the very end of September, she felt so very cold.

The emergency department of the local hospital was brightly lit and bustling despite the late hour. Several rows of hard plastic seats were filled with people with various ailments and injuries. Rico strode to the front to talk to the triage nurse while Halina sank into a seat, desperately trying to hold onto her composure as well as her hope. Her stomach still cramped, off and on, off and on.

Rico strode back to her then sat down next to her and took her hand. 'You're freezing,' he said, and chafed her hand between his own. Halina gave him a shaky smile.

'I feel like I'll never get warm. Maybe it's shock.'

'It's going to be okay, Halina.'

'I know you want that to be the case, but it might not be.' Her voice wobbled. 'It might not be. This isn't in your control, Rico, just like the sandstorm. I know you hate that, but it's true.'

'I do hate it.' Rico's voice was low and fierce. 'I hate it absolutely.' His hands squeezed hers. 'But I also believe it's going to be okay. It has to be.'

Looking at the agony written in harsh lines on his features, Halina knew he meant that with every fibre of his being. Rico couldn't take this not being okay. She couldn't cope with it, just as he couldn't, and it made her cling to him all the more.

'Signora Falcone?'

Halina gave Rico a startled glance as she heard the nurse call out her soon-to-be name.

'It seemed easier,' he muttered, and rose from the seat before helping her to her feet. 'We're here,' he called to the nurse.

Halina focused on staying calm as she followed the nurse to a cubicle in the hospital's busy emergency department. After a short wait a doctor bustled in, smiling in a slightly distracted way.

'What seems to be the problem?' she asked as he soaped her hands at the little sink.

Haltingly, Halina explained about the cramps and bleeding. The doctor frowned as he dried his hands.

'You're about sixteen weeks along?'

'Yes, just sixteen weeks.'

'It can be normal to have a little bleed during your pregnancy, but it can also be a sign of something wrong. Why don't we have a listen for the heartbeat?'

Halina nodded and lay back on the examining table, her mouth dry, her heart thudding. Rico stood by her, his hand still encasing hers.

The doctor turned on the Doppler and began to press Halina's belly, looking for the heartbeat. All they heard was the whoosh of her own body and blood, not the lovely, galloping sound of their baby's heart.

Halina closed her eyes, willing to hear that wonderful sound. This couldn't be the end. It just couldn't be. *Please, baby,* she prayed silently. *Please live.*

The doctor switched off the Doppler, looking serious. Halina risked a glance at Rico and saw his jaw was clenched tightly, his eyes dark and focused.

'I'll send you to the ultrasound department for a scan,' the doctor said. 'Sometimes it can be difficult to find the heartbeat.' He gave them both a sympathetic smile. 'But of course, it could also be that something has gone wrong. We'll only know when we see the scan.'

Halina nodded. She felt icy and numb now, too numb to be afraid any more. She'd feared the worst already, and it seemed likely. Wordlessly she pulled her top down and she and Rico went back to the waiting room to wait until she was called for a scan.

Neither of them spoke as they sat in the brightly lit room while people bustled and moved around them—children sleeping on mother's laps, babies crying. Halina looked away from the tear-filled eyes of a chubby-cheeked cherub. What she wouldn't give to have a baby in her arms right now, even one that was crying and in pain.

'It's going to be okay,' Rico said in a low voice, and Halina turned to him with a sudden, surprising spurt of fury.

'Stop saying that,' she returned, her voice just as low. 'You don't know. You can't know. And at the moment, Rico, it looks like things aren't going to be all right. The doctor couldn't even find a heartbeat—' She broke off with a shuddering breath and looked away.

'You're right,' Rico answered after a moment. 'I don't know, and I hate that, because I don't know what to do, Halina. I want to help you and I can't.'

Tears stung her eyes and she blinked them back. 'You can help me by just walking with me through this, whatever happens,' she said steadily. 'Don't try to fix it or control it, Rico—just be with me. That's what I want.' She turned to him, blinking back more tears that threatened to fall. 'Can you do that?'

He looked at her seriously, his mouth a firm line, an agony in his eyes. 'Yes,' he said. 'I can do that.'

He hated everything about this. He hated watching Halina's fear and pain, feeling it himself, twice the agony. He hated having their carefully constructed world break apart, shatter into pieces. He thought of the baby nestled in Halina's womb and willed it to live. He hadn't realised just how much he wanted this child until it was at risk. Until everything he'd shared and built with Halina was at risk.

The knowledge jolted him, like missing the last stair. This wasn't just about their baby; it was about him and Halina. Their relationship. Their marriage. Over the last few weeks he'd got used to having Halina with him; he enjoyed it, counted on it, even. And he wasn't willing to give that up.

But if their baby had died…there was no reason to get married. No reason at all, and with an uncomfortable, prickling sensation Rico realised that Halina would no doubt be glad to get away from him. She'd made it clear several weeks ago—hell, all along—that she was willing to marry him but she didn't actually want to… because she wanted someone who would love her. Who could love her.

And he couldn't.

'Signora Falcone?'

Halina looked up, her face pale, her lips set in a firm line. Rico reached for her hand and together they walked towards the nurse, braced for the worst.

The ultrasound room was dim and quiet as Halina lay back once again on the examining table and the technician squirted cold, clear gel on her bare belly, her baby bump barely visible. She looked so vulnerable lying there, waiting, worrying, and Rico's heart ached for her. Ached for them, because he was so afraid it was all slipping away.

He knew that fear. He knew it far too well, because he remembered feeling it when his father had dropped him off on the steps of the orphanage in Salerno, his face grim but determined.

'They'll take care of you here,' he'd said while Rico had fought tears as he'd begged for his father to keep him. Not to leave him. He'd cried like a baby; he'd clung to his father's sleeve and his father had had to push him off.

Then he'd watched his father walk away; he hadn't looked back once. And in that moment Rico had resolved never to let someone hurt him like that again.

'Rico, look.' Halina grabbed his sleeve, just as he had

with his father, and he blinked back the memories as he was startled into the present. 'Look, Rico. Our baby!'

He focused on the ultrasound screen, and the beautiful sight of their tiny baby wriggling around like a jumping bean.

'Baby looks fine,' the technician said with a smile, and Halina let out an incredulous, shuddery laugh of joy. Rico's smile nearly split his face. 'It looks, Signora Falcone,' the technician continued, 'as if you've had a subchorionic haematoma.'

'A what?' Halina asked, her voice filled with nervousness.

The technician gave her a quick, reassuring smile. 'Basically a bleed between your baby and the uterine wall.'

'Is it dangerous?' Rico asked, his voice harsher than he'd meant it to be.

'It doesn't have to be.' The technician gave them both a sympathetic smile. 'Of course, any bleeding in pregnancy can be a cause of concern, and a haematoma of this size is definitely something we need to keep an eye on.'

None of which sounded particularly good. 'So what now?' Rico asked. 'What do we do?'

'Signora Falcone can continue as normal,' the technician said. 'Which is what we'd advise. But we'd also advise slowing down a little if possible—not being on your feet too much, or carrying anything heavy, that sort of thing.' She smiled at Halina. 'Giving both you and your baby the best chance possible. And, if you have any more bleeding, don't hesitate to call.'

Rico's mind was still spinning as they drove back home, dawn lighting the empty streets of Rome and touching them with rosy gold.

Back in the penthouse Halina went straight to bed, and Rico tucked her in as if she were a child. 'See?' he said as he brushed a kiss across her lips. 'I told you it was going to be okay.'

Halina gave him a wan smile; she looked utterly exhausted. Within moments she was asleep.

Back in the living area Rico pulled his laptop towards him and spent several hours finding out everything he could about sub-chorionic haematomas. The information was mixed, with some specialists saying they heightened the chance of miscarriage, and others saying they had no effect.

His eyes gritty and aching, Rico stared out at the city and vowed to do everything he could to keep Halina and their baby safe. They'd come so close today to losing it all and it had scared him.

It had scared him even more how devastated he'd been at the thought of not losing just his child, but Halina too. He was starting to care for her and that prospect terrified him more than anything.

How could he make Halina happy, love their baby and yet keep the emotional distance from her he knew he needed? The lines were blurring more and more every day. Soon it would be impossible...and what then?

'What time is it?'

Rico looked up, startled out of his thoughts, to see Halina standing in the doorway, her hair in a dark cloud about her face, her expression still sleepy.

'I don't know.' He checked his watch. 'About ten in the morning. You should get back in bed.'

'I can't spend the next five months in bed, Rico.'

'You heard what the technician said.'

'Yes, I did. Did you?' With a wry smile she crossed the room and curled up on the opposite end of the sofa. 'She said I needed to take it a bit easier, not that I needed to be bedridden.'

'Still…'

She turned to him, her smile gone, her expression serious. 'Don't you think I'm going to do everything in my power to take care of this baby?'

Slightly abashed, Rico nodded. Yes, he believed that. Of course he did.

Halina drew her knees up, resting her chin on top. 'Still, it could all go wrong,' she said quietly. 'We have to be prepared for that.'

'Just as we have to do everything we can to make sure that doesn't happen,' Rico returned. 'I'm going to call off the wedding.'

'What?' She turned to him, startled, her eyes wide and dark.

'It's too much strain and pressure on you. We can have a quiet wedding later, or reschedule a big ceremony, if that's what you prefer.'

'But all the preparations…all the money you spent…'

'What does money matter? Your health is more important. Our child's health. Besides, perhaps if we wait a while your father will come round and decide to attend.'

Pain flashed across her face and she nodded slowly. 'Yes. Maybe.' She sounded so sad that Rico ached to hold her, but he didn't, because something about Halina right now was cool and brittle, as if she were trying to maintain a certain distance. Her next words confirmed it.

'But Rico…if I do lose this baby…we need to talk about that.'

He tensed, his jaw clenched. 'Let's not court disaster, Halina.'

'Let's also be prepared,' she returned evenly. 'Isn't that your motto? Wasn't that why you had all those provisions in the car when we were trapped in the sandstorm in the desert? Because you like to be prepared.'

'Yes, but—'

'So let's be prepared for this,' Halina said steadily. 'If I lose the baby, we don't have to marry. You're free.'

Why did he now hate that thought? 'And what about you?' he asked. 'Are you free?'

'Yes,' Halina returned after a pause. 'Yes, I will be. I told you before, I never wanted a marriage without love.'

He fought to keep his expression neutral when everything in him wanted to cry out, to resist and deny. 'So what will you do, in this worst-case scenario? Return to Abkar?'

She let out a small huff of sad laughter and shrugged. 'Maybe I'll get that apartment in Paris I always dreamed about, with a piano and a terrace.'

But how would she do that? She had no money, no resources, and if she was free from him, her father might plan another marriage for her. But maybe Halina would prefer that, rather than be shackled to him for the rest of her life. The knowledge hurt, far more than Rico wanted it to.

'Well, then,' he said in a hard voice. 'Now we're prepared for the worst. So let's hope for the best, hey? And keep you on bed rest.'

She smiled faintly. 'In control, as always.'

'Yes,' Rico answered, but he didn't feel in control at all. Now, more than ever, he felt as if things were spinning out of his grasp...especially his own heart.

CHAPTER FOURTEEN

TODAY WOULD HAVE been her wedding day. Halina gazed out of the window of her bedroom at the buildings and streets of the Eternal City, feeling more in limbo now than ever. The last week had been endless, lying in bed, waiting for the worst to happen.

Since the first terror-filled visit to the hospital, thankfully she hadn't had any more episodes of bleeding, but she still lived in fear, and so did Rico. They were both tiptoeing around each other, a constant strain between them, caused, Halina supposed, by the new uncertainty that had opened up like a yawning chasm, sending them both into tense isolation.

Any day, any week, and it could all be over. Their child's life, the little family they'd been creating, the marriage they'd both intended to embark on. All of it could be reduced to nothing. It was exhausting, living with that kind of uncertainty, and Halina spent most of her enforced bed rest sleeping, in part just to escape the strain. How long would it last? The next five months? Or maybe not long at all. Maybe today would be the day it ended. It was impossible to know.

What she did know was that she'd fallen in love with Rico and it was tearing her apart. At every turn her fears were confirmed and the knowledge that he didn't love her, didn't want to love her, reverberated through her all over again, a loss she could never get used to. A tiny, treacherous part of her almost wondered if losing this baby would bring its own bitter relief, because then she wouldn't be faced with a loveless future with Rico. She hated herself for thinking that way for even a single second, and guilt scorched through her, making her even more miserable.

Rico had berated her for not taking care of herself, and had tried to make her eat when she had no appetite due to fear and worry. She knew he was feeling it too, and she wished they could comfort each other in their shared anxiety and sorrow. But that never seemed to be the case; like the ninth circle of Dante's terrible hell, they were frozen in their own isolation, doomed to a life of loneliness.

The sound of the intercom of the flat buzzing had Halina turning from the window in surprise. Rico was at work, and no one called at the flat; deliveries were left with the building's doorman.

Cautiously she went to answer the intercom. 'Hello?'

'*Signorina?*' The doorman's disembodied voice came through the speaker. 'You have a visitor.'

'A visitor…?'

'Sultan Hassan Amar,' the doorman said in a tone of utmost respect. 'He says he is your father.'

For a few seconds Halina couldn't think. She couldn't even breathe. She simply stood there, blinking, one finger pressed down on the intercom.

'*Signorina?*'

'Yes, I'm here.' Her voice sounded strangely tinny and faraway. 'Send him up.'

As soon as she'd said the words she half-regretted them. What if her father was here to take her back home against Rico's wishes? What if she got kidnapped yet again? But then she reasoned that he wouldn't have come to do such a thing on his own. And in any case, if he was on his own she could resist. If she wanted to.

The treacherous flicker of wanting made her pause. Could she really be thinking that way, even for a moment?

The lift doors pinged open and then her father stepped into the open area of the penthouse. Halina turned to him, her mind spinning, her heart beating wildly as her throat dried.

'Father.'

'Halina.' His gaze dipped down to the gentle swell of her belly. 'You are looking well.'

'Am I?' She laughed uncertainly because lately, despite all the rest, she'd been looking as worn out as an old dishrag. 'I don't feel all that well.'

'You don't? Is something wrong?'

The note of alarm in her father's voice caught her on the raw. 'Why do you care?' she couldn't keep herself from retorting bitterly. 'You never wanted this baby to live.'

Her father's face contorted with a spasm of grief and he started towards her, his arms outstretched. 'Halina, *habibi*...'

'Don't.' Halina stepped back quickly, nearly tripping over her own feet. 'Why are you here, Father?'

'I was intending to come to your wedding, and then Falcone informed me he'd called it off.'

She flinched, in part because of the stark fact of her father's words, and in part because Rico hadn't even told her that her father had called, or that he'd changed his mind and had been planning on coming to their wedding after all. The relationship between her and Rico, if she could even call it that, had broken down even more than she'd realised... But perhaps nothing had been built up enough to be broken. It had all been in her head, the intimacy, emotion and love. All on her side.

'Why don't you sit down, Halina?' her father suggested gently. 'And let us talk.'

She wrapped her arms around herself, feeling cold despite the warm October day. 'What do we have to talk about?'

'There is much I wish to say to you. Much I sincerely regret.'

Halina hesitated, then she nodded. 'All right.' They moved towards a pair of luxurious grey suede sofas; she'd spent many happy evenings there curled up next to Rico, watching television or reading a book, pleasant hours they'd whiled away together. It felt like a dream world now.

'What is it?'

'I want to apologise for my conduct to you,' Hassan said seriously. 'I regret the way I acted very much.' He bowed his head, seemingly overcome, and Halina stared at him, too shocked to feel gratified or hopeful. Yet.

'Do you...do you really mean that?'

Hassan looked up, tears gleaming in his dark eyes. 'Yes, I do. Events overtook me, my daughter, and I let them carry me away. I couldn't think properly with everything that had happened. Prince Zayed's kidnapping attempt, your situation... There was so much to deal with.'

'I know,' Halina whispered. 'For me too, Father. And I... I know I acted improperly. Recklessly. I regret that very much. I do.'

'And I acted recklessly as well,' the Sultan returned seriously. 'But let us have no more regrets, Halina. Now that the wedding is called off, I am here to take you home.'

Halina stared at her father in shock, his words penetrating her overwhelmed state and leaving her cold. 'Take me home…?'

'Where you belong. Where you'll be happy. This is no place for you.'

'Rico Falcone is the father of my child.'

'I have had investigators research his past,' Hassan returned, his tone becoming cold. 'Do you know this man, Halina? Do you really know him?'

She loved him. 'What did you find out?'

'That he grew up a gutter rat, and then made his fortune in property investments, and has been known for years as being a cold, ruthless, heartless man. That he has had many women, more than you can imagine, and they never lasted for more than a week. That he has been quoted as saying he doesn't believe in love and he doesn't have time for marriage. This is not a man you want to marry, *habibi.*'

Nothing her father had said about Rico was a surprise to her, but to hear it spelt out so plainly, so terribly… It was hard to bear. Hard to accept. And yet Halina knew she had to.

'This is not the man for you,' Hassan said definitively. 'Or for your child.'

'Rico would never leave his child,' Halina said, unsure what she was really saying. That he would leave her? That she wanted to go but couldn't? She felt a welter of confusion and grief, and it didn't help that things had been so strained between Rico and her recently. She was filled with doubt and fear.

'Are you sure about that?' Hassan asked, his tone gentle. 'Has he said so?'

'He took me from the Palace of Forgotten Sands,' Halina reminded him bitterly. 'Where you'd left me to rot.'

'That is not true, *habibi*. I put you there to keep you safe.'

Her father had a penchant for viewing things through his own singular lens. He always had. It hadn't mattered when she'd been treated like a spoilt pet, but now it made a difference.

'That's what it felt like, Father,' Halina said quietly. 'And I don't have any desire to return to such circumstances.'

'That's not what I'm suggesting at all,' Hassan protested. 'Halina, I am asking you to return to your home, your family. Your sisters long to see you, and so does your mother.'

'You forbade me from seeing my sisters.'

Hassan bowed his head. 'An impetuous decision that I regret. Halina, come home. We all want you to come home. Falcone can't force you to stay here, and in all truth I suspect he would be relieved if you left. Such a man is not made for marriage and family.'

Halina flinched, because her father was only voicing her own terrible suspicions. What if they were both right? What if Rico secretly wanted her to go? Yes, he had a protective streak a mile wide, and he'd been determined to look after her and their baby. But she didn't sense any joy from him, any gladness that he had to do it, that she was here. In her darkest moments she'd even wondered if Rico would be relieved if things ended, if they had no child together.

'Halina,' Hassan said gently. 'I have the royal jet at the airport. We can be heading back to Abkar, to your family, in an hour.'

She ached to see her sisters, her mother. To feel safe and loved, instead of restless and uncertain.

'I can't leave without telling Rico,' she said, hardly able to believe she was saying the words.

'Telling me what?' Rico demanded as he stepped through the doors of the lift and surveyed them both with a dark glare.

Rico gazed between Sultan Hassan's impassive face and Halina's frightened and confused one and felt his stomach and jaw both clench. Whatever they'd been talking about, it hadn't been good.

'What do you need to tell me, Halina?' he asked in as mild a voice as he could manage. 'What's going on?'

'Tell him, *habibi,*' the Sultan said.

The endearment did not go unnoticed. So that was how Hassan was playing it. The doting father had returned. Rico had often wondered how he would act if his father had ever returned. What he would have said, whether he would have opened his arms to him. He'd known what Halina would do. He saw it in her face, in the unhappy guilt written on her delicate features.

She was leaving him. At least, she was thinking about it. God knew the last few weeks had been hard. He knew that; he'd felt it. Halina's admission that she wanted love from him, from their marriage, the terrible uncertainty shrouding her pregnancy…all of it had taken its toll. Had made her doubt, made them both doubt, if they were doing the right thing getting married. Because he was honest enough to admit he'd started wondering too, and somehow that made this moment all the harder to bear.

'Halina?' he prompted, an edge entering his voice, and she stared at him unhappily, her lips trembling.

'Let me talk to him,' the Sultan said, and Rico swung his gaze over to appraise his real adversary. He didn't trust this man. Not a single inch.

'I can…' Halina persisted, but she looked so pale and miserable that Rico took pity on her.

'Let him say what he wants to say. We can talk later if needed. You should rest.'

They stared at each other for a long moment, a world of yearning and regret spinning out between them, then she nodded and walked wordlessly to the bedroom. As the door clicked shut behind her Rico turned to face Hassan.

'Well?' he said coolly.

'The Princess is coming home with me.'

Rico kept his expression neutral, refusing to give the man the satisfaction of seeing him affected by anything he said. 'That was your suggestion, I presume?' he drawled.

'My suggestion and her desire.'

'She said as much?'

'I know it. She's my daughter.'

'And she's the mother of my child.' Rico stared at the man, refusing so much as to blink. 'We are to be married.'

'Yet the wedding was called off.'

'For health reasons only.'

'Come now, Falcone.' Hassan smiled, the genial expression so close to a smirk that Rico itched to wipe it off his face. His fists clenched and he forced himself to unclench them and relax. 'Let's be honest with each other, now it is just the two of us.'

'I am being honest.'

The smile dropped from Hassan's face like the mask Rico had known it was. 'I have had people look into you and your background,' he said in a low voice, his lip curling in an ugly sneer. 'Seen what a gutter rat you truly are. No matter how many billions you have now, you were born a beggar boy and you still are one now. I will never allow you to marry my daughter, a princess of the royal blood. How could I?'

'What you will allow is not my concern. Halina is of

age and in this country, my country, she is not bound by your archaic laws.' Rico spoke calmly even though the blood was boiling through his veins.

'So you would shackle her to you, all because of a child you've never wanted?'

'I'll always want my child.'

'Oh, yes, I understand that certain code of honour—'

'Do you?' Rico interjected, unable to keep the venom from his voice. 'Because, by all accounts, you do not possess it.'

'Halina has spoken to you about that unfortunate incident, I see.'

'You tried to make your own daughter get an abortion she didn't want.'

'I am King of a country, Falcone,' Hassan said sharply. 'With it comes responsibilities and expectations, some of them unfortunate. For my people to see my own daughter shamed in such a way…it would be disastrous. For them, for my rule, for the stability of my country and for Halina herself.' He took a step towards Rico. 'She sees things from her own view, a simple child's view. Trust me, the truth is much more complicated. But we are both men of the world. We know that.'

Rico stared at him, his jaw clenched so tight he thought he might break a tooth. He recognised the truth in the Sultan's words, a truth he had not wanted to see before. He didn't condone the man's actions; he could never do that. But he could understand them.

'Halina belongs in Abkar with her own people, her own family.'

'And would you marry her off to a man of your choosing, a stranger?' Rico demanded. 'Because those do not seem the actions of the loving father you are professing to be now.'

'Come, Falcone.' Hassan smiled. 'We both know that her marriage to you would be no different, and in some ways worse, for there would be no political benefit to you. You would tire of her eventually, whether you are willing to acknowledge it or not.' The Sultan levelled him with a starkly honest and challenging stare. 'Do you honestly think you could ever make her happy?'

Rico tried not to flinch at that question and the lack it revealed in himself. Because the truth that he'd been trying to avoid staring in the face for the last few weeks was that he didn't. And he knew in his gut, in his heart, that Halina deserved more than he could ever give her.

'Would you marry her off against her will?' he asked, the words dragged from him, scraping his throat.

'Against her will? No. In time, when she has recovered from this and longs for a husband and a family? We would make the decision together. That much I have learned.' The Sultan met his gaze unblinkingly; Rico knew he had no choice but to trust him.

'And the child?' he asked painfully, the sting of tears behind his lids, in the back of his throat.

'Would want for nothing. He or she would grow up in the palace, a member of the royal family.'

'Your people would accept that?'

Hassan smiled grimly. 'They will have to.'

Several moments ticked by; it took all of Rico's energy and effort simply to breathe. To keep standing. 'Fine,' he said finally. 'Leave us now. I want to talk to Halina.'

'I'll return in an hour.'

'An hour…'

'It will be better if it's quick,' the Sultan said, then walked towards the lift.

Rico stood where he was, waiting for the man to leave before he moved. Before he told Halina what he intended.

As the doors pinged open and then shut Rico let out a shuddering breath. So this would be the end. He would let her go, because he cared for her too much to shackle her to him. He saw that now.

And, in a jolt of sorrowful realisation, it occurred to him that he finally had a glimmer of understanding of what his father might have gone through in leaving him at the orphanage all those years ago.

Perhaps, just as Rico had, his father had come to the grief-filled conclusion that he could not make the person he loved most in the world happy. That he could not provide for them in the way he longed to. That leaving was the better, and harder, choice.

With a leaden heart, Rico walked towards the bedroom door.

CHAPTER FIFTEEN

HALINA HEARD THE rise and fall of low, tense voices from behind the door but she couldn't make out any words and she didn't think she wanted to. What was her father saying to Rico? And what was Rico saying to her father?

She paced the room in a ferment of anxiety and fear, wondering if the two men she loved most in the world were deciding her future without her. Here, then, was the ultimate loss of freedom. Her fate was completely out of her hands, even while she waited in the next room.

Then she heard the lift doors open and closing. She stilled where she was by the window, one hand resting on the sill. She couldn't hear a sound from the other room; had Rico gone?

Just when she was about to go and find him, the bedroom door opened and Rico stood there. The haggard and grim look on his face struck a cold note of fear in Halina's heart.

'Rico…'

'Your father will return in an hour.'

'Return? Why?'

'It's better this way, Halina.'

'Better?' She stared at him wildly. The doubts that had been festering in her heart burst into painful reality. 'What are you saying? You want me to go?'

'It's not a question of want or whim. It's what is best for you—'

'Best for you, you mean!' Halina cried, pain lancing every word.

'I can't give you what you need.'

'You mean you can't love me.' Even now it hurt to say it. Rico hesitated, his jaw tight, and then he nodded. 'And what if I was willing to live with that?' Halina asked painfully.

'Do you remember what you said to me? That if my loyalty or affection wasn't grounded in love it would eventually fade?'

'Yes, but—'

'Are you no different? Eventually you would come to resent me for not loving you. Hate me, even. And I would hate that. So would you. We'd end up living separate lives, festering in bitterness and resentment.'

She stared at him, hating the bleak, bleak picture he painted with his grim words. 'It wouldn't have to be like that.'

'Maybe not, but the risk is too great. I can't make you happy, Halina. I can't give you what you want.'

'And that is a reason to walk away?' she demanded, her voice shaking. 'You're a coward, Rico Falcone—'

'Do you think this is easy for me?' he cut across her, his voice a ragged roar. 'Do you think I am doing this lightly? I am talking of abandoning my child, as my father once abandoned me. Do you think I would ever want to do that?'

'Then don't—'

'I am trying to do the right thing, hard as it is for both of us. You have to think of the future, Halina. Your future. Perhaps one day you'll find a man you love, a man who can make you happy...'

'Perhaps,' Halina answered in a choked voice, 'happiness is overrated.'

Rico stared at her. 'Do you really mean that?'

Halina simply stared back, confused and miserable. She didn't know anything any more. She didn't understand why Rico was doing this, even as she feared she did. Because their relationship had been doomed from the start—forced into a marriage neither of them wanted for a child they never should have conceived. But even now she couldn't regret her baby, their baby, and she pressed a trembling hand against the soft swell of her bump.

'What of your child? What shall I tell him or her about you?' She shook her head slowly. 'You're really going to give up all your rights?'

'It's better this way,' Rico said. His face was as blank as his voice; it was as if he had already left her, emotionally if not physically. Halina knew she would never reach him.

'So that's it?' she said hollowly. 'After everything that's happened...the way you pursued me, how determined you were to marry me...that's it?'

A full minute ticked by as Rico stared at her, his jaw clenched, his eyes pitilessly blank. 'That's it,' he said flatly.

Everything happened in a fast, unhappy blur after that. Halina packed, leaving behind the couture gowns and outfits that she and Rico had shopped for together. She couldn't bear to bring away clothes that held so many memories, beautiful as they were. Her father arrived, nodding graciously to Rico before he turned to Halina.

'Are you ready, *habibi*? The plane is waiting. So is your family. I called your mother and she is eager to see you.'

Everything in Halina cried out to resist. She stood in

the living room, trying to work up the courage to turn to Rico and tell him she loved him. She'd never said the words. She'd never confessed how she felt about him, only that she wanted him to love her. Would it make a difference? Didn't she have a duty to try?

She opened her mouth, her heart beating hard, but before she could say a word Rico spoke first.

'Goodbye,' he said, and walked out of the room.

Halina stood there for a moment, stunned and blinking, then she followed her father out of the apartment.

She didn't talk much on the ride to the airport; grief swamped her, a fog surrounding her that made it difficult to think, much less speak.

Sultan Hassan was all gracious solicitude, asking how she felt, if there was anything she needed. Once they were on the royal jet Halina went to lie down; she couldn't face anyone, not even the servants. She slept the entire journey, only waking up when it was time to land.

She stared out of the window of the jet at the bleak, undulating desert of Abkar and her heart cried out for Rome. For Rico.

'Everyone is waiting for you,' Hassan said as he guided her from the jet to the waiting SUV. Halina slid inside, resting her head against the seat. She felt too listless to ask what was going to happen now, what her father intended.

Would she live in the royal palace? Raise her child there, under the benevolent eyes of her parents? It was so far from the fury and sick disappointment they'd shown her before, she couldn't quite believe in it. Somehow it didn't much matter any more, because Rico had rejected her.

Throughout the journey, even as she remained dazed, one hard truth had emerged from the fog of her mind.

His claim that he was thinking of her, of her happiness, was nothing more than an excuse. Of course it was. Rico would never give up his child unless he wanted to. Unless he'd decided that marriage and fatherhood wasn't for him, after all.

Bitterness rooted in her heart as she replayed their last conversation in her mind. He was a coward. He should have had the courage to tell her the truth—that he'd changed his mind, that he didn't want to marry her—instead of dressing it up with fine sentiments about thinking only of her happiness.

Back at the palace her sisters swarmed her, and Halina hugged each of them in turn, her heart emerging from its chrysalis of grief as she realised afresh how much she'd missed her family.

'Halina.' Aliya pressed her cheek against her daughter's. 'We are so glad you have returned home.'

'Thank you, Mother,' Halina whispered.

'We have much to do,' Aliya said as she gestured for Halina to sit down in the family's private living area. A member of staff poured glasses of mint tea.

'Much to do?' Halina's youngest sister was curled up on her lap and Halina put her arms around her, grateful for the easy affection.

'Yes, for the wedding.' Halina stared blankly at her mother and Aliya's eyes narrowed. 'To the Sultan of Bahari. Surely your father told you?'

'No,' Halina said numbly. 'He didn't tell me.'

'But the wedding is in a week! The Sultan wants to marry you before you show too much.' With her lips pressed together, Aliya glanced repressively at her younger daughters. 'You are lucky to have such a match arranged for you, Halina.'

'Lucky?' Halina stared at her mother in disbelief as

realisation bloomed poisonously inside her. Her father had duped her with his words of love and regret. He'd wanted her home only so he could marry her off again to his political advantage, this time to a man over three times her age.

She knew the Sultan of Bahari. She'd sat next to him at one of those stuffy diplomatic receptions; he had to be at least seventy, and he had two wives already. And it seemed she was to be the third. Bile churned in her stomach and rose in her throat.

'Mother,' she whispered, 'Are you really intending this for me?'

Aliya folded her arms. 'It is all you have left.'

'Rico Falcone, the father of my child, a billionaire in his own right, was willing to marry me,' Halina retorted, even as a treacherous little voice inside whispered, *Was he?* 'Surely he is more appropriate than an aging lecher with two wives already?'

'Do not speak so disrespectfully. Falcone is not appropriate because he does not offer any political alliances, and his reputation is quite beyond the pale. This is your duty, Halina. Surely you see that? After all your disgrace, this is the least you can do for your family.'

The *least*? She'd be giving up her whole life, and in far worse a way than any future she could have envisioned with Rico. But Rico didn't want her, and Halina was left yet again with no freedom, no choice, in the worst situation she'd ever had to face.

She turned from her mother, tears blurring her eyes. She could hardly believe she was right back where she started, only worse. So much worse.

Rico. Her heart cried out his name. She should have told him she loved him. Even if she had to marry the Sultan of Bahari, at least Rico would have known. It would have been small comfort during the bleak, barren years that stretched ahead of her now.

Three days had passed since Halina had walked out of his flat, his life. Three endless days. It was long enough for Rico to reconsider his decision, which now seemed unaccountably rash. What had he been thinking of, letting her go? Letting his child go?

Sultan Hassan had played on all his doubts, all his fears of inadequacy and commitment. The fear he had of risking his heart for someone, holding it there for her to crack or crush. Halina had been right. He was a coward. He'd chosen to let her go rather than fight to hold on. To tell her the truth, which had come to him in a shocking moment of naked realisation: that he loved her. He'd loved her for a while, but he'd been hiding it from himself because he'd been so afraid. Afraid to fall, to risk, to beg her to stay. So he'd chosen the cowardly option of walking away.

Now he would live the rest of his life knowing he'd loved and lost. It was the price of his cowardice, his shame. And all he could do was pray and hope that she had a better life without him.

Then, on the fourth day after Halina's departure, Rico read the headline in the society section of the newspaper: *Abkaran Princess to Marry Sultan*.

Everything in him stilled as he scanned the few scant lines.

Princess Halina of Abkar, recently engaged to billionaire tycoon Rico Falcone, is now poised to marry the Sultan of Bahari on Saturday. The Sultan has two wives already, and the Princess will be his third.

Rico's head jerked up from the newspaper, shock slamming into him, leaving him breathless. The *third* wife? He glanced back down at the article and saw a grainy black-and-white photograph of the Sultan, a paunchy old man with jowly cheeks and a smug smile. His skin crawled. He hadn't let go of Halina for this. He hadn't sacrificed his own happiness, his own heart, for her to be married off to some old lecher.

And he was sure, with a stony certainty, that she hadn't known what she was walking into when she'd returned to Abkar. Her father had tricked them both.

Rico swore out loud, viciously and fluently. His emotional cowardice had led to this disaster. He'd wanted the very best for Halina, and instead he'd dumped her in the worst situation possible. With his mouth hardening into a grim line of determination, Rico reached for his phone. He'd rescued Halina once before. He could do it again. Only this time it might take a little more finesse.

Several hours later, Rico had found his way forward thanks to a few crucial phone calls. He booked a flight to Bahari and within hours of landing he had a royal audience with the Sultan. Forty-five minutes later, their business was concluded and, after spending the night at a hotel in the desert country's capital city, he booked another flight to Abkar.

He stood in front of the royal palace, soldiers barring his way, the golden stone of the palace shimmering under the hot desert sun.

'You may tell the Sultan I am here in regard to Princess Halina's forthcoming marriage. I have crucial news that I know he will want to hear.'

The soldiers glared at him uncertainly before one gave a terse nod and spoke Arabic into an intercom. Several tense minutes later Rico was admitted to the palace and led to a small, spartan waiting room.

The Sultan kept him waiting for nearly an hour before he finally deigned to make an appearance. Rico didn't mind. He wasn't going to play the man's petty games, and he wasn't going to fall prey to them either. Not any more.

'How surprising to see you here,' the Sultan remarked, his eyes cold, any pretence at friendliness dropped. 'I cannot begin to imagine what you have to say to me in regard to the Princess's marriage, but I decided to humour you.' He folded his arms. 'So, say what you will and then be gone.'

'The Sultan of Bahari has called off the marriage.'

Hassan's eyes narrowed. 'You are talking nonsense.'

'I am not. If you wish for it to be confirmed, you may call him.' He held out his phone, his eyes glinting with challenge. 'I have access to his private line.'

'What have you done?' Hassan ground out, staring at Rico's phone as if it were a snake poised to strike.

'Why don't you find out?'

Wordlessly Hassan snatched the phone and swiped to dial. Seconds later they both heard ringing and then the Sultan of Bahari's unctuous voice. Hassan listened for several taut seconds, his expression becoming grimmer and grimmer, before he ended the call and flung the phone at Rico. Rico caught it neatly.

'Very clever, Falcone. Very clever.'

'It is too bad for you that the Sultan prefers racehorses to wives.'

'How much did it cost you to buy him that horse?' Hassan asked scornfully. 'Millions? Money wasted. I am not letting Halina go.'

'Yes, you are,' Rico said evenly. 'Because, if you don't, I will do everything in my power, give everything I have, to ruin you. And trust me, Hassan, it can be done. I've only just begun, and I enjoy a challenge.'

Hassan stared at him for a long moment, his eyes cold, his jaw tight. 'What does it matter so much to you?' he finally asked. 'You've had dozens—no, hundreds—of women. She's but one. Why can't you leave her alone?'

'If she wants me to leave her alone, I will. But that's her choice,' Rico returned. 'Not yours.'

Another minute passed, taut with suppressed tension and resentment. Then Hassan shrugged. 'Fine. She's damaged goods anyway, and I would be hard pressed to find someone suitable to take her now. Do what you like with her, but she will not be welcome back here.'

'That,' Rico answered, 'is your loss.'

A short while later he stood in front of the doors to a more ornate reception room, his heart beginning to hammer as doubt chased him yet again. He'd acted precipitously, out of concern for Halina, but what if it had cost her her family? What if she would have rather married the damned Sultan? There was only one way to find out.

Taking a deep breath, Rico opened the doors. Halina was standing on the far side of the room, once again looking pale and gaunt despite the roundness of her belly. She whirled around as he came into the room, her mouth dropping open in shock.

'Rico...'

'Did your father not tell you I was here?'

'No one's told me anything.' She drew a shuddering breath. 'I'm to marry the Sultan of Bahari...'

'No, you're not. The wedding's off.'

She stared at him in confusion. 'What?'

'I made a deal with the Sultan of Bahari. He agreed to call off the wedding, in exchange for a racehorse he has been wanting for many years.'

'A racehorse!'

'The owner wouldn't sell it to him, so I bought it instead.'

'How…?'

'It is done easily enough, when you know the right people and offer the right amount of money. But first, Halina, tell me you're all right. The baby…'

'The baby's all right.' She gave him a wan, tremulous smile. 'I haven't had any more bleeding and I've felt movement—tiny little flutters.'

'Thank God.'

'But why are you here, Rico? Why have you done this?'

'Because I read about your engagement in the newspaper and I didn't believe for a second that you wanted that. I feared your father had tricked you into coming home.'

'He did.' Halina closed her eyes briefly. 'I should have known better.'

'*Cara,* so should I. I will never forgive myself for jeopardising your life, your happiness, in such a way.'

'Let's have no more recriminations, please, Rico. There has been far too much regret already.'

'I need to ask.' Rico looked at her seriously. 'Is this what you want? Because your father made it clear that, if you left with me, you would not be welcomed back by your family. It's a high price to pay, Halina, and one I should have foreseen. Only you can decide if you wish to pay it.'

'And what is the alternative?' she asked, staring at him with wide, troubled eyes. 'To marry a man old enough to be my grandfather, and live in shame and seclusion as his third wife with an illegitimate child that would no doubt be taken away from me? Rico, it's a hard price to pay, but I pay it willingly. You need not fear that.'

'Good.' He took her hands, which felt small and icy, in his. 'Then it's time we departed.'

'Are we going back to Rome?'

'No,' Rico said, his heart full of both love and pain. He finally knew what love was, and he understood it was so much more than he'd thought. It wasn't an ephemeral emotion; it was life itself, duty and sacrifice, joy and feeling. He would do anything for Halina because he loved her. He would even let her go.

'Rico…? Where are we going?'

He smiled at her, his heart aching with both love and loss. 'We're going to Paris.'

CHAPTER SIXTEEN

YET AGAIN, WITHIN the space of a week, Halina found herself on a private jet, crossing the world. She felt such an overwhelming mix of relief and sadness that she could barely begin to process the emotions. To have seen her sisters, her family, again only to say goodbye so soon. It filled her with grief, even as she acknowledged the sweet and overwhelming relief at being rescued from a fate so grim she hated even to imagine it.

But what was going to happen now? She'd asked Rico why they were going to Paris, but he'd refused to be drawn. And, instead of seeming happy to have got her back, he'd withdrawn even more into himself, seeming so quiet and sad that Halina feared the cost her rescue was to him. Were they really better off than they'd been a few days ago before her father had arrived? It felt as if nothing had really changed; Rico was still remote and she still loved him. An impossible situation.

The plane finally touched down in Paris and, as they drove into the city, Halina gazed out of the limo's window in awe and wonder, her nose nearly pressed to the glass.

'There's the Eiffel Tower!' she exclaimed. 'I've only seen it in pictures…'

'You'll have time to do all the sightseeing you want,'

Rico assured her, and she turned back to him uncertainly. Why did he sound so resigned?

Realisation began to dawn when the limo turned onto a street of eighteenth-century townhouses, tall and elegant. It parked in front of number eighteen, a lovely old building covered in vines, just like in the children's story *Madeline*.

'What...?' Halina began in a disbelieving whisper. Rico drew a key from his pocket.

'Come,' he said, and she followed him out of the limo and up the stairs to the front door painted a shiny red. 'Sorry, there are quite a few stairs,' he remarked as he fitted the key in the door. 'But you did say the top floor.'

'My dream...' she whispered, feeling as if she were in one. She followed Rico into an old-fashioned lift with a grille for a door, up to the flat on the top floor. He unlocked the door and ushered her inside.

Halina stepped into the little hallway with its antique flocked wallpaper and colourful prints. She turned the corner and gazed in amazement at the living room—the squashy sofa, the grand piano, the shelves of books. It was as if he'd conjured it straight out of her head.

'How did you...?' she began, walking slowly around the apartment. There was a cosy kitchen with dishes in different colours and fresh flowers on the table. The bedroom had a double bed with a cover decorated in *broderie anglaise*, the window's bright-blue shutters open to the October sunshine.

And the balcony... She pushed open the French windows from the living room and stepped onto the tiny balcony with its wrought-iron railings and pots of herbs and flowers. Below her the streets of the Latin Quarter bustled and the smell of freshly baked croissants drifted up. Halina turned to Rico, shaking her head in amazement.

'It's as if you pulled this right out of my dreams.'

'Well, you did describe it to me in some detail.' He smiled faintly, but his eyes still looked sad.

'Yes, but how did you arrange it all?'

'It took some doing. I had very specific requests.' Rico's smile deepened. 'But it was worth it.'

'Rico, I don't know what to say.'

'The deed is in your name, of course,' he continued, and Halina blinked.

'What?'

'I've engaged a housekeeper to come once a week, but of course that's up to you. I thought you'd want your privacy.'

'I don't understand.'

'Of course this place might feel small once the baby comes, but we can cross that bridge when you come to it. If you'd like to move somewhere more suitable eventually, it can be arranged.'

'Now I really don't understand.' Her voice and body both shook. 'What are you telling me, Rico?'

He smiled sadly. 'I'm giving you what you've always wanted, Halina. Your freedom.'

Rico watched Halina's eyes widen in shock. Seeing her delight in the little flat had brought him such painful joy. She would be happy here. He'd make sure of it. Because, when you loved someone, you wanted their happiness more than anything. More than your own.

'My freedom,' Halina repeated slowly. 'You mean, you're leaving me again?'

'I'm giving you what you want,' Rico insisted. He'd thought long and hard about what to do when he'd been flying to Bahari and then Abkar. What Halina needed to be happy. 'You told me—many times you told me—

that you wanted your freedom, the chance to choose your own destiny. Well, here it is.'

'But I'm not choosing it,' Halina said, her voice growing in force and volume. 'Am I? You're still choosing it for me.'

Rico blinked, surprised by her fury. He'd thought she'd be pleased. He'd wanted to please her. Or, he wondered with an uncomfortable pang, had he been trying to assuage his own guilty conscience for backing out on her once before?

'If you don't want to live here, you don't have to.'

'I thought… I thought when you came for me you'd come to bring me back with you, because that's where you wanted me.' Her breath thickened. 'With you.'

'I'm trying to do the right thing, Halina—'

'Are you? Or are you trying to do the safe thing? Rico, I love you.'

The words fell into the shocked stillness.

'I've loved you for a while, and I should have told you sooner, but I was afraid. But I don't want to be afraid any longer. I've been batted back and forth like a ball in a game and I don't want that either. I want the freedom to choose, yes, and I choose you. If you'll have me.'

His stunned mind couldn't make sense of her words.

She continued determinedly. 'I know you don't love me, and I'm willing to accept that. I hope in time you might at least come to care for me a little, but in the meantime I want what we had before. I'll let it be enough. I want us, Rico. I want our family.'

'Stop.' His voice was so choked he could barely get the single word out. 'Stop, Halina. I can't let you say any more.'

Her eyes clouded and her lips trembled. 'You can't?'

'No, because you're wrong. So wrong. I won't come

to care for you a little in time, because I'm already completely, hopelessly in love with you.' Her mouth dropped open and he started walking towards her. 'I've been fighting it for a while, maybe even since we first met. Fighting it, because I was so scared of loving someone again, letting myself get hurt. Left. And so I did what I thought I'd never, ever do and I left you instead. I convinced myself I was doing the right thing, the noble thing, but really it was just cowardice. You were right to call me a coward, Halina. *Lina.* My Lina.'

He took hold of her hands, drawing her towards him. 'To hear that you love me…to know it and believe it… I wish I'd told you first. I wish I'd had that much courage. But I'm so honoured, so privileged, to be loved by you. I don't deserve it. I know I don't.'

'Deserving doesn't come into it, Rico,' Halina said softly as she came into his arms. 'Love is a gift, freely given, gratefully received. And that's how it is for me.'

'And for me. I love you so much. So much.'

'And I love you just as much.'

He kissed her then, because he needed to feel her in his arms, against his mouth. Halina wound her arms around his neck, her pliant body pressed to his as the sun spilled through the windows, and the whole world sang.

EPILOGUE

Six months later

'HE'S A HUNGRY little fellow, isn't he?' Rico gazed down at his son's rosebud mouth sucking greedily at his mother's breast. Halina stroked her baby's hair and looked up with laughing eyes.

'I don't mind.'

'As long as you're getting enough rest.'

'Plenty.' They shared a loving smile as he touched her hand, still incredulous, and so incredibly grateful, that she was here. That they shared this rare and precious happiness.

The last six months had been tumultuous, with their quiet wedding ceremony taking place when Halina had been seven months pregnant. Her friend Olivia, wife to Prince Zayed, had come, as had her husband, and Rico had found he liked the man. Halina's mother had come too, the first step of many to healing her fractured family.

After ten gruelling hours of labour his son, Matteo Falcone, had been born. Named after Rico's father, because all this had taught him that everyone made mistakes as well as hard choices. He didn't know which his father had made, but he knew he finally had it in his heart to forgive him. Because of Halina, and the light and love she'd brought to his life. The healing.

'I think he's had enough.' Halina lifted their sleepy son up to him. 'Do you want to hold him?'

'Of course.' Rico never tired of cradling his precious, tiny son. He marvelled that marriage and family had been gifts, treasures that he'd scorned, and he thanked God that he'd learned otherwise.

Now he balanced Matteo on his shoulder and gently jiggled him while Halina watched, a faint smile curving her face. She'd blossomed in the last few months through a difficult pregnancy, a tough labour, and then moving house to the villa outside Rome where they lived now, perfect for a growing family. Through it all she'd grown in grace and beauty, basking in his love for her, a love he'd never tire of showing and feeling…even when life was hard. Especially when it was.

'What are you thinking?' Halina asked softly, and Rico smiled.

'How blessed I am.'

'And I am, as well.'

'Yes, we both are.' He drew her up from the rocking chair and put his arm around her so they were together in a tight circle, the people he loved most in the world. His family. Their family. Together at last for ever.

* * * * *